Praise for *The Agency for Scandal*

"Witty, fiercely feminist, and deliciously
romantic, Laura Wood has outdone herself with
this thrilling tale of scandal and subterfuge"
Louise O'Neill, author of *Idol*
and *The Surface Breaks*

"*The Agency for Scandal* is glorious! Clever,
funny, charming, and achingly romantic, it
is a delight from start to finish. Laura Wood
always writes about love and friendship with
a deft hand, and this is her best work yet"
Katherine Webber, author of *Twin Crowns*

"Incredibly charming"
Sophie Irwin, author of *A Lady's
Guide to Fortune Hunting*

"A perfect mash up of Bridgerton and Enola
Holmes with plenty of Laura Wood's own magic
dust sprinkled on top. A wallflower who's more
than she seems, a dashing duke hiding a secret
and plenty of intrigue, romance and snappy one
liners make this the perfect comfort read"
Sarra Manning, author of

Published in the UK by Scholastic, 2023
1 London Bridge, London, SE1 9BG
Scholastic Ireland, 89E Lagan Road, Dublin Industrial Estate,
Glasnevin, Dublin, D11 HP5F

SCHOLASTIC and associated logos are trademarks and/or
registered trademarks of Scholastic Inc.

Text © Laura Wood, 2023
Cover illustration © Mercedes deBellard, 2023

The right of Laura Wood to be identified as
the author of this work has been asserted by her under
the Copyright, Designs and Patents Act 1988.

ISBN 978 0702 30324 1

A CIP catalogue record for this book
is available from the British Library.

Printed by CPI Group (UK) Ltd, Croydon, CR0 4YY
Paper made from wood grown in sustainable forests
and other controlled sources.

1 3 5 7 9 10 8 6 4 2

This is a work of fiction. Names, characters, places incidents
and dialogues are products of the author's imagination or are used
fictitiously. Any resemblance to actual people, living or dead,
events or locales is entirely coincidental.

www.scholastic.co.uk

The Agency for Scandal

LAURA WOOD

SCHOLASTIC

To Gen, Louise and Sophie –
making books with you is so much fun.

"The human heart has hidden treasures,

In secret kept, in silence sealed;

The thoughts, the hopes, the dreams, the pleasures,

Whose charms were broken if revealed."

—CHARLOTTE BRONTË

PART ONE

London
June 1897

CHAPTER ONE

When hunting for secrets and scandal during the London season, then there is really only one place to go: the opera.

All those people dressed up in their finery, packed in tight, pretending to watch the drama onstage while actually watching each other? The place is a perfect hotbed for intrigue.

Which is precisely why I was there.

I've always thought the Royal Opera House looks like something from a confectioner's window, all white and gilt, as if those scrolling acanthus leaves were piped out of sugar paste – good enough to eat. Then there are the boxes full of plush crimson velvet seats, one hundred and twenty-one of them, arranged in golden splendour in a towering horseshoe shape, beneath a soaring domed ceiling. When the place is full it holds almost two thousand people – two thousand pairs of eager eyes, two thousand gleeful voices breathless with gossip. It's quite something.

"Izzy," a voice rang out then, close to my ear. "Isn't that the Earl of Rathmore over there? Because if it is, that's *definitely* not his wife with him."

Teresa Wynter has been my best friend for eighteen years, and she is many things, but subtle is not one of them. If the carrying sound of her voice or the infectious charm of her wide grin wasn't enough to draw attention, then the eye-watering lemon yellow of the gown that she wore would certainly do the trick ("It looked much more of a pale primrose at the dressmaker's, Iz, I'm sure it did…"). Several heads swung towards the box where we were sitting to stare in our direction. Or perhaps I should say to stare in *her* direction. Those gazes slid right past me. As usual, I was little more than a shadow, barely a flicker somewhere in society's peripheral vision. Which, actually, was perfect for my needs.

When you worked for a secret agency of female investigators, being invisible was something of an advantage.

"Eh?" The noise came from Teresa's Great-Aunt Louisa, who seemed to shudder to life for a moment, sitting upright in her red velvet seat. "What was that?" She eyed us suspiciously. Whenever she roused herself it was usually to make her disapproval of our conversation felt.

Teresa's smile was angelic. "Nothing, Aunt."

Louisa sniffed but returned to her dozing without further comment. Teresa's great-aunt was a lady of advanced years, deaf as a post, and seemingly happy to fall asleep anywhere. In other words, she was the perfect chaperone, particularly for Teresa. My friend always maintained she had been born about eighty years too late because she'd most certainly have had a tawdry affair with Lord Byron given half the chance. I absolutely believed this claim, and I'm not sure Byron would have known what had hit him.

"I wouldn't worry too much about Lady Rathmore," I whispered back to Teresa once Louisa had definitely settled. "I hear she got fed up of her husband's infidelities and has gone on an extended tour of Europe with a certain handsome young footman."

I could hardly keep the satisfaction from my voice. It had been a pleasing outcome for one of our trickier cases. Lady Rathmore was a client, and providing her with the blackmail material that forced her philandering husband to give her financial freedom had been extremely satisfying work. After all, she had been the one who'd brought that money to their marriage in the first place.

Teresa's eyes widened. "How on *earth* do you always know these things?"

"I have my sources." I smoothed down the skirts of my pale grey dress, drab and ordinary in the best of circumstances, but spectacularly outshone by the women attending the opera, whose gowns gleamed against the red velvet, like gems lining a jewellery box.

Father had died two years ago, but despite my friend's protests I was finding the idea of dispensing with my mourning clothes surprisingly difficult.

Moments later, and almost directly across from where Teresa and I were seated, Sylla Banaji drifted in on the arm of her father, Sir Dinshaw Banaji. She did not so much as glance in our direction. Plenty of heads swung in *hers,* however. The candlelight glinted off more than one pair of twitchy opera glasses as necks strained to see how the baronet's beautiful daughter was dressed and if anyone interesting was accompanying her.

At nineteen, Sylla, with her easy, cat-like grace and scornful attitude towards society, was often the centre of attention wherever she went. I watched now as the crowd greedily took in her appearance, a hum of appreciative chatter breaking out at the picture she created, clad in a pale blue-and-silver gown that emphasized the raven's-wing shine of her hair and the tawny gold of her skin, with cuffs of slender silver bangles that climbed her wrists.

"How ... *original,*" I heard a woman mutter, her tone like the sharp taste of a wine turned sour.

As the daughter of Lady Anne Stanton and her Bombay-born, Oxford-educated husband, Sylla occupied a complicated place in society. Her father may be a retired dragoon, who was made a baronet almost a decade ago, thanks to his vast fortune and philanthropic efforts (as well as his friendship with the Prince of Wales), but there would always be plenty who couldn't see much past the colour of his skin. Or Sylla's, for that matter.

Eventually, Sylla's cool gaze drifted towards me, caught mine – only for a fraction of a second – before moving on. Still, it was enough for me to get the message, loud and clear: *don't you dare mess this up.*

I huffed a sigh. I was not in the habit of making mistakes, but Sylla still treated me like the green recruit she'd approached a year and a half ago. I pulled Father's pocket watch from my reticule where it sat beside a small glass perfume bottle, a folded fan and a handkerchief. There were more than thirty minutes before the performance began; plenty of time.

I leafed through my programme, trying not to let my impatience show. I had seen *Manon Lescaut* when it premiered here at Covent Garden almost three years ago. I was sixteen then, and Father had been alive. We had sat in our own family box that we had since given up. I claimed this was because Father had been the one who loved the opera and it now had little use – when really there was no way on earth I could afford to keep it.

That was when my days had been all party dresses and wide eyes and husband hunting. It felt like a lifetime ago, as if all of that had happened to another person, and if I was being honest, there wasn't much that I missed. Of course I'd give anything to have Father back ... but the rest of it? Life was *so* much more interesting these days.

"Ooh, I love that shade of pink!" Teresa's exclamation snapped my attention right back to the scene in front of me. "Do you think it would suit me?"

I followed her pointing finger to a dress that was a nightmarish hue sitting somewhere between puce and salmon. "I think you'd look lovely in any colour," I said, partly because it seemed the most diplomatic answer and partly because I thought it was true.

Teresa scoffed, but I could tell she was pleased. "I'm wearing pink to the Devonshire House ball, but it's a much lighter shade, now I wonder if that's quite right..." She tipped her head to the side. "Perhaps I should speak to my dressmaker again."

"Leave that poor woman alone!" I said. "I've lost count of how many times you've changed your mind about that gown."

"It's for the social event of the year." Teresa's tone was scolding. "Probably the decade. If you ask me, you're not taking it seriously enough, especially when it's fancy dress. I heard the Duke of Marlborough has spent five thousand francs on a costume from the House of Worth; you can't turn up in any old thing."

I only shrugged. No one was going to be paying any attention to what I wore so it hardly seemed worth worrying about. Teresa let out a tsk of irritation, but went back to scanning the crowd.

Suddenly, I felt the hairs on the back of my neck stand up, a shiver tingled across my skin. I didn't need to turn my head to know what had happened.

Max Vane had arrived.

"That man," Teresa said, her eyes focused hazily over my shoulder, "really *is* the handsomest I have ever seen."

Almost against my will I turned and felt the same physical jolt that I always did when I saw Max. I should be used to it by now – I saw a great deal of him in society life – and yet I still felt that curious shock that was half-pleasure, half-pain. He stood, illuminated in the doorway to his own box, the one adjacent to the Queen's, and only two along from Sylla, impossibly handsome in a perfectly fitted black tailcoat and plain black silk waistcoat. He looked around the theatre with a steady gaze, seemingly unmoved by anything he saw.

I'd been in love with Max Vane for eighteen months now. He, however, had no idea that I existed.

Teresa was not exaggerating about his good looks. Max Vane was built like one of those statues of classical Greek heroes, over six feet tall, and no amount of prim tailoring could hide his impossibly broad shoulders, the well-defined muscles. His face was perfectly proportioned, with a square jaw and full lips, usually set in a firm line. His hair was blond with a slight curl, cropped shorter than was currently fashionable.

The fact that, with all of this in his favour, it was his eyes that everyone noticed first should tell you how extraordinary they were. A deep, warm green, with flashing lights in them – the kind of eyes people might write poems about ... if they were the sort of people inclined to write poems, that is. (I had only tried it once, with excruciating results and all evidence had been immediately destroyed in the fireplace in my bedroom.)

"It's a shame he's always so proper and serious," Teresa mused. "I don't think I've ever seen him so much as crack a smile."

I had. In fact, I had seen Max Vane laugh.

CHAPTER TWO

Eighteen months ago I'd just come out of deep mourning for Father. I'd always been ambivalent about society life – much of it seemed dull, if necessary – but now the same social events felt claustrophobic, airless. The drawing rooms filled with watching eyes left a crawling sense of panic in my chest that I didn't understand or know how to master. It was also becoming increasingly clear that Mother, Henry and I were in financial difficulties and the grinding worry about how we could survive – with Mother unwell and Henry at school – kept me awake at night.

One particular evening, I was at a house party in Kent along with about two hundred other people for a dance in the grand ballroom.

It was hot and crowded, the press of bodies making me want to wriggle out of my own skin. Teresa wasn't there and I had spent most of the evening tucked in a gloomy corner, clutching a glass of warm lemonade and fanning myself with my empty dance card. In the end I couldn't face it any longer and I slipped outside. It wasn't appropriate for a young lady to be walking the grounds alone at night, but no one ever took much notice of what I was doing.

Those first gulps of cool air had felt like a draught of clean water. I wandered further into the parkland, away from the noise and activity, moving silently on my slippered feet, as I melted into the darkness. Each step I put between myself and the ballroom eased the tightness in my chest. Soon, I found myself beside a stream, following along the banks until it widened, the water rushing silver under the light of the moon. It was peaceful and I felt the rapid beating of my heart begin to slow, my shoulders relax.

That is, until I heard the words ringing through the air, deep and commanding: "Come here."

I froze, bristling at the peremptory command. I turned towards the voice, an angry retort ready on my own lips, but the words were coming from the other side of a large oak tree and the instruction was not directed at me at all.

I peered around the trunk. Standing there, frowning down towards the water, and wholly unaware of my presence, was Maximillian William Spencer Vane, the eighth Duke of Roxton.

I was not – at this point – in love with Max Vane. I had seen him before of course, across crowded ballrooms, and felt slightly awed by the sense of power and privilege he exuded, the way that people flitted around him like moths around a flame. We may have attended the same parties but we moved in vastly different circles. The distance between a duke and the daughter of a minor baron was a vast one, and Vane seemed well aware of his position – an imposing and unsmiling figure at any social gathering, with a reputation as a stickler for propriety.

It was curious that he would be out here and I wondered who he could be talking to as I edged a little closer. I could hear a high-pitched whining sound and realized that there, on the other side of the river, was a small dog of indeterminate breed. It was standing mid-stream, as though it had begun to cross and then frozen in fear. Now it was trembling and whimpering, seemingly unable to commit to swimming across the deeper water, or to turning back the way it had come.

Vane sighed loudly. "I said, *come here*," he tried again encouragingly.

The dog's ears pricked but that was all. The trembling continued, the whine growing louder.

"Don't make me come over there and get you." His voice was low, rich and polished with all the drawling confidence of the position he was born into. "My valet will have a fit."

The dog remained unmoved, and I bit my lip to stifle a laugh at the look on Vane's face.

With another sigh, he bent down and began to unlace his shoes. I felt my eyes widen in shock as it dawned on my addled brain that the most handsome man in the country, the greatest catch of this – or any other – season was about to disrobe in front of me.

I shouldn't look, my brain said sternly. *I definitely shouldn't look.*

(Believe it or not, we still haven't reached the part of the story where my heart was hopelessly compromised.)

At that moment, the dog seemed to find some previously undiscovered font of courage and pelted with a sort of yowling war cry across the water towards Vane.

The poor man, who was in the middle of removing his trousers, had only time to turn his head before a very wet, very muddy dog flew at his chest, barking ecstatically and knocking its would-be rescuer clean off his feet and straight back into the muddy riverbank with an audible splat.

The dog – ungrateful creature – pelted off into the night, leaving the Duke of Roxton lying in the dirt.

I don't know what I expected. Anger? Annoyance? Frustration? I was sure that dukes were all quite aware of their dignity. I thought there would be shouting, swearing, an imaginative curse or two thrown in the direction of the fast-retreating dog.

Instead, this duke threw his head back, getting even more muddy in the process, and he laughed. His laugh was as beautiful as the rest of him – starting as a low growl, and becoming something warm and giddy.

That was it. The moment when I felt a jolt run through me. It was as instant and unexpected as an electric shock, and I put my hand to my chest, as if I could feel a change in the way my heart was beating.

Watching him lie there, in the dirt, laughing easily at himself, he stopped being the Duke of Roxton, and became in my mind, simply, Max.

Falling instantly and unexpectedly in love with a virtual stranger who doesn't know you exist is actually quite an overwhelming and inconvenient feeling, and I was barely aware of my surroundings as I turned and began quickly picking my way back to the path.

His laughter stopped. "Hello?" he called. "Is someone there?"

But I carried on moving, hurrying back to the party, my brain still trying to catch up with the bizarre flood of emotions that had been released by a nice but perfectly ordinary laugh.

Soon after the encounter, I watched from the edge of the room as Max appeared back at the party, immaculately turned out, not a hair out of place. I have no idea how he did that – I suppose a duke must have his ways. No one knew what had happened. No one but me. He looked quite stern and serious again, and the fact that I knew the sound of his laugh felt startlingly intimate.

I could not make sense of how swiftly I had tumbled into infatuation. I turned over the bewildering events of the previous half-hour in my mind like they were a puzzle, as if I could make sense of them if I only tried hard enough. I had just watched a duke fall in the mud from behind a tree (like some sort of terrible lurker), and then – what? – fallen in love with him? Ridiculous. Up until this point I had always been quite a sensible person. I didn't even believe in this idea of love, the one that struck a person in the chest like an arrow.

On the other hand, however, at least I was feeling *something*. After the grief of losing Father, after the shock of discovering the dire financial situation we had been left in, this reckless plummet into infatuation felt momentous. It was a new feeling, one that seemed to break through the hard shell of grief and panic. Despite knowing that my feelings would remain unrequited I felt the once-familiar stirrings of something I had been missing recently: hope.

And that night had been momentous in more ways than one. It was also the night I met Sylla.

"Actually, I take it back." Teresa's voice hitched, shaking me from my memories and back to the theatre where I had a job to do. "*That* is the handsomest man I've ever seen."

My friend was sitting upright, taut as a bowstring. She was looking at the man standing beside Max now. I frowned. The stranger was good-looking, with his reddish-brown hair, neatly trimmed beard and laughing brown eyes, but he was – objectively, at least – not the *most* handsome man in the room. Still, my friend had the look of a person who could hear a choir of angels singing. I wondered if that was how I had looked hiding behind the tree.

At that moment, the man's head turned in our direction. His eyes locked on to Teresa's. She smiled. He smiled. She let out an involuntary "Oh!" His expression grew dazed. He turned to Max and said something. Max looked at us, and I felt my own pulse gallop – but he wasn't looking at me at all, he was looking at Teresa. Then they turned and left through the door to their box.

Teresa released a long, slow breath. "Izzy," she squeaked. "Izzy, did you see…"

"Of course I saw!" I laughed.

Teresa giggled, fanning her face with her programme. "I wonder who he is."

She didn't have to wonder for long, because moments later there was a sound behind us, and there they were. I rose to my feet in surprise, the reticule that had been in my lap falling unheeded to the floor. Teresa too jumped up, her mouth split in a delighted grin.

"Miss Wynter." Max's voice had a pleasant gravelliness to it that did something strange to my insides. "I hope you'll forgive the intrusion."

Of course Max knew Teresa – he was friendly with her cousin Nick, the new Earl Wynter. Thanks to her, I had now been introduced to Max on more than one occasion. I was always torn between misery and amusement that he never seemed to remember who I was.

"Your Grace," Teresa purred, her eyes fixed firmly over Max's shoulder. "How nice it is to see you, it's no intrusion at all."

I took in the scene with interest, trying not to dwell on the heat that rushed through my body in Max's presence. I might be the victim of an unrequited passion, but I refused to allow it to turn me into an idiot.

Max's eyes slid towards Louisa, who was still sound asleep, the odd snuffling noise issuing from between her lips. Uncertainty flickered across his face, and it was easy enough to tell what was running through his mind. There were proprieties to be observed, and he wanted to observe them.

Teresa grinned. "I shouldn't wake her," she said confidingly. "She'll be put out to be woken from such a pleasant nap, even by a duke."

Max frowned, but the man behind him gave a bark of laughter.

"Miss Wynter," Max said a bit stiffly. "May I present my good friend, Mr James St Clair."

James St Clair stepped forward and bowed over Teresa's hand. "A pleasure to meet you, Miss Wynter," he said.

I liked him at once. For one thing there wasn't a hint of Byron about him. He seemed solid, reassuring; there was an ease to the way he stood, the way he spoke, a glimmer in his eye as though he would always be the first to see the humour in a situation. Teresa's usual taste leaned more towards men who looked like they slept in caskets inside a Transylvanian castle, supped on the blood of virgins, and burned with a crackling intensity as they read their own terrible, endless poetry.

Now, however, Teresa was gazing at this perfectly ordinary-looking young man with the same expression she'd worn as a child when we were offered a trip to Gunter's Tea Shop. It seemed just about possible that James St Clair would win out in a contest against strawberry ice cream.

"The pleasure is mine, sir," Teresa – an expert flirt

of many years – twinkled at him. They stood for a beat, her hand still in his, and then Max cleared his throat.

Spoilsport.

A slight flush appeared on James's cheek, and he released Teresa's fingers. Teresa turned to me, her own cheeks pink with pleasure.

"And I'm sure you remember my dear friend, Miss Isobel Stanhope." She flashed me a brief smirk. Although I had never said a word, Teresa had long suspected my interest in the Duke of Roxton and enjoyed teasing me about it as much as possible.

"Mr St Clair." I bobbed a curtsey. "Your Grace."

The gentlemen bowed formally. There was not a flicker of recognition in Max's eyes and I swallowed a sigh, reminding myself that being forgettable was all part of what made me effective at my job.

Speaking of which... I looked over at Sylla and this time she was fixing me with a glare, the sort of glare that required little skill to interpret. *Stop dithering around with irrelevant men and get to work.*

Quite right. I glanced down to the circle and saw that my target had finally put in his appearance. Adrenaline rushed through me. I did enjoy this bit.

"If you'll excuse me," I said, turning towards Max with a sunny smile. "I've just seen someone I must have a word with before the performance starts."

He looked startled, as did Teresa. I suppose the most eligible bachelor in the country wasn't used to ladies making speedy exits when he deigned to visit them.

"I'll be quick," I said to Teresa, already moving forward. "I promise. I'll be back before the curtain goes up."

"I believe you've dropped your reticule," Max called. He held the small silk bag out towards me and I took it from him. My fingers brushed his for a fraction of a second, and even through my gloves I felt the touch all the way down to my toes. Our eyes met, and I allowed myself a luxurious moment of being the focus of his attention. My gaze dropped to his mouth, and I remembered how he had looked when he smiled, when he laughed.

"Thank you," I managed, and then, bobbing a hurried curtsey, I slipped out.

It was time to work.

CHAPTER THREE

I entered the circle, elbowing my way through the crowd. It was much warmer down here. People were milling about drinking and talking. I spotted my target again. He was in a group with some friends – a rowdy set of students who had obviously been drinking quite heavily. I took a moment to study him. It was barely perceptible, but he was swaying a little when he moved. He had a drink in his hand. Good, that would make things straightforward.

I looked at my watch again. Almost nine, there should be...

And then, yes, there, appearing as if from nowhere, was Maud, another of my colleagues. She was dressed in a low-cut gown, her cheeks heavily rouged, her red hair falling down from its pins. She moved as if there was music playing that only she could hear, and admiring glances followed in her wake. She caught my eye and gave a brief, bawdy wink.

Our intended target, Mr Wyncham – a twenty-four-year-old man who we believed had been making some unsavoury new friends – was all too easily distracted by Maud's swaying hips. He turned towards her, leering quite openly. Maud giggled – a high, coquettish titter that she would never make in real life – and Wyncham's smile widened. It was all so painfully predictable.

Keeping my gait steady I approached the pair, and then – just before I reached them – I pretended to trip slightly, falling into Wyncham's side, and knocking the drink in his hand down his front.

"I'm so sorry," I exclaimed. "How clumsy of me. Oh dear, you've spilled your drink, and it's all my fault! My aunt always says I must watch where I'm going because if there's a crack or a bump in the floor I'm bound to find it and go flying!" I wittered on, grasping Wyncham's arm as Maud came still closer. I had come to realize that the more I chattered like this, the less attention people – particularly men – seemed to pay.

"No harm done," Wyncham cut in, barely sparing me a glance. I caught Maud's eye and she gave the tiniest shake of her head.

The document we needed wasn't in his outer pockets. It must be tucked inside his jacket. I did a quick assessment. I was extremely familiar with men's coats, and this one was decently made, but shabby, repaired several times. The lines, however, were clean and it fitted well. There were no hidden pockets, I decided. It would be inside on his left.

I pressed my hand over my heart and Maud picked up the signal at once. "Why don't you let me dry you off a bit, sir," she purred, dusting down the front of his coat. Meanwhile, I pulled the handkerchief from my reticule, the one I had sprayed with "perfume" before I came downstairs.

As the man laughed at Maud's teasing, she extracted the letter from his breast pocket. Using the cover of her skirts she palmed the letter to me and I covered it in the handkerchief, pressing the back of the paper to my stomach and using the firm surface of my corset to apply pressure while I counted silently to three and prayed that Winnie's latest trick was going to work. Then I handed the letter back to Maud who had no difficulty returning it to Wyncham's pocket. Whatever it was she was whispering in his ear meant he was not at all worried about her wandering hands. The whole affair was over in seconds. Wyncham wouldn't be able to pick my face out of a crowd – even if he realized anything had happened.

The bell rang to indicate the performance was about to begin. As I walked back to my seat I pulled a silver fan from my reticule. Snapping it open to reveal an empty frame, I clipped the handkerchief swiftly into place, folding it back together in a smooth motion while I made my way up the stairs. Another one of Winnie's tricks.

Sylla appeared from the doorway to her box. "No, no, I'm sure I dropped it out here, and it's one of my favourites," she said, over her shoulder.

"Are you looking for this, Miss Banaji?" I asked, holding the fan out with a curtsey.

Sylla's fingers curled around the fan, which matched her gown perfectly, snapping it open for a brief moment before flicking it closed again.

"Indeed I was, Miss..." She looked down at me from her superior height.

"Stanhope," I murmured.

"Miss Stanhope," Sylla said lazily, her eyes already passing over me. "My thanks."

With that, she turned back to her box. "Found it," she called, dismissing me as she returned to her family.

I headed back along the corridor to my own seat, pushing through the doors and taking my seat with the minimum of fuss.

"Where have you been?" Teresa hissed, her eyes enormous. "They stayed for almost ten minutes, and he's *wonderful*, and I've had no one to talk to apart from Great-Aunt Louisa." She gestured towards the prone figure of her chaperone who was still sleeping with her mouth slightly open.

I didn't need to ask who *he* was. "Love at first sight!"

Teresa sighed, slumping woozily back in her seat, a beatific smile on her lips.

Teresa had been known to fall in love no less than three times in a single season, so I wasn't sure how seriously to take this declaration. Still, I had liked James St Clair on sight, and my skill at reading people had been honed considerably over the last year. "I'm glad you like him," I said lightly. "You've liked many a stupider person."

"*Like?*" Teresa's nose wrinkled. "I don't merely *like* him. Such an insipid word. Honestly, Izzy, we must try and find someone for you to have a passionate love affair with. You're always so sensible and, and … cheerful. It's not at all poetic."

"I'm sure there's plenty of cheerful poetry," I said mildly. "Only think of Wordsworth's daffodils. There's nothing more cheerful than a daffodil."

Teresa made a scoffing sound at this, which I took to be a scathing critique of Wordsworth's skills, and I knew I had successfully distracted her.

Fortunately, this conversation was cut short when the lights in the theatre were dimmed and silence fell across the audience. I glanced down towards Wyncham; Maud was nowhere to be seen. As I watched, I saw the man press his hand absently to his chest, right over the pocket that contained the letter. Clearly having reassured himself it was still there, his hand dropped and he sat back.

I couldn't help the grin that spread across my face then. It was so satisfying when a job went well.

There was a round of applause as the orchestra struck their first note.

I settled back, ready to enjoy the opera, but I found I couldn't miss the opportunity I had been presented with – when the lights were low and all eyes were focused on the stage – to turn and sneak a look over my shoulder at Max.

James St Clair was sitting forward, his forearms rested on the ledge in front of him. He was focusing intently on the opera and I gave him points for not sitting and mooning Byronically over Teresa. Even if mooning was precisely what I was about to do. Completely at ease with that bit of hypocrisy I let my gaze skate over to Max...

...who was looking straight back at me, his eyes glittering in the shadows, a small frown between his brows. Even his eyebrows were handsome, but now was not the moment to be distracted. Despite the hammering of my heart I forced myself to smile, and then turn, unhurriedly, to face the scene onstage.

I didn't hear a single note for the rest of the performance.

CHAPTER FOUR

Hours later, Teresa kissed my cheek as her carriage drew up outside my home. As usual, the house was wrapped in a thick darkness, unbroken by any sign of light from inside.

"Are you sure you're all right?" she asked, casting a doubtful look at the unlit façade. "It looks as if there isn't a soul at home!"

"Of course," I said cheerfully. "Mama is here, and she'll be waiting up to hear all the gossip. You know her rooms face on to the garden where she'll be less bothered by the noise from the street."

"And the servants will be waiting up as well, I suppose." Teresa nodded. "You really should ask them to leave a light burning for you."

"I really should." I smiled at her. "I'll come over tomorrow so that you can tell me all about James St Clair."

"Sounds delicious," Teresa agreed, easily distracted.

"GOODNIGHT, MISS TRENT," I bellowed at Great-Aunt Louisa.

She opened one eye and scowled at me. "No need to shout," she grumbled.

I jumped lightly down from the carriage and waved as it pulled away before hurrying through the wrought-iron gate and up the small path towards the house. Then I dug the key out from its hiding place in a nearby plant pot and let myself in.

Inside, it was so dark that I paused for a moment to allow my eyes to adjust. At least it wasn't completely freezing, as it had been over the winter. Thank goodness for these warm summer months when I didn't have to worry about the coal bill.

Grasping the stubby candle that I had placed on

the table in the hallway before I went out, I struck a match, the leap of the flame sending shadows chasing one another around the enormous, empty room. With the candle held in front of me I made my way along the hallway and then down the stairs to the kitchen. Setting my light down on the big, scrubbed table I proceeded to fill the kettle with water and place it on the stove. I went into the (mostly empty) pantry and took down the tea tin, giving it a hopeful shake. There was definitely something in there, though when I lifted the lid it was less than I had hoped. Well, I suppose no one ever died of weak tea.

I carried the tray up the stairs towards my mother's rooms. Along the way I passed room after room stripped of furniture, artwork, even curtains in some cases. I was used to it now – I suppose you can get used to most things. Not so long ago, it had left an ache in my chest seeing our home scraped clean as an oyster shell, but now I was able to walk past the empty rooms without being assailed by memories of different times. It was simply how things were and there was no use weeping and wailing over it. Much better to concentrate on fixing things than to dwell on them being broken in the first place.

When I reached Mama's bedroom I knocked gently, and the door swung open to reveal the scowling face of Button, my mother's maid.

"And what sort of a time is this to be bothering Her Ladyship?" Button demanded without preamble.

Button had been my mother's personal maid since Mama was younger than me, and she wasn't about to let a little thing like not being paid stop her from looking after "Her Ladyship". If Button had another name I had never heard it, she had simply been Button for my whole life – a bad-tempered angel who not only put up with my mother's hypochondria but cosseted her as though she were a precious, helpless infant. It was a relationship that I knew better than to interfere in.

"Is that Izzy?" Mama's excited voice came from the room, and Button's frown deepened.

"Come in, come in! I must hear all about it. Did Lady Farnworth really arrive with her new cicisbeo? Darling Andrea said in her last letter that it was absolutely *frightful* the way she had him fawning all over her, you'd think she'd have a bit more dignity at her time of life, but then, you know the rumour always was that she and her husband…"

Mama's chatter continued in this gleeful vein as I came in and laid out the tea service, Button looming over me at all times to make sure I didn't do anything unforgivable like spill a drop of tea or disturb Her Ladyship's carefully arranged bedside table.

The contrast between these rooms and the rest of the house was absolute. Despite the summer weather, a fire crackled merrily in the spotless fireplace. The deep red papered walls were crammed with oil paintings, the floor laden with richly coloured rugs. A vase stood on the ornate gilded dressing table holding a bouquet of blowsy silk roses. (It had taken only the merest suggestion that Mother's allergies were getting worse for her to agree that silk flowers would be better than real ones, thus abolishing my weekly bill from the florist with Mama none the wiser.)

In the middle of the room, my mother lay in an enormous canopy bed swathed in velvet throws and piled high with plump pillows. She wore a beautifully embroidered, lace-trimmed nightgown, and a little silk cap that tied beneath her chin. The table beside her was scattered with dozens of letters – correspondence with her friends that she kept up compulsively, often sending six or seven letters a day. I was surprised the news from the opera hadn't beaten me home. Sometimes, even with all my contacts, my mother was unwittingly the best source of information at my disposal.

"I don't think people use the word 'cicisbeo' any more, Mama," I said, bending to kiss her on the cheek and throwing myself into the cosy armchair she had had Button place by the side of her bed for when I came to sit with her.

"No, really?" Mama frowned. "But it's such a lovely word, so nice to say. *Cicisbeo*. What should I call him?"

"Her lover, I suppose." I took a sip of my tea.

She sighed. "I wish things would stop changing. But then the world must move on, without old ladies like me."

"Mama, you know perfectly well that you are not at all an old lady. Why, Mrs Tipton is always telling the story of that party when I was fifteen, and the general thought we were sisters..."

Mama leaned back into her pillows, a pleased smile on her lips. "The dear general, I'm sure the man needed eyeglasses."

"Nonsense, Your Ladyship," Button interjected briskly. "You barely look a day older than you did at sixteen."

"Oh, you pair of flatterers," Mama said, but she darted a glance at her reflection in the mirror above the fireplace and fluffed her hair.

"Izzy, you must have a word with Cook," Mama said then. "This tea is too weak."

I started guiltily. "Oh, do you think so?" I asked. "Certainly, I will mention it to her." I cast a look at Button, whose face took on a long-suffering expression.

Mother had declared herself bed-bound only days after Father's funeral, a combination of grief over losing her husband and lifelong hypochondria, we thought – until Dr Roberts diagnosed her with a genuine and serious heart complaint. She must avoid sudden shocks or overexerting herself, the doctor had said firmly. She had not left her small suite of rooms since that day, and I had assumed total management of the household ...

which now consisted only of me, Mama and Button. Not that Mama knew that.

After years of Mama treating every single sniffle as if it were a full-blown case of pneumonia, the diagnosis of a serious illness came as a horrible surprise, especially so close on the heels of Father's unexpected passing. The idea of losing another parent – of losing my sweet, funny, eccentric mother – was unthinkable. With the doctor's warning about shock ringing in our ears, Button and I had decided that what she didn't know couldn't hurt her, and in her room, in this little bubble, everything was as it had always been. My mother was perfectly happy to write to all her friends – far too vain to let them come and visit her in person – unwittingly keeping my reputation intact and the family secrets buried.

In fact, no one knew the whole truth about my situation.

No one except, perhaps, Mrs Finch.

CHAPTER FIVE

I should explain.

My father was a lovely man. Kind, gentle, clever, but absent-minded. The Stanhope name and line stretched back well into the annals of history and he had inherited a small estate and a dwindling fortune. He also had a peculiar skill: he was fascinated by locks. He spent hours tinkering with the things, and as a small child, while other little girls were playing with their dolls, I had been presented with a shiny set of lock picks. My father began to teach me to pick various locks, sometimes racing against a timer, sometimes against him. I remember the first time I ever beat him. I was twelve and the look on his face was one of pure, shining pride.

Father's skill meant that several companies consulted with him on their own security and provided him with an income, which was information he kept quiet, because it didn't do for a baron to work for a living. In fact, it was such a secret that even his family knew nothing about it, not until the night he died, suddenly, in his sleep.

My brother Henry became the new baron at eight years old, Mama fell quite spectacularly to pieces, unable to deal with any of the practicalities, and I found myself in possession of my father's big secret: the Stanhopes were almost penniless.

Henry was away at school, a school that the boys in our family had attended for centuries, a school that he loved, and his tuition was paid up until the end of the year, but that was the only blessing. The lawyer explained it to me in fairly simple terms: the financial decisions my father had made in a desperate bid to rebuild something of his family's fortunes had been catastrophic. Father was many things but a shrewd investor he was not. He had lost almost everything, throwing good money after bad – emptying out what remained of Mama's marriage settlement and even my own small dowry in his increasing panic. The only thing that had been keeping us afloat was Father's work, and his death had been so quick, so unexpected, that he simply hadn't left us provided for.

"I think he believed he had all the time in the world to steady the ship," the lawyer sighed. "He was always certain something would turn up and things would sort themselves out."

Yes, that sounded like my father, the eternal optimist. However, in this case that optimism had been misplaced and it fell to me to try and untangle the mess we were in.

The first thing I did was to contact the companies that Father had worked for. I was practically his apprentice – even better than him. But of course not a single one wanted to employ a woman, let alone a gentlewoman who, as one reply said, should be focused on more important things, like finding herself a husband.

It wasn't that simple. I would have considered marriage to save my family from ruin, but I wasn't exactly being flooded with offers. The small, mousy daughter of a lesser baron with no real fortune was hardly an appealing prospect. A penniless one who came with a family to support was actively to be avoided. And I knew that I would never be able to lie – if someone *did* want to marry me then I would have to tell them the truth about the money. After all, I'd be expecting them to look after Henry and Mama too, at least until Henry came of age. So I had taken Button into my confidence, dismissed the rest of the staff, and puzzled over how I was to find a way to keep Mama comfortable, to keep Henry in school, to keep the house running – at least for the foreseeable future.

It was around this time that I came out of deep mourning and returned to society. Mama may not have any idea about the reality of our situation, but she was as invested as the next woman in getting her daughter married off, and through her network of friends she made sure that I was invited and chaperoned everywhere, and she received plenty of updates on my progress. Or lack thereof.

"I can't think why you've become such a wallflower, Isobel," she would sigh. "There was nothing I used to love more than the excitement of a party."

Mama had been the toast of her own season, as she liked to listen to Father tell me while feigning embarrassment, and it was easy to see why. She was bright and vivacious, small and slight like me, but she had a cherubic face, huge violet eyes and a mop of golden hair. She looked like the angel on top of the Christmas tree, and despite only a modest dowry, she could have married almost anyone – but she married my father because they fell instantly and irrevocably in love. Father, who was mild and bookish and hated socializing, spotted her across a crowded ballroom and promptly asked for every slot on her dance card. They waltzed the entire evening away, oblivious to the scandal of it, only smiling and talking and dancing and knowing they would never be parted.

It was a wonderful story, one of my favourites. But it had seemed to me, as I tossed and turned at night trying to find a solution to our predicament, that a love like that didn't come along often. Certainly not one that was so wholeheartedly requited.

I am – as Teresa is quick to point out – quite a sensible, cheerful person. An optimist, like my father. I generally believe that things will work out. But after Father's death, and with Mama unwell, for the first time in my life I found myself under a dark cloud that I couldn't shake. Panic started to creep in, in ballrooms, in places with too many people. I would feel like I couldn't breathe, my hands would get clammy, then begin to tingle, my heart would start to race. It was as if the grief and the worry were coiling tighter and tighter around my chest, choking the life out of me.

That was how I felt the night I escaped from a party and fell for Max Vane.

The same night I met Sylla, and my life changed for ever.

I was in the lady's retiring room, ostensibly to fix the hem of my dress, but really because I wanted to hide in this warm, quiet room like a hibernating woodland creature, away from the mass of people I didn't know or care about, to digest what had just happened in the gardens where I had heard Max Vane laugh and apparently completely lost my wits.

Then Sylla Banaji walked in. I knew *of* her, of course, but we had never actually spoken. That evening she looked regal in a rich burgundy gown, enormous sapphires sparkling at her ears. She walked straight up to me, where I was sitting on a slightly scratchy, heavily embroidered chaise longue, and looked me over appraisingly, as one might do a horse they were considering purchasing.

"Can I help you?" I asked, not precisely politely. It had been an emotionally fraught evening.

Her eyelashes flickered as she reached into the pocket of her gown – a ball gown with pockets! – and pulled out a crisp white card, which she handed to me using the tips of her fingers.

"This is for you," she said shortly. "Make sure you're there." Then she turned and left in a swirl of red skirts and gardenia perfume.

I looked down at the card, which seemed to be for a business.

The Aviary

Mrs Finch

Proprietress

1 St Andrew's Road

London

The card was thick, heavily embossed in dark ink. On the back someone had scrawled: *Wednesday 5 p.m.*

I had no idea what was going on, but I could swear that my fingers tingled, that I felt something dance up and down my spine. Something like anticipation. I had no idea what awaited me at the Aviary, but I knew I would be there at the instructed time. And the tiny spark of hope that had awakened in my chest that night was fanned, if not quite into a flame, then at least into a flicker.

Thinking about the Aviary reminded me that my evening was far from over, and as comfortable as it may be sitting here in Mama's cosy rooms, I still had work to do.

"I think I had better go to bed and let you get some rest," I said, with a yawn that I didn't have to feign.

"Yes, Your Ladyship is looking a mite pale for my

liking," Button said, fussing with Mama's bedcovers, snapping them into perfect smoothness.

I looked more closely at Mama and felt a pang of worry. She *was* looking pale and drawn. While she was always reliably determined to elevate a cold into a case of the Spanish flu, she was also peculiarly dismissive of any actual symptoms or sign of serious illness.

"I'm fine," she said now, and the feeling of worry instantly grew, clenching tight in my belly.

Something of this must have shown in my face because Mama patted my hand reassuringly and Button's face softened fractionally.

"Don't you worry, miss," Button said firmly. "Nothing a good night's sleep won't fix, and she'll be right as rain in the morning."

"Oh, I don't know about right as rain," Mama sighed. "My neck has been aching *dreadfully* when I wake up. I wonder if we should get Doctor Roberts out … it could well be an early symptom of consumption."

I hid a grin of relief, and I thought even Button's mouth tugged up at the side.

"Let's see how you feel in the morning," Button said

placidly. "For tonight we can always try some of my medicine."

Mama fell silent at that, grimacing at me behind Button's turned back. I tried to smother my laugh by turning it into a cough, but I wasn't sure Button was fooled. Her "medicine", which she made herself (out of who knows what, though the doctor assured us it was perfectly harmless) and which lived in an enormous brown bottle, was used to treat everything from scraped knees to sore throats in our house. I had no idea about its efficacy, but it tasted absolutely vile and had a slimy consistency; I always imagined it was what swallowing a frog would feel like. Button swore by it, however, and it had been a strangely reassuring presence throughout my childhood.

"I'll check on you in the morning," I said, leaning down so that Mama could wrap her arms around me. "I'm going to call on Teresa, but not until the afternoon."

"Well, not too early, darling," my mother said, snuggling down into her pillows. "You know what a strain the morning light seems to be on my poor eyes."

Holding the candle in front of me, I made my way

down the corridor to my room. This room was not so bad either, really. I'd sold anything of financial value, but there were plenty of things that held another kind of value that I'd held on to. As well as a small bed, a wardrobe and an old chest of drawers, I had dragged Father's old workbench up under the window. Spread over that was his collection of locks – all kept in perfect condition by me. Although I could open them with ease I still tried to practise cracking them for at least twenty minutes a day – a routine that had been drilled into me by my father.

On the walls were framed watercolours that Mama had painted when I was small and she had developed a short-lived enthusiasm for the activity, of lopsided bluebells and a pastoral scene containing a collection of wobbly little sheep. The bookshelf was well stocked with novels from the circulating library, and I kept everything scrupulously clean, the pleasant smell of lavender and beeswax rising from each surface. It might be basic, but it was comfortable.

Now I made my way in quick strides to the other piece of furniture in the room, a locked chest from which I extracted a roll of bandages as well as a shirt, trousers, jacket and cap.

After a quick outfit change, I stood in front of the mirror to inspect myself. I had once overheard someone describing me as a "little dab of a thing". This was obviously quite lowering, but it was precisely why I had the dubious distinction of being the only woman at the Aviary who could pass herself off as a twelve-year-old boy.

I'll admit, it's perhaps not an achievement one dreams of as a young girl, but I couldn't argue with the results. Staring back at me from the mirror was a young man in worn clothing. Yes, I saw my own wide brown eyes, my slightly snub nose, covered in a smattering of freckles, my soft, round jawline, but with my mousy hair tucked carefully up under a shorn wig of the same indistinct colour, my cap pulled low, and my chest tightly bound, no one would question my identity. Even if they did, *who* in their right mind would make the connection between the Honourable Isobel Stanhope, society's most indistinct wallflower, and Kes, the light-fingered boy whose skills as a thief had earned him quite the reputation among a certain crowd? No one would. It was laughable. Half the time I didn't even believe it myself.

In a practised movement, I opened my window and slung my leg over the sill, shimmying easily out and down the conveniently placed trellis that climbed up this part of the house. I didn't want to be seen leaving through either the front door or the back; I had so far kept my job secret from both Button and Mama and I planned to keep it that way.

My feet hit the ground, and I let myself out of the back gate, sticking my hands in my pockets and whistling a jaunty tune as I turned and headed in the direction of the Aviary.

When Mrs Finch had first started training me in the role of Kes, over a year ago, I found every bit of it difficult. Unlearning years of feminine etiquette was no small thing, but now I slouched along comfortably, giving the impression of a young man at home walking the streets of London alone at night.

In fact, I enjoyed going out in my disguise. Isobel Stanhope couldn't walk around alone at night, but

Kes could. There were a whole lot of rules that Kes didn't have to follow – and not only because he was, I suppose, something of a criminal. Kes didn't have to worry about how he spoke or who he spoke to, Kes didn't have to dress properly, to walk properly, to eat properly or read properly, to have proper hobbies and proper manners. He didn't need to ask for anyone's permission to do *anything*. I didn't feel like a boy when I dressed as Kes; I felt like a girl with the *freedom* of a boy. And I liked it.

It wasn't a long walk from my house to the Aviary, and the streets were quiet. It was past midnight now but the air was still warm. Summer had started in earnest and the heat was about to turn stifling. The darkness was punctuated by the odd street lamp, casting its ghoulish-yellow glow in hazy circles. This part of town was pretty respectable, but I remained alert even as I presented the picture of ease, still whistling chirpily. It was all part of my training – only a fool let their guard down, but a clever person might let people *think* their guard was down. Being unpredictable was a real asset if there was any kind of fight. Not that I anticipated any trouble this evening.

When I reached the quiet, well-heeled street on which the Aviary was located, I slowed, casually examining the sole of my boot while doing a quick check up and down for anyone who might be watching. The Aviary was a well-kept secret, but that was because we practised extreme caution.

Above the door a sign hung, the words on it painted in swirling calligraphy.

The Aviary
For all a lady requires

CHAPTER SIX

I remembered the first time I had seen that sign.

I had presented myself at the Aviary that Wednesday at 5 p.m. exactly. My heart had sunk as I took in the shopfront. Why on earth had Sylla Banaji sent me to a haberdashery? Was it some not-so-subtle insult about the state of my wardrobe? That seemed unnecessarily cruel. Still, I had been told to be here, and I wasn't going to leave without seeing Sylla or this Mrs Finch – whoever she was.

It had been cold outside, grey and drizzling. The

lights were still on inside the shop, and the window glowed invitingly, filled with large glass jars of buttons in a hundred different colours. When I pushed the door open a musical little bell rang, and I was engulfed in an explosion of warmth and colour.

There were beautiful polished wood cabinets lining the walls, and the drawers had hand-painted gold labels, proclaiming them full of beads, or buttons, or skeins of thread. Ribbons and trims made of satin, lace and silk were on display, ranging like a rainbow all the way from a crimson so dark as to be almost black to rich, deep violet. Gilded bird cages hung from the ceiling, only instead of birds they contained intricate, climbing arrangements of beautiful silk flowers. I couldn't help dipping my fingers into one of the dishes of tortoiseshell buttons that sat on a small table in the middle of the room. They were smooth and cool to the touch, like pebbles.

"May I help you?" a voice asked, and I saw that there was a girl about my age standing behind a desk with a large brass till at the back of the shop, wearing a dark dress. She smiled at me from beneath a white lacy cap.

"I was given this card," I said hesitantly, pulling it

from my reticule. "It said to come here at five o'clock…"
I trailed off uncertainly, but the girl's smile only grew.

"Miss Stanhope," she said. "To see Mrs Finch."

"Yes. That's right."

The girl lifted the heavy velvet curtain on the wall behind her to reveal a door.

She opened the door, and beyond it I saw a small hallway with a staircase running steeply up one side. "Mrs Finch is waiting for you upstairs."

I paused. After all, what did I actually know about this place? If anything happened to me then what would become of Mama and Henry? But I couldn't ignore the feeling that *something* happening was precisely what I needed, precisely why I had come here today. I stepped past the curtain and began the climb upstairs.

The girl locked the door behind me, which was not especially reassuring, but I tried not to dwell on that. I was taking my destiny into my own hands. Or was I placing it in this Mrs Finch's? Either way it felt as if my feet had been set on a certain path the moment I crossed that threshold.

The stairwell was dark and at the top was another

closed door. This one had a brass sign nailed to it with no words at all, only the image of a small bird.

I held my hand up, hesitating again for a moment before knocking as firmly as possible.

"Come in." The words came, crisp and absolutely dripping with authority. Something about that voice made my spine stiffen, like a soldier being called forward for inspection, and I turned the handle.

I'm not sure what I was expecting, but it certainly wasn't what I found. The room I stepped into was something like a sitting room, but larger … a salon, perhaps. It must have taken up the entire second floor of the building. There were deep red curtains swagged around tall windows, and an enormous chimney breast in the middle of the room indicated there had once been a wall running down the centre that had been removed. Now, groups of mossy-green chairs and dark plum velvet sofas were gathered cosily around the double-sided fireplace. Scattered elsewhere were inviting armchairs, next to low tables covered in newspapers and periodicals. Three tables with chess sets flanked one wall – each one looked as though it had been abandoned in the middle of a game. There were bookcases too, stuffed to overflowing with books that looked as though they were in no particular order at all, and an upright piano sat in one corner.

The walls had been painted white, but someone had covered them in tall, twining murals of plants and flowers, though not the sort of flora one usually found in the English countryside. These were spiky, vivid things, a snarl of vines and hothouse blooms.

Along the back wall, the artist had left the white paint untouched, except for the words, painted starkly in tall, bold letters,

I am no bird; and no
net ensnares me:
I am a free human being
with an independent will.

I recognized it at once as a quote from *Jane Eyre*, a favourite of mine (not least because I had always heartily identified with its heroine in feeling *poor, obscure, plain and little*).

The woman who was sitting in one of the armchairs

cleared her throat and my attention turned to her. She was, I would guess, in her late thirties, and very pretty. Her light brown hair was pulled away from her face, which was soft and round. Her generous figure was wrapped in a delicious blue gown trimmed with silver ribbon. Her eyes were the same bright, striking blue as her dress, and in contrast to the rest of her – which screamed soft, delicate, feminine – those eyes were shrewd and calculating.

She stood with a rustle of sapphire-blue skirts and looked at me for a moment. I felt the weight of interrogation as her gaze darted over me from top to toe. A small smile seemed to curl in the left-hand corner of her mouth.

"Miss Stanhope, I presume," she said. "I am Mrs Finch."

I sketched a curtsey. "It's nice to meet you," I said.

She gave a short, dry laugh. "We shall see if that continues to be the case. Please, won't you join me?" She gestured towards the seats nearest the fireplace, and I noticed there was an ornate tea tray waiting for us.

"Thank you," I said, as I sank into one of the chairs,

as if the situation was completely normal, as if this sort of meeting took place every day. I still had absolutely no idea why I was here. In fact, the more I saw of this place, the less of an idea I had. The glass cabinet I had glimpsed on the way to my seat appeared to contain an extensive collection of antique firearms.

"You are wondering why you've been invited here," Mrs Finch said, pouring the tea with a graceful ease.

Her words were not a question but I nodded anyway, accepting the fine china cup and saucer from her outstretched hand. "I suppose I am," I said. "I don't..." I floundered for a moment. "What *is* this place?"

That smile again, the one that wasn't really a smile, more the promise of one to come.

"This..." she sat back in her seat and looked at me over the top of her cup, "is the Aviary. It is both a place of business and a ... *refuge* for like-minded women."

"A sort of club?" I ventured. "Like gentlemen have."

"Something like that," Mrs Finch agreed. "Though we provide a much more important service, one to women in need."

I sipped my tea, mulling over her words. The tea

was perfect, steaming, liquid amber, neither too hot nor too cold, too strong nor too weak. "Women in need?" I repeated.

She nodded. "As you are no doubt aware, the married women's property act, which passed fifteen years ago, has helped to address a small handful of the more urgent problems facing women today. A married woman is now legally recognized as a person in her own right, rather than simply an extension of her husband – which seems to demonstrate the bare minimum of common sense required from our law makers." Her voice held obvious distaste, and I nodded eagerly in agreement as she continued. "However, there are still a multitude of problems faced by women, both married and unmarried, that the courts and the laws of this land fail to adequately address. That," she lifted an eyebrow, "is where *we* come in."

"The Aviary?"

"Yes. The Aviary is an agency run by women for women. We do not advertise our existence, our clients tend to find us, or – occasionally – we find them. We work for women in every level of society – some women pay us large sums, some don't pay us at all, some make generous donations so that we can continue to fight for the most vulnerable. We investigate all sorts of different cases from thefts to infidelities to the occasional murder, but we specialize in acquiring the necessary leverage for our clients to live their lives as fully and peacefully as possible."

"Necessary leverage?" I asked blankly, trying to look unmoved by the casual mention of "occasional murder".

She took another sip of her drink. "I suppose if we were being vulgar we might call it blackmail material. We secure information that certain men would not like to be shared publicly, and then we hand this over to the women who may use it as they require, whether that's to gain money or freedom to travel, or a safe space away from their husband where they will be left in peace." Her nose wrinkled. "It is not always a pleasant business, but it is, unfortunately, a necessary one. I do not exaggerate when I say such interventions have literally saved lives. A wife can be sadly expendable to a certain kind of man."

I stilled at that. It was an idea that I had never looked

at head on, though it hovered on the edge of my mind, like a twinge of toothache that you tried to ignore whenever the pain flared. Mama and Father had been deeply in love, in many ways they had been a model for wedded bliss, and yet now – thanks in large part to my father's actions – my mother's future was shaky and uncertain. And that was a *good* marriage. Not all partnerships were as successful; society gossip was full of unhappy or poorly treated wives. However, I still didn't understand why I was here.

I frowned. "Forgive me, Mrs Finch," I said. "I think there's been some mistake. Your organization sounds very interesting, but I don't require your services at the moment. My own problems are … of a different nature."

"Oh, I didn't invite you here because I thought you were a *client*," Mrs Finch said breezily. "I invited you here to offer you a job."

"A job?" The words came out in an undignified squeak.

Mrs Finch took her time, topping up our teacups, and stirring sugar into hers, the slow, deliberate circles of the teaspoon chiming against the side of her cup, the sound loud in the otherwise silent room.

"I knew of your father's work," she said, surprising me into spilling some of my own tea on to my skirts. "I also know that he was training you, and that you were rejected from the companies that he worked for on the basis of your gender." She handed me a linen handkerchief, embroidered with a small bird – a goldfinch, I dimly registered, as I set about dabbing at my dress.

"How do you know *that*?"

This time she did smile, a wide smile that showed off her teeth. "Miss Stanhope, you will soon find that there are few things I don't know."

I was beginning to believe that.

"So you wish to offer me a job because of my skill with locks?" I said.

"As you may imagine, your skill set could prove extremely useful in our line of business." She inclined her head. "Along with your social connections. You have access to the sort of places where the information we trade in is ... plentiful."

She was right. Our financial situation might be

dismal, but my family name was an old one that carried with it just enough lingering social cachet. Not only was I frequently invited into the homes of the kind of men that the Aviary may be investigating, but there was not a locked door that could stand between me and anything that Mrs Finch was looking for. There was also the fact that I was so nondescript that no one paid any particular attention to me. I was certain that Mrs Finch had already made that observation as well.

But could I really do such a wild and risky thing?

Something of these feelings must have shown in my face, because Mrs Finch continued. "You will of course be generously compensated for your time. Enough to keep your brother in school with a tidy sum left over." I didn't even bother asking how she knew about Henry's school fees. "There will also be a clothing allowance, as we will require you to continue your social engagements. And you will be trained in the arts of disguise, self-defence, that sort of thing."

"So you really are offering me the job?" I asked.

"I'm offering you the opportunity to become one of the Aviary's Finches." Mrs Finch placed her teacup down on the table and got to her feet, and for the first time it occurred to me that "Mrs Finch" may not be her real name at all. "We are the agents of the Aviary, and the last line of defence for many women in this country. It is serious work, Miss Stanhope, important work, and I am inviting you to take part in it. However, it would be wrong of me not to … *illuminate* the risks for you. You would have to keep your work completely secret, we operate effectively from the shadows. One word of this agency gets out and it could jeopardize our entire operation. Not to mention the fact that should your involvement be discovered you and your family would be ruined in the eyes of society, *utterly* ruined." Her eyes were hard, and her words matched.

"There are plenty of powerful men with reason to resent us and what we do. The world that you inhabit, the one that you wish to remain in for the sake of your mother and your brother would not take kindly to knowing that one of their own had been digging into their grubby little secrets." Her gaze met mine. "This path is not the safe one, Miss Stanhope, but our cause is righteous, and it is one that I believe to be worth the sacrifice. The question is whether you do too."

Her words clanged like a bell through my whole body. This job could easily destroy our reputations – mine, Mother's and Henry's. It could sully the Stanhope name for ever. It was a scandal waiting to happen.

Or it could save us all.

I got to my feet and held out my hand. "When can I start?"

CHAPTER SEVEN

It had been a year and a half since I had accepted Mrs Finch's invitation and I had not regretted it for a moment. Alongside the money, there was the bone-deep, all-encompassing thrill of it. The adrenaline that came with doing a job, the joy of feeling not only useful, but *necessary*. It was not something many eighteen-year-old girls of my station got to feel.

Now, I – or rather Kes – let myself in through the back door of the shop, and made my way through the storeroom and then up the stairs and into the salon. It was a busy night, and despite the late hour there were over a dozen women in there, some of them deep in conversation, some of them bent over a map spread out on a table, a couple playing what looked to be an intense game of chess. The room was filled with the sound of chatter and laughter, and something jaunty on the piano. It looked like the good malt whisky had been broken out.

Several of the women called a greeting as I passed through – even in my boy's clothes they knew who I was. I pushed through the door in the corner, revealing another staircase, this one lit by a single branch of candles. The noise of the salon dropped away as the door swung shut behind me and I made my way up to the real base of the Aviary.

The third floor of the building was where Mrs Finch's office was to be found. There was also a training room where we practised everything from fencing to scrappy street fighting; a storeroom that contained all sorts of weird and wonderful objects; and a workshop and small laboratory. I headed straight for the office to debrief on this evening's activities. I only hoped that Winnie's experiment had worked.

Upon opening the door I discovered I was the last to arrive. Sylla was in a tall, straight-backed chair, examining her fingernails, and Mrs Finch was sitting behind her enormous desk, poring over some papers, while Maud – her face scrubbed clean of the rouge she had worn at the theatre – sprawled across the battered Chesterfield sofa, her head resting in Winnie's lap.

Within the Finches, there were different groups who were assigned to work together, and this was mine. The groups were called charms – the collective noun for a group of finches – and assigned a number for all administrative purposes. Our group was charm number four, and we were good. Really good.

Winnie looked up to greet me with one of her sweet, vague smiles. The third daughter of the third son of an earl, Winnie Phillips and I had occasionally run into one another before I joined the Finches, though she attended far fewer social events than I did. We had been recruited at the same time, and swiftly put into a charm with Maud and Sylla – who was the head of our group.

Winnie was a genius; a scientist and a world-class mathematician rolled into one. She had an incredible memory and created the most useful pieces of equipment for our various activities. Not that anyone outside the Aviary knew any of that – all they saw was a dreamy, scattered young woman who rarely remembered to do things like brush her fine blonde hair or wear matching stockings.

Her clever fingers were gently untangling the knots in Maud's hair and Maud was practically purring, looking up at Winnie adoringly.

Sylla's eyes fell on me then, and she jumped to her feet. "Finally," she said.

"Did it work?" I asked.

"It's a little late in the day to be asking that, isn't it?" Sylla muttered.

"Of course it worked," Maud grinned, pulling herself upright and giving Winnie a smacking kiss on the cheek. "My girl's a genius."

Winnie blushed. "It was only a matter of formulating a simple solvent for you to soak the handkerchief in."

"And creating the fan to hide it in," I said.

Winnie waved a dismissive hand, as if to indicate such a thing wasn't even worth mentioning.

I moved over to Mrs Finch's desk where the handkerchief was spread out. One side of it was covered in an almost perfect transfer of Wyncham's letter.

"Some of the letters are a little smudged," I said, tracing the lines with my finger.

Mrs Finch shrugged. "They're still legible, and if Wyncham's letter is smudged he will put it down to the drink you spilled on him."

"He spilled it on himself," I said, moving back from the desk. "I only helped."

"It was a good plan, Sylla." Mrs Finch tipped her head towards our leader. Sylla's lips pressed together, ever so slightly, as if to try and fight a smile.

"We could have been faster," she said, fixing Maud and I with an accusatory glare. "You two were too slow on locating the letter and, Maud, you hung around far too long afterwards."

Maud snorted. "*You* weren't the one who had to disentangle yourself from the man. He was like an octopus."

"I bet that didn't last long," I suggested.

"Let's just say he might be walking with a bit of a limp the next few days," Maud smirked.

Of all of us, Maud was undoubtedly the toughest. She had been one of the Finches for a long time, ever since she had arrived on the Aviary's doorstep at the age of twelve, having been sent by a friend of her mother's. Her mother – a factory worker with no family of her own – had died, and the Aviary had taken her in. She still lived in a small room up in the eaves of the building.

"Is it enough?" I asked Mrs Finch, who was laying the handkerchief out next to her typewriter, ready to be copied several times before adding it to the fat file on her desk.

"I believe so. The letter details where the missing girls are, we were right to think that Wyncham had been recruited as a go-between and these instructions for him explicitly implicate Sharpe. We should have everything we need to shut down Sharpe's entire enterprise." She flexed her fingers. "My contacts at the police have already secured the girls' release."

I was glad to hear it. Andrew Sharpe had come to our attention when we received reports of several young girls going missing in the seedier part of town. The sort of young girls no one was likely to miss. Our investigation that had been ongoing for the last three months revealed that Sharpe had his fingers in many pies, but the main one included buying and selling young girls like pieces of cattle. Discovering a weak link in the chain of men working for him had led us to Wyncham, a down-on-his-luck chancer who had recently been drawn into Sharpe's employ by the promise of quick, easy cash, and we had it on good information that he had received a letter from Sharpe, full of incriminating details. Now, there would be no way for Sharpe to avoid punishment – not when the police force and the press received such ironclad evidence of his crimes.

"Good," Sylla said, already on her way to the door. "Then our business is concluded."

"Will you come and have a drink downstairs?" Winnie asked, though Sylla rarely joined us in our post-job celebrations.

"I should get home," she replied.

Winnie's face dropped, but I caught a glimpse of relief on Maud's, and I understood. It was always difficult to feel relaxed around Sylla, as if she were about to produce a list of all the mistakes we had made on a job and tell us how incompetent we were. (Actually, she had done this on several occasions, and so it wouldn't come as a surprise at all.)

Sylla also had a harder time keeping her secrets than the rest of us, because she had a large, busy household who actually paid attention to her. From what I understood there was an elaborate system in place which involved several members of the household staff and some heavy bribes whenever she needed to attend this sort of meeting.

"Izzy," Mrs Finch said, halting me on my way to the door. "Can you stay back for a moment?"

It seemed *my* evening was not done. The others trooped out as I held back.

"I need you to head down to the King's Head," Mrs Finch said without preamble. "Sally will meet you there. She has messages to pass over to me."

"All right," I said, fighting the urge to yawn. I knew she wouldn't ask if it wasn't important.

I made my way back down to the salon, where

I waved at Winnie and Maud – who were deep in conversation with a couple of the salon's regulars – and gestured to indicate that I still had work to do. Winnie looked sympathetic, Maud rolled her eyes, and I departed with a wave, back out into the night.

This time I headed towards Whitechapel and through the twisting, turning streets in the direction of the docks. I walked with practised ease, but kept to the shadows, my blood thrumming and all my senses alert. Even in my disguise as Kes, these streets were dangerous, the stuff of all-too-true horror stories.

I remembered vividly the first time I had ventured down here at night, not alone but with another of Mrs Finch's agents. The cacophony of noise, the press of people – even so late at night – coupled with the eerie silence of other, smaller winding streets and alleyways that appeared empty but still throbbed with menace, was completely overwhelming. I had actually worried that my knees were going to give out at some points, they were trembling so hard. No amount of training at the Aviary could truly prepare you for the reality of this part of the city.

These days I was wise enough to be wary, but my knees were pretty sturdy. I made my way as quickly as possible to the King's Head, which was located on Back Church Lane, a spindly, soot-streaked brick building with a battered sign hanging over the door.

Inside I found the usual handful of unsavoury characters, nursing their glasses of gin and eating the greasy sausage rolls that Sally, the landlord's wife (the person who actually ran the place while her husband drank himself into a stupor upstairs), made in the small kitchen. The place was dingy, full of the sort of shadowy corners where shadowy deals could be hashed out.

"All right, Kes," Sally nodded at me from behind the bar. "Have a seat and I'll bring your usual."

"Cheers, Sal," I replied easily.

I chose a table in the back and took a seat facing the door, ever alert to danger, propping my elbows on the slightly sticky surface of the table, and trying not to inhale too deeply the smell of tallow candles and stale beer that permeated the air. I drew one or two looks, but nothing worrying. I was known around here.

Once I'd had the requisite training in self-defence

and had mastered the art of shimmying up and down drainpipes in perfect silence, Mrs Finch had set "Kes" up as a low-level criminal with a talent for picking locks, on the lookout for work. The thieves I worked with were specially chosen by Mrs Finch; they were targeting people we also needed to steal something from. It was a clever plan, but then cold-hearted efficiency was a trademark of my employer's schemes.

I had slipped into the role of common thief with worrying ease; but there was a Robin Hood quality to the whole affair that stamped out any potential moral qualms I might feel simply enough. I only stole from bad men, men who had something I needed, and anything of value that I did steal went back to fund work at the Aviary, work that protected their victims. I didn't feel a moment of worry over that side of things, though the fear of being caught always added a certain amount of tension to proceedings.

Mrs Finch had not been exaggerating when she said that my work for the Finches could destroy the Stanhope name and reputation for good. A baron's daughter running around Whitechapel in boy's clothes?

Stealing from her fellow aristocrats? They'd probably cheerfully wave me off to Highgate Prison, never mind what would happen to Mama and Henry. The stakes were so high that it felt constantly like walking a swaying high wire. Still, I'd be lying if I said it wasn't fun, or maybe even that it was the element of danger that added to the thrill of it all.

Sally appeared then, a pint of watered-down beer in her hand, along with one of the sausage rolls wrapped up in paper.

"'Ere you are," Sal said, sliding the items across the table towards me.

I pulled a coin from my pocket and pressed it into her hand and she bustled away.

I carefully unwrapped the pastry, folding the thick papers that surrounded it into squares and tucking them inside the pocket of my jacket. Then I turned hungrily to the sausage roll. I was starving by this point, and as long as one didn't spend any time considering what might be in them, Sal's sausage rolls were actually quite tasty.

I was nonchalantly sipping my beer and thinking I could probably slip out now without drawing any attention, when a man appeared and dropped into the seat across from me.

He was tall and spare, dressed in dark, ragged clothing, and his face was sharp beneath a thatch of pale, greasy hair. He had a series of dots tattooed across the back of the hand that was grasping his drink. I knew him by reputation, but we hadn't spoken before.

I took a slow, deliberate sip of my drink and leaned back in my chair. "Rook, isn't it?" I said, pitching my voice in the gruff tones I used when I was playing Kes. "What can I do for you?"

"Heard you're a decent screwsman," Rook replied in a rasping voice that was almost a whisper. "Might have a job for you if you're interested?"

"Might be," I said offhandedly. If Rook was looking for a lock pick then whatever he was up to may well be of interest to Mrs Finch. "What's the job?"

Rook sat back in his chair, mirroring my posture and pursed his lips, his eyes scanning my face appraisingly. He was deciding exactly how much to tell me. Too much and I could snake the job out from under him, not enough and I might not be interested.

"Got a cove who wants us to nab some jewellery," he said at last. "Big score, and he's only interested in one piece. The rest's for us. He can help get us into the house. It's easy money, but I need someone who's fast with the twirlers to get us in and out, sharpish."

"Why's he only want the one piece?" I asked.

Rook shrugged. "Dunno. Didn't ask. He's one of the nobs himself, only interested in a ruby brooch. Says it's not even the most valuable thing in there. It's a big haul. Really big."

A gentleman, organizing a dangerous robbery – who only wanted one item. Now that *was* interesting. I was about to ask another question when I saw movement by the front door, and my whole body stiffened. I felt my eyes widen, and Rook darted a look over his shoulder, following my gaze.

He cursed impressively under his breath, sliding from his chair and heading for the back door without another word. I barely noticed, too focused on the men in front of me.

Standing by the door was James St Clair, and with him was Max Vane.

CHAPTER EIGHT

I blinked. What on earth was the Duke of Roxton doing in one of the seedier pubs in London's East End? Clearly, Max and James had made *some* efforts at blending in. Gone was the tailored evening wear from the opera, and in its place they wore dark, heavy overcoats, and caps pulled low. But everything about them was too clean, too expensive. By society's standards they looked big and dangerous, but here … well, here they looked like what they were, a pair of toffs well out of their depth.

They walked to a table in the corner and took

their seats. The hum of conversation in the room did not falter, no one glanced their way, yet I could feel every person's attention focused on the two men, with an intensity that simmered like a pan over a flame, threatening to boil over at any moment.

Sally went over. "What'll it be?" she asked roughly.

"Pint of arf-an-arf," Max growled in a passable working-class accent. I was surprised that he even knew to order the drink – a mixture of half a pint of dark porter and half a pint of ale.

"Same," James grunted.

Sally went off to fetch the drinks, and Max and James sat back in their seats, speaking occasionally to one another in low voices. Gradually, I could feel the atmosphere in the room relax, ever so slightly.

I gestured to Sal for another drink of my own, and pulled a knife from my boot. In my pocket was a small piece of wood that I was whittling vaguely into the shape of a bear. At least I think it was going to be a bear. It could have been a chicken. I was not a skilled whittler, but Mrs Finch had taught me that in times like this it was important to have something to do with your hands, to be the apparent focus of your attention. It stopped me from doing things like openly staring across a dangerous bar at the man I was infatuated with.

The minutes ticked past, and Max and James nursed their drinks. Two men came through the door. They were, I knew, the sort of men who were quick to raise their fists and – perhaps more worryingly – they were frequently paid to do so. I saw their gazes settle, for a fraction of a second, on Max and James.

I could feel tension, taut like a piano wire about to snap, spreading around the room. I wasn't sure if Max felt it too. He gave no indication of the fact. His eyes travelled around the bar, and at one point his gaze fell on me, lingered only for a second before travelling on.

Whoever or whatever they were waiting for, it didn't appear to be happening. It was well after one o'clock in the morning now. They must have reached the same conclusion, because James muttered something in Max's ear. A flicker of irritation passed over his face, before he jerked his head in a nod.

Reaching in his pocket, James fished out a couple of coins which he slapped down on the table, then the pair of them got up and made their way back towards the door and out on to the street.

Only seconds passed before the two men I had noticed earlier peeled themselves away from their seats and casually followed.

I looked at Sal and she rolled her eyes. She was right. A pair of daft men getting in a scrap with a load of other daft men was hardly any concern of mine. Except ... this was Max.

I hesitated for a moment longer. I knew what Mrs Finch would say. I shouldn't get involved. I should leave Max Vane to fight his own battles and make my way back to the Aviary quick sharp, to deliver the information currently residing in my pocket.

I pulled myself to my feet and walked towards the door. Back Church Lane was a long, narrow street, poorly lit and full of dank shadows. As I expected, I emerged to find trouble.

The two men I had seen must have had friends waiting outside. Max and James were fighting for their lives against six men. Rather unexpectedly they were doing a decent job of it. James had just delivered a punishing right hook to another man's face, knocking him almost clean off his feet. Max was facing off with one of the bigger assailants, and if it hadn't been for sheer numbers I'd have said that he had the advantage.

He had at least two inches on even the tallest of the men coming at him, and was doing an excellent job of communicating that he was, in fact, a solid wall of muscle. However the numbers *weren't* on his side and another man threw himself into the action, bringing the total they were fighting up to seven.

With a sigh I flung myself into the fray, intercepting a blow that was aimed at Max's back with my forearm, and kicking the surprised-looking attacker hard between the legs. He fell down with a noise that was somewhere between a wheeze and a howl, and Max spun round to face me.

"What are you—" he began, but he didn't get very far with his question because one of the other men – I recognized him as a bruiser called Nero – lamped him in the jaw.

"For God's sake, pay attention," I grumbled, pulling the knife from my boot and swinging it round to the fleshy part of Nero's leg, above his knee. I made only a shallow cut but Nero gave a sound of alarm. He hadn't been expecting the weapon, and he seemed to properly notice me now for the first time. I didn't have much of a reputation for violence – Mrs Finch was clear that we were taught to fight *defensively* – but I knew how to handle myself. I wiped the knife casually on the dark sleeve of my jacket.

"I'd stay out of this, Kes," Nero growled. "We've got our instructions."

"And I've got mine," I replied, smiling coldly.

That was enough to give him pause. I had all sorts of friends in high – or rather low – places, and although Nero's fists clenched at his sides, he nodded, dragging himself to his feet and stumbling away. "Come on, lads," he barked.

The others backed off, glaring at me.

Max was looking at me as though I had fallen from the sky.

James was standing with his hands braced on his knees, clearly winded after a blow to the stomach. In the distance I could hear footsteps running in this direction. Reinforcements who may be far less inclined to listen to me.

I put my hand on Max's arm. "Come with me," I said. "Both of you. Now." Without waiting for an answer, I turned and ran.

I might have been taught how to fight, but the far more important lesson had been learning when – and where – to run. It was a rule that had been drilled into me. *Only fools stay and fight if they don't have to.* I had spent hours poring over maps of the city until I could hold them in my mind, then more hours walking the streets to find anything the maps might have missed. I knew every blind alley, every twist and turn, and I ran light-footed now with the two of them following behind me.

Fortunately they were fast, but unfortunately they were neither small nor quiet, and the footsteps behind us persisted. It took a long and circuitous route before I felt confident we had lost the men on our tail. Eventually I came to a stop in a quiet lane that was a loading area for a wine merchant's premises, with several conveniently stacked crates providing cover.

My breath was coming hard, and I knew that my legs would be aching tomorrow, but it seemed like we were reasonably safe at least. For now. Max must have thought the same, because he took this opportunity to grab me by the collar of my jacket.

"Who," he demanded, "are you?"

"A nice way to treat the person who saved your skin," I protested, aiming a kick at his shins. He released me. I couldn't help but notice that our escape had left him looking rather ... dishevelled.

"The lad's right," James put in. "There were too many of them. They must have known we were there."

And who exactly were they? I wondered.

Max made an impatient noise. "I know, God damn it," he said shortly, and he looked like he too would like to kick someone.

Then he turned to me and held up his hands in a placating gesture. "Sorry. I'm grateful for your help. I don't know what we'd have done without it."

I dusted off my jacket. "You'd be in an alley with a knife stuck in your belly," I said matter-of-factly. "You had no business being in the King's Head."

He gave me an amused look. "And who are you to be telling me where my business should be taking place?"

I glowered at him. "I'm someone who knows better than to turn up to a place like that looking like a toff wearing his coach driver's coat." A look of chagrin passed over Max's face and I rolled my eyes. "That's exactly what you're wearing, isn't it?"

James St Clair burst out laughing and turned to Max. "I told you they wouldn't pass muster."

Max scraped a rueful hand across his jaw. "We were in a tight spot and time wasn't on our side. I improvised."

"Well, if you're going to do any more improvising I'd suggest you keep your drivers in shabbier gear," I replied.

"The point is taken," Max said, casting a quelling look at James who was still laughing. Then he turned his attention to me. "So," he said, and I reached up to tug my cap a little lower, shadowing my eyes. "Now do we get an introduction?"

I shrugged, digging my hands in my pockets. "Name's Kes."

"Well, Kes, I wonder if – now that you've gone to the trouble of saving us – we might trouble you for a little information?" A flash of silver appeared in Max's hand, like he was a magician plucking coins from the air.

"Depends what kind of information," I replied. I kept my eyes on the coin, which is what they'd expect. A magpie distracted by something shiny.

"We're looking for a man, tall, angular, light hair. Prison tattoo on the back of his right hand. Have you seen him?"

I kept my face bland. Why on earth were Max and James looking for Rook? No wonder he'd scarpered as soon as they arrived. Had he been the one who'd sent the toughs after them? Nero had certainly done work for Rook before.

"Might have done. More than one bloke with tattoos in that place."

"How about," Max said, holding the coin out, "you take this for now, and if you can bring me any information about that man then there'll be plenty more where that came from."

My brain was going a mile a minute. "Why are you looking for him?" I couldn't help but ask.

Max considered me. "Let's just say ... we want to ask him some questions."

There was something in his voice, something dangerous that didn't seem to belong to a gentleman at all, something that belonged here in the world where things were vicious and cut-throat.

"All right," I said, snatching the money from his hand. "How do I find you?"

"Number 27, Grosvenor Square," Max said. "Ask for Roxton."

It was his home address, one of the most fashionable in town. Strange that he would willingly hand it out to a boy like Kes. I had obviously passed some sort of test.

I whistled. "Coo-ee, you really ain't from round here, are you? No wonder you nearly got yourself killed."

Max smiled then, a proper smile, and it shot right through me. "*Nearly* being the operative word."

And with that he turned and walked away, James limping after him. I stared at his retreating shadow.

Who on earth was this man?

CHAPTER NINE

By the time I returned to the Aviary the sun was struggling up over the horizon. The sky was beginning to burn pink around the edges, and I felt as though I could fall asleep standing up.

When I dragged myself up to Mrs Finch's office I found her – as I had expected – waiting for me. She looked as fresh and unruffled as ever, not at all like a woman who had stayed up all night working, and when I entered the room she said nothing, merely looked at me with her eyebrows raised.

I expect I made quite a picture. My jacket had been ripped badly enough that one sleeve was all but torn off. There was blood spattered on the front of my shirt (not my own blood) and oozing from an ugly cut on my arm (very much my own blood). I walked stiffly to a chair, collapsing into it and pulling the papers Sal had given me from my pocket. At least they were still in one piece. I threw them on top of the desk with a wince. My arm was throbbing.

Mrs Finch pulled a tin from her drawer which I knew contained a medical kit – she had them in every room in the place – and helped me shrug off my shirt before setting to cleaning and bandaging my arm. She worked for a while in silence. My eyes fluttered closed. I was in safe hands.

No one at the Aviary seemed to know about Mrs Finch's history (and I had definitely asked), but at some point it was clear she had received some kind of medical training. She was efficient when it came to treating all sorts of injuries, and had once – so the story went – successfully removed a bullet from someone's shoulder on the desk in this very room.

"Keep still," she said when I flinched away from the sting of the alcohol on the wound.

It was several wince-inducing minutes before she finished. I pulled the ragged remains of my shirt over my head and filled her in on everything that had happened this evening. She interrupted my story only twice.

"A ruby brooch?" she asked when I got to the part about Rook approaching me about the job. "And a gentleman setting the whole thing up?" to which I nodded; and, "You told him nothing?" when I revealed that Max had also been looking for Rook.

"Of course I told him nothing," I said. "But what I can't understand is why the Duke of Roxton was out in Whitechapel looking for Rook in the first place!"

If I had expected Mrs Finch to share in my bafflement I was to be sorely disappointed. "Oh, *that*," she waved an airy hand, "must be to do with his work for the intelligence agency."

"His ... *what*?" I gasped.

Mrs Finch looked at me, her eyes blinking closed in an expression that was decidedly feline.

"Maximillian Vane has for some years been an agent

of the Crown, working under the aegis of Lord Samuel Morland."

My mouth remained open as this news soaked in. I did not bother to question if it was true. If Mrs Finch said it, then it was a certainty.

"Lord Morland," I murmured, focusing on the rest of the information for now. "The Lord Morland who's supposed to be our next prime minister?"

Everyone knew about Morland, the man who had risen rapidly through the political ranks over the last few years to become one of the most influential figures in Westminster. He was in the process of trying to pass a big defence bill, I knew, concerned about keeping England's green and pleasant lands as green and pleasant as possible by being armed to the teeth.

Mrs Finch nodded. "The wheels of change grind slowly, but Morland has been attempting to put together an official intelligence division within the government for some time. He's obsessed with national security, and I anticipate his efforts will be successful before long, but for the time being there remains a more shadowy organization who see to the government's secrets. Your duke is part of that."

"*My* duke?" I spluttered. "He's not *my* duke, I barely know the man. He doesn't even know who I am..." I trailed off as Mrs Finch regarded me calmly.

"I can't say that I blame you, Isobel," she said. "We've all been drawn to a handsome face every now and then."

Mrs Finch wore a wedding ring although no one quite knew if Mr Finch was either alive or indeed real.

"Have you and Mr Finch been married long?" I asked, pushing my luck.

She eyed me narrowly, refusing to rise to my question.

"I wonder you hadn't discovered this about Vane yourself," she said instead. "You seem to pay him a great deal of attention."

I gritted my teeth. Bad enough that everyone seemed to know about my feelings for Max, but I had *missed* something that should have been easily uncovered. It was a matter of professional pride. I made an effort to pull myself together.

"Then James St Clair must also work for this

agency?" I asked.

"Yes." Mrs Finch leaned back in her chair and picked up a pen, twirling it in her fingers. "A fairly new man on the scene. He's been working in France for several years. I don't have much on him yet. Your being invited into the duke's confidences may end up being extremely useful. It is always helpful to have a sense of what the government are looking towards ... usually because it means we should be looking the other way."

I nodded, but my thoughts turned to Teresa. Her flirtations tended to die out fairly quickly – but to be safe, I needed to do a bit of digging on this James St Clair.

"Here's what we'll do," Mrs Finch said. "I will think on the matter of Rook's offer and decide what information we can safely feed Vane. You stay close to him and find out as much about his investigation as you can. You will hear from me in due course."

With that I was dismissed, and I gratefully took my leave. In the short time I had been sitting down, all the muscles in my legs had seized up, and I limped home, a sorry sight indeed. I was glad there was no one around to witness me going back *up* the trellis I had climbed down all those hours ago. It was certainly a sloppy break-in by the Aviary's standards.

I stripped off my filthy clothes and fell, face down on to my bed, where I slept until well past midday.

It was, therefore, quite late in the afternoon when I arrived at Teresa's house. I had been to sit with Mama for a while; she had spent almost all of that time lamenting her many and varied ailments, and asking me whether I thought the Black Death was likely to stage a return. It would seem that Button's medicine had done its job.

There was also a letter from my brother Henry, full of happy boyish news of cricket matches and frogs and an upcoming visit to the seaside with his friend's family. It was a relief that my plan was working and that Henry was so obviously enjoying himself, but letters like these were always another reminder of how precarious our situation was. The fine families of Henry's school friends would not be so quick to extend invitations to the brother of a disgraced young lady mired in scandal. Sometimes the fact that I held my brother's and my mother's fragile happiness in my hands was overwhelming. One misstep, any tiny slip-up and everything I had built would come crashing down around us all.

Teresa's parents' house was only a short walk from my own. It was a pleasant, elegantly furnished home; Teresa's father may only have been a second son, but the Wynter family fortune was substantial and Teresa wanted for nothing. Their butler, Wilkins, greeted me at the door and showed me through to the drawing room where I discovered that Teresa had company besides me – her grandmother, Lady Wynter, the dowager countess.

Teresa's grandmother was – aside from Mrs Finch – the most intimidating person I knew. In fact, as she had been intimidating me since I was in the nursery, I would have to rank her top of the list. She was tall and elegant, with silver-white hair and piercing blue eyes. When she looked at you it felt as though she could see every single time you had allowed a library book to become overdue. Her posture was extremely rigid, and she turned any seat into a throne. Today I noticed that she was wearing a new gown in dark grey trimmed with black ribbon. It had been barely a year since her son, the earl, died and the last time we met she had been in full mourning. After Teresa's mother died when she was thirteen, Lady Wynter had become her sometime chaperone but following the earl's death that job had been taken over by Great-Aunt Louisa, to the relief of all involved. Lady Wynter saw far too much for Teresa's liking.

"Izzy!" Teresa cried, jumping to her feet from her own seat by the fireplace and flinging herself at me. "I thought you were never going to arrive. You won't believe what's happened."

"Teresa," the dowager countess snapped. "Please desist from bouncing around like a Labrador. It is uncalled for. You and Isobel have hardly been separated for years. You saw the girl last night." She fixed me with her beady gaze, the one that made me certain she knew that as a child I had routinely fed my vegetables to Teresa's pug, Reginald.

Reginald himself was currently curled up, snoring in

a plush armchair.

"Isobel." Teresa's grandmother inclined her head. "You are looking … pale."

I smiled. "Thank you, Lady Wynter, you're too kind."

The dowager countess harrumphed, but her eyes softened a fraction. "It's those dreadful clothes," she declared. "Washing you out. It's time you left them off. Not what your father would have wanted."

I felt a pang at that, a neat twist of pain and guilt and anger and sadness all wrapped up together. "It is hard to let go," I said pointedly, my eyes resting on her own outfit.

She gave another derisive sound.

"Enough of that," Teresa said, grabbing my hand. "Your awful taste in gowns is not important at the moment."

"*My* awful taste in gowns!" I exclaimed, eyeing the frilly lime-green monstrosity that clung to Teresa's generous curves this afternoon.

"Oh, stop it." Teresa was actually dancing from foot to foot now. "Izzy, look … at *this*!" With a flourish she gestured to a small glass vase that held a pretty posy of pale yellow roses.

Reginald lifted his head, blinked at the vase, and then yawned widely.

Teresa looked at me expectantly, and I regarded the flowers. "They're ... lovely?" I ventured.

"They're from *him*!" Teresa cried, clasping her hands to her chest and pretending to swoon into the sofa.

"Ah," I smiled. "Mr St Clair." Perhaps it was impressive that he'd thought about sending her flowers in between running around London and fist fighting with criminals. Or perhaps he was playing a different game. I would have to find out.

"And now, Isobel." Lady Wynter's voice was commanding. "*You* are a person with at least a modicum of good sense. Perhaps you can tell me your impressions of the young man whom my granddaughter informs me is this season's soulmate."

"Grandmother!" Teresa pouted, as I fell laughing into the seat beside her.

"I didn't see much of him," I said. "He seemed a perfectly nice young man."

"Nice!" This from both women, neither of them

pleased.

"How ... how..." Teresa began.

"Nondescript," Lady Wynter finished.

"Yes! Exactly!" Teresa put in, for once in agreement with her grandmother.

I laughed again. "But he *was* nice! I don't know how much help I can be when I hardly spoke to the man. He's good-looking and neatly turned out, he has kind eyes, and he's an acquaintance of the Duke of Roxton. That's really all I know." I could hardly add that he also had a very solid right hook.

"Hmmm," the dowager countess sniffed. "Well, it doesn't matter much. I imagine you will have moved on to a tragic poet or tortured watercolour artist by the end of the week, Teresa."

Teresa folded her arms over her chest, her expression militant. "This time is different. You'll see. There was something about him, something that spoke to me. What is it that Catherine says in *Wuthering Heights*? *Whatever souls are made of his and mine are the same.*" Her eyes grew dreamy.

"Yes, but she says it about *Heathcliff*," I pointed out.

"Look how things turned out for them."

Lady Wynter gave a bark of laughter, but before Teresa could rise to deliver a fervent defence of Heathcliff (the man who marries a woman just so that he can be as cruel to her as possible) we were interrupted by a knock at the door and Reginald began a passionate fit of yapping.

Wilkins entered with a silver tray on which a letter had been laid. "Forgive the intrusion," Wilkins bowed, as Reginald – clearly feeling he had proven his point – flopped back into a comfortable position, "but there's a message for Miss Stanhope, and the messenger was insistent that it was urgent."

I jumped up from my seat, my thoughts flying instantly to my mother. The letter when I opened it, however, was not from home, but from Mrs Finch.

Come at once, was all it said, on the Aviary's letterhead. It was unusual for the Aviary to contact me while on a social visit like this, though I was not remotely surprised that Mrs Finch knew where to find me.

"I'm afraid I have to go," I said, turning back to

Teresa and her grandmother with an apologetic smile.

"Is your mother well?" Teresa came towards me, clearly worried.

"She's fine," I said. "I forgot about an appointment with my dressmaker. I can't believe I was so scattered."

"It's not like you," said the dowager duchess, shooting me one of her piercing looks. "See if she can get you out of that hideous shade of mauve," she called after me by way of a goodbye as I was already moving towards the door.

Teresa, though, followed me out to the hallway, her brows pinched. "Izzy," she said, putting a hand on my arm, and gently pushing me round so that I was facing her. "Is anything the matter?"

"No, no," I said brightly. "Nothing except that I'm a widgeon. I really did want to hear all about Mr St Clair. How thoughtful of him to send roses."

This time Teresa didn't take the bait; in fact, the narrowing of her eyes told me she had seen straight through that distraction tactic. "*Something* is going on," she said. "You've been acting strangely for months now. Is everything well at home? You know that if you needed help – with *anything* – I would be there for you. There's nothing you couldn't ask of me."

Moments like these made keeping my work from everyone difficult. Until recently, Teresa and I had never had secrets from one another, and it took everything in me to smile lightly and make my voice teasing as I replied, "Up to and including disposing of a dead body, I know. But there isn't anything amiss other than my poor timekeeping."

"I really would help you with a dead body," Teresa said earnestly. "We could bury it in the garden under dead of night."

"Reginald would promptly dig it up and deposit one of the limbs at your grandmother's feet."

"And she'd probably tell us that a real lady buries her bodies at *least* six feet deep," Teresa giggled, and I joined in.

My friend sighed. "Fine. Don't tell me. But, Izzy, you're *not* alone. Remember that."

I nodded, swallowing the lump that had risen in my throat and making my way back out on to the street.

CHAPTER TEN

It was not typical for me to be called to the Aviary so soon after a job. Something must have happened, and so I walked quicker than usual, my heels clipping along the pavement.

I was even more surprised to find the entire charm waiting in Mrs Finch's office – I was the last to arrive.

There was also another person in the office, a girl of about sixteen, pale and clearly nervous, dressed in the simple dark dress of someone who worked in service.

Her gown was plain but of good quality, and she had a general air of being well looked after.

"Ah," Mrs Finch said. "Now we're all here, we can get to business. Ladies, this is Lorna Smith." She gestured to the girl who nodded weakly, her eyes wide. Mrs Finch was always careful not to use *our* names around clients – often we did not even meet them in person. Our identities needed to be kept secret.

"Miss Smith here has come to me with an interesting problem, and I think it important that you hear her story in her own words." Mrs Finch smiled at the girl. "Forgive me, I know it's difficult, but do you think you could go over the events one more time?"

Lorna visibly relaxed under the warmth of Mrs Finch's regard and she nodded. "Of course, miss, if you think it will help."

She twisted her hands in her lap, darting glances at all of us. Then she took a deep breath and began her story.

"The truth is I don't know what to make of any of it myself. I wasn't even sure if there was anything worth telling and if there was, I didn't know who to tell it to, but a friend of mine, she said her mistress had come to you for help once before and so..." She trailed off anxiously, and Mrs Finch nodded in encouragement.

"That's right," she said soothingly. "You've come to exactly the right place. Please, tell the others what you told me."

"Something ... strange is going on, in the house where I work." Lorna's words came haltingly. "I'm a lady's maid, and my mistress is a kind, sweet-hearted lady. Everyone loves her. But I'm beginning to think ... to think that someone is trying to do her harm." She bit her lip. "In fact, I think ... I mean, I suspect that perhaps her husband ... well, that he might be ... going to kill her." The words came out in a desperate rush, as though they had been torn from her throat.

There was silence in the room. It was not the first time we had heard something like this, but it was always shocking.

"Lorna." Mrs Finch's voice was low. "Tell them who your mistress's husband is."

Lorna gave her a look of pure anguish before she choked out three words: "Lord Samuel Morland."

113

I couldn't stop a gasp escaping my lips; my eyes flew to Mrs Finch, but her attention was on Lorna.

"Thank you," she said to the girl. "Now, carry on."

It seemed that getting Lord Morland's name out had been the worst bit, and Lorna continued in a firmer voice. "My mistress, Lady Morland, is Lord Morland's second wife. She's a lot younger than His Lordship, and they've been married for less than a year. Until recently it seemed like a happy match. I mean, His Lordship is old enough to be her father but that's not so unusual. And he was always so sweet to her, giving her gifts and teasing her and making her giggle. She's a sweet soul is Lady Morland – Katherine is her name but all her society friends call her Kitten, and that's just what she's like. A pretty little thing with not a malicious bone in her body."

Lorna's voice grew almost fierce when speaking of her mistress. I tried to recall what I knew about Kitten Morland. I had seen her occasionally at parties and Lorna's description sat comfortably with my own impression. Extremely pretty and only eighteen years old, Kitten had a reputation of being generous and impulsive and more than a little silly.

"Anyway," Lorna continued, "Lord Morland is an important man, and because of his job he has to be very sociable, and that suits my mistress right down to the ground. She's a real asset as a politician's wife, you see. Like I said, everyone likes her. She enjoys being a hostess in her own home and throws the most wonderful parties, and treats everything like a lovely game. What I mean is, there wasn't anything amiss in their marriage until recently."

She bit her lip, clearly gathering her thoughts. "It all started a couple of weeks ago. His Lordship is forever showering his wife with gifts, ever since they were courting – nothing was too good for her. One of the gifts he gave her was this brooch. It was quite big and old-fashioned, with an engraved ruby in the middle of it."

A ruby brooch. I stilled at that. This time Mrs Finch did meet my gaze, though her own eyes were unreadable.

"Well," Lorna carried on anxiously. "My mistress, she hated the brooch and I must admit it was not her style *at all*, but His Lordship would ask her to wear it on certain occasions, and it was clear he was quite fond of it. Lady Morland didn't want to hurt his feelings, she never would hurt anyone on purpose, but she used to groan every time the brooch came out – said it didn't go with any of her clothes. And you have to remember, you see, she's a fashionable lady, and used to having things her own way. Then it was at one party that the Duke of Devonshire was there, and he took a shine to the brooch, said he collected things like it and it reminded him of a family heirloom lost for ever, and how he would give anything to have such a piece back. So of course that gave Her Ladyship a bit of an idea as she told me later that night."

"Lord Morland is hoping to be the next prime minister, and the Duke of Devonshire has an awful lot of influence, and so my mistress thought that if she sent him the brooch with Lord Morland's compliments then she would be helping her husband while getting rid of something she didn't want. You must understand," Lorna put in earnestly, "that it's how Her Ladyship is. So generous, always giving gifts. She's never wanted for anything and often all it takes is for someone to admire something for her to give it away. She doesn't give it a thought. She's even given me old gowns and things, just because I've commented on how lovely they are, and I'm only her maid."

"And was His Lordship pleased?" prompted Mrs Finch quietly.

"No, miss." Lorna's face paled. "I've never heard anything like it when he found out. Screaming and shouting so as I thought he was going to murder her there and then, calling her a little fool, telling her she had no right to give the brooch away, and that everything she owned, down to her last pin, was his by marriage and she'd be sorry she ever interfered with his plans. Poor Lady Morland was trembling and crying for hours afterwards. His Lordship calmed down in the end, and then he apologized to Her Ladyship, and said not to think of it any more. I thought that would be the end of it."

She took a breath. "That was almost two weeks ago and ever since then strange things have been happening in the house. On the surface, everything did go back to normal. But then ... things started being misplaced. Nothing important – my mistress's embroidery, her book, her favourite boots … nothing seems to be where she left it. The items always turn up, just in different places, as if Her Ladyship left them there and forgot. She found it funny at first, said she'd always been scattered, but then it kept happening. She started getting embarrassed, then scared. Then there were the appointments that she forgot she had. Guests arriving, and His Lordship telling her she organized the visits weeks ago. It was always all right in the end – His Lordship laughed it off – but still, it bothered her. She came down dressed for an important luncheon the other week and His Lordship told her she was quite mistaken, that no plan had ever been made. She started having nightmares, seeing things at night. She wakes up screaming that someone is in her room but when the servants come no one is there."

Sylla's lips were pressed together in a thin line, Maud was glowering, and even Winnie's sweet gaze was clouded.

"She's changed," Lorna said, in almost a whisper. "It's been so quick, but I've watched her turn from a bright, vivacious lady into a shadow these last two weeks, and I'm afraid if it goes on much longer something terrible is going to happen. Lord Morland has started sending for the doctor a lot and then yesterday I heard them talking about sending her away. For a rest, he said, but I know the sort of places they send *nervous* ladies, and so does my mistress. He's punishing her for giving away that brooch, I know he is. And, you know, there's the matter of his first wife…"

Mrs Finch stiffened.

"What happened to his first wife?" Maud asked.

"She had an accident," I said, trying to remember the details that Mama had told me. It was a couple of years ago now – a terrible tragedy. "She fell down the stairs?"

Lorna bit her lip again and nodded. "Yes. His first wife was a shy, retiring lady, so they say below stairs – not a bit like my mistress, who is happy to play hostess to his political friends. She wouldn't have been so useful to him. Everyone says he was heartbroken after she died – but then he was hardly out of mourning before he was looking for another wife and there's the money my lady brought with her … I don't know what to think."

She sat back in her chair. "That's it," she said. "That's the whole thing. I can't even say for certain that something is going on, but, oh, I've such a feeling about it – starting right after he tore up at her like that, and I couldn't just sit back and wait for her to do herself an injury or for His Lordship to send her away … or worse."

"You did absolutely the right thing, coming to us," Sylla said grimly, echoing Mrs Finch's words.

"You mean, you can help?" Lorna asked, sitting up straight, hope creeping into her voice.

"Oh, yes," Sylla nodded. Winnie squeezed Lorna's hand.

"You can leave it to us," Maud said.

"This is what we do," I added.

Lorna slumped back limply in the chair and burst into tears. Clearly, she had been under great strain. Mrs Finch passed her a handkerchief and helped her to her feet, hustling her gently from the room and murmuring reassuring words in her ear. The rest of us waited in silence until our employer returned.

"I'd like to get my hands on this Morland character," Maud growled.

"There will be a queue." Sylla's voice was ice-cold.

"That poor woman," Winnie sighed. "She must think she's losing her wits. It certainly seems that her husband is trying to break her down, get her locked up somewhere. What an extreme reaction to the loss of this brooch. Why do you think he's doing it? Is it about the money somehow?"

"It always is," Maud said, her voice heavy with weary experience.

"But as a public figure, surely Morland doesn't want word to get out that his wife has been shipped off to an asylum?" I asked.

"That's not how he'd frame it." Sylla shook her head. "She'd be described as being fragile and he'd tell his society friends that she was off resting in some European spa or other. If he played his cards right he'd have people telling him what a kind and doting husband he was."

"Well, now we're on the case." Maud glanced at Sylla. "What's the plan?"

Sylla took a pace or two about the room. "First, we need to get someone into the household. Can we get

Maud in as a maid? If we pay Lorna to take some time off – a family emergency or something similar."

It was obvious Mrs Finch was riffling through her mental list of contacts. "I think it can be arranged. The Morlands use the Wright Agency for their domestic engagements. I can contact Mrs Wright personally."

Of course Maud would have to be the one we sent in – it was one of the things that made her so important to the team. She was from a different world and could slip easily through society, unnoticed, smiling and trailing havoc in her wake. It was a role she seemed to relish – but I sometimes wondered whether she ever minded being set apart from the rest of us.

"If Maud goes in, she can look for any signs of foul play," Sylla said. "Find some solid evidence that her husband is behind this, perhaps – if we can convince her of that fact – it will set Lady Morland's mind at rest. It's the not knowing that is causing the most damage; she will begin to mistrust herself."

"If she's seeing things and hearing things at night then getting a look around her bedroom will be a good place to start," said Maud.

Sylla's eyes snapped on to me. "You're being quiet."

"I'm angry," I said. And I was, but that wasn't all. Rook had mentioned a planned theft – and the only thing his employer wanted was a ruby brooch. Lord Morland had lost such a brooch, and had been furious about it. Max was working for Lord Morland. And now Max was looking for Rook. It was such a strange tangle. What did it mean?

If Mrs Finch wanted the others to know about what had happened last night then she would have said something, so of course I kept the information to myself. None of this worked unless we trusted Mrs Finch. We each had our moves to play, but she was the only one who could see the entire chessboard.

After discussing Maud's role a little more, the meeting broke up and the others left. I didn't need to be told to wait behind this time, I simply closed the door quietly after them and leaned back against the wall. I did not miss the hard stare Sylla delivered on her way out. She knew something was up, and the thinning of her mouth told me she wasn't happy to be excluded.

"This can't be a coincidence," I said. "Morland is the man who hired Rook."

Mrs Finch nodded. "Yes. He wants that brooch back, badly."

"But why?" I wondered aloud. "Kitten Morland has plenty of jewels. She brought an absolute fortune to her marriage. He even told Rook that it wasn't the most valuable piece he'd be stealing."

"*That* is the question." Mrs Finch tapped her fingers across the top of her desk. "The one we need to get to the bottom of."

"And what does the Duke of Roxton have to do with it?" I asked. "He's working for Morland. He was looking for Rook last night, and it didn't seem like he was after a friendly chat. Then he seemed to think that Rook had sent those men to attack him. Why would Rook do that if they're both working for the same man?"

"I don't know," Mrs Finch said reluctantly. I don't think it was a phrase I had heard her utter before. "But I will say this; the way that Morland is setting about undermining his wife speaks to a level of calculated cruelty that troubles me. It troubles me deeply. We must tread carefully here." She lapsed into silence. "Still." She stood straighter, visibly brightening. "By some peculiar twist of fate you have an in with both Rook *and* Vane. Go to Rook and tell him you'll take the job. Then, if possible, confirm that Morland is the one pulling the strings."

"And the duke?"

"Give him just enough information about Rook to keep him on the line." Mrs Finch's face was impassive. "And then find out how the hell he fits in to all of this."

CHAPTER ELEVEN

I had my orders, and I wasn't going to waste time before setting things in motion. As soon as I had changed into Kes's clothes again, the first call I needed to make was to my friend Joe.

Joe was a contact of mine, a fence who Mrs Finch had put me in touch with soon after I began visiting Whitechapel. He managed to dispose of any stolen items that I acquired with absolute discretion and for a good price, he knew everything about everyone, and had a reputation as a dangerous man behind his elegant façade. He co-owned a gambling den on Goulston Street, with a piratical young rascal named Ash. The Lucky Penny was known for its deep play and surprisingly good food. When the nobility wanted a taste of danger they headed to the Penny, as it was called, and vast fortunes had been won and lost over their tables.

The stories about Joe were largely about how ruthless he was, but he and I had always dealt together extremely well and wary respect had gradually turned into genuine friendship. You didn't break into a circus and liberate a poorly treated capuchin monkey with just anyone. As a long-time friend of Mrs Finch's he knew about the Aviary, and that made him an important ally in the darker underbelly of the city.

Like me, Joe had a secret. Joe had been born Josephine, but – unlike me – Joe wore men's clothing because that was who he was. He had seen through my own disguise easily enough but had kept the knowledge to himself. I, on the other hand, had only come to know *his* secret when he confided in me some months ago. It was not a confidence that I took lightly.

It was too early for the Penny to be open to the public, but the enormous thug that Joe hired to man the door knew me by sight and gave me a brief nod, before letting me inside. The gaming rooms were shrouded in gloom, a far cry from the blazing candlelight that would fill them in a few hours. Already there was a buzz of activity as staff rushed about, getting the tables set up, the food and drink and entertainment ready. Soon enough this big space would be heaving with patrons, silly on cheap alcohol and happily parting with their cash, pouring coins into Joe and Ash's coffers. I dodged around the tables, slipping behind a dark green curtain and up the stairs to Joe's office.

I found him sitting behind his desk looking over his books. He raised an eyebrow in greeting

"Looking for Rook," I said without preamble.

Joe narrowed his dark eyes at me. "What do you want to get involved with that snake for?"

I shrugged. "Offered me a job."

Joe leaned back in the seat behind his desk, and took a swig of his drink, something swirling golden in a heavy crystal glass. Only the best for Joe. "If you'll take my advice, you'll stay away from that particular job."

I was instantly alert. "What do you know about it?" I asked.

"Only that there's someone pulling Rook's strings. Someone you don't want to mess with."

"Who?"

An expression of annoyance flickered over Joe's face. "I don't know," he said. "But whoever it is has got money. A lot of it. And influence too. Got a lot of people running scared, the kind of people who don't scare easy. I'm ... concerned."

That was interesting. Especially if the person was Morland.

"I need to take that job," I said.

After a moment, Joe nodded shortly. "Rook's in a house on Varden Street," he said, writing down the address for me.

"Thank you." I took it, slipping it into my pocket. "And about that other matter ... it's been taken care of."

Joe sat up, instantly alert. "Sharpe?"

I nodded. "We got the evidence we needed. The police have it now – and the press. You can expect to see all of his operations closed down over the coming weeks."

Satisfaction gleamed in Joe's eyes. "And the girls?"

"Mrs Finch has taken care of it."

That was good enough for Joe, and he relaxed back once more into his seat. "Thank god for that," he muttered into his glass, taking another deep sip. The relief in his voice didn't surprise me – it had been Joe who had brought the issue of the disappearing girls to us in the first place. He had been the one to notice the pattern, had known that Mrs Finch would do whatever she could to help.

"Will you let me know if you hear anything more about Rook's string puller?" I asked.

"Of course," Joe said. "But I mean it, Kes ... watch your back with this one."

"I always do," I replied cheerfully, already wheeling out the door.

I made my way in the direction of the house on Varden Street, near the London Hospital. The place was small but looked respectable enough from the outside. Still, I knew far better than to trust appearances.

I didn't bother with the front but went round to the back, hammering on the door with my fist.

It opened a crack and a boy of about thirteen looked out at me, his eyes alight with suspicion. "What d'you want?" he grunted.

"Here to see Rook," I replied, hands dug in my pockets. "You can tell him Kes's here. Reckon he'll want a word."

The door closed without any further conversation, and I waited for several minutes before it opened again, revealing Rook standing in the doorway. He darted a look around before inviting me in.

"Nah." I jerked my head. "Let's take a walk."

The smile Rook gave me was grim, but he didn't argue. No one wanted to walk into a house like that when they didn't know who was waiting in there, no one with brains anyway. And Rook was after a screwsman with a brain.

We ambled along the street, and Rook pulled a rolled

cigarette from his pocket, which he paused to light with a match.

"Well?" he said.

"Tell me more about this job," I said. "I might be interested."

He eyed me narrowly. "Heard you helped those two blokes last night. You got in the way of something there."

I glared at him. "Help them? Told them to take it somewhere else, more like. I happen to have some sensitive business going on at the moment and the last thing I need is two fancy coves like that turning up dead in Whitechapel. We'd have the peelers all over us."

Rook eyed me, then nodded, seemingly satisfied.

"Who were they anyway?" I rubbed my nose. "You scarpered fast enough when they arrived. Should I be worried?"

"Nah." Rook shook his head. "Our man on the inside'll manage 'em. Let's just say they'd like to stick a spoke in the wheel, but they don't know enough to give us any real trouble."

So whatever this scheme of Morland's was, it didn't

sound like Max was involved. "What's the idea?" I asked.

"Big party happening at Devonshire House next week. All the nobs'll be there."

The Devonshire House fancy-dress ball. I frowned, trying to hide my shock. It was the last place I'd have thought of staging a robbery. It was the event of the year – maybe of the decade, as Teresa was constantly reminding me. It had been the talk of the town ever since the beginning of May when the season began, and had been arranged as a celebration of the Queen's diamond jubilee. Though the Queen herself was too frail to take part in such public events, other members of the royal family were to be in attendance. In short, it was not the sort of event Rook and Kes would typically attend.

"And I s'pose we're invited," I said with a derisive snort, even though I actually *was* invited – as Izzy, of course.

Rook grinned. "Good as. We've got a way in. The duke has some big jewel collection that he's putting out special, on display for his guests to have a gawp at. The party is the only time the stones'll be together in one place and not locked away in some bank vault. When the toffs sit down to eat, we'll be in and out before anyone knows about it. It's an easy job, easy money. And I need someone who can get into the display cases, quick as you like. Heard from Trundle that you're good for the job."

I shrugged, nonchalant, even as my heart was thumping. A jewel heist during the Devonshire House ball? What was Morland thinking? It had to be the most audacious plan I'd ever heard of. "What's in it for me?"

"We're splitting the take five ways. Like I said, there's only one piece spoken for."

I saw an opening. "Who is this mystery man that only wants a single piece?" I asked, making my words heavy with suspicion.

"That I can't say." Rook shook his head.

"You can if you want me." I kept my voice firm. "I'm not going into business unless I know who I'm in business with."

Rook seemed to consider this for a moment, taking a long draw on his cigarette. "More than my life's worth to give you a name," he said finally. "But let's just say it's someone in high places. Very high."

Morland. It was as much of a confirmation as I was ever likely to get.

I allowed myself to nod reluctantly. "All right," I said. "I'm in."

After talking over the plan in more detail with Rook, I turned and headed – by the most circuitous route possible, just in case Rook had put a tail on me – for Grosvenor Square, my final destination of the day, where I presented myself at the service entrance.

"I'm here to see Roxton," I said. The maid who had answered the door gave me a highly dubious once over.

"And I'm off to visit the Prince of Wales later," she said.

I gave her my most impish grin. "I hope he pulls out the good silver."

The maid's face remained stony, unmoved by my charm. I sighed. "He told me to come so you'd better get him a message. Name's Kes. Gave me his card." I fished the card from my pocket, crumpled and lightly stained.

Once again I found myself staring at a closed door,

only this time I wasn't sure anyone was going to come and open it again.

I leaned against the iron railings that edged the stairs back up to the street and turned over everything that Rook had told me. It didn't seem as though Max was working with Morland – Rook didn't think so, at any rate. In which case, what was Max doing trying to track Rook down? Was he unwittingly working against his own employer?

Hopefully I would learn more from the man himself.

At last, the door opened and an incredibly upright and dignified man looked down his long nose at me. You didn't need the Aviary's training to deduce that this was the butler.

"If you will follow me," he said, in frigid tones which effectively communicated that he viewed me as something lower down on the food chain than a grub in the dirt.

I smiled sunnily. "Right you are, guv," I said, and whistled as I was guided through the kitchens, up a staircase, down a long and impressive hallway and into the most luxuriously appointed dining room I had ever seen.

The walls were papered in a rich plum design, there were Turkish rugs on the floor and not one, but two spectacular crystal chandeliers hung over the table, which seemed comically long and must have been capable of sitting at least fifty people.

At one end of the endless mahogany dining table, polished to such a shine that it acted as a perfect mirror, Max was sprawled in a chair, reading a newspaper, a plate of bread and cheese in front of him, a glass of wine beside it. He looked up over the pages and his eyebrows rose.

"You did come after all," he said. "That's a quid St Clair owes me." Then he turned to the butler. "Thank you, Wheeler, that will be all. Unless my guest here would care for some refreshment?"

I couldn't resist the invitation – not only because I was absolutely starving, having trotted all over London today, but also because the expression on Wheeler's face made it clear how little he wanted to wait on me.

I grinned again, patting my stomach in an elaborate pantomime, laying the accent on thick. "Now you mention it, Your Lordship, the old bread basket is right empty. A bit o' that bread and cheese would go down a treat."

Max's mouth twitched, but he turned to Wheeler and said, quite composedly, "Have Cook make up a plate for my young friend."

"Certainly, *Your Grace*," Wheeler said, with particular emphasis on the correct form of address – the one I had purposely failed to use.

"Yer Grace, is it?" I said, pulling out a chair a few seats down from Max and making myself comfortable.

"That is the traditional way of addressing a duke," Max said, folding the paper neatly in half and laying it down beside his plate. "But Roxton is perfectly acceptable, or Vane. After a man saves another man's life I believe his name is the least he is entitled to."

There was an earnestness to the words that surprised me. I swallowed, willing down the blush that I felt certain was about to spring to my cheeks. He was just being so ... nice. For the Duke of Roxton to speak so easily, to extend his hospitality, to a boy like Kes – well, let's just say it was unusual. I was almost used to the idea of being in love with him, but I hadn't expected to begin to like him also.

"Well," I said roughly. "That's good 'cos I never can remember all the Your Graces, and My Lords. The lot of you have about sixteen different names."

"Very true."

Wheeler appeared then with a tall glass of lemonade and a plate of crusty bread, creamy butter and sharp cheddar cheese, as well as a couple of slices of perfect pink ham. I fell on the meal hungrily. It had been a long day and I'd worked up a tremendous appetite along the way.

"Mmm, 's'good," I said thickly.

Wheeler looked openly appalled now. I badly wanted to laugh. Isobel Stanhope wouldn't get away with talking with her mouth full, nor having her elbows on the table, nor taking big, satisfying bites – but no one expected Kes and Isobel Stanhope to behave in the same way. I caught Max's eye and winked, and this time he was forced to smother a laugh, clearing his throat before dismissing the butler.

I could barely take it all in. I had dreamed, of course, of sharing a cosy meal with Max, but never like this.

"Well," he said after a quiet moment. "Now that you've filled your face and horrified my butler, do you want to tell me what you're doing here?"

I took a swig of lemonade and drew the back of my hand across my mouth. I was going to have to walk a careful line – working out what Max knew without telling him much at all. "Man you're looking for goes by the name of Rook."

"Go on," Max said, unhelpfully bland.

"Hangs about in Whitechapel. Hear he's got a job on the go."

"What kind of job?" Max leaned forward.

I raised my eyebrows. "What's a bloke like you want with a bloke like Rook? He's dangerous, you know."

"I can be rather dangerous myself," Max said. He was a big man, but prior to these last couple of days I had never imagined him using those muscles for more than a bit of gentlemanly boxing. Now, I wondered.

"Hmmm," I said. "I was a bit surprised to find you going blood-or-beer with them bashers in the alley last night."

Max frowned. "Yes, it seems our friend Rook had people watching out for me."

"Why would Rook be worried about you?" I asked, as innocently as possible.

Max was clearly not fooled. "Because I have a habit of stopping people like Rook from getting what it is they want."

"Oh, right, and what is it that Rook wants, then?" I asked.

"I believe you already know the answer to that, Kes," Max said, leaning forward. "And I will pay you a pretty penny to tell me."

I nibbled thoughtfully on my bread. "I hear Rook likes shiny things," I said, keeping it vague for now. "If he's planning a job then likely there's jewellery involved."

Max frowned. "That hardly narrows things down," he muttered.

"Well," I said cheerfully. "I can't do all the work for you. I did hear Rook's got a new friend. Man in high places, they say. One of *your* sort."

Max looked startled. "One of my sort?" he said. His look of confusion certainly seemed genuine.

"Yeah," I said, watching him from under my cap. "Posh. Society bloke."

Max's expression relaxed and he shook his head. "I think you must be misinformed there," he said. "That's something I *would* know about. If you hear any more about what Rook is planning, I want you to bring it straight to me, do you understand? There'll be a fat purse in it for you if the information is good. I hear that whatever he has planned it's going to be soon."

Little did he know how soon.

"Right you are, guv," I said, getting to my feet. "Sorry, I mean *Your Grace*. What about today's work? Don't I get paid for that?"

Max reached into his pocket and flipped a coin at me, which I snatched out the air, before biting it between my teeth.

"Do you think I'd try to cheat you?" Max said, clearly torn between amusement and insult.

"It's always best to check," I said. "You never know who you can trust."

With that warning, I walked out of the room.

CHAPTER TWELVE

Mrs Finch's reaction to all of my gathered intelligence was to suggest a shopping trip.

Madame Solange was a dressmaker with a growing reputation in London, and she was the only modiste that Mrs Finch frequented. For several years, Madame's shop had been one of the city's best-kept secrets, but word of the beautiful garments she created had spread, and she had recently relocated from her old premises to a more stylish address in the West End. Madame's shop was by appointment only, and her business was discretion, so Mrs Finch, Sylla and I could shop together undisturbed.

I hasten to add that I did not typically shop at Madame Solange's. Mrs Finch paid me a generous clothing allowance, but rather than spending it on expensive gowns, I simply bought what was passable and squirrelled the extra money away with the rest of my savings. I was determined to restore as much of our family fortune as possible by the time Henry came of age. Besides, my bland outfits usually contributed to my ability to do my job, but this case was different. I would be attending a fancy dress ball with the wealthiest and most influential people in the country – including the future king – and I was doing so both as Isobel Stanhope and as Kes.

"I'm sure I have something suitable at home," I had said, trying to put my employer off as I had with Teresa at the opera, but Mrs Finch had shaken her head.

"Max Vane does not seem to be an idiot," Mrs Finch said, almost regretfully. "Now that he's seen and conversed with Kes up close we cannot risk him making a connection with Isabel Stanhope. People so often underestimate the power of one's wardrobe. You've used it to fade into the shadows. Now, you must use it to become the precise opposite of Kes. Madame will know just what to do."

She had also enlisted Sylla to help me. I was not looking forward to it. I didn't care for gown shopping, and going gown shopping with Sylla (who had ordered her costume from Madame weeks ago) was going to make everything worse. It wasn't as if I couldn't stand to look at myself in the mirror – I liked my wide eyes and long eyelashes, I was fond of the sprinkling of freckles on my nose, I knew that if anyone really took the time to look closely at my mousy-brown hair, they would see the hint of chestnut when the light hit it, and my body was small but strong – it could run and hold its own in a fight, it had seen me through plenty of adventures in the last eighteen months.

But I would defy the most confident person in the world to stand next to Sylla Banaji in a ball gown and not feel at least a quiver of insecurity.

And so when I pushed through the door to Madame Solange's, setting the bell over the top ringing merrily,

I was not in the most optimistic mood. This was not improved by the sight that greeted me.

Sylla was dressed as an actual Valkyrie.

She stood on a block, while Madame went into spasms of delight beside her.

Mrs Finch's attention too was on Sylla, and it was a testament to the dramatic success of the costume that even she did not immediately swing round when I entered.

I couldn't blame her: Sylla did look wonderful. The simple sleeveless white silk dress was overlaid with a heavy embellished tunic of gold chain that reached down to her hips, trimmed with a row of gold tassels, her waist cinched in tight. Gold cuffs were wrapped around her upper arms and wrists, her long dark hair tumbled down her back and on top of her head was a gold helmet with a pair of wings on top of it, made of pure white feathers. There was even some sort of spear for her to hold.

It was ridiculous. It was amazing. Even here, totally out of context, Sylla looked breathtaking – fierce and powerful and beautiful. I began to see why I had been told I couldn't simply throw a mask on with one of my old gowns.

"I think the neckline needs altering slightly," Sylla said, eyeing her reflection critically. "The chainmail is not sitting quite right here." She gestured at the minor imperfection that only she could see, and Madame nodded, making a note. That was the thing about Sylla; she didn't miss *anything*. Including me.

Her eyes met mine in the mirror, and she nodded a greeting that looked even more regal than usual, thanks to her outfit.

"That is really something," I said, stepping forward for a closer look.

"Ah, good morning, Mees Stanhope," said Madame Solange, in the heavy French accent that I was fairly sure was put on. If Madame was from further away than Essex I'd eat my hat. "I am certain we weel be able to make something spectacular for you to wear to zee ball as well. Although the timings are now rather tight..." She looked me up and down with professional curiosity. "Perhaps you can look around and see eef there is anything you are drawn to?"

I turned to the counter where several rolls of fabric had been partially unfurled for closer examination. I rubbed my fingers lightly over a green silk that was, I noticed almost reflexively, the exact colour of Max Vane's eyes.

As I continued to wander around the shop, I thought how strange it was to suddenly be thrust into the orbit of the man I had lusted after from afar for so long, and I felt a mixture of frustration and relief that he was proving himself to be a complicated, interesting person. Frustration, because I think I had always believed that if I actually got to know Max, then it would dispel the illusion, that my heart wouldn't hammer at the sight of him, that I wouldn't find myself daydreaming about teasing him into laughter. That would have been better – more sensible. But still I felt relief. I hadn't been wrong, that night in the trees. There *had* been something special about him.

It might be silly, but I had quite enjoyed my infatuation – it harmed no one and it was light, *fun*. Now Max was caught up in something messy and complicated, and I was going to have to be careful if I wanted to keep him safe, and even more careful about guarding my own secrets.

I was so engrossed in my thoughts, I hadn't even noticed that I had passed through the shop and into the employees' area, until I came face to face with a girl who must have been a couple of years younger than me.

"Oh!" I exclaimed. "I'm sorry! I'm afraid I was daydreaming, not paying any attention to where I was going."

The young woman observed me levelly, and my first thought was that she could teach Sylla a thing or two about delivering a quelling gaze. My second thought was that she had to be the most beautiful girl I had ever seen. She was dressed plainly – on her feet she wore stout boots, her gown was unadorned navy wool, her honey-blonde hair was pulled back into a severe knot – and yet rather than playing down her good looks, it all only served to highlight her delicate bone structure, enormous blue eyes, and clear, peaches-and-cream complexion. I recognized at once someone who was trying simply to blend into the shadows, and yet – unlike me – this girl was failing miserably. Always would.

"I'm Isobel Stanhope," I said, holding out my hand.

After a moment the girl shook it. "Iris Grey," she said. "You're not supposed to be back here."

"Sorry," I said unrepentantly, looking about me with interest. The workroom was small but bright and airy, tall windows were flung open and flooded the place with drowsy summer sunlight. Iris stood next to a workbench that contained a sewing machine with a half-finished gown of ivory silk bundled up around it, and several sheets of paper covered in sketches.

"Did you draw these?" I asked, moving towards them.

I knew that she couldn't be rude to a customer; but I could tell how much she wanted to be. She gave a nod. "They're good," I murmured. I touched my fingers to one that showed the outfit Sylla had just been modelling. The lines on the page had been sketched by a confident hand.

My eyes narrowed. I let them wander over the rest of the scene. The stack of neatly labelled boxes, the dressmaker's dummy wearing a fragile tulle creation, the jam jar full of pencils next to the fat sketchbook.

It seemed that I had found the source of Madame's success.

She met my eyes then, and shrugged.

"The dress you made for my friend is wonderful," I said sincerely. "Though I worry she might set a fashion for feathered helmets and spears. Once she buttoned her pelisse wrong and several young women instantly rearranged their own garments so they wouldn't fall behind on the latest style."

Iris gave a reluctant chuckle. "I'll tell Madame to invest in more white feathers. And you, Miss Stanhope? Have you come for a costume as well?"

I nodded glumly. "I don't really care for clothes – or for shopping. Somehow it always seems to be a lowering experience. I'm not even sure anything can be made up in time."

"The current style doesn't suit you," Iris said, not mincing her words. She gestured at my gown. "You are too petite for all this heavy material; you're being smothered by your own sleeves. Silhouettes are becoming narrower now... You should perhaps aim to set the fashion rather than follow it. That shade also does very little for your colouring. You need warmer tones."

"I'm sure you are right." I fingered the sleeve of my dress, which was a largely unadorned pale grey. "It's time to come out of half-mourning for my father," I said, unsure where the words were coming from or why I was sharing them with a stranger.

Iris said nothing, only pressed her lips together and picked up a pencil.

"I'm finding the idea … difficult," I admitted. "It's hard to let go of the appearance of grief, when you're still carrying that grief around with you. It would be like I was saying I was forgetting him. I find I am afraid of that."

"Then we shall have to make you something that will help you feel brave." Her voice was surprisingly gentle.

I blinked back unexpected tears and gave a smile. "That sounds like a good plan."

CHAPTER THIRTEEN

With the matter of costuming left in Madame Solange's (or rather Iris Grey's) capable hands, it wasn't long until I found myself back in the sort of clothing I was certain would not pass muster with the fashionable designer.

The next afternoon, dressed once more as Kes (I was beginning to feel as though I spent more time in his clothes than my own), I headed for the Morlands' residence. The house was in Mayfair, around the corner from Grosvenor Square, and a world away from Whitechapel. It was a big building, stern and imposing, and grand in a way that loudly announced that its inhabitants were both wealthy and influential.

Despite what Max's butler may think, Kes could be rather charming when he wanted to be and so I set about looking as winsome and malnourished as possible, until the secretly soft-hearted cook invited me in for a cup of tea and a bite to eat.

"Now, mind you sit here," she said, pointing to a seat at one end of a scrubbed table – not dissimilar to the one in my own kitchen. "I don't know how I've ended up waiting on you, and now the word'll probably get around and I'll be feeding every waif and stray that comes near the place."

"It's right kind of you, miss," I said, ever so humbly.

The cook crossed her arms and made a sound that implied she wasn't buying what I was selling. I peeped up at her and grinned, and her face softened. There was even a twinkle in her gimlet eyes as she bustled around fetching me a cup of tea and a bit of cake. It was a Victoria sponge, light as air and layered with home-made raspberry jam, and I fell on it with enthusiasm.

The kitchen was as busy as any in a flash house like

this, a constant stream of kitchen staff and maids and footmen rushing through. A row of bells attached to the wall were labelled with the names of different rooms, and I watched as the one marked "Blue Sitting Room" trembled, emitting a shrill ring. I sat as quietly and unobtrusively as possible, waiting for everyone to forget I was there. Unfortunately, the cook was a sharp lady, and she kept an eye on me at all times.

At last, Maud came in. There was a slight hitch in her step as she noticed me, but otherwise she gave no reaction. She looked completely comfortable in her uniform, moving through the kitchen with a sharp efficiency, and I thought I even detected reluctant approval in Cook's eye as she came to a stop before her.

"Her Ladyship would like some tea," she said. "And perhaps one of your ginger biscuits."

"She shall have a plateful," Cook announced happily. "I'm glad to hear she's eating anything at all after these last few days. Barely touched her dinner last night and I made her favourites."

Maud helped Cook and the kitchen maid to prepare the tray, deftly arranging the china. As she worked, her eyes met mine and then flickered to the back door, and she pushed a strand of red hair away from her face with her hand, showing me all five fingers. At least five minutes, then, but she would meet me out the back.

Once she had left with the tray, I got to my feet.

"Thank you, miss," I said to the cook. "That was the best cake I ever ate. I feel like a new man."

Cook pursed her lips but she looked pleased. "Well, don't you go getting used to it," she grumbled.

I hurried back out through the kitchen door and up the short staircase that led to the street. Here, I hovered, tucked behind a well-placed hedge, waiting. It was a fair bit more than five minutes when Maud appeared, a dark cloak over her uniform, a basket over her arm, and I reached out, pulling her behind the hedge with me.

"Oof." She stumbled into my side. "A bit of warning next time," she said, straightening her hat.

"Sylla sent me for an update," I said.

"I guessed as much," Maud replied. "Though how you managed to wheedle Cook into cutting a thick slab of her precious Victoria sponge for a grubby little street urchin, I genuinely do not know."

"It's my natural charm."

Maud scoffed. "Right," she said, getting down to business. "I can't stop long because they've only sent me out to pick up some more ginger in case Her Ladyship wants more biscuits. She's not been eating much the past couple of days and Cook's desperate to tempt her appetite."

I grimaced. "Is it bad?"

Maud nodded. "I'd say Lorna painted a pretty accurate picture. Kitten is a mess, nervous and twitchy, not sleeping or eating. There's plenty of stuff being 'misplaced' as well, only little things like her embroidery, a letter she was writing, a pair of gloves – easy enough to understand, but it's the regularity of it. And I've been keeping an eye out as much as I can but I've yet to catch anyone actually in the act of moving things. She also says she hears screaming in her room at night but no one else does. There's already some rumblings among the servants that her mind is wandering."

"What about Morland?" I asked, curious as to what the great man himself might be like.

Maud wrinkled her nose. "Barely had anything to

do with him, but when I have seen him he's polite. The other servants all treat him with respect. But there's something..." She hesitated, considering. "I don't know, he gives me the creeps. I'll only have another couple of days to poke around because he's taking Kitten to the country, for a *rest*, on Tuesday, apparently, and he's not even letting her take her lady's maid with her. They've got a house just outside the city and it has its own staff." She paused here. "Which tells us something else as well... They've got a *lot* of money, keeping two big houses fully staffed like that, and Morland wants to make sure Kitten has no allies with her."

"So they won't be attending the Devonshire House ball," I murmured, almost to myself. It was unusual for someone of his status to miss such an important social occasion. Morland was going out of his way not to be anywhere near the scene of the crime he was paying Rook to commit.

Maud frowned. "No, I guess not. I haven't been able to get near Kitten's room at night yet – after she's asleep, I mean, but I've had a good nose round during the day and I can't see how these noises are being made. Hopefully I'll be able to creep down and have a look round after lights out at some point." Maud reached under her cloak and produced a small, red leather notebook. "I've managed to swipe her diary, but you'll have to get it back to me sharpish. She writes in it every night and the last thing I want to do is be responsible for something else going missing from where she left it."

"Anything useful?" I asked, tucking the book into my pocket.

It was Maud's turn to pull a face. "Nothing as far as I can see, but you never know, do you?"

Maud was right about that, it was something Mrs Finch drummed into us right from the start: you never knew what detail would prove the key to unlocking a case, so you had to gather all the information you possibly could.

I nodded and pulled out my pocket watch, making quick calculations. I needed to get it to Win for copying. "I can have it back in two hours."

"Fine," Maud said. "You might have to wait around for me, I'm not sure when I'll be able to get away."

"I'll be here," I promised.

When I reached the Aviary, I found Winnie in her laboratory, bent over various liquids in glass vessels.

"I've got a job for you," I said somewhat breathlessly. She didn't look up. I cleared my throat. I knew better than to surprise her – sneaking up on Win when she was holding chemicals was a particularly stupid thing to do, as I had previously learned the hard way. It was fortunate that only the front of my hair had been singed – and that at least the current style was quite forgiving.

"Win?" I said, more loudly.

She looked up, blinking at me, her eyes coming back into focus. "Oh, hello, Izzy."

"Hello, Win." I stepped forward, holding out the diary that Maud had acquired. "Maud sent me with this."

Winnie's face lit up. "How is she?" she asked.

"She's fine," I said. "Ten fingers, ten toes, plotting the imminent downfall of the master of the house. The usual."

Winnie's smile was soft and she chuckled. Watching her and Maud together was so sweet it should be sickly, but even a notoriously tough nut like Sylla couldn't do more than roll her eyes at them.

I handed Winnie the book and she laid it on her worktop, hunching over it as she began reading the pages. Winnie's memory was extraordinary. When she looked at a page of writing, it was if her brain took a photograph of it and filed it away, able to recall it in perfect detail whenever she needed. It was – as you might imagine – an incredibly useful skill for an organization like ours.

Winnie's lab managed to retain an air of dishevelled elegance, rather like its owner. The walls were lined with gleaming mahogany cabinets similar to the ones in the haberdashery downstairs, only here instead of "beads" and "buttons" the drawers read "chemicals: Ammonium–Zinc" and were full of stoppered glass bottles. On the long wooden work surface that ran along one whole side of the room were all sorts of strange apparatus, and wooden racks lined with glass test tubes. There was Winnie's precious microscope, and a series of glass bell jars on brass vacuum plates that held what looked like plant specimens.

Above the worktop, the wall was lined with bookshelves that reached up to the ceiling, but which were still groaning under the weight of all the tomes there. The Aviary kept Win supplied with all of the latest publications and while Winnie herself, as a woman, was not admitted to the Royal Society, her library rivalled even theirs. (Which was some comfort, I suppose. You'd think that anyone of intelligence would welcome a genius like Win's, regardless of gender, but I still found it staggering how stupid even clever men could be.)

There were also piles of paper scattered about, covered in Winnie's scrawl or rough pencil drawings. In the corner of the room was a deep armchair where Maud often sat and read while Winnie worked.

"I need to go and speak to Mrs Finch," I said. "I'll be back in a minute."

Winnie nodded, already absorbed by the task in front of her.

I found my employer alone downstairs in the salon.

She had clearly just come in herself and was unbuttoning her pretty light green coat.

"I've been thinking about Morland's scheme," I said shortly. "And I believe there's only one thing to do."

"What's that?"

"I'm going to have to steal the brooch myself."

Mrs Finch gestured to me to sit. "I had something of the same idea myself," she said. "That brooch must be the key to this whole affair, but we won't know how until we can examine it. And it will certainly throw a spanner into the works for Morland. But it's risky – it means stealing it *during* the job."

I nodded. "While we're doing the break-in. I'll go to the ball as myself, then change into Kes's clothes and meet Rook for the job. When I pick the cases I'll have to palm the brooch before he sees it, convince him it wasn't there in the first place."

Mrs Finch frowned. "Rook is dangerous. I don't like it."

"I can handle Rook," I said with a steadiness I didn't precisely feel. Too much was riding on this now for me to let nerves get the better of me.

Mrs Finch gave me a long look. "I think it's time to inform the others of everything we know," she said. "We'll let the group decide."

Which meant Sylla would have the final word. I hoped she'd agree with me.

I returned to the lab where Winnie was finishing up her reading.

"Is there anything useful, do you think?" I asked when Winnie finally closed the book. It was possible that Winnie's analytical mind might have caught something that was not immediately obvious to the rest of us.

She held the book out towards me. "See what you think."

I flipped through the pages, aware that time was ticking by. For a diary, it was almost painfully uninteresting. I had been expecting lengthy outpourings of feeling, but instead the book was a meticulous record of mundanities. Kitten recorded every meal she ate, everything she wore, what the weather was like, every activity she undertook and who was there ... and quite often what they were wearing as well. It certainly contained no clue as to why the ruby brooch might be important to her husband, or why he would be trying to get rid of her – unless he didn't care for how often she had their cook serve pork chops.

Seeing the disappointment in my face, Winnie smiled. "You never know when such scrupulous record-keeping may come in handy. I'll start writing up a copy now."

"Thanks, Win," I said, returning the book to my pocket. "I'd better get back. Any messages for Maud?"

"Tell her I miss her," Winnie said. "And, Izzy." She put a hand on my arm. "You will all be careful, won't you?"

"Everything will be fine," I said cheerfully, but I felt an unwelcome pang of apprehension. I wasn't so sure I believed that.

PART TWO

The Devonshire House Ball, London

July 1897

CHAPTER FOURTEEN

"I can't wear this!" I exclaimed, holding the dress up in front of Teresa's mirror while my friend danced around in the reflection behind me, a hand clasped to her mouth in obvious delight.

"Why not?" she asked. "I think you'll look marvellous!"

"Teresa! It's … it's…" I was lost as to how to finish this sentence, save that it was not the sort of costume that the Honourable Isobel Stanhope, drab little wallflower, would be seen in. "Practically indecent," were the words I settled for in the end.

It was the night of the ball, and I didn't know how Iris had pulled it off, but my dress had been delivered straight to Teresa's house that afternoon.

"I wonder where on earth Madame got the idea of turning you into Medusa from?" Teresa ignored my protests, brushing the soft silk of the skirts admiringly. "I can't *believe* you managed to get an appointment with her and didn't take me!"

"I think it's supposed to make me feel brave," I said weakly.

The dress was made of the green silk I had absently compared to Max's eyes. Dark and gleaming and slipping coolly through the fingers like water, it was the sort of scandalous creation one could only get away with at a fancy dress party (which was, presumably, why people kept throwing such events). It had a low, curved neckline and long, narrow skirts, and the silk had been embroidered in rectangles outlined in gold thread, like scales. It had no sleeves to speak of, but rather two thin straps over my shoulders, and attached to these were two snakes made of gathered gold lamé, which were arranged so that they would coil down and around my arms. There was also a small gold crown made of writhing snakes to wear on my head.

I could almost hear Iris Grey laughing.

Teresa, who was already dressed as Marie Antoinette in an elaborate and outrageous powder-pink confection, heavily embroidered with pastel-blue roses, that showed off a good deal of her enviably ample cleavage, and a towering pale blue wig that contained – among other things – a small bird's nest, was gleefully undoing the hooks at the back of the dress I was currently wearing.

"Come on, come on," she chided. "You have to put it on – what else are you going to wear?"

She had a point there. It wasn't as if I had any choice about attending the ball either. I had to be there, because there was the small matter of stealing a valuable ruby brooch out from under the nose of a gang of dangerous criminals.

Yet it was the thought of putting on the dress that made my hands clammy. When I had told Iris that I wanted to feel brave, I had been thinking, perhaps, of introducing a slightly deeper shade of purple to my wardrobe. This was going to make me look ridiculous.

I turned my back on the mirror, and allowed Teresa and her maid to help me shimmy into the new gown. It fell smoothly over my hips, and the lightness of it, compared to the hefty weight of a typical gown, was shocking. I adjusted the gold snakes so that they wrapped around my arms from shoulder to wrist, their heads lying flat against the back of my hands. Another snake formed a collar at the back, draped over my shoulders like an expensive mink. My hair was long and poker straight, refusing ever to hold a curl as was the fashion. Teresa solved this problem by having her maid plait it into lots of thin, snaky braids before coiling them and pinning them up. Then she set the crown on top of my head. Teresa stood back to admire her work, and her grin threatened to split her face in two.

"Izzy!" she managed.

I steeled myself to turn and look at my reflection.

"Oh!" I exclaimed.

Let me preface this by saying that I was not the ugly duckling who had turned overnight into a magnificent swan. I still looked like me, but I looked like a version of me I had never seen in the mirror before. Now, I realized, Iris hadn't been having a laugh at my expense.

The dress with its sleek lines made me look taller, more graceful. If I had been drowning in fabric before then now I was certainly coming up for air. My skin – usually a bit wan and colourless, as Lady Wynter had pointed out only recently – looked almost pearlescent against the rich green fabric, and the slight touch of red in my hair was more obvious too. I stood straighter in the mirror (wearing a crown seems to have that effect, and I wondered idly if women should wear them all the time). I didn't look small and meek, like a shadow. I looked powerful and a little bit wild. I looked like I could turn a man to stone just by glancing at him.

I liked it.

"You should dress like this all the time," Teresa declared ardently.

I laughed at that. "It would certainly turn heads, walking down Piccadilly."

"You know what I mean!" my friend huffed. "You don't have to cover yourself in snakes. But the silhouette, the colours ... honestly, Iz, you look wonderful."

I shrugged off the compliment with another laugh, but I actually felt quite wonderful too.

Now that we were ready to go, we wasted no time in setting off. Sitting beside me in the carriage, Teresa was practically vibrating with excitement – a dangerous thing when one was supporting an entire family of birds in one's hair. James St Clair would be there tonight, and that particular infatuation showed no sign of waning. Great-Aunt Louisa was in her usual place as chaperone, resplendent in some sort of ancient funereal garb complete with a black lace veil which seemed like rather a damning comment on the evening's festivities, and – for the moment, at least – she remained awake.

The pavements outside Devonshire House were heaving with bystanders, hoping to catch a glimpse of some of the esteemed guests peacocking in their elaborate costumes. Our carriage pulled up the drive, part of a long line of vehicles delivering their guests through the huge wrought-iron gates adorned with sphinxes and bordering Piccadilly.

The exterior of Devonshire House was plain, almost to the point of austerity, but what lay behind the front doors was another matter altogether. The enormous entrance hall, with its marble columns, was crammed with ferns and hothouse flowers sent down from the greenhouses at Chatsworth, and there was a huge marble basin filled with water lilies. It was warm, and the smell was dizzying, sweet and musky. The famous crystal staircase with its carved glass handrail had been festooned with flowers. An orchestra by the foot of the staircase was playing jauntily as we waited to climb the stairs for our audience with the duke and duchess who were holding a receiving line.

"What delightful costumes," the duchess said warmly, and though I was sure she must have said the same to everyone, I felt myself light up. She herself was dressed extravagantly in a gold dress covered with diamonds, emeralds and sapphires, her train was green velvet and also jewel encrusted, and she wore white ostrich feathers in her hair. The overall effect was one of dazzling wealth.

The duke was dressed in a more sombre dark velvet costume, but his coat was embroidered all over with gold thread, a jewelled sword tied around his waist.

He beamed as he welcomed us, while I tried to ignore the pang of guilt that flared as I remembered that I was planning to burgle the man later.

We moved through the hallway to the grand salon, where we were announced by a master of ceremonies in Elizabethan dress. There we found an enormous room, cleared of furniture, but full once more of beautiful flowers, lilies and orchids and roses spilling from urns and vases, banked up around the room. Footmen in eighteenth-century buff-and-blue livery meandered between guests, holding great trays of champagne. At one end of the room a set of open double doors led through to further entertaining space, and at the other an ornate dais had been erected, complete with two gold thrones, awaiting the arrival of the prince and princess. The walls were hung with huge, heavy oil paintings, and a crystal chandelier the size of a carriage sent rainbow light refracting around the room.

The dancing hadn't started yet, but it was already heaving – the rumour was that over seven hundred invitations had gone out. I strained my neck looking for Sylla in the crowd. I had supposed that her feathered helmet would make her easy to spot, but most costumes were equally elaborate. The Countess of Westmoreland passed us, dressed in a diaphanous gown with an entire stuffed eagle perched on her shoulder, wings outstretched. I shouldn't imagine it was going to make dancing very comfortable.

"Can you see him?" Teresa asked. She too was standing on tiptoes, trying to see through the crowd. We had already deposited Great-Aunt Louisa on the edge of the room with the other chaperones.

I didn't need to ask who we were looking for. "No, I can't," I said. "Shall we have a look round?"

Teresa nodded, and we moved through the crowds to the next room where refreshments had been laid out, and men in costumes were pouring cold glasses of champagne, which we gratefully accepted. The balmy summer evening and the press of bodies meant that it was getting warm.

Beyond the refreshment room was a saloon with comfortable chairs clustered in groups. Here people could retire to hold more intimate conversations without shouting over the crowds. It was cosier in this room, wood panelling and an enormous fireplace, bookcases lined with leather-bound books, and the faint smell of pipe tobacco. My heart raced as I spied the glass-fronted cabinets that ran along one side of the wall. Sylla's intelligence had been correct: this room held the duke's collection of carved jewels, which he was displaying specially for his guests for this one single night.

It was well known that the duke's collection of precious jewels – each engraved with an image – was one of the finest in the world: several of the previous dukes, including his grandfather, had been prolific collectors. The display cases contained an enormous variety of carved stones: carnelian, amethyst, garnets, emeralds, sapphires and diamonds, all engraved with pictures of people or animals or scenes from mythology, and there was even a portrait of Queen Elizabeth carved in a green enamel locket. The collection was largely being ignored at the moment, the focus instead on who was arriving and what everyone was wearing. I had heard the duke was going to introduce the display after dinner, and that suited me – it was easy enough to drift over and quietly study the contents of the cabinets in peace.

The collection was extensive, and it featured the famous Devonshire parure, which was actually seven different pieces of jewellery, commissioned by the current duke's grandfather for his niece to wear to the coronation of Tsar Alexander the second in Moscow. It was incredibly elaborate, a most unsubtle display of wealth and power.

"Izzy," Teresa whined. "What are you doing?"

"Look at these!" I exclaimed, gazing down at the ridiculous stomacher, a sort of gold breastplate covered in stones.

"It looks like it would be terribly uncomfortable to wear," she said, glancing at it. "And why is it covered in all those funny jewels with people's faces on? Some of them look quite shabby!"

"They're engraved gemstones, you philistine," I said. "They belonged to the second duke, and some of them look shabby as you say because they are actually from the ancient world! Extremely valuable. Irreplaceable, in fact."

So this was what Rook was planning to steal. He'd never be able to fence such distinctive pieces; I don't suppose Morland had been in a hurry to tell him that.

I wandered a bit further down, pretending to be interested in the jewels on display as I gauged the locks on the cases. They looked fairly flimsy and would present me with no problem. Clearly the duke was relying on the burly footmen hovering nearby to provide the necessary security.

I came to a stop when I spotted my target. There, in a cabinet on the end, was a gold brooch with a ruby at the centre. I could see why Kitten resented having to wear it – it was not a pretty piece at all, bulky and old-fashioned, made of a heavy, braided gold that was slightly tarnished with age. The large ruby in the centre was carved with a rose. A Tudor rose, perhaps.

So this was the brooch that Morland had been so upset to lose. The question was – why?

"Enough staring at ugly jewellery." Teresa pulled my arm impatiently. "You're not standing about in the shadows tonight, not in *that* gown. Let's go back to the ballroom."

This time Teresa had more luck. James St Clair had arrived, and with him was the Duke of Roxton. My heart clattered in my chest as I took in the sight of him in his costume. It turned out that Max in the powdered wig and gorgeously embroidered frock coat of a sixteenth-century nobleman was an unanticipated visual treat that would now occupy many of my daydreams. I think it was the stockings. That was the thing about today's fashions, simply not enough muscular men in stockings.

Teresa squealed in my ear. "Have you seen his costume?"

"Oh, yes," I breathed.

My friend looked at me, and then at Max. "Not your duke, you idiot, Mr St Clair!" I tore my gaze from Max to James St Clair. He was dressed as Louis XVI, Marie Antoinette's husband, as depicted in the famous Callet portrait, swathed in sumptuous coronation robes, all cream and gold and burgundy, a powdered wig on his head.

"Do you think he knew?" Teresa whispered. "That I was coming as Marie Antoinette?"

I thought that James St Clair, agent of the Crown, would have had no trouble finding out such information. "I have no idea," I said. "Perhaps it's a coincidence."

"Or *destiny*." Her eyes shone.

"And he's not *my* duke," I said, my brain catching up to her words. The same Mrs Finch had used.

The look Teresa gave me was one of complete disbelief. "Isobel Stanhope, I am your best friend. If you think I don't know you've been lusting after the Duke of Roxton for the best part of the last two years…"

"I have not been *lusting*!" I exclaimed hotly. Because even if that was precisely what I had been doing, it was not the sort of thing one admitted in a crowded ballroom.

"Shhhh!" Teresa hissed, which I felt was a bit rich given she was the one who started this. "They've seen us, they're coming this way."

"Miss Wynter." James St Clair bowed over my friend's hand, brushing her fingertips with his lips. "You look ravishing."

"And you, sir," Teresa replied. "It seems we have come as a matched pair."

"Destiny, perhaps." Mr St Clair twinkled, and his eyes held such mischief that I was certain he had found out what Teresa's costume was going to be. From the blissful smile spreading across my friend's face, she had reached the same conclusion.

With obvious reluctance, James let go of Teresa and turned to Max. "You are, I know, already acquainted with my friend, the Duke of Roxton."

"Of course," Teresa replied, regaining her poise. "You'll remember my friend, Miss Isobel Stanhope."

"Miss Stanhope." Both men bowed. Max, as usual, said the name as though he had never heard it before.

There was a moment of silence, while Teresa and James gazed moonily into each other's eyes, and Max and I stood awkwardly beside them.

"Miss Stanhope," Max said at last. "I wondered if you'd do me the honour of the first dance?"

I stood staring at Max's proffered hand for a beat, as I struggled to comprehend what was happening.

"I—" My voice came out as a squeak, and I cleared my throat. "Certainly, Your Grace," I managed.

I took his hand. Dimly, I registered that the music had started, that James St Clair was extending the same invitation to Teresa who accepted with a good deal more dignity than me. But really, all I was aware of was the feeling of Max's warm hand wrapped around mine. When we reached the dance floor and he placed the other around my waist I flinched, as though scalded. Indeed, it was almost the sensation. His fingers burned through the thin silk of my dress like a brand.

The dance began, and then we were moving, and that was a relief because I had to concentrate on the steps and not the fact that up close, Max smelled delicious – clove and peppermint and fresh, clean air. He was so much taller than me, that my eyes were barely level with the top button of his waistcoat. With my heart pounding, I focused on that gold, embossed button as if my life depended on it.

Time passed – I couldn't tell you how much – and then Max spoke.

"So." I could feel the words, vibrating in his chest, and for a moment my mind emptied completely. "Are you enjoying the party?" His tone was polite.

"It's very nice," I said. "People certainly took their costumes seriously."

"Indeed they did," Max said easily. "Though I think some of them are going to find the evening a long one while they're juggling their stuffed animals and longswords."

I laughed. "To think I was only going to wear a domino mask – but my dressmaker had other ideas. I never imagined I'd be dancing at Devonshire House wrapped up in snakes." I looked up at him,

A mistake. Max was looking back at me, that almost-smile on his lips, and I was close enough to be able to see the tiny flecks of gold in his green eyes. I had never noticed those before, but I suppose that was because there had always been at least several feet between us. Not so, now.

I lowered my eyes at once. I was supposed to be staying *away* from Max, who knew Kes, who was alert to Rook's plans, not waltzing around in his arms and staring into his eyes. What on earth was wrong with me? It seemed a particularly cruel trick of the universe to offer up this opportunity precisely when I was unable to enjoy it.

We kept on dancing, and I tried to give dull, colourless answers to any question that Max asked. Meanwhile my brain screamed through all the ways in which the plan tonight could go wrong. Was it possible that Max knew about the break-in happening tonight?

He seemed relaxed – not like a man planning to thwart a jewel heist, but then hopefully I didn't seem like I was about to take part in one either.

We spun faster and faster, and the room was so hot, and it seemed to be filling up with more and more people. Seven hundred invitations. How many people was that? A thousand? More? Could a thousand people even fit into this room? Panic began to creep in and I closed my eyes for a moment. *Oh no. Not now.* It had been so long since I'd had one of these attacks that I thought perhaps they had finished with my joining the Aviary.

Not now. The words drummed inside me. *Please. Not now. Not now. Not now.*

CHAPTER FIFTEEN

My throat tightened, my chest felt like an iron band had been wrapped around it. I struggled, but couldn't get enough air into my lungs. The room seemed to tilt around me for a moment.

I felt Max's arm steady me, and I realized he had waltzed us over to the edge of the dance floor, nearest the windows, careful not to draw attention.

"It's all right," he said, his voice low. "Breathe in through your nose..." He waited. "And out through your mouth. In and out. Just breathe." His words were soothing, hypnotic, and he held me gently, just the lightest touch that left space between us. I concentrated on the slight breeze coming through the window, slowed my breathing in time with his words, felt the pulsing in my temples ease.

"Thank you," I said, when I felt I could speak almost steadily.

The music ended.

"It was nothing." Max placed my hand on his arm. "Now, shall we go and find those friends of ours? I don't think I will be telling you anything you don't already know if I reveal that Mr St Clair is most taken with Miss Wynter."

I managed a smile. "I had my suspicions."

As we reached Teresa and St Clair, I saw that the pair were standing a fraction too close together, and my friend's face was glowing up at him from beneath her towering wig, her heart in her eyes. I felt a stab of worry. Was James a part of Morland's schemes? I needed to find out more before I knew whether my friend could trust him with her heart. The last thing I wanted was for Teresa to be hurt.

An elegant figure cutting through the crowd caught my eye. Sylla. If I had thought that her costume would be overwhelmed in the scrum, then I had underestimated her presence. If anything she looked more spectacular than ever, and eyes – some friendly, some less so – followed in her path as she moved towards me.

We did not have a chance to talk, however, because we were interrupted by the arrival of the royal party. There was an enormous amount of fanfare (literal as well as metaphorical), the orchestra played the national anthem, and the Duchess of Devonshire led the prince and princess to their golden thrones, set amid the hothouse flowers on a dais at the end of the room.

There followed a lengthy procession where the most prestigious guests trooped past the royal couple in their finery, ready to be admired. This had been organized as a sort of "parade through history" with people and costumes grouped into different time periods. It was almost comically elaborate, and when the Duchess of Devonshire entered the room on a palanquin carried by six men I actually began to think there might have been some truth in the wild story I had heard that one of the guests had tried to borrow an elephant from London Zoo to complete her costume.

Teresa was beside me, shifting impatiently from foot to foot. James and Max had been ushered ahead of us. Sylla too had been presented with her father, thanks to the latter's friendship with the future King of England.

"Will this never end?" Teresa grumbled. "I'm starving. It's always such a chore when the royals turn up."

"You'll find yourself locked in the tower if you don't keep your voice down," I teased, but the truth was that I was restless too. Once everyone went through to dine, my evening would truly begin. I could only hope that Sylla, Maud and Winnie had all done their parts.

It was after eleven when the moment came, the prince and princess were led out, and the rest of us could follow down the sweeping staircase.

We were shown through to the garden, which, like the rest of the house, was enormous, reaching all the way to Berkeley Square. For those who wished to sit outside on such a beautiful night, a temporary veranda had been built, topped with crimson-and-cream striped awnings, under which numerous seats and sofas were arranged banked by mossy-green ferns. A vast marquee had been erected, swathes of beautiful printed silk making up the sides. It was a warm night, and the sky was a black, star-spangled backdrop.

In the centre of the lawn shone an eight-point star, flanked by smaller stars at each corner, with the monogram "DD" and the crest of the House of Devonshire – a serpent – picked out in flaming torches. The oak and elm trees were outlined with green lamps, while the avenues to the east and west were festooned with luminous, multicoloured lamps of pearl and green. Japanese lanterns hung from the trees, and the flower beds along the back of the house were lit up red, white and blue. In fact, there were lamps everywhere, hanging from every tree branch, every shrub, dotted along the ground, casting everything in a soft, golden haze.

"I heard the duchess ordered twelve thousand of them," Teresa whispered in my ear. "Can you believe it? How extravagant." My friend's words were laced with approval.

Extravagant was the right word. The fact that

everyone was dressed in the most fantastical costumes only added to the strange otherworldliness of it all. It was like stepping into the sort of peculiar scene you might accept unquestioningly in a dream. To experience it while awake was bizarre indeed.

Beyond the marquee I noticed another, smaller tent, in which I had heard that the London photographic firm of Lafayette were to be taking portraits of the guests, an enormous undertaking that had created a real stir of excitement. Beyond that tent, a number of small alcoves had been erected, archways bedecked in roses, ready and waiting for intrigue and indiscretions to take place in the shadows. It always struck me as funny that society hostesses had to plan for such things, while we all pretended they weren't happening – but this time it was to work to my advantage.

"Mr St Clair said that we would be sitting with him at dinner," Teresa said.

I froze. "With the duke too?" I asked, trying and failing to sound casual.

"Yes!" Teresa was obviously delighted. "Apparently Mr St Clair arranged it himself!" She dimpled. "He said he would very much look forward to continuing our conversation."

"How thoughtful of him," I said. What I was actually thinking was that my friend's latest love affair was proving extremely inconvenient for me. The last thing I needed at such a delicate moment was to be in the company of two intelligence agents.

We stepped into the marquee, and the setting drew gasps from the crowd. If I hadn't known better I would have said we were standing in another grand room inside the house. The floor was covered in a thick crimson carpet, the walls draped with gold and blue, covered with mirrors and elaborate tapestries. Heavy crystal chandeliers hung suspended from the ceiling and at one end of the tent, there was another display of wealth: a collection of beautiful gold plate, brought down from Chatsworth to be shown off. Each round table, seating twelve people, was arranged around its own palm tree strewn with electric lights.

James St Clair had been busy indeed and Teresa and I, along with Great-Aunt Louisa, who was practically somnambulant at this point, found ourselves at a table that was several rungs above our usual spot on the social ladder.

"Allow me," Max said, getting chivalrously to his feet and pulling out my chair.

"Thank you, Your Grace," I mumbled, catching Sylla's eye. She was glaring daggers at me as though I had intentionally sat myself beside the one person I was supposed to be avoiding.

"I hope you're feeling better. The ballroom was overheated." He really was being scrupulously polite.

"You're right," I replied, as crisply as I could manage. "The fresh air is much nicer."

It would have been wonderful to take advantage of this turn of events, to draw Max into conversation, to find out more about him – perhaps even to hear that laugh again – but I turned instead to speak to the man on my other side. I had seen no flicker of recognition in Max's eyes, and I doubted he had made the connection between Kes and Isobel Stanhope, but I knew I shouldn't push my good luck. After all, he may not know it but we had recently shared a very different meal.

The man I was talking to was older,

distinguished-looking with a large, bristling moustache, and dressed as a soldier from the civil war. After we had made our introductions I tried to focus on what he was saying – something about fishing, I think. He clearly took my glazed look as a sign I was deeply interested in the subject.

While nodding along mindlessly I found my attention actually focused on the conversation on my other side. Max was sitting with Teresa and James, and I didn't have to look to know that my best friend was blooming like a flower under the attention of two handsome men.

"So you are recently back from France, sir?" Teresa's voice was almost a purr.

I could hear the smile in James's response. "I am indeed, and after several years of languishing on the continent I find myself extremely happy to be home again."

"You grew up here?"

"I did, and had all my schooling here which is where I met Roxton."

"Ah!" Teresa exclaimed happily. "You're old friends, then! Now you can tell me all of each other's scandalous stories."

James laughed. "Scandalous? Not us. We were the picture of good behaviour."

Max made a humming sound. "Is that what you call putting toads in the master's desk drawer?"

Teresa giggled as James feigned indignation. "I was simply trying to put them somewhere warm and cosy. It was cold outside."

"A very commendable act," Teresa said. "And what about His Grace? Was he often in trouble?"

It was James's turn to laugh again. "Rox? Not he. A proper duke indeed. We used to tease him for it."

"I just believe in sticking to the rules, as you well know," Max said lightly.

"And a good thing too, because you were always there to bail me out of trouble," James said. "But when we first met I thought he was insufferable."

"No!" Teresa gasped, clearly delighted.

I wished I could see Max's face, but his voice held affection when he replied, "And I thought you a rascally troublemaker."

"Which I was," James agreed. "Though I am reformed now, Miss Wynter, I assure you."

"Not *too* far reformed, I hope," Teresa replied and I could practically *hear* her eyelashes batting. "A little trouble is always a good thing, I think."

"I'm afraid he's turned respectable these days," Max said.

"Oh, don't," James groaned. "You'll make me sound a dull dog indeed. I shall have to fill your desk with toads, Rox, and restore my reputation."

Teresa went off into peals of laughter again, and I couldn't help smiling, which was all the encouragement that my dinner partner needed to launch into another description of a particular trout he had caught that week.

The food was brought out then – course after course, with great ceremony – and I had something else to focus on as the time ticked on past twelve. There was a cold consommé, roast chicken, mutton and roasted quail to start, followed by salmon mousse with cucumber, lamb with hazelnuts, crab remoulade, sliced tomatoes that tasted like summer sunshine, and tiny birds in aspic.

I wasn't about to let a little thing like planning to commit larceny deter me from doing such a meal the justice it deserved, and so I dug in with gusto. If anything, I was feeling less nervous now. The thought of picking locks and outwitting Rook seemed easier than negotiating a society ball.

After almost an hour – and approaching one in the morning – I saw Sylla rise from her own seat and walk towards us. I cast a rueful look at the dessert I was about to miss out on: fat, rosy strawberries with Chantilly cream, as well as jellies and a selection of cream-filled pastries *almost* too pretty to eat. I moved so that my skirt spilled slightly out into her path and as she stepped on it, I turned. There was an audible tearing sound.

I winced, sending up a silent apology to Iris Grey, and then let out a little squeal of alarm.

"Oh dear!" Sylla was all apologies. "Forgive me, Miss..." She trailed off.

"Stanhope," I said.

"Miss Stanhope, of course." Sylla's eyes widened. "Your beautiful gown, I am so sorry. We must mend it for you before you have your photograph taken."

"I'm sure it will be all right if I just pin it," I demurred.

"Nonsense." Sylla was brisk. "I have my maid with me, we can go to one of the retiring rooms, and she'll be able to mend it so that no one will ever know the difference. She's an excellent seamstress, and I must insist. I feel terrible."

"That's kind," I said. "If you'll excuse me." I nodded to the table – noting that Teresa was still engrossed in conversation with St Clair – then I followed Sylla from the marquee, picking our way past the comical number of swords and spears and shields and enormous feathered fans that had been left propped against the walls.

"Shame about the dress," Sylla said in a low voice. "If I'd known you were going to wear something decent for once, I'd have suggested a different plan."

"You could just tell me that I look nice, like a normal human," I grumbled under my breath.

We made our way down through the garden and towards the little alcoves. We kept our heads close together. If anyone did see us they would think nothing of two ladies slipping into one of the hidden bowers to share secrets, or even a secret embrace. That was what parties like this were for, after all.

When we reached the agreed upon alcove, the third from the left, Sylla and I ducked through to the small clearing where a red velvet love seat had been placed as if in suggestion.

It was certainly a suggestion that had been heeded as it was currently occupied by two women locked in a passionate embrace.

"For goodness' sake, you two," Sylla huffed. "We're *supposed* to be working."

The women broke apart, and Maud grinned. "You can't blame us for taking advantage of the situation."

"You have Winnie's moustache in your hair," Sylla said acidly.

Blushing, Winnie reached to gently untangle the large white moustache from Maud's hair. "That new glue must not have been as good as I thought," Winnie said, looking sadly at the moustache as if it had let her down. I had to stifle a giggle, because Sylla was still doing her stern headmistress bit, and I didn't want her attention turning to me, but I caught Maud's eye and winked.

Winnie pressed the moustache above her lip, and I

had the opportunity to admire her full outfit. She was dressed in some sort of regency military garb. Her body was heavily padded so that she was extremely rotund, her face hidden beneath a high cap and the lustrous moustaches. It was – in dim lighting – a passable impression of Winnie's father. While Winnie had not made the guest list for tonight, her father had just about warranted an invitation. Fortunately for us, Winnie's father was a vague man who rarely attended such events and pilfering his invitation had been easy work. Winnie had simply slipped in late, waved her invitation in the right faces, and headed for the garden to wait.

Maud's entrance was more simple. She had come as Sylla's maid.

Winnie began unbuttoning her shirt, revealing Kes's clothes and boots strapped into her ample padded belly. As swiftly as possible I exchanged these for my gown and petticoats – as well as my snakes – and Winnie strapped the stomach back into place.

The three of them tried, with varying levels of success, to help me get into Kes's outfit, and I ended up smacking their hands away.

"I don't need the three of you to tie my boot," I hissed. Again, I felt laughter rising as I imagined someone interrupting us during this whole process. It probably wouldn't even be the most scandalous sight on offer tonight.

"Right," I said, once my transformation was complete, my wig firmly anchored. "How do I look?"

Sylla circled me, her eyes flicking from the top of my head down to my toes. "You'll do."

And on those rousing words I slipped off into the shadows.

CHAPTER SIXTEEN

Rook had told me to meet him and the rest of the team near the stables just after one. I didn't even have to be too careful because if anyone spotted me there they would simply take me for a particularly grubby stable boy.

When I arrived at the designated spot it was to find Rook and two others waiting for me.

"Harvey, and Clink." Rook growled the introduction, gesturing to the two burly gentlemen beside him, who nodded briefly at me. All three of them were dressed in drivers' coats of good quality, the first sign of Morland's presence in this plan. They were smoking cigarettes in the shadows, looking for all intents and purposes like a trio of bored men waiting for their wealthy employers to need driving home.

The area around the stables was a hive of activity, with horses, carriages, grooms and drivers, mixing with kitchen and waiting staff who were diving in and out from the back doors of the kitchen which were set nearby in the basement of the grand house.

Though I would never have thought to do so, these were ideal conditions for staging a break-in, if you were bold enough – and if you had a little help. There were so many strangers, all concentrating on their own work, that a handful more could pass by unnoticed. Particularly if your wealthy benefactor had greased enough palms in the kitchen to smuggle you inside.

In the end it was laughably easy. The entire party were outside in the garden so only the staff remained in the house, with their minds on feeding and watering the guests. A footman dressed in full Elizabethan regalia and carrying a tray with two drinks let us in. We moved through the kitchens in the general hurly-burly and soon enough found ourselves in an empty corridor that ran away from the direction of the ballroom.

"Through here," hissed the footman, gesturing to a small wooden door, before walking off.

Rook opened the door, revealing a narrow stone staircase behind. We followed Rook up the stairs. My heart was beating wildly now. It would not be an easy thing to explain away our presence if we got caught, and I didn't like the look of the two toughs Rook had brought with him. It was possible someone would get hurt.

The stairs were dark and dank, and they ran steeply up, so that it felt like we were climbing a great way. Rook lit matches as we went, to provide us with enough quavering light to keep our footing. No one spoke.

When we reached the top of the stairs, Rook looked over his shoulder to check we were all there, then tentatively pushed at the door. It didn't look like anyone had used this staircase for a long time, but the door swung open on silent hinges. Morland's touch again – clearly someone had oiled them.

With the door partially opened, Rook paused, pressing his face to the gap, checking the coast was clear. I held my breath. This bit of a job always felt like bracing yourself to dive under ink-dark water: frightening, unknowable, exhilarating.

Rook opened the door the rest of the way and gestured for us to follow.

When I stepped through the door, my jaw dropped. We had come out straight into the saloon. The door was hidden behind one of the bookcases, which had swung open to allow us entry.

Rook held a finger to his lips and moved over to the door that led to the refreshment room, which was now closed. He pressed his ear to this door and stayed there for several long seconds. I took the time to eye the cabinets. The brooch was there, right where it had been earlier.

We continued to stand in place and I wondered what precisely we were waiting for. Then there was a muffled thud outside.

I thought I heard a brief, slurred exclamation before another, similar thud occurred. Rook shot a gleeful smile over his shoulder and a shiver weaselled its way up and down my spine.

"Right," he said, low and gravelly. "Let's go."

With that, he opened the door and in a twinkle, he, Harvey and Clink had pulled the two unconscious footmen inside and shut the doors. Before they closed I noticed the cups the footman who let us in had carried on his tray lying on the floor. It seemed that Morland had been busy. The dissemination of whatever drug the guards had been given to knock them out had clearly been managed with military precision.

Harvey and Clink removed their heavy drivers' coats, revealing pale blue-and-buff livery that was a perfect match for the Elizabethan costumes all the footmen were wearing tonight. Harvey winked at me, before the two opened the doors and disappeared to stand where the now unconscious guards had been placed only moments before. No one happening upon the scene would ever know anything was amiss.

"Get to it," Rook snapped to me, as he pulled a rope from the bag at his side and began tying up the guards. I did not delay, but made my way to the cabinet on the end where the brooch was. I pulled my picks from my pocket, and the locks barely needed touching before they sprang open like they were pleased to help out.

As an experienced pickpocket I knew that hesitation was the enemy. I scooped up the brooch in a fluid motion, transferring it to the hidden pocket in my jacket and moving the piece beside it a little to the left to cover the gap. I didn't so much as glance towards Rook, trusting that he was focused on his own job, before I turned to the next cabinet, cracking the lock on that one even quicker.

I worked my way down the row, and by the time I got to the end, Rook was finished, and the two men, still unconscious, lay gagged and bound, face down on the floor.

"That was quick," Rook said with approval. He pulled out several thick cloth bags, handed one to me, and began scooping the jewels unceremoniously inside. I tried not to wince as he handled the beautiful stones that had survived centuries of upheaval, war and disaster, as though they were glass marbles children might play with on the street.

"Where is it? Where is it?" I heard him mutter as

we worked our way down the line. He was watching me now, watching my hands. I kept calm and worked carefully. When we reached the end he swung round to me, suspicion blazing in his eyes.

"Where's the brooch?" he demanded.

I widened my eyes. "There's a hundred of them."

"The ruby brooch! Where is it?"

I shrugged. "Probably in one of the bags."

Rook shook his head. "You've taken it." The words weren't a question, but a statement. He moved towards me, radiating danger.

"Why would I do that?" I asked. "What do I want with a brooch? You said it's not even worth much."

"Turn out your pockets."

I did as I was asked, making a great show of pulling them right out so that he could see that save for my lock picks and a couple of mint humbugs they were empty. Something flickered across his face ... anxiety, perhaps. It was possible I was going to get away with it, but then his expression hardened.

"Take your jacket off and give it here," he said. "I'll search it myself."

My heart leaped unpleasantly. I was certain he could see the pulse beating wildly at the base of my throat. "Stop wasting time," I said roughly. "We need to get out of here. It's in the bag, I tell you."

A knife appeared in his hand – I hadn't even seen where he'd pulled it from which probably meant he'd had it up his sleeve. The blade was long and narrow, and it looked as if it had been used before.

"Give. Me. Your. Coat." He whispered the words, which only made them more terrifying.

He was standing between me and the door to the hidden staircase, and Harvey and Clink were waiting outside the other exit.

Rook took a step forward and I turned and ran for the window behind me. Thanks to the heat of the evening it was already open and I leaped up on to the sill and out the other side as quick as a wink. Even so I felt Rook's fingers brushing against the cuff of my trousers. I didn't stop; instead I sprang to my feet on the narrow ledge and edged my way along, my back pressed flat against the wall.

Rook stuck his head out, and grinned. "Where d'you think you're going, boy?"

He had a point. This window faced out on to the east side of the house, which was the only good thing about it. There was nothing set up down below, no people around, only a large gravel area that led to the driveway, and flower beds and shrubbery cut through with winding gravel paths, lit with more of the coloured lanterns. People were still at dinner, but they would finish soon and come strolling past. There was *nothing* else ... no well-placed tree, no trellis, no vine, not even an open window where I could take my chances. Just a long, long drop down with nothing to catch me.

Rook's eyes glittered in the dark, and he leaned further out of the window. I had absolutely nowhere to go. Still, desperately, I shuffled further away from him. Perhaps one of the windows further along was unlocked, perhaps I could force it open. The ledge was so narrow that my toes hung over the edge. I pressed back into the wall as much as I could, trying to melt into the stonework.

"Hey!" a voice shouted from below. I looked down, then closed my eyes, swallowing the curse that rose instantly to my lips.

Max Vane. Of course. I barely even felt surprised.

He was staring up at me, and I wasn't sure whether it was coincidence that had brought him here or design, but it was certainly a blow to all my well-laid plans.

Not that things were exactly going smoothly.

I glanced to my side, and noticed that Rook had withdrawn into the shadows – or had he left, to dispose of Max? I let fall the stream of curses I had swallowed.

"Kes?" Max called. "Is that you? What are you doing?"

"Oh, just taking in the sights, enjoying the balmy evening, trying to keep myself – and you – from being killed, you great handsome lummox," I muttered. Max wandering into the middle of Rook's plan made him an obvious target for Harvey and Clink.

That was when I heard the whistle. It was quiet but distinctive, no doubt a signal from Rook to those henchmen. I turned instinctively in the direction of the sound, and my left foot slipped from under me.

With a cry of alarm, I tried to scramble back towards the wall, but my feet hit only air. I was falling, sliding, and I gasped, reaching out with

212

desperate fingers, clawing out at the ledge. I had my eyes tightly shut, but when I peeled them open it was to find myself hanging, suspended twenty feet in the air. When I made the mistake of looking down at the dark ground below, I felt my stomach heave, my mind go woozy.

"Kes!" Max barked, hoving into view beneath me. "You'll have to let go. I can catch you."

"Let go?" I managed. "You must be mad."

"Well, I doubt you can hang on indefinitely," he said dryly. "You're only small. I'm pretty certain we'll manage."

"*Pretty* certain," I said, the words somewhere between a sob and a laugh. "That's reassuring." I could already feel my hold on the ledge slipping. My arms were shaking. He was right. I couldn't hold on much longer.

"Trust me," Max called. "I've got you."

Sending up a silent prayer, I released my grip on the edge, and then I fell through the dark, velvet sky, so fast that I heard the air whoosh past me, and I braced my brittle, fragile body to land. Which it did.

"Oof!" Max exclaimed, as I cannonballed into his arms, knocking him off his feet and flat on his back.

I was alive.

The idea took a moment to sink in, but there it was. I was undeniably alive.

I laughed.

"I'm glad you're so amused," Max gasped, clearly winded. In fact, I realized, I was still draped rather inappropriately across his torso. And now was not the time to be enjoying the sensation.

I scrambled to my feet. "Sorry," I said dazedly. "Sorry." I held out a hand and helped him up. He winced a little, brushing dirt off his costume. I mourned for the state of the pale silk stockings.

"Now, explain yourself," Max said sternly, running his eyes over me. "What on earth is going on?"

I cast a glance up at the salon window. There was no sign of Rook and that made me nervous.

"We haven't got time," I said, taking hold of his sleeve. "We have to go."

Max shook his head. "We're not going anywhere, not until I get some answers."

"You stupid, stubborn man!" I exploded. "Listen to me, we have to go!"

Max frowned. In my urgency I had not adopted Kes's rough voice.

"Wh—" he began, and then Harvey and Clink burst from behind us, knocking Max back to the ground.

I pulled my knife from my boot, only to find the two of them already bearing down on me.

"Fink you can double-cross us, do ya, lad?" Clink hissed, advancing steadily. That was when I noticed that he had a knife in his hand, and that it was already slick with blood. My eyes skittered to Max, who wasn't moving.

Something chill ran through my veins. It was as if the panic fell away and all I felt was an ice-cold fury. "If you've hurt him, you'll be sorry," I said.

Clink looked at Harvey, and the two of them laughed.

I sprang forward. I was small but I was well-trained. I knew how to defend myself, and these two were brutes, big and strong, but unwieldy, like blunt tools. I whipped around low, slicing out at Harvey's leg, and when he bent down in surprise I thrust the heel of my hand up into his nose, with an ominous crunching sound. He staggered back, howling in surprise, but Clink already had one meaty arm around my waist. I kneed him between the legs as hard as I could, but he didn't let me go.

I still had a hold of my knife and my arm was free so I slashed it towards his face. He dropped me then, his hand going to his cheek, a low roar in his throat.

I darted to Max and dropped down beside him. He was clutching his side, blood coming up between his fingers. He looked up at me, eyes wild.

I bit back a sob. The two men were already advancing on me.

I crouched again, holding the knife out in front of me. I was *not* going to die here. I was not going to let Max die here.

At that moment, there was a sound from the direction of the driveway. A carriage rounded the bend on two wheels, coming to a shuddering stop in front of us, sending gravel flying everywhere.

The driver on the box, a shadowy figure with a

luxurious moustache, muffled in black, cocked a pistol with a sound that seemed to echo through the air. The threat was clear, and Harvey and Clink dropped back in wary surprise, their hands lifted up in front of them. With the gun trained on them they stood frozen, clearly unsure what to do next.

I knew we had to move fast. Their indecision wouldn't last long, and it was a miracle no one had yet stumbled on our little scene.

"Max," I pleaded, close to his ear. "You have to get up." With the air hissing between his teeth he managed to stagger, a good deal of his weight leaning on me, to his feet, and together we stumbled forward and half-fell on to the floor of the open carriage.

"Go! Go!" I shouted, and the horses sprang forward, turning on a sixpence as we headed back for the driveway and from there to the street. I would have to commend Winnie on a superlative piece of driving later, but first I had other things to see to.

I was kneeling with Max's not insignificant weight lying across me. His eyes were closed. I felt for his pulse and was relieved to find it going strong. I tore off my jacket, leaning over him and pressing it hard to the injury, hoping to slow some of the bleeding.

It must have hurt because Max's eyes opened, and he let out a low groan. We juddered over an uneven surface, and I raised a hand to the side of the carriage to stabilize us. My cap and wig had come off, presumably now lying somewhere on the floor of the carriage underneath him. He looked up at my face now, my hair escaping from its pins as he continued to bleed all over my lap, and his eyes widened.

"Miss Stanhope!" he gasped, before his eyelids fluttered closed and he was rendered, once more, unconscious.

Well, at least this time he'd remembered my name.

CHAPTER SEVENTEEN

There was never any question as to where we were headed. After checking to make sure we weren't being followed, Win drove us at a smart clip to the Aviary where we were met outside by Maud and Mrs Finch. Between us we managed to get Max inside and up the stairs (no small task, that), and into Mrs Finch's office where she had swept the desk clear.

Her eyes travelled quickly over me, a brief flare as she took in the sight of blood on my shirt, that died away when she seemed to realize I was uninjured.

"Put him on there," she said shortly, already rolling up her sleeves and reaching for the medical supplies she had laid out. We did so, and then Maud and Winnie left to gather more hot water and towels.

"How did you know?" I asked, dazed. "How did you know we would need all this?"

She snapped her fingers. "Hand me those scissors." She began cutting Max's shirt away from his side. "I knew what you were doing tonight, you think I wasn't prepared for there to be bloodshed? I will admit, however, I had not anticipated that it would be the Duke of Roxton's blood."

I waited as she examined the wound. "It's deep," she said at last. "And he's lost a fair amount of blood, but I don't think anything has been hit. Let's clean him up, and then he'll need stitches."

She was cleaning the wound when Sylla swept in. She was still dressed as a Valkyrie, though the spear had been discarded.

"Bloody hell," she growled succinctly. "What is *he* doing here?"

We did not have men in the Aviary, particularly men

who worked for the villain we were trying to bring down. The situation was far from ideal, and that was even before Max suddenly roared back to life, and sat upright.

"Where am I?" he demanded. "What the hell is going on?"

"You are bleeding all over my desk," Mrs Finch replied. "Please lie back down and be still."

Max's eyes landed on me. "Miss Stanhope!" he exclaimed. "I thought... I remembered... But how..."

"You've been wounded," I said gently. "You need to have stitches."

Max glanced down then, seeming to notice for the first time that his shirt had been shredded and that he was bleeding profusely. The word that came from his beautiful mouth then was not one I had ever expected to hear a duke say, and I trained my eyes on the ground.

"Well, quite," Sylla said, unruffled.

"Miss ... Banaji?" Max's brow crumpled in confusion.

"Don't overthink it," was Sylla's advice. "Just let Mrs Finch stitch you up."

"Would you care for some brandy?" Mrs Finch

asked solicitously, brandishing a bottle at him. "This part is going to hurt."

"Take it," I said, reaching for the bottle myself and stepping forward, holding it to his lips. "It will help."

I don't know if it was my nanny-ish tones, or if the pain was bad enough to demand it, but Max accepted the brandy from my hand and took a long drink, straight from the bottle.

"Much obliged," he said weakly, slumping back on the table. Without another word Mrs Finch returned to her ministrations, which involved threading a wicked-looking needle.

I felt my own head spin when she dug this into his flesh, and though he didn't make a sound, any remaining colour leached from Max's face. Without thinking, I stepped forward and placed my hand over his, squeezing his fingers. He squeezed back, tightly, so tight that it hurt, but I remained there, silent and unmoving while Mrs Finch finished. The wound, though deep, was thankfully not long, but the time passed slow as treacle.

"So this is quite a mess," Sylla broke in sharply, after

the first three stitches had been set in place. "Did you at least get the you-know-what?"

I nodded, gesturing to my jacket, which was soaked in Max's blood and crumpled up in the corner. Sylla went over, slipped her hand in the hidden pocket and pulled out the brooch.

"Oooh, you did get it!" Winnie exclaimed, hustling back through the door with another clean bowl of steaming water, which she placed beside Mrs Finch. "Well done, Izzy!"

"Rook wasn't happy," I said, and I felt Max's fingers twitch around my own, though the pained expression on his face didn't change.

"And what exactly were you doing there, Roxton?" Sylla asked, clearly having decided that undergoing surgery was no excuse to avoid questioning.

"Heard something." Max forced the words out. "A rumour. Didn't believe it, too ridiculous, but something about Rook and Devonshire House. Thought I'd better check on things. To be safe."

"Well, that went well," Sylla said.

"Thought I saw someone," Max mumbled. "Man

I know of, unsavoury sort, but he was dressed as a footman. Very odd. Followed him, but he disappeared."

"That'll be the footman who let us in," I said.

"So what's so special about this thing anyway?" Maud dumped the towels she was carrying on the sofa, and took the brooch from Sylla's hands, turning it over and peering closely at it. "Apart from being ugly?" She passed it to Winnie, who was probably the best person to examine it.

"I don't know," I sighed. "I think the stone might be Tudor. It's possible it really is about how valuable or rare a piece it is."

"Well, Morland *is* the sort to care about prestige," Maud mused.

"Morland?" Max said, struggling to sit up.

"Steady," Mrs Finch hissed. "I'm almost finished."

"I see we're not too concerned about keeping our secrets," Sylla put in acidly, glaring pointedly at Max's prone form.

"What's the man going to do?" Maud chuckled. "He's in no state to move."

"How could we keep it from him now?" I asked, exasperated. "Convince him that this was all a dream?"

"Feels more like a bloody nightmare," Max said through gritted teeth, his eyes remaining tightly shut.

"We still don't have to spill *all* our confidential affairs out on the table like a handful of loose change," Sylla snapped, and I winced. She was right, of course.

"There," Mrs Finch said. "If you can sit up, Your Grace, then Miss Stanhope can help me with the bandage."

"*I* can help you with the bandage," Max said hoarsely, levering himself into a more upright position. In doing so he seemed to notice that we were holding hands and he dropped mine like it was a hot coal.

His gaze met mine. "So that part was real," he said softly. "Miss Stanhope and Kes are the same person?" He glanced from me to Mrs Finch as though asking for confirmation, but my employer remained unmoved.

"Well, obviously," Sylla said. "It hardly takes a spy to work that bit out." She turned to me. "I thought you said he was clever."

Max's eyes narrowed but he knew better than to betray himself. "You said that *Rook wasn't happy*." He

225

frowned at me. "So he *was* there. Are you working with him?"

"Not precisely," I hedged. "Why have you been looking for him?"

Max exhaled slowly. I got the impression that between the blood loss and the brandy he was having trouble keeping his thoughts straight. "Heard some rumours that he was planning a robbery. Something big." He rubbed his forehead in a bewildered sort of way. "It turned out I was right."

I nodded and he gave a wry smile. Then he returned his attention to Mrs Finch. "May I know to whom I'm so indebted this evening? I am grateful, madam, for your help."

Mrs Finch considered Max. "I am Mrs Finch," she said. "This is my place of business."

"And may I ask," Max continued, frighteningly calm as he wrapped a long bandage around his torso, securing the pad that Mrs Finch had placed over her handiwork, "what *kind* of business you are in?"

"It's a haberdashery," Mrs Finch said tranquilly.

Max blinked. "Which no doubt explains the needle

and thread."

"Enough of this," Sylla interrupted. "We need to see how much damage has been done after tonight. Izzy, was your identity compromised?"

"No," I said. "I don't believe so. But Rook's men saw Roxton." I gestured to Max. "Obviously."

"Which puts us in a very awkward position," Sylla said. "But we have the brooch. Presumably they got away with the rest of the jewels?"

"As far as I know. Though they'll have trouble shifting such recognizable pieces."

Sylla nodded. "Was anyone else hurt?"

"Two guards were rendered unconscious and tied up. That's all that I saw. I don't think Morland wanted to get his hands dirty."

"Miss Stanhope!" Max snapped. "I really must insist you tell me what is going on. This Morland you keep mentioning, do you – you can't mean *Lord Morland* is mixed up in any of this?"

Sylla glared at him down her nose. "Your Grace, I would ask you to keep your unnecessary interruptions to a minimum while we try to untangle the mess you have made."

Max's mouth dropped open, and he gaped wordlessly at Sylla. A muffled snort of laughter came from Maud's direction, and even Mrs Finch was trying not to smile.

"So," Sylla mused, unaffected. "By now it is likely that Morland will know that his plan has failed, and instead of thinking that the brooch was stolen by the elusive Kes, he will be looking for the incredibly visible Duke of Roxton, who is in fact in his employ." She shot me a look. "Am I correct in thinking his ruffians will assume that you and the duke are in cahoots?"

I pictured myself standing over Max's body, a knife in my hand, ready to defend him, and nodded glumly. "Yes," I exhaled. "They'll think he was involved in double-crossing Rook."

"Then Morland will believe it too. He'll think that Roxton is on to him, that he and Kes were working together to obtain this brooch. And so we must add protecting the duke to our endless list of things to do. This is what happens when *amateurs* wade in." Sylla scowled at Max, who scowled right back.

"Miss Banaji," he said, getting stiffly to his feet. "I'm

truly grateful for your assistance tonight. However, I should perhaps explain who I am. It's not necessary to protect me. My business is that of Queen and country, and if *you* are in need of protection I will do my best to provide it."

To this noble speech Sylla paid absolutely no attention whatsoever. "Winnie," she said, turning to face her. "Have you discovered anything unusual about the brooch?"

Winnie shook her head reluctantly. "I'd like to look at it under my microscope, though."

"We might get an expert opinion on the valuation," Mrs Finch mused. "Perhaps it's worth more than we think or has some relevant history. There's no one we can trust in London – with his resources Morland will have every jeweller in the city under surveillance. I know someone who could help, but he's in Yorkshire."

"I'd go," Maud said. "But the Morlands will be back from the country soon, and I think it's going to be a good idea to keep someone in the house. Something is really wrong there." She bit her lip. "Do you think this interference with Morland's scheme will put Kitten in greater danger?"

I felt my stomach twist at that.

"I could go," I said quickly. I had travelled for such things several times before. It was fairly easy to arrange for me to sneak away for a day or two – Mama didn't miss me immediately, and I could always tell her I was staying with Teresa.

"You can tell people you're staying with me," Sylla said, as if reading my mind. "We can say we struck up a friendship at the ball."

"Fine," I said. "I'll go as Kes."

"You can't go as Kes," Mrs Finch pointed out. "Kes can't appear at all, not for the time being. Between them, Rook and Morland will have everyone looking for him, high and low."

"Then I'll go as a widow," I said. "One in reduced circumstances. No one will look twice."

Max's gaze was bouncing between us, like he was watching a tennis match.

"That would work," said Sylla. "One of your dowdy gowns—"

"Enough!" Max yelled, slicing his hand through the

air. "Can someone *please* tell me what the hell is going on?"

There was a silence. He looked at me, and his eyes were pleading. I opened my mouth, searching for the right words.

"Lord Morland, your employer, is a scoundrel," Sylla said in clipped tones. "He is trying to drive his wife out of her mind for some nefarious purpose of his own – perhaps to punish her for giving away this brooch of his to the Duke of Devonshire. He hired a gang of miscreants to burgle the Duke of Devonshire this evening in order to acquire that same jewelled brooch. We don't know why he is so desperate to get it back *yet*, but we intend to investigate. As he is the frontrunner to be the next prime minister I'm sure that even you can understand the significant consequences of this information."

Once more, Max was robbed of speech. He looked at me, the plea still in his eyes.

"I'm afraid," I said, "that about sums things up." I turned to Sylla. "You might have broken it to him a little more gently."

"He asked." She shrugged. "We don't have time to

coddle him. The question is, what are we going to *do* with him?"

"We could stash him in one of the safe houses?" Maud suggested. "Camden?"

Winnie shook her head. "Not possible, because of the—"

"Ladies," Max interrupted. His expression was serious yet composed, he stood straighter, his words were clipped and formal – as if he were addressing parliament. "I'm sorry to say you're acting under a misapprehension. I'm not sure precisely what this set-up is, but I can assure you that Lord Samuel Morland is a man of unimpeachable character. He had absolutely nothing to do with the burglary this evening; on the contrary, his agency will do their utmost to get to the bottom of it. Everything the man does is about keeping this country and its citizens safe."

The silence that greeted this was only broken by a derisive snort from Sylla. Just then, there was a hammering at the door downstairs.

We all froze.

"Wait here," Mrs Finch said calmly, sweeping out of

the room. The clock on her mantelpiece ticked loudly as the seconds passed. The quiet was fraught, pressing down on us like a heavy blanket on a hot day. Winnie cleared her throat, a nervous sound.

Mrs Finch reappeared with a piece of paper in her hand. Her face was grim. "I'm afraid Lord Morland has wasted no time."

She passed the message to Sylla, who read it before passing it on to me. It was a telegram. I scanned the lines, the message short and to the point:

RECEIVED INTELLIGENCE ROXTON TRAITOR
TO CROWN. STOLE JEWELS TONIGHT FROM
DEVONSHIRE HOUSE. BELIEVED IN COMPANY OF
BOY, AGED BETWEEN TWELVE AND FOURTEEN,
ORIGINS UNKNOWN. APPREHEND AT ALL
COSTS. MATTER OF GREATEST URGENCY.
THREAT TO NATIONAL SECURITY. ALL
RESOURCES DEPLOYED. AM EN ROUTE LONDON.

– M

I glanced at Mrs Finch. "One of my runners intercepted this," she said. "But there will be plenty of others. He'll have sent them out to all his agents."

"What?" Max demanded. "Who are you talking about?"

I turned to him and held out the telegram. "I'm sorry," I said softly.

Max snatched the message from my hand and read it. "This is obviously a mistake," he said, his voice calm although I detected a tremor in it. "The circumstances were confusing and Morland has been misinformed – I will put him straight at once."

"So," I mused. "This is Morland's plan. To have every man who works for him on the hunt for you."

"It is rather clever," Sylla admitted. "He knows someone is on to him and believes the duke to be working with them. So he discredits the duke – anything Roxton says now about Morland will be dismissed as the ramblings of a traitor. Morland has the whole country out looking for both Roxton *and* the missing brooch, under the guise of catching a thief. It seems he's still desperate to get the brooch back."

"*Too* desperate," I said. "He's worried. Worried that Roxton knows whatever secret is attached to the brooch. Worried enough to have the entire intelligence service looking for one man. To accuse a duke of treason. This brooch is definitely more than it seems. It has to be."

We all turned then to look at it in Winnie's hands. For a moment I could have sworn the ruby glimmered with some malevolent force that sent a shiver through me. I gave myself a shake. For goodness' sake – this was not some Penny Dreadful, and there was work to be done.

"Winnie, you examine the brooch while I prepare to travel to Yorkshire," I said. "We'll get to the bottom of why Morland wants it back so badly."

"This is ridiculous," Max said. "Everything that has happened tonight has obviously been a misunderstanding and it will be simple enough to sort it all out. I must go home and—"

"You can't go home!" I yelled, my patience utterly worn away. "Can't you understand that, you idiot?"

An uncomfortable silence fell and Max's eyes narrowed. "I do not require your permission,

Miss Stanhope."

And with that, despite being bandaged and dressed in the blood-soaked rags of a fancy-dress costume, he drew himself up to his full height, looking every single inch the duke, as he swept past me and out of the Aviary.

CHAPTER EIGHTEEN

"We'd better send someone after him," Mrs Finch said.

"Yes, before he gets himself killed," Sylla ground out. "The fool."

I was already pulling my wig back on, and flinging myself towards the door.

"Not you, Izzy!" Sylla was shouting, but I ignored her.

"Take the dark greatcoat on the way out," Mrs Finch called after me, her tone resigned. "Your duke is looking remarkably eye-catching tonight."

I caught up with Max not far down the dark street. He was already drawing interested glances.

"Wear this," I said, shoving the coat in my hands towards him. I saw his jaw clench under the lamplight, but he said nothing as he pulled the jacket on. It would have fallen to my toes but was too short for him. At least it covered his costume, and helped him to blend more quietly into the shadows.

We walked on in silence. He made no acknowledgment of his injury, but he held himself stiffly. We were heading in the direction of his home – and I had no idea what we would find there. I kept my eyes open, my steps light, I felt for the reassuring presence of the knife in my belt. There was another in my boot.

"So," Max said, breaking the silence. "Miss Stanhope goes about town dressed as a boy?"

His tone was neutral but his words sent a sharp spike of panic straight through me. I felt my step falter. In all of the excitement, with the adrenaline pumping – between the burglary, fighting, bleeding and running – I hadn't even registered this simple fact: the worst had happened. My secret was discovered.

"I – it's complicated," I managed, my words coming out a terrified wheeze.

"I take it no one knows?"

"No one outside the Aviary," I said. "I hope to keep it that way." I glanced at him, desperate for some sign that he would keep my secret, but his face was set, impossible to read.

He spoke no more as we approached Grosvenor Square. I could see Max's house now. The lights were on and there were two men posted outside.

Max saw them too and our pace slowed. We moved in silent agreement out of the path of the street lamps. Already I noticed there were huddled shapes in the shadows.

"Do you—" I began in a whisper.

"I see them," he said shortly. He changed course, cutting down an alley between two houses so that we would be approaching the house from the back.

"You can't do this," I whispered as we crept down the side of his house. Standing at the corner we could more closely see the two men at the front door. "If you go in there, they'll arrest you ... or worse."

"They can't arrest me," Max said. "I haven't done anything wrong."

I was saved from having to reply to this piece of idiocy by the noisy arrival of a coach and horses outside the front of the house. James St Clair jumped down before the carriage had come to a complete stop. He was wearing a long dark coat over his costume, the white wig had been removed. His face was devoid of its usual light, and was set in grim lines.

"What the hell is going on, Keene?" he barked at the men on the door. "What's this I hear about Roxton being a wanted man?"

"Morland's orders," Keene replied. "Roxton had been compromised. We believe he may be trying to flee to France."

"Nonsense." James sounded furious. "This is madness. I need to speak to Morland at once. Roxton would never be involved in anything underhand, the very suggestion is ludicrous."

"Don't let your friendship cloud your judgment, St Clair," Keene warned, his voice hard. "Morland says he's been selling state secrets for years." He sighed.

"You've been betrayed, St Clair. We all have. Do you think Morland would make an accusation like that without solid evidence?"

"I – no." James came up short. "But surely there's been a mistake … it's not possible…"

"More than possible, I'd say," Keene cut in coldly. "We've had an order to bring him in, by any means necessary." He paused significantly. "*Any* means. Do you really believe Morland would give that kind of order – about Roxton of all people – if it wasn't certain?"

James paled. "Roxton … a traitor?"

I felt Max still beside me.

"No. I—" James's shoulders sagged. "For god's sake let me inside. I need a drink."

With that he shoved through the door.

"Straight for the good whisky," Max murmured. His voice was wooden, his face drained of colour, a wan smudge in the darkness.

"Do you see now?" I said. "We have to go back to the Aviary. We have to go this instant."

There was a pause. Then he gave a short, jerky nod, and I exhaled in relief.

This relief however was short-lived. Almost as soon as we moved away from the house I was aware of the net closing around us.

We walked steadily, and there was something shifting through the darkness off to the side. Someone was following us. I didn't react, but picked up the pace ever so slightly. I darted a glance at Max who was still moving stiffly. Would his injury allow us to make a run for it? I wasn't sure. If there was only one man, perhaps there were other ways of dealing with him. I chewed my lip, and we carried on doggedly, turning corners almost at random, trying to cling to the shadows.

A figure stepped out into the road, another moved to my left.

My hand went to my knife. "Two of them have seen us," I murmured.

"Three now," he replied, and I noticed another figure peel away from the gloom.

We had no choice. "Run," I hissed.

We ran. How he managed it with the wound at his side I don't know, but Max kept pace with me as we darted from street to street. A cry went up. Footsteps thundered behind us, then receded, then began again.

There was a loud bang and I felt something whiz past me, far too close for comfort.

"Are they actually shooting at us?" I gasped.

Max's face was grim. He said nothing, clearly all his energy focused on putting one foot in front of the other, but my mind was racing. It seemed that Morland's orders of *any means necessary* didn't specify that Max was to be brought in alive. No wonder James had looked so horrified. We carried on running with ragged determination, and once again I tried to hold a map of the area in my mind, calculating a route that might guide us to safety. I don't know how long we ran like that, dipping and weaving through the darkness until eventually we lost our pursuers and arrived, panting, back at the Aviary.

"So," Sylla sniffed when we burst into the room. "You're back, then."

Max's face was absolutely grey as he collapsed into a chair in Mrs Finch's office. Maud and Winnie were gone, but Sylla and Mrs Finch were still there, a bottle of brandy open on the desk and two empty glasses beside it. They had been scheming. Without a word, Sylla passed the bottle to Max who tipped it straight into his mouth.

I filled them in on what we had seen. Mrs Finch rolled her glass between her fingers as she listened.

"I think I'd better head off to Yorkshire as soon as possible," I finished. "There are orders out to use all force against Roxton. The sooner I find out what this brooch means, the sooner we can begin to clear his name."

"I think you're right," Mrs Finch said, setting her glass down.

"No, I'll go," Max broke in.

"You will not," three voices exclaimed in unison.

"It's far too dangerous," I pointed out. "You need to hide."

"Which I would have thought was obvious," Sylla muttered.

"I know you're a man of action," Mrs Finch said. "But the best thing you can do for the investigation right now is to lie low and let us handle it."

Max's expression was stony. He was no longer slumped in the chair but had risen to his feet. He took up quite a lot of space.

"No," he said. "I refuse to believe that Morland is behind some traitorous scheme." I let out a groan, but he held up his hand. "I know him. He's my mentor, my friend. I would *know*. Someone must have passed him false information – or want to frame me, for some reason. I have to get to the bottom of it. To clear my name, yes – but it's more than that. It's my duty to find answers. It is *my* job. I *cannot* hide away and leave someone else to unravel this mess."

His words were quite stirring and I felt my heart fluttering, but fortunately my brain was on hand to tell my heart to pipe down.

"It would be of no help whatsoever," I told him crisply. "You have no resources. You cannot trust a single person you usually work with – those people will be trying to throw you in prison. Morland has agents everywhere looking for you, and most likely from what we've seen they've all been given orders to bring you in dead or alive. I'm sure I know Morland's preference."

"Miss Stanhope," Max interrupted. "For goodness' sake, you can't expect me to let you go jaunting off to Yorkshire! A young, single woman, alone, travelling up and down the country. Think of all the things that could happen! Think what would become of your reputation if anyone found out!"

A more dangerous silence filled the air then. I fixed Max with a hard stare and then looked pointedly down at Kes's clothes that I was still wearing, smeared with his blood. My hair was a tangled mess, and I'm certain that a glance in the mirror would have shown that I had dirt and dried blood on my face.

"I think, Your Grace, that ship has sailed," I said dryly. "It's also *my* job that we are talking about, and I will do it to the best of my ability. You are not going to *let* me do anything. I go where I choose."

My heart was thumping and I knew my words were dangerous – this man knew my secret, could ruin my reputation – but I was almost vibrating with anger. To be thinking about my reputation at a time like this, to be trying to curb my own agency when I could do something useful to help prevent a great wrong ... it was everything that I hated about society's rigid, foolish conventions.

Max had the good sense to look sheepish.

"You should both go," Sylla said.

"What?" Max and I turned as one towards her.

"They'll be looking for the Duke of Roxton and Kes, together or apart. Your little appearance at Roxton's house will only have confirmed that. They *won't* be looking for a married couple taking a tour up north. It's actually one of the better ways to keep Roxton hidden from Morland's men."

Max opened his mouth and then shut it.

"You would be travelling to remote parts, which would keep you out of the way," Mrs Finch mused. "That is a good idea, Sylla." She stood up, imperious as a queen. "That's decided, then. Izzy and the duke will travel to Yorkshire as soon as arrangements can be made."

With that, she and Sylla hurried away to begin making those preparations. Max and I stood in the middle of the empty room, staring at one another.

"I have some questions," Max said evenly.

"Yes," I sighed. "I thought you might."

CHAPTER NINETEEN

In the end we didn't have much opportunity for a private chat. Within the hour a parcel arrived containing clothes for Max – trousers, a jacket, several linen shirts, stout boots and even a dark shaggy wig to go under a hat. All of the clothes struck a perfect note of tattered respectability and, remarkably, all of them looked like they might fit.

I was much easier to provide for – several of the older gowns from my standard wardrobe hit much the same note. I returned home briefly, to collect the essentials that I needed for the journey, and to leave a note for Mama which explained that I had been whisked away to Sylla's house outside the city for a couple of quiet days to recover from the drama at the ball. Word of the robbery was already snaking its way all over town, so I had no doubt Mama would be informed by the first post. Fortunately, she'd also be informed about my disappearing with Sylla.

I left her Sylla's address, safe in the knowledge that Sylla would intercept any post and that, given she was a gifted forger of handwriting, she would even be able to pen a reply from me if needed. Mama would be delighted to think I was staying with such a tastemaker, and would count on me returning with plenty of gossip.

On arriving back at the Aviary I found Max, dressed in his new clothes, eating a cheese sandwich with a slightly dazed expression, while Mrs Finch fussed over papers on her desk. Sylla had returned home.

"Izzy!" Mrs Finch looked up. "Perfect timing. I've already sent a message ahead of you to my contact, Lockhart. Let's go over the details of the journey." She turned to a map, which was spread over the desk, and pointed to a spot somewhere to the north of York, which seemed to be in the middle of nowhere. "Here's where Lockhart lives. The nearest village is Helmsley but even that is several miles away."

"He's certainly not easy to find," I said.

Mrs Finch smiled. "That's the way he likes it."

"We'll have to go by train," I mused. "Otherwise we'll be gone a week at least."

"Mmm. But Morland will have people watching the London stations. I've already had reports of agents at Victoria."

"We can travel to Hatfield by carriage." I ran my finger across the map. We were all well versed in the various unobtrusive routes around the country. "Then we can get the train from there to Peterborough and change on to the fast train to York."

Mrs Finch nodded. "I can arrange a carriage from here, and for one to collect you in York."

I leaned back, my eyes scanning the map. "He might have Hatfield under surveillance," I said.

"Hatfield will be fine." Max spoke up. "They won't expect me to leave London." He was quiet for a moment. "They'll be waiting for me to use one of my contacts. If I hadn't met you I would have no other option." He rubbed a hand over his tired face.

"I think you're right," I said, fighting the urge to smooth away the frown between his eyes.

Max turned to Mrs Finch. "You really think this man will be able to give us information about the brooch?" Clearly, while I was at home collecting my things, she had filled him in on some of the details.

"Winnie found nothing using the microscope," Mrs Finch said. "She didn't want to undertake more tests for fear of damaging the piece. If anyone can tell us anything I'd lay money on it being Oliver Lockhart. He has an eye for unusual pieces."

It was good enough for me, and Max nodded. It was the only path open to us.

"We should leave at once," I said, my eyes moving towards the window, where the sun was already up, and the sounds of the city coming awake drifted through: a symphony of street sweepers and paper boys and jangling carriages, a sharp clip of hooves, and doors and windows banging. I pulled out my pocket watch;

almost six o'clock. "We could make the 12.12 from Peterborough if we hurry."

Max nodded and reached for the dark wig, which he placed on his head, before pulling his cap over the top. His face was slightly shadowed.. Apart from his size, which we could do little about, he was not easily recognizable. I noticed that his posture had changed, loosened, his head dipped low. I thought back to seeing him in the King's Head, to the way he had ordered his pint. In all the confusion I had almost forgotten this about him – that he had some experience of this game too.

"Let's set off, then," he said, and even his voice was different, taking on a lower timbre.

"You'll need this." Mrs Finch held something out to me and I took it from her. In my hand was a simple gold ring, and I looked at it in confusion for a moment, before feeling a flush creeping over my cheeks.

"Oh, thank you." I slipped the ring on to my wedding finger, finding it difficult to meet Max's eye. When I curled my hand into a fist, I could feel the ring there – the unfamiliar, cool weight of it. I flexed my fingers, trying to shake the feeling away. It was only a costume.

"You're newly-weds," Mrs Finch said. "Taking a tour of the north for your honeymoon. Sylla was quite right that it's the last thing Morland will be looking for. I don't need to tell you that you must play the parts with conviction. More than one life is at stake here."

I nodded, my eyes still trained on the ground. I couldn't decide if I was delighted or horrified that Max and I were going to pretend to be madly in love with each other. I suppose that at least I had plenty of practice.

We descended to the street through the back door, where Mrs Finch had a discreet black carriage waiting. Our small bags were thrust inside, and then Max handed me in through the open door, his hand warm and steady. The interior was small, the air stuffy, the blinds were pulled almost all the way down over the windows, leaving it in shadow, and Max and I were forced to sit pushed up alongside one another. The entire left-hand side of my body, from shoulder to ankle was pressed against him, and I tried very hard to ignore any fluttering feelings this created. We were here to work. I squeezed my fingers together, running my thumb across the underneath of my wedding ring.

Max must have noticed because, as the horses set off at a clip, he turned his head slightly towards me. "I really am sorry to have dragged you into this, Miss Stanhope," he said.

I leaned back in my seat, wedging myself into the corner and turning as much as possible so that I could look at him. He mirrored the action.

"I think we'd better get this cleared up once and for all, Your Grace," I said stiffly. "You haven't dragged me into anything. I was already investigating Lord Morland's misdeeds, and had you not stumbled across me last night, you would not now be a fugitive from the law with a knife wound in your side. Please, let me apologize for dragging *you* into this."

I knew it wasn't easy on his code of honour to hear such things, but then again, his code of honour was extremely silly and unnecessary. I was no helpless maiden waiting for a knight in shining armour. Perhaps he would begin to realize that soon enough.

"*Your Grace*," Max murmured, surprising me then, a half-smile on his lips. "Is it my imagination or did you call me Max when you were busy defending me from ruffians?"

I had been hoping he wouldn't remember that part. "Er – I'm not sure," I hedged. "I forget. Did I? It was quite a stressful situation."

"Perhaps, while we're in disguise, you could call me Max. No one does any more, you know, apart from my sister … even my mother calls me Roxton." He paused. "I like hearing it."

"Well, I can hardly go around calling you *Your Grace* the whole time," I agreed, trying to cover my confused feelings with light words.

"It would probably get us caught quite quickly. I can't imagine Miss Banaji would be impressed with my skills then. I think I'm even more afraid of her than I am of a prison cell." He gave a brief shiver.

"She can be quite intimidating."

"Terrifying," Max said, but there was respect rumbling through his voice. "And you, Miss Stanhope?" he said.

"I don't think I'm particularly intimidating."

"No." The touch of a smile. "I meant what should I call you?"

"Oh." I was flustered. "Isobel, I suppose – or Izzy. That's what my friends call me."

"Izzy," he said softly, as if he were trying it out, the way my name felt in his mouth. It was wonderful. I wanted to make him say it again. Instead, I coughed into my hand, trying to hide my obvious pleasure, worried that I was lit up like a Christmas candle, simply because he'd said my name.

"Now, will you answer my questions?" Max lifted an eyebrow. "This is the most privacy we'll enjoy before we reach York."

I nodded. "I'm not sure if I'll be able to answer everything," I warned. "But I'll try."

Max ran a hand over his jaw (which was currently stubbled, lending a rakishness to his appearance that I had never seen before and shouldn't currently be admiring). "Mrs Finch filled me in on some of the background of the agency you work for. You take on female clients who fall into difficulty?"

"That is the general idea," I said.

"What I don't understand is why these women turn to *you*." He frowned. "Surely their issues can be resolved through legal avenues, the authorities, I mean, or else they can turn to their father or their husband. Forgive me, but a shadowy society of female agents seems a rather ... risky choice to handle such delicate matters."

I hesitated, wondering how honest to be. He returned my look, clear-eyed, really oblivious to the flaws in his argument.

"That question is one that only a man with your privilege would ask," I said, deciding not to hold back. "When a woman marries, she becomes her husband's property. It has taken centuries for a married woman even to be recognized as a separate individual under the law, rather than simply an extension of her husband, like a limb, as if we were an extra arm or leg incapable of any separate thought, feeling or action. When a woman finds herself in difficulty it is, more often than not, *because* of her husband or her father, or her brother – whichever man is responsible for her at the time. There is no legal avenue open to them, because it is the *law* that is the problem."

I paused to draw breath; he continued to watch me quietly.

"The law protects men, but it *assumes* that men will protect women. I can tell you that in my short time at the Aviary I have seen dozens of cases in which this is patently not the case. The law, the authorities, the government, our entire social system fails women over and over again. You ask, why do they come to us? They come to us because they have *nowhere else to go*."

I was proud that my voice had remained steady throughout this speech, though I could feel my pulse racing and I was panting slightly, heat in my cheeks, as though I had just run at great speed.

The expression on Max's face was hard to read. It wasn't an unpleasant look; in fact it was doing something peculiar to my insides.

"I see," Max said finally, the words an exhalation.

"Do you have any other questions?" I asked.

He tilted his head. "How did *you* end up joining this agency?"

I sighed. "That's a long story. The short version is that I was invited to join at a time when my family found itself in a difficult situation. I needed to get a job, and the Aviary provided me with the perfect opportunity. Of course, for me to work efficiently it has to be a secret. The same goes for all of us." I shot him an uneasy look. He knew about us now and we had no idea what he would do with that information. The Duke of Roxton's interference could pose a very serious threat to our operation. It could also mean the end of my own fragile peace.

We drove for a while in silence but it wasn't precisely uncomfortable – it was more like I could tell Max was absorbing what I had said, turning the words over in his mind. At last, he said, "I think I'm beginning to understand."

It wasn't much, it wasn't a promise to keep our secret – but it was something. His world was being turned upside down and it would take a while to adjust. Whether he helped or hindered us was yet to be seen.

I let myself imagine for a moment the idea that someone who benefitted so completely from the system as it stood would still have the desire to change it. Perhaps – surely – it was possible.

I felt the familiar lift of optimism inside me, my equilibrium returning with each mile that the horses put between us and the city. We would solve this mystery, we would clear Max's name, we would protect Kitten Morland, and we would find a way to bring her husband to justice. I ran my fingers down the side of my pelisse. The ruby brooch was sewn into a hidden pocket, and I could feel the weight of it against my hand. When we reached York we would finally unlock its secrets.

PART THREE

Yorkshire
July 1897

CHAPTER TWENTY

When we reached Hatfield, I was half-expecting Morland to spring from behind the ticket office, twirling his moustache like a villain in a vaudeville production, but there was no sign of him or his cronies. I kept a tight grip on Max's arm, my heart in my mouth as I tried to covertly scan the faces of every single person milling around. We had acted quickly, and Morland didn't know about the Finches' involvement, but his network was enormous – he had government resources and apparently no qualms about involving a criminal element either.

Max gave no indication that he was similarly anxious. When we arrived he began an excellent impression of a solicitous husband, so that it seemed all his attention was for me and nothing else. I swallowed a smile when we headed for the third-class carriages – not at all what he was used to, I'm sure – but again he didn't bat an eyelid, only took my bag in hand and followed me down to our compartment, checking I was settled and fussing over me – was my seat comfortable enough? Did I think I'd rather be facing the other direction? Certainly, I should sit by the window because there was a fine view out over the countryside on this route. Nothing was too much trouble.

I allowed myself to enjoy it. It had been a long time since anyone had fussed over me, even if it was pretend. I was playing the role of a happily cosseted wife, so I told myself it was all part of doing a good job when I sat close beside him, or picked a piece of lint off his lapel, the light bouncing off my gold ring. Max glanced down at me then and once again there was that look, the slight wash of rose pink over his cheekbones. His eyes were soft, his pupils enormous. He was a very good actor.

We drew into Peterborough with plenty of time to connect to the 12.12 to York. I felt my shoulders tense as we changed trains, though I kept my expression neutral. It seemed to me that any of the people thronging the platform could be working for Morland. At one point a man loomed up in front of us, and my hands clenched instinctively into fists, ready to fight, before he handed me a glove that I had dropped. I smiled and thanked him, as Max wrapped an arm tightly around my waist.

When we were stowed safely in our compartment on the next train, with the miles piling up between us and London, I relaxed so far as to actually doze off for a couple of minutes, waking up comfortably propped against Max's shoulder.

"Oh, sorry!" I exclaimed, springing upright and desperately hoping that I hadn't been drooling.

"Don't be," Max said easily. "You haven't slept. It's been a long day."

He hadn't slept either, but I didn't point that out. In fact, as the hours passed and the miles sped away from us, scenery slipping past the window like

265

seaweed streaming alongside a ship, Max's face looked increasingly drawn.

When we reached York at three o'clock, the fine summer day had clouded over. The sky was velvet grey, and the air felt heavy with the promise of rain. We were both feeling weary by now. It had been a long and incredibly hectic twenty-four hours, and it was hard to believe that in the early hours of *this* morning we had been at the ball at Devonshire House when now we were stumbling from the train station some two hundred miles away.

As promised, Mrs Finch had a carriage waiting for us under her name, and Max and I dragged ourselves wearily inside. The driver, a friendly man in his fifties swathed in an enormous rainproof cape and high hat greeted us in a broad Yorkshire accent and introduced himself as Barker, Mr Lockhart's aide-de-campe.

"Which is the master's fancy way of saying I do a bit o' everything, and he don't want a house full of servants," he grinned.

He'd been sent from Mr Lockhart's house to fetch us, and he'd have us out on the moors in no time. It was going to take another couple of hours' journeying over some fairly rotten terrain to reach our destination, and I was bracing myself to be rattled about like a penny in a tin can, but this carriage was even smaller than the last, and I found myself firmly pressed into Max's uninjured side.

"Sorry," I murmured, the first few times the wheel hit something, sending my body crashing into his.

Max shrugged, or attempted to, given the confines of the carriage. "Situations like this always make me feel like an overgrown oaf. I'm a severe disappointment to my valet." His mouth remained in its typical straight line, but I could detect the humour in his eyes.

"I would imagine so," I said. "Didn't he used to have the dressing of Sir Percival Marsh? A *very* dashing figure, so handsome and elegant, and I would guess hardly above five foot, nine inches."

"Now, how on earth do you know that?" Max asked.

"We Finches know everything."

Max was silent for a moment. "Sir Percival is not *that* handsome," he said at last.

We had been travelling for about an hour when the rain began, a persistent drumming against the roof of the carriage.

"It's going to thunder," Max said, looking out of the window where raindrops raced one another along the glass.

"Perhaps it's just a summer shower," I said hopefully.

Max sighed. "Haven't you read *Wuthering Heights*? It was always pouring down whenever those poor idiots were out on the moors."

"That was poetic licence," I replied. "Meant to reflect stormy temperaments and fraught passions." The word *passions* seemed to linger in the air for an unnatural amount of time.

"I think it was meant to reflect the terrible weather," Max said prosaically, and then, with frustratingly perfect timing, a rumble of thunder split the air.

We carried on in silence for several more minutes, but the carriage was trembling like a wounded animal.

"Do you think Barker's all right?" I asked. "Surely he can't stay up there much longer."

"I'm certain he's had the same idea himself," Max replied. "But look out of the window, what do you see?"

I pressed my face to the glass, my fingers leaving smudges on the cold surface as I leaned forward. The rain was driving harder now, and the world outside was a muddy swirl of green and brown and grey. I couldn't see much, but I could make out enough to know that we were in the middle of nowhere. I shouldn't have been surprised – I'd seen the route we were taking on the map – but even so, it felt as though we had been cut adrift in an unfriendly sea.

It was only a few tense minutes later that the carriage lurched drunkenly to the side with an ominous groan, followed by a loud cracking sound. I let out a shout of alarm as, this time, Max was thrown on to me. He reached out instinctively to brace himself with one arm, turning to shield me, as the carriage swayed for one frozen, unbelievable moment and then crashed on to its side.

Several seconds ticked by, in which the world was curiously silent. I had squeezed my eyes closed and I forced them open. For an instant I was completely discombobulated, and then the world of shapes and sounds rushed back in and I realized that the window in the side of the carriage was now above me. Rain was falling down through the shattered glass and on to my prone body. I wriggled my toes and fingers experimentally, and was relieved to find them working.

"Izzy!" Max loomed over me then, his hand clamped to his side. "Are you hurt?"

I pushed myself up on my elbows, and as I did so, tiny pieces of glass fell from my hair like glittering beads. I winced. My knee was hurting, I must have jarred it, but otherwise I felt pretty much all right. "I'm fine," I managed, my eyes going to his side. "What about you? Have you opened your stitches?"

He grimaced, glancing down. "I don't think so – pulled them, maybe." Well, that was something, at least. His eyes widened with concern. "But your head is bleeding!"

I raised my fingers to my face. When they reached my hairline they came away bloody. I frowned. "I think it's just a small cut from the glass. Head wounds always do seem to bleed like the devil."

He huffed. "Had a lot of experience with head wounds, have you? Of course you have." His fingers were sifting gently through my hair, examining my scalp. I was bruised and battered, lying in a carriage that was the wrong way up, sprinkled with broken glass, but I wanted to curl up like a cat and purr.

"I think you're right," he said. His hand was cupping my cheek as he scanned me for injury.

I resisted the urge to lean into his touch. "Oh, goodness," I said instead. "What about poor Barker?"

I scrambled to my feet, but even I had to stoop in the cramped space. The carriage was much smaller widthways. Max was almost bent in half, the window on the other side of the carriage now crunching beneath our feet.

"Hello!" I called. "Hello out there! Barker, are you there?"

The rain continued to fall on us, and I blinked it out of my eyes. The glass left around the window frame was jagged, glinting like blades.

A face appeared on the other side, the anxious face of Barker, a gash over his eyes, his hat missing, and rain plastering his grey hair to his head.

"Oh, Mrs Finch, Mr Finch!" he exclaimed. "What a thing!"

"What happened?" Max asked.

"Axel's snapped." Barker's face was crumpled in frustration. "Been telling Mr Lockhart the whole thing needed seeing to, but he never leaves the house do he, so he's not at all particular about his carriage. Not a thing I can do to fix it here, it's barely worth trying to salvage, great heap." He climbed up on to the side of the carriage and tugged at the door, but it was clearly stuck. Max came and put his shoulder against it, pushing hard, though that only succeeded in creating another shower of glass.

Barker shook his head. "It's no use. There's an inn, only a few miles along the road. I'll take the horse and bring help back with me. Can you hold on?"

"It doesn't look like there's much choice," Max said resignedly. "Go careful, it's hard weather for riding."

"Don't you worry about me, sir," Barker grinned. "Me and Pepper here could find our way blindfolded." With that he disappeared from view and soon we heard the hoofbeats of his departure.

Max and I remained in silence for several minutes. The rain intensified, falling so hard through the window that it stung my face and arms.

"Well," I said eventually. "This is not exactly ideal."

"The queen of the understatement." Max looked down at his feet. As if things weren't bad enough, the rain was beginning to pool in the bottom (or should that be the side?) of the carriage. "At this rate we'll probably drown in here."

"But neither of us are hurt," I pointed out. "Just a bit damp and uncomfortable. I'm sure Barker will be back to rescue us in no time."

"I don't know about that." Max rubbed his face. "The conditions out there are not exactly ideal for a rescue mission."

The rain continued to fall and I was starting to feel miserably cold. Time to take action.

"Then maybe we should try to effect a rescue ourselves. The window's too small to get out of, even if we could safely clear it of glass, but there's still the door." I stooped so that my face was close to the handle. "There's something stopping it from opening."

I pulled a pair of hairpins from my head. They had been made for me by Win for Christmas last year, and I loved them. They were long, thin and perfectly shaped for a bit of spontaneous lock picking. "It looks as though the latch mechanism has jammed. It probably got jarred when the carriage overturned." I clucked my tongue, trying to gently force the spring back into position.

It took me a minute or two, but finally I felt the satisfying click of it returning into place. I pulled on the handle and the door swung easily open above us.

"Perfect," I said. Then I turned to Max, who was staring at me with a stupefied expression.

"Did you just unlock the door ... with your hairpins?" he asked.

"Don't tell me Her Majesty's secret agents don't know how to pick a lock," I said. "Anyway, now that we *can* get out, do you think we should?"

"I'd rather be walking towards this inn than shivering in here," Max said. "What do you think?"

"I agree. Hopefully we'll meet Barker's rescue party on the way."

"Well, then." Max boosted himself up through the door in a single easy movement and held his hand out to take our bags before reaching back for me. "By all means, let's make our way towards the buttered rum."

CHAPTER TWENTY-ONE

The side of the carriage was slick with water, and while the rain had momentarily eased, it seemed still to hang in the air in a diffuse grey mist that stuck my clothes to my skin.

"Wasn't it summer this morning?" Max grumbled.

"This morning was a long time ago." I scrunched up my nose, looking at the ground. "It looks like Barker headed off in this direction." I pointed to the hoof prints in the mud.

"I hope this inn has ale," Max said, as we began

marching down the dirt track. "And food. A nice hot bowl of soup, a slice of pie, a capon or two."

"And blankets, and a big, soft armchair," I joined in.

"And roast potatoes," Max added with a fervent glint in his eyes.

We trudged along, our heads down, for what seemed like hours. My legs were starting to hurt, and I was soaked through.

"Izzy," Max said finally. "I hate to say it but I can't see the hoof prints any more."

"I know," I said. "Do you think it's possible we went wrong somewhere?"

"More than possible, this landscape is impenetrable in this weather." His frustration was clear. "We could be walking in circles for all we know."

"If we were walking in circles we'd end up back at the coach," I said reasonably. "I'm sure we'll find the inn soon. Or if not, somewhere we can dry off and get warm."

"Are you always this optimistic?" Max asked. "We haven't seen a single sign of civilization for miles, what makes you think we'll see one now?"

"I think there's a sort of shepherd's hut up ahead." I pointed. A low stone wall cut through the rolling green landscape, and there in the distance a small, grey stone structure slumped drunkenly alongside it.

"Did you make a cottage appear with your mind?" Max demanded, picking up the pace. "Why didn't you do that an hour ago?"

I tried to laugh, but my teeth were chattering too hard. We sped up, a final burst of energy pushing us forward until we reached the little hut.

Max banged on the door but there was no reply. I put my fingers around the handle and it turned easily. No need to even pick a lock. We practically fell through the doorway. The inside of the hut was a single room, clean and dry with a small fireplace.

I was shivering hard now, and Max was pale as a ghost.

"Fire," I managed, pointing at the fireplace where a pile of chopped wood was neatly stacked, as if waiting for us.

Max said nothing, simply set about building the fire while I headed for the wooden cupboards ranged along the back wall. There were blankets neatly stacked, and I even found a tin of dusty tea and a heel of bread.

"Tea and toast," I said. I turned to Max who was coaxing the wood to catch light in the grate with middling success. "We need to get out of these wet clothes." The words left my mouth and I was instantly flooded with mortification. "I mean... I mean..." I stammered incoherently.

Fortunately, Max decided to simply ignore my flustered stuttering. "Here, hand me those blankets," he said.

Once he had them he folded them quickly over a line of string that ran across the width of the room near the fire – presumably some sort of drying line – creating a screen, behind which we could both change into some of the spare clothes we had packed. I did this as fast as was humanly possible, wriggling out of my sodden dress with a relief that brought the sting of tears to my eyes. Apart from anything else, my skirts weighed a ton. Men's fashions were much more suited to traipsing across tricky terrain in all weathers.

I stripped off on my side of the blankets, painfully

aware that Max was doing the same on the other side. I could hear the sound of him shucking off his jacket, the gentle thud of his boots hitting the stone floor, the pop of buttons and the scrape of fabric against skin. I was blushing so hard I thought I might combust. At least I was warming up. I tugged on a shapeless navy wool dress.

"Ready?" Max asked finally.

"Yes," I replied, and he removed the blankets, holding one out to me. I accepted it gratefully, pulling it round my shoulders for extra warmth. My bare toes peeked out of the bottom and I moved towards the fire that Max had built, which was crackling now.

I draped my wet clothes over the line, trying not to let my embarrassment show. We were simply like soldiers, working in close confines. Max Vane wasn't interested in the sight of my sensible stockings hanging beside his wet shirt. It meant nothing. In fact, he didn't so much as look at them, instead busying himself setting the kettle to boil over the fire, cutting the bread and spearing it on a toasting fork, holding it over the flames. I had nothing to do but curl up on the floor and concentrate on getting warm.

All of this was accomplished in a silence that was surprisingly comfortable. The Duke of Roxton was well-known as a taciturn sort of fellow, but now that I had been thrust into his company, I began to realize this wasn't – as some people thought – from a sort of haughty reserve, but simply his natural state.

"You're very quiet," I said, breaking the silence.

He looked surprised. "Yes," he replied. "I apologize. My sister frequently reminds me that it's off-putting."

"I don't think it's off-putting." I stared at my toes, luxuriating in the warmth of the fire. "I think it makes sense. With your job, I mean. You listen more than you talk."

I felt him shoot me a look. "You seem perfectly capable of doing both," he said. "In fact, the other night at the opera I'd say you talked plenty while you and your friend were picking that gentleman's pocket."

My eyes shot to his. "What do you mean?"

"I was watching you that night. I thought something funny was happening at the time. Then back at the Aviary the other girl was there too, the one with red hair. Maud."

"I'm surprised you noticed," I said, dodging his original question. "You never seemed to remember my name and we must have been introduced countless times."

The words came out sounding petulant, and I wished straight away that I could take them back. There was a pause while Max gazed into the fire.

Finally, he began to speak. "The first time we met officially was at the Perrys' ball last year. You were wearing a grey gown with lilac trim, and you didn't dance once. You *did* stand in the corner with Miss Wynter and laugh a lot, and you also spent some time sitting with Perry's grandmother who is extremely cantankerous and very lonely."

My mouth dropped open. "How do you..." I trailed off.

"I remember every time we were introduced. I remember things." His words held a smile. "I am quite good at my job usually, you know."

"But then why did you pretend not to know me?"

He had the good grace to shift uncomfortably. "A careless duke doesn't remember every young woman he meets."

"That's ... that's despicable!" I sat up straighter, outraged.

"It's a role I play." Max shrugged. "Just as you do. It's what you want, isn't it? You've been *trying* to blend into the shadows. You expected me to forget you, wanted me to forget you. You can't be offended by the fact that I did *and* use the exact same thing to your own advantage."

"I find I am perfectly capable of doing both, thank you," I grumbled. "I contain multitudes."

Max pressed his lips together but I saw the smile there. More and more, I was seeing the humour behind the serious mask he wore.

"I don't think the rain is going to stop, do you?" I asked finally.

"No," Max sighed. "I think we're stuck here for the night. It's already getting dark."

I glanced at the window and saw that he was right. What I had taken for more gloom was actually night-time drawing in. I pulled out my pocket watch. It was almost nine.

"Do you think Barker is all right?" I asked. "I hope he hasn't got a search party out looking for us."

"He's a sensible man," Max said. "And he knows we're together. He'll probably assume that we've found shelter somewhere. Hopefully the rain will have stopped in the morning and we'll be able to track each other down. The best thing we can do now is to get some sleep."

The words hung in the air. Ever since we'd entered the shepherd's hut I had been trying to ignore the small bed tucked in the corner.

"Right, yes." It came out in a squeak and I cleared my throat. "Then we can get an early start in the morning."

"You take the bed and I'll sleep here on the floor," Max said.

"You can't sleep on the floor!"

"I'm so tired, I think I could sleep standing up," Max admitted.

I looked doubtfully at the cold, hard stone. "Well, if you're sure..."

I got to my feet and made my way over to the bed. It wasn't terribly soft, but it was covered in a clean sheet, a woollen blanket folded at the bottom, a single thin pillow on top of that. Whoever looked after this place was very neat.

I lay down on top of the bed, fully dressed, and the wave of exhaustion that crashed into me made me feel woozy. The room was dim, lit by the fire, and I could still hear the rain falling outside.

"You can't sleep on the floor," I said, and the words slurred a little, too tired to enunciate properly. "You're a duke."

I heard Max huff. "I don't know what being a duke has to do with it."

"And you're injured!" I pushed myself up on my elbow, remembering. "Your stitches! You have to have the bed."

"If you think I'm sleeping on the bed while you sleep on the floor then you've a funny idea about how dukes behave."

"You're being chivalrous," I grumbled. "I don't need you to be chivalrous. I'm quite tough, actually."

"I absolutely know that," Max said.

We both fell quiet.

"We ... could both sleep in the bed?" I said quietly.

There was a pause. "I-I'm not sure that's appropriate," Max replied, his voice strained.

I had been feeling a bit nervous about the offer, but now his stiff tone made me laugh. "For goodness' sake, Max, I'm not going to force you to defend your honour. We've both been through a lot today, we're tired and cold and there's one bed. We left propriety behind a long time ago – probably around the time I was fighting off your assailants on the streets of Whitechapel. It's up to you if you want to sleep on a stone floor, but you're going to be less useful tomorrow if you don't get some actual sleep." With that I plumped the pillow with an unnecessary amount of violence and turned to face the wall.

It seemed that the argument was compelling enough because moments later, the side of the bed depressed as Max lay down with a quiet groan. We were both fully dressed, touching less than we had in the carriage earlier, but I worried that he would be able to hear my heartbeat, the way I could, drumming loud in my ears. I remained resolutely facing the wall.

"You're sure you don't mind?" Max asked softly.

"Don't be silly." I closed my eyes. "Go to sleep."

Then, despite the fact that I was sharing a bed with the Duke of Roxton – an idea which only a few hours ago would have seemed nothing but a distant dream – I followed my own advice, and within seconds I was completely unconscious.

CHAPTER TWENTY-TWO

I awoke the next morning aware only that I was warm and deliciously comfortable. I snuggled into the bed covers, only to find that the covers felt firmer and significantly more alive than usual. My eyes popped open, and I had to stifle a mortified squeak.

I was wrapped around Max Vane like a clinging vine, like I had grown around him overnight, twining over his limbs. My cheek was on his chest, my arm thrown over his shoulder, my legs tucked over his. I was holding on to him like I was about to drown and he was the only thing keeping me afloat.

I lay silently for a moment, frozen, feeling the even rise and fall of his chest under my head. Cautiously I pulled my arms and legs back – those treacherous limbs that had betrayed me in sleep – and waited again. Max still didn't move, his breathing didn't alter.

Slowly, slowly, I lifted my head. His eyes were closed and I didn't even take advantage of the opportunity to watch his perfect face while he slept like the infatuated idiot I was, instead I rolled my body away so that I was firmly back on my side of the bed, facing the wall. Only then did I let myself exhale a long, slow breath.

Thank goodness I had woken up first. The thought of Max waking up and finding me draped all over him was mortifying. I had told him in no uncertain terms that I wasn't going to accost him if we shared a bed and then look what happened! I shuffled even further away, my knees pressing into the wall. The movement must have been enough to wake Max, because there was the sound of a leonine yawn and I felt him stirring beside me.

I did my own elaborate enactment of regaining

consciousness, and turned over on the pillow. As Max was now lying on his side facing me, this meant that we found ourselves almost nose to nose. His green eyes looked steadily back at me, and for a moment I thought I saw a flicker of laughter there, but it was gone again in half an instant. His fair hair, always so neat, was tousled, and I longed to reach out to push it back into place. The shadow on his jaw was darker now too. He looked rumpled and delicious.

"Good morning," he said, his voice low, still rasping with sleep.

"Good morning." I blinked, and then, unnerved by our closeness, I sat up. "It's light," I said inanely.

Max propped himself up on his elbows. "Just," he murmured. "It must be early."

I clambered from the bed, and hunted around for my pocket watch. "It's gone six." I glanced at the window again. "It's stopped raining!"

"I suppose it had to at some point," Max said, swinging his legs over the side of the mattress and rolling his neck. "I slept surprisingly well in the end. Plenty of room for both of us."

My eyes darted to his, unsure if he was teasing me, but his features were utterly bland. Almost suspiciously so.

"Well, you must have been tired," I said in a matter-of-fact voice.

"Mmm," Max nodded. "Staying up all night, burgling people, falling from buildings, getting into knife fights, travelling most of the length of the country, and then being thrown from a carriage may be all in a day's work for you, but I must admit I was grateful for a moment's respite."

"These pampered dukes," I sighed. "It's no wonder you can't keep up."

"But I'm rested now," Max protested. "Bring on your Herculean tasks. What will it be? A bit of light mountaineering before breakfast?"

"Only a gentle climb. We'll see if we can find your inn full of roast potatoes."

Max clutched at his stomach. "By all means, let's go at once."

It took little time to gather our belongings, which had dried nicely, and we left the place as tidy as we had found it. Max dropped a handful of coins on the side, and we made our way out through the door.

A very different scene greeted us this morning. The sun was coming up over the horizon, bathing everything in rippling liquid gold. A patchwork of fresh, bright greens undulated around us, neatly bisected by grey stone walls. We were some way up a large hill that I had barely even noticed climbing the day before in our mad scramble, and the landscape was laid out in front of us, like a well-dressed table, a feast of pastel-blue sky and tumbling violet heathers.

"Beautiful," I exhaled.

"Hard to believe it's the same place we were slogging through yesterday," Max said, squinting into the distance. "There's the road down there." He pointed to a sort of valley that ran between the hills.

It was much easier now that we could see where we were going. The air was clear and sweet, and the scene was perfect, full of fat, drowsy little bees, and spiky yellow flowers, clustered together like constellations. We even found a cloudberry hedge, the amber fruit perfectly ripe with the merest blush of pink.

"Teresa would be delighted," I said. "Breakfasting on cloudberries and drinking cool water from the stream. What could be more romantic?" I tilted my head. "Of course, then later she'd be starving and complaining that what she really wanted was hot buttered toast and a cup of tea, which is an eminently more sensible start to the day."

"Eminently," Max agreed. "Perhaps we could make her a jar of cloudberry jam as a compromise."

I was assailed at once by the perfect pastoral image of Max and I living in our cosy little hut, making our own cloudberry jam, living off the land. Perhaps we'd have a sheep ... did one keep solitary sheep? No, you'd have to have a flock. A goat, maybe. Much less work than a cow, but we could still have milk...

"What are you thinking about?" Max asked. "You've gone all dreamy."

"Jam," I replied sharply.

Max nodded solemnly. "I get a bit dreamy over preserves myself."

I laughed then, and he smiled, without meeting my eye.

We followed the road for about forty minutes and then, like a mirage in the desert, a small village appeared, a smattering of stone houses clustered around the road, and a larger building with a weather-beaten sign that proclaimed it the Blacksmith's Arms.

"We found it!" I exclaimed. "Now, let's hope we find Barker as well."

We were in luck, because we had barely pushed our way through the door before the man himself was wringing our hands and exclaiming in pleasure.

"We were getting the search party together!" Barker beamed, gesturing to the woman behind him. "Saw you'd bailed out of the carriage last night, which was probably the right thing to do given the thing were half-full of water. We guessed you'd gone off the path and found shelter but with no tracks to follow there weren't much we could do to chase after you."

"I hope we didn't make you too anxious, Mr Barker," I said. "We found a shepherd's hut and spent the night there, waiting for the storm to pass."

We were interrupted then by the formidable-looking

woman who bustled over, clucking and shoving Barker aside.

"This is Mrs Crantock," Barker said. "She and her husband Ned own this particular establishment."

"I'm sure the young couple are absolutely famished," she said, looking Max up and down and sighing as though he were in danger of wasting away. "Let's get some hot food in you. I've got a pot of porridge on the go, and we'll have some toast and some bacon, and a sausage or two. I daresay Mr Crantock will be back with some eggs from the chickens in a minute and I can fry up a plateful of those."

Max was looking at her, starry-eyed with appreciation. "That sounds wonderful," he said, sounding almost tearful.

"Thank you. But then we really must set off," I said, smiling apologetically at Mrs Crantock. "We were supposed to arrive at Mr Lockhart's home last night, and I'm afraid our business is quite pressing."

Mrs Crantock's bright eyes looked at me with undisguised interest. "Of course, of course. We'll feed you up and then Barker will have you on your way. Don't get many visitors for Mr Lockhart, do we, Barker?"

Barker sniffed, immediately less affable. "Who the master does and doesn't see is none of our concern," he said stiffly.

Mrs Crantock rolled her eyes. "Oh, don't be so buttoned up, it's only a bit of village gossip. Now, let me go and fetch that food."

It took the best part of an hour to do justice to the lavish attentions of Mrs Crantock. I'm sure Max ended up eating half a dozen eggs as well as half a pig. He put it all away with an enthusiasm that had the landlady pink with pleasure.

"That's a fine strapping young man you've got yourself there," she whispered to me at one point. It was the sort of whisper that could be heard across the room.

"Mmmm," I murmured non-committally, but my eyes lingered on Max's forearms, bare to his elbows where he had his sleeves rolled up, and corded with muscle.

Eventually, we were able to leave the inn, a parcel of food under Max's arm "for the journey". Barker had assured us we had less than an hour ahead of us, this time in an open cart borrowed from the Crantocks.

"Best I could do in the circumstances," Barker sighed.

It was a lovely way to travel on such a beautiful day. I lounged back, feeling the sun warm on my face as we trundled along the winding dirt road.

Finally, we rounded a corner and the landscape opened up in front of us.

The house was perched atop a high hill on the edge of a jutting stone cliff. It looked like something from Grimm's fairy tales, all twisting turrets and high, arching Gothic windows and ... was that a drawbridge? It was indeed, and as we trundled over the lowered bridge that crossed a steep drop down to a stream below, I realized that when raised the house – though really it was more like a castle – would be impossible to reach.

"Oh!" I exclaimed, loud enough that Barker heard me and turned over his shoulder to grin at me.

"That's what most people say," he chuckled.

"Though you're lucky to be seeing it on a pleasant day like today. When the storms are wailing it's quite a sinister aspect."

"I can imagine," I managed.

I leaned out of the side of the cart as we pulled through the gate cut into the high stone wall, and arrived in a small, square courtyard.

"Of course it has gargoyles," I said gleefully. "Of *course* it does. Tell me, Mr Barker, are you much troubled by restless spirits?"

Barker pulled the horse to a stop and turned to me. "Let's just say I wouldn't go wandering too far on your own late at night, miss."

I wasn't sure whether he was being serious or not, and I found myself looking for reassurance at Max who only shrugged and helped me down from the cart.

We stood in front of an enormous wooden door that looked as though it had come out the winner in many an attempted siege, and Barker reached out, turning the handle.

Inside was a large entrance hall, double height and shockingly dark and gloomy after being outside in the sunshine. I blinked as my eyes tried to adjust to the difference.

"Now, I'm sure after last night you'll be wanting to clean up and rest a bit." Barker glanced back at the sunlit morning spilling through the doorway. "Mr Lockhart won't be up for hours yet. I shouldn't think he'll be able to receive you until this afternoon."

"I see," I said. "I hope Mr Lockhart isn't unwell?"

Barker gave a short snap of laughter. "He's not unwell, miss, he's a layabout and he doesn't like people." It was said with affection, and I was puzzled by the relationship between Barker and the master of the house. Max and I exchanged a brief look, and he gave another small shrug. So much for the dazzling insights of Her Majesty's finest.

We were led up the great stone staircase, and down a long, dark corridor before Barker ushered us through a door on the right.

"This here was the mistress's room," Barker said in a low and reverential voice. "I thought this was the best for you, miss." He gestured to a door at the side of the room. "And through there is the old master's room. Seemed proper to give you the connected suite."

At least now Max and I would have a whole bed each. Which I was definitely not disappointed about. Definitely not.

"It's perfect, Barker, thank you," I said.

The man smiled. "I'll fetch up some hot water for the bath." He gestured to the enormous tin bath in front of the fireplace. "And then either me or Beth will come and get you when the master shows his face downstairs. Beth'll be up with a tea tray too. Can I send anything to eat?"

"No, thank you, Mr Barker." I returned his grin. "It feels like I'll never be hungry again, after that meal from Mrs Crantock."

Max opened his mouth as if to protest but then visibly recollected the food parcel under his arm, and remained quiet.

Barker nodded and left the room, whistling jauntily, leaving Max and I alone.

I glanced away. The room we were in had been kept clean but obviously left largely untouched for several years. The yellow paper on the walls was faded, as were the drapes which may once have been rose coloured but were now a sort of dirty pink. There was an old-fashioned bath in front of the stone fireplace, a dressing table which held a tarnished silver-backed hairbrush and an almost empty bottle of scent, and a huge four-poster bed draped in faded chintz. Apart from a wardrobe there was nothing else in the room. It smelled slightly musty, cut through with beeswax and lemon. Someone had made an effort to freshen the place up for me.

"Well," Max said, striding to the door that joined our rooms together. "I'll leave you to your rest." He stepped through the door and shut it behind him with a definite click.

I flopped down on to the bed with a sigh. As I did so I felt the jewelled brooch in my pocket dig into my hip and I took it out, holding it up to the light.

"What's your secret?" I murmured, turning it this way and that, the red stone gleaming.

Hopefully the mysterious Oliver Lockhart would have some answers.

CHAPTER TWENTY-THREE

In fact, it was not until late afternoon that Oliver Lockhart deigned to make an appearance. In that time I had had a bath and the maid Beth had even offered to do my hair for me. She was around a decade older than me and clearly related to Barker – her face was a younger, softer version of his underneath a mop of dark curls. She also sported the same winning grin, and I got the feeling she enjoyed having a lady in the house to fuss over.

"Oliver is easy enough to work for," she said.

"But I do miss doing the ladies' hair and the pretty gowns and such." She looked down at my drab gown with more than a touch of wistfulness and I felt sorry that I had let her down on that front. It seemed the absolute least I could do to offer up my wet hair to her ministrations.

"Oliver?" I said curiously.

Beth chuckled. "Mr Lockhart, I mean ... but I've known him so long, and usually it's just the three of us: him, Da and me. Oli— I mean, Mr Lockhart, he's not particular about the niceties. In fact, he gets furious when I call him Mr Lockhart. I only do it when he's acting the tyrant."

"Does he often act the tyrant?" I asked.

Beth's gaze dropped, and she sifted her fingers through my long hair. "He can be difficult," she said softly, and there was sadness in her face. "But then, he's got better reason than most."

Mrs Finch had taught me that sometimes, simply leaving space for the truth invited it forward, and so I remained still and quiet for a long moment.

"He lost his mother and his sister," Beth said finally.

"In difficult circumstances." Her lips pressed together and it was clear that was as much as I was going to get out of her.

We made small talk, and I relaxed under Beth's nimble fingers as she coaxed and braided my hair into a soft chignon.

I was fielding questions from Beth about the London fashions when I looked up to see Max reflected in the mirror behind me. He was standing in the doorway, clean and freshly shaven. He had forgone wearing the dark wig since we arrived in Yorkshire, and, even in the borrowed, second-hand clothing, he looked so handsome that my words to Beth died on my tongue.

For his part he was observing me with his usual sphinx-like expression. Beth, following my gaze in the mirror, gave a start and turned.

"There you are, sir." She bobbed a curtsey. "I've finished on Mrs Finch's hair." She returned her eyes to the mirror and winked at me in its reflection. "Pretty as a picture."

This was something of an overstatement.

"She is indeed," Max said, playing the doting

husband to perfection. Well, Mrs Finch *had* told us to make sure our cover story was clear for all to see.

I got to my feet and put a hand to his cheek. "I expect you were glad to be able to have a shave at last."

For a second Max's hand covered mine, pressing it to his face, and then he pulled it away and pressed it to his lips.

Beth gave a sigh. *So in love,* were the words I could see in her eyes. What an excellent job we were doing.

"Now, I'd better go and get started on the dinner," Beth said. "Shall I show you down to the library? That's where Oli— Mr Lockhart will be."

"Wonderful," I said, and as soon as she had bustled past us I dropped Max's hand, trying to look unaffected as my fingers tingled.

We followed Beth back downstairs and through several rooms that had the same feeling of faded grandeur as my bedroom before reaching the library. "He's in there," Beth said, gesturing to the door and then scurrying away down the corridor, presumably in the direction of the kitchen.

The library was clearly where Oliver Lockhart did

most of his living. The room was handsomely furnished, the walls lined with books that showed signs of being well read rather than simply there for display. There was a wooden desk, piled high with papers. In front of the fireplace a single, battered armchair was occupied by a large orange cat. Otherwise the room was empty.

"Well, I don't think you're Oliver Lockhart," I said, stooping to pet the cat.

"Of course not," snapped a disgruntled voice. "That pampered, overstuffed carpet-bag is Marmalade."

With those words, Oliver Lockhart strode out from the bookcase.

My mouth dropped open in surprise. Not only because he had entered the room through a hidden door, but because Oliver Lockhart was absolutely, jaw-droppingly beautiful.

I felt a moment of relief that Teresa was not here, because the young man in front of me was the embodiment of all Teresa's wildest fantasies, and the presence of him in this Gothic monstrosity of a house would simply have been too much for my friend to handle. I had been expecting someone much older but he was actually around the same age as me, with tumbling dark hair, brooding dark eyes, light brown skin, and the sort of sensual mouth that looked as though it would always be spouting poetry. His body was lithe and graceful, his cheekbones so sharp they looked dangerous, and even his deep scowl only added to the image of a tortured artist. I found myself picturing him striding across the moors in a long, flapping coat, and actually felt a bit dizzy. Teresa would have swooned dead away by now.

I realized then that I was still bent over the cat and I snapped up straight.

"Mr Lockhart," I said, smiling warmly at him.

His scowl only deepened. "You," he said, marching forward and pointing a finger at me, "are not Mrs Finch. Mrs Finch and I have corresponded for several years and she is much older than you."

"How old were you when you started corresponding *several years* ago?" I said, needled. "Twelve?"

"Fifteen, actually," Oliver said disinterestedly. "So who are you?"

"I am a colleague of Mrs Finch's," I said, regaining

some poise. "I assumed she would have made that clear when she wrote to you."

"Her telegram was clearly sent in great haste," he said shortly. "She said only that I should expect Mr and Mrs Finch to arrive imminently. It is extremely inconvenient timing – I am busy with my work." He turned towards Max, his eyes filled with suspicion. "And you? Because if this isn't Mrs Finch, I take it *you* are not her husband."

Max hesitated for only a fraction of a second. "I am also an associate of Mrs Finch," he said.

"You can call us Izzy and Max," I said, trying to retain control of the situation. "We're sorry to disturb you at such a busy time, but we are here on an urgent matter."

"The telegram said something about a piece of jewellery?" Oliver's eyes flicked in my direction.

I pulled the brooch from my pocket and walked towards him. He took it from me, his fingers a cold brush against my own skin. I felt myself shiver. I don't think I'd even have been surprised if he'd revealed himself to be a vampire at this point. It seemed entirely plausible.

His attention now was entirely devoted to the brooch. His eyes brightened with interest and the glowering look lifted. "Intriguing," he murmured, and with that he turned and disappeared through the bookcase.

"Hey!" I exclaimed, and his head popped back around the door.

"Well, come on, then," he grumbled. "Both of you," he added, regarding Max sourly, as if he didn't want to leave him unsupervised in the library.

We followed him. The door was part of the bookcase, swinging open on a hinge, and beyond it a steep flight of stairs led down into darkness. Max and I exchanged a brief glance, then we descended after Oliver.

I'm not sure what I expected. Given Oliver's appearance and general demeanour, I suppose it could have been some sort of dungeon. Candlelit, perhaps, with iron rings and chains in the wall. Instead we emerged into a clean and extremely tidy workshop. There was even electric lighting, though I was sure I hadn't seen that elsewhere in the house.

The room was square and the walls had been painted white. Light filtered in through a couple of grates high up on the left-hand wall. Two long workbenches stretched the width of the room, separated into separate work areas, with vices clamped to the sides and small, intricate tools laid out neatly on strips of red fabric. There was also a furnace built into the end of the wall, and it groaned away, making the room very warm.

"I suppose that's where he disposes of his victims," Max murmured in my ear, and I smothered a laugh.

Oliver's eyes snapped to us with displeasure. "Is something funny?" he asked.

"No, no," I said quickly. "Just admiring your workshop."

Oliver made a harrumphing sound and whisked the brooch over to one of the work areas, sliding it underneath an enormous brass microscope.

I stepped closer to the worktops and realized that they were covered in pieces of jewellery. Glittering stones in every colour were strewn about as if they were nothing more than sweets in a confectioner's window, half-finished rings and bracelets and even an elaborate sapphire necklace were held in clamps.

I stepped closer to the necklace. It looked familiar,

somehow. It was a heavy design, a little old-fashioned, containing an enormous blue sapphire in the centre and then ropes of smaller sapphires and diamonds creating a spider-web effect around it. As my eyes slid away I realized that there was an identical necklace, only this one was perfect and complete, on a velvet mat alongside it.

I reached out my fingers towards it, but Oliver's voice came sharply. "Don't touch anything."

I snatched my hand back, and glanced at him. He hadn't even looked up from the microscope. I looked at the necklace again, frowning as I tried to place where I had seen it before.

Oliver stood up from the microscope and carried the brooch to another part of the workshop. Here he screwed a sort of monocle into his eye and peered more closely at the piece of jewellery.

"Hmmm," he murmured.

"I don't know if Mrs Finch mentioned it in her letter," I said. "But we're trying to work out why someone would be so keen to get their hands on this particular piece. If it's simply a question of it being valuable, or if there's—"

"Please be quiet," Oliver cut in coldly.

My mouth snapped shut and I felt Max shift at my elbow. We waited in silence as Oliver moved around the workshop, subjecting the brooch to various examinations, even applying drops of several different chemical solutions with the precision of a doctor performing surgery.

Finally, he set the brooch down on the tabletop and looked at us, as if finally remembering we were there.

"Well, the stone is Tudor," he said. "A fine example of the kind of engraving that was fashionable at the time. The engraved rose might represent the House of Lancaster in which case it would more likely date to the time of Henry VII. Of course, it could be a representation of the Tudor rose in which case it's possible it is later, but I doubt it – the style is too simple. The setting however is not so old. I would put that around the mid-1600s. Civil war possibly, given its purpose."

"Valuable?" Max asked.

Oliver shrugged. "Quite valuable, although what

price it would fetch, I'm not sure. Historically it's interesting, but it's not in the current style at all. A piece for a collector, but not – I would think – for any lady of fashion to covet."

"You said *given its purpose*," I said then. "What do you mean?"

"Well, you know, with all those state secrets flying around the country I'd imagine it would be useful in some way during the civil war." He absorbed our confused expressions for a moment and sighed. "It's not really a piece of jewellery at all, is it? It's a key."

CHAPTER TWENTY-FOUR

"A key?" I exhaled.

Oliver gestured to us to come closer. "It's quite ingenious," he said, turning the brooch between his long, elegant fingers. "Do you see this join here?" He pointed to the side of the braided gold setting. Max and I both leaned over.

"I don't see anything," I said. "Do you?" I turned to Max, and found his face was close to mine. For half a second I luxuriated in his nearness and then I stepped back. Max shook his head.

"I don't see anything either."

"Here." Oliver handed me the monocle he had looked through earlier and I held it to my eye. It was an intense magnifying glass and, with Oliver pointing, I could make out the join he was referring to. It was no bigger than a hairline crack.

"It looks like a bit of damage to the setting," I said, handing the magnifying lens to Max so that he could see.

"It's a hinge," Oliver said, as if I were a simpleton. He twisted the brooch sharply between his hands before pulling the two halves apart. The brooch moved smoothly – still in one piece, but now there was a gap under the stone. With a click, one side of the setting dropped down and I could see that the metallic braid was actually hollow and when Oliver nudged his finger inside it he unfolded a long, thin metal stick with a serrated edge.

"A key!" I squealed.

"As I said," Oliver sighed wearily.

"A key to what?" Max stepped forward, his eyes alight with interest. My own heart was beating rapidly.

Here, finally, was the reason that Morland was so interested in this thing. Here was the answer to all of our questions.

"How the devil should I know?" Oliver said icily, turning the brooch back so that the key was hidden away once more. "I should think that bit will be your department."

I chewed on my lip, the euphoria draining out of my body. Of course we had only solved half the puzzle. Where would we even start to work out what the key unlocked? Even my optimism wavered for a moment. I glanced over at Max and saw the storm of frustration in his eyes. It was his life, his reputation on the line here.

"Quite right, Mr Lockhart," I said with a smile. "Now that we've uncovered the secret of the brooch I'm sure we can locate the lock it opens. We've cracked much harder cases with little more to go on."

Oliver clearly couldn't care less, but my words hadn't been for him; they had been for Max. I knew he still wanted to believe the best of his mentor, but the existence of a secret key, and the lengths Morland had been going to to retrieve it must surely be raising some alarm bells for him.

For a moment it seemed as though my thought had been taken literally when we were interrupted by the shrill ringing of a bell.

"Dinner is ready," Oliver said, casting a dark look at us both. "I suppose you two will be joining me – it's too late to head back to London."

"Thank you," I replied, as politely as if the invitation had been sincere. "We'll be grateful for your hospitality tonight and then we'll be out of your hair first thing tomorrow."

"Fine," Oliver conceded gracelessly. "Let's go and eat, then. I hope to God it's not fish. I don't know how Beth does it, but she's got a real talent for making the simplest dishes inedible. She cooks things until they bend."

Fortunately for us, Beth had made chicken and though it was slightly rubbery, it was not inedible. We ate in a large, formal dining hall, crowded round the end of a long table. It was clear that Oliver Lockhart did not typically eat in here, and also that he was annoyed that our presence meant he was required to do so.

"Here we go, Mr Lockhart," Beth said, laying a plate in front of him as she bobbed a wobbly sort of curtsey.

Oliver eyed her narrowly. "You don't have to go putting on airs because we have guests," he growled. "No one cares what they think."

The look Beth gave him was almost maternal. "And there's no need for *you* to behave like such a scapegrace, Oliver," she said.

Oliver ignored her, digging into his food.

"Is your dinner all right, sir?" Beth asked Max anxiously.

Oliver daggered him with a glare. It seemed that he was the only one allowed to complain about Beth's cooking. He needn't have worried.

"It's delicious, thank you," Max said, and he smiled at her so warmly that Beth blinked, looking suddenly slightly dizzy. I knew the feeling well. She headed back to the kitchen and Oliver grudgingly topped up Max's wine glass.

"Will you tell us about your work, Mr Lockhart?"

I asked.

"Why do you want to know?" came the sullen reply.

"I thought it might be interesting," I said a little desperately.

"Your workshop is certainly an impressive set-up," Max waded in, bravely taking up the baton.

Oliver snorted into his glass. A thick silence fell.

It was then that I remembered where I had seen the sapphire necklace downstairs. "Lady Brandwick," I murmured.

"What?" Oliver didn't move, but his eyes were alert and watchful.

I looked at him for a moment, the wheels turning in my head. "That necklace you have downstairs. I know where I've seen it before. It was at a party several months ago, Lady Brandwick was wearing it. She said it had been in her family for generations. I know, because my friend Teresa admired it, and Lady Brandwick doesn't tend to wear much jewellery."

I remembered Lady Brandwick's face when she had spoken about the jewels and how her mother had worn them. She had put her hand to her neck and her usually timid face had shown something like pride. What was it doing in Oliver's workshop now? And why was he making a copy?

"Didn't Lord Brandwick have a bit of financial trouble recently?" I said slowly, turning towards Max.

Max looked uncomfortable, as if discussing another man's finances with me went against some sort of code. "I believe Lord Brandwick had some gambling debts called in."

I stilled, my eyes sliding towards Oliver who was peering disinterestedly into his wine glass. Now the connection between Mrs Finch and Oliver Lockhart made sense.

"You're making the copy for Lady Brandwick," I said. "So that she can keep the real one safe from her husband, in case he tries to pawn it."

"What?!" Max exclaimed.

I leaned forward, my eyes still on Oliver. "It's true, isn't it? You're working with Mrs Finch to help a client."

"It seems you have it all figured out," Oliver said sourly, toying with food on his plate, and careful not to confirm or deny what I was saying.

"But that's terrible," Max said.

I wheeled round on him. "What do you mean it's terrible?" I demanded.

"Making counterfeit jewels," Max said, looking confused. "Deceiving her husband. It's ... well, it's illegal, for one thing."

"It's only illegal because the law is idiotic," I said. "Those jewels belonged to Lady Brandwick's family, they had nothing to do with Lord Brandwick, and yet now, because they're married, they belong to him. Never mind that he's a reckless gambler. If he chooses to he can sell off her precious family heirlooms just so that he can play another hand of cards. *That's* what's terrible. *That's* what should be illegal. What Mr Lockhart is doing is protecting her from the actions of her husband because the law won't."

The room fell quiet again, and Max blinked at me, that odd look on his face, the one that made him look troubled and a bit shaken, but also something else, something that I couldn't put my finger on, something that spread like an itch across my skin.

Oliver cleared his throat, and then reached out and

topped up my wine glass. I took a defiant sip.

We finished up our meal in silence, which seemed to suit Oliver perfectly well, though it made me feel jittery, almost nervous. The sound of my knife against my plate seemed too loud as I pushed my food around. I avoided Max's eyes, but couldn't help watching his hands as they moved, his fingers wrapped around his glass.

"I'm tired," I said, once the plates had been cleared. I dropped my napkin on top of the table and got to my feet. Max and Oliver rose as well. "I hope you won't mind if I retire. We'll make an early start in the morning – shall we try for the 8.45 train from York?"

Max nodded.

"Barker will take you back to the station," Oliver said. "You'd better leave by six. I certainly won't be up so I shall say my goodbyes now." He gave an almost indiscernible bow. "Please pass on my regards to Mrs Finch."

With that he strode from the room.

The clock on the mantelpiece ticked. "What an … unusual man," I said finally.

"He certainly is that," Max agreed.

There was a pause that felt, for the first time between the two of us alone, slightly awkward. "Well," I said. "I think I'll go to bed."

"Let me go with you," Max replied quickly, and then I had the pleasure of watching him blush. "I mean," he said, the words coming out slightly strangled. "Please allow me to escort you up to your room."

We made our way up the stairs together, still not talking. With Max that was hardly unusual, but his silence definitely felt different now, strained and uncomfortable.

We reached the door and he turned to me. "Are you angry with me?"

I blinked. "I—" I hesitated. "I'm not angry," I said finally. "I'm ... frustrated, I suppose. You're bound so tightly into a system that I've come to resent. My work, the things I've seen..." I trailed off.

He nodded. "I understand that, but surely society only works because of the laws which govern it?" He rubbed his face, in a weary gesture. "I don't think it's right to break the rules."

"That's because all the rules were designed with you

in mind."

The silence stretched out. His eyes scanned my face with an intensity that felt like a touch. It was as if I were a book he was desperately trying to read, in a language he didn't understand.

But perhaps he could learn.

"Goodnight, Max," I said quietly, slipping through the door.

"Goodnight, Izzy." I heard the soft words following me into the dark.

PART FOUR

Back to London
July 1897

CHAPTER TWENTY-FIVE

We made the early train to London the next day. Max was back in his dark wig, and we were – once more – the newly-weds who could barely keep their hands off each other. It was a peculiar type of torture, this game of pretend.

Things between Max and I felt increasingly complicated. We were almost friends, but we saw things so differently. There was of course the inconvenient fact that I was besotted with him and he had no idea. Still, there was one thing I knew for sure: once the case was over we would return to being strangers. Max would go back to his work, his life, and I would go back to mine. Which was a good thing, I reminded myself. Max knew too many of my secrets.

"I'm still not sure this is the best idea," I murmured as the train drew into Kings Cross. "Morland is sure to have people here looking for us."

Max nodded, glancing out of the window. "But no one will expect us to be coming back *in* to London. They'll be focused on departures. And this will give us a chance to see how Morland is organizing his search, how many men are here and if I know any of them."

I looked at him. "Do you still think Morland has nothing to do with this scheme?" I asked quietly. "That it's all a terrible mistake?"

Max's gaze remained fixed on the window, but I saw his expression tighten. "I don't know," he said at last. "But I know I need to avoid capture, until I can clear my name. Whatever the reason – by mistake or by design – Morland has ordered my arrest."

I nodded. That would have to be enough – for now. Max stood, gathering our bags and holding out a hand to me. "Shall we?" he smiled softly, and I felt a now familiar tingle in my fingers when he twined them through his own.

We stepped from the train, Max taking my arm so that my hand rested possessively in the crook of his elbow. His hat was pulled low, shadowing his face, and he affected a slight limp – barely noticeable, but one that changed his posture.

He wasn't the only one who didn't want to be recognized: Isobel Stanhope would have a lot of trouble explaining away the man on her arm and the wedding ring on her hand. I had worn a fashionable little hat with a light veil that covered the top half of my own face.

We walked with our bodies pressed close together. Max kept turning to murmur in my ear, and I would giggle or swat playfully at his shoulder. To anyone watching it looked like we were wrapped up in each other, newly-weds in love. The reality of the sweet nothings Max was whispering, however, would have come as a severe disappointment.

"Those two over by the newspaper stand are Morland's men."

I flicked a glance from under my eyelashes and saw the men he meant. One of them shifted and I noticed that beneath his jacket he wore a harness for carrying a gun. Their attention was focused on the platforms with trains departing for the north, but I still felt my blood run cold. If I had needed a reminder of the danger we were in then that was it.

The criminal element was present too, I saw. "That man in the corner – the one in the green jacket – is one of Nero's boys," I whispered back.

"Your friend from the King's Head?"

"Yes, and someone who does work for Rook from time to time."

"Could be a coincidence." Max pulled me gently to a stop in front of a flower stall, our bodies at least partially hidden by towering bunches of irises and greenery.

"Do you think so?" I asked, smiling at the girl who was already trying to sell Max a posy "for the pretty lady".

"No, probably not."

Max took a moment to admire the blooms, and I

was both impressed and unnerved by his boldness. He was hiding in plain sight, right under the noses of the men who wanted to arrest him, and he didn't betray a hint of unease, didn't hurry along or draw attention. Instead, he was the picture of a relaxed man spending time with his sweetheart.

"The violets, I think," he said, handing over a coin. "My wife's favourite."

A lucky guess, but they really were my favourites, and I felt myself flush as he handed me the small bunch of velvety purple flowers.

We made our way towards the exit, blending into the crowd. We were almost out of the station when I spotted a familiar face and let out a muttered curse. Squeezing Max's arm slightly, I guided him over to a corner and took out a timetable from my reticule.

"James St Clair is here," I murmured, bending my head over the timetable, and pulling him around so that he had his back to his friend, shielding him from view.

I saw Max's body stiffen but his face betrayed nothing. "Where?"

"He's blocking the way through the door, scanning

the crowd. He's in disguise. I almost didn't recognize him."

Max smiled but it didn't reach his eyes. "He's always loved his disguises."

Today, James's efforts to look like a working-class tough were much more effective than they had been that night at the King's Head. He was scruffy, his beard longer and untrimmed, his clothes shabby, and he held himself like one of Nero's boys. It was no wonder people were giving him as wide a berth as the busy station would allow. He stood looking unperturbed, scratching his cheek and observing the crowd with interest.

"We'll have to go out the other way." I gestured towards the exit at the other side of the station.

Max nodded. "He won't expect me to be with a woman. Keep walking."

"But he knows me," I whispered, nerves singing through me and sending my breathing ragged. "Not just as Kes, he knows Isobel Stanhope. If he sees me he'll want to know who I'm with."

"I won't let him see you," Max promised.

I felt my eyes widen. "He's coming straight towards us."

Suddenly Max was very close, his arm coming up to rest on the wall by my head. His body pressed against mine, and I felt my breath catch as I was abruptly confronted by his broad chest. He reached for my chin and lifted it gently so that I was looking up into his eyes.

"W-what are you doing?" I managed.

"A recently married man takes any opportunity he can to snatch a kiss from his wife," he said, his own voice low.

"Oh, of course," I said, hoping that he couldn't actually feel my heart about to beat out of my chest. Was he really going to kiss me? It seemed as though the whole world had slowed down, and I was dimly aware that I had a million life-or-death things I should be worrying about, but all I could do was stare at Max's perfect mouth.

His face came closer to my own, so close that it would only take the tiniest movement and my mouth would be on his. I glanced up at his eyes and his pupils were enormous, I could see the pulse beating at the base of his throat. I hoped that the veil covering my eyes was also hiding the feelings I was certain were on display there. His breath mingled with mine, and the tension in my body ratcheted up again, as if something coiled inside me was readying itself to strike.

This was it. He closed the gap between us and my lips parted softly, my eyes fluttered closed … and then at the last second he turned his face so that his lips trailed lightly along my jaw and up over my cheek until they reached my ear.

At that point I made a noise that I would rather never think about ever again, and which Max politely ignored.

"Has he moved past us?" he whispered into my ear.

"Um." I tried to unscramble my thoughts, to focus on something other than Max's warm body and the feeling of his breath against my skin. I peeked around his shoulder. "Yes," I managed. "He's gone past."

Max pulled away from me so fast that I almost fell forward, except then he was taking my arm once more and we were walking out of the door towards freedom.

"I'm sorry about that," Max said politely.

"Think nothing of it." I was amazed my voice sounded so calm. Thank goodness. Now that my brain seemed to be receiving oxygen once more I was able to remember the job at hand. And that's what this was, I reminded myself. A job. One with incredibly high stakes, and more than one life in the balance.

By the time Max handed me up into the carriage he had hailed I was completely calm. I was even almost able to convince myself the near-kiss hadn't meant a thing.

Almost.

CHAPTER TWENTY-SIX

We arrived at the Aviary to find the shop empty except for the girl behind the counter, who nodded at me and showed not a flicker of interest in my companion.

As I led Max up the back stairs from the shop, I saw that he was looking around with curiosity. The conditions in which he'd been here last time probably meant he hadn't been up to noticing much, but he was certainly noticing now. I felt a pang of anxiety, thinking again about how many of our closely kept secrets Max had access to.

"I am no bird," he murmured when we stood in the salon, looking up at the dark letters painted on the wall. "*Jane Eyre.*"

"One of my favourites," I said. "I always thought that's where Mrs Finch took the idea of the Aviary from. All those pretty little birds kept in gilded cages."

"Not you, though." Max kept his eyes on the writing. "Hidden in these walls, a charm of wild finches."

We were interrupted by the arrival of Mrs Finch who was already unpinning her hat as she strode through the door.

"I got your message," she said. "Come and tell me all about it."

We followed her up the stairs to her office. Once more, Max was clearly taking in the sight of the corridor with rooms coming off it. The door to Winnie's lab was slightly ajar, and his eyes widened. "This place is extraordinary," he murmured.

Mrs Finch smiled. "Izzy will have to give you the tour," she said lightly. I glanced at my employer in surprise. It seemed that she, at least, had decided to trust Max. I wasn't sure how the rest of the charm would feel about that. I wasn't even sure how *I* felt about it.

"So," Mrs Finch said briskly, standing behind her desk and stripping off her gloves. "Report."

I pulled out the brooch, twisting it as Oliver had shown us, revealing the key inside.

Unlike us, Mrs Finch didn't look surprised by this development. "It's a key." She held out her hand and I placed the brooch in it. "I suspected something like this – that it had to hold a message or unlock something. It's the only reason Morland would go to these lengths."

A message. Something in her words tugged at me, as if there was an important piece of information I was missing, but I couldn't quite see what it was.

"Do you know what the key opens?" Max asked.

She shook her head. "No, unfortunately I don't."

"Well, there's nothing else hidden inside," I confirmed. "Oliver Lockhart was extremely thorough. He sends his regards, by the way."

Mrs Finch laughed. "Does he? That's terribly polite for him, I wouldn't have expected it."

"He's quite a character." I grinned.

"But you liked him?" Mrs Finch asked.

"I really did," I said. Oliver Lockhart was extremely rude and dazzlingly bad-tempered, but still, underneath that, I saw a glimmer of something else in him. Something I admired. "He's a very interesting man. I hope I have the opportunity to work with him again."

"So we're no closer to finding out what is going on," Max cut in, surprisingly curt.

"We'll work it out," I said, thrown by the sharpness in his voice. "We always do."

"Izzy is quite right," Mrs Finch said, and amusement danced in her eyes, though I wasn't sure what had caused it. "Mr Lockhart has provided a crucial piece of the puzzle, and now we must get to work on finding out what the key opens. When we have that information, we'll finally be able to make sense of Morland's actions and counteract them. Speaking of which, we've had reports that the search for Kes and the duke is going from strength to strength – Morland has pulled in men from all over the country. He's keeping it very quiet for the moment, but at some point the public is bound to find out."

Max's face dropped, and his fingers curled into a fist at his side.

"We saw several of his men at the train station," I said. "Some of Nero's thugs were out too, which I don't think is a coincidence. It seems that Morland has spies on both sides of the law."

"You did well to get past them," Mrs Finch said.

I fought the flush that I knew was rising to my cheeks. "Sylla was right – they're not looking for a couple. It was a good idea for us to stick together."

"What about Kitten Morland?" Max asked, and I started. It was a question I should have asked myself.

"She has returned to London with her husband," Mrs Finch said. "Maud is there now, and reporting back as often as possible. The situation seems largely unchanged. She's still hearing things at night – noises in her room. Still forgetful, although she is largely confined to her bed at present. The doctor visits regularly. Her friends are told she is indisposed. Maud says that even Kitten herself is starting to agree that she's delicate and possibly in need of a rest cure. Morland's schemes certainly seem to be doing the trick."

"I still can't understand why Morland is doing this to his wife," I said. "Why is he so determined to drive her to madness?"

"Because it makes her a less credible witness," Max said hollowly.

Mrs Finch and I both turned to look at him. He cleared his throat. "If she knows something, if she's seen something that could harm Morland, then he needs the world to believe she is mad. It's the same reason he's branding me a traitor – so that no one will believe anything I say." He gave me a wry smile. "I didn't want to believe it for the longest time," he said quietly. "I *still* don't want to believe it, but I can't bury my head in the sand. Morland has gone to extraordinary lengths, *criminal* lengths to recover this key, and something is clearly wrong in his home. Whatever is really going on here, it's dangerous, and Morland is behind it."

I swallowed. Despite his calm voice, I could see the hurt on his face.

"Yes, Morland is behind whatever is going on here," Mrs Finch said, moving to place the brooch in her safe. "And this key is at the centre of it. We need to discover its purpose. I will have our own surveillance on Morland increased, and we should get the others in for a meeting so that we can strategize. Sylla has been trying to dig into Kitten Morland's background some more, perhaps she will have something useful to add."

"In the meantime," I said, "we need to keep Max somewhere safe."

"I have places I can go," Max said. "I'm perfectly capable of taking care of myself."

"Are any of these places unknown to Lord Morland?" Mrs Finch asked, her eyebrows raised.

A muscle ticked in Max's jaw, and he shook his head with reluctance.

"Then let's not go undoing all the good work we've done so far to keep you out of prison," she said acidly.

Max made a sound of frustration. "You're right," he said finally, though it was clear it cost him to do so. "I'm sorry."

"However," Mrs Finch said. "As it happens, circumstance has been conspiring against us and we do not currently have access to a suitable safe house in the city."

"Could he stay here?" I asked.

Mrs Finch shook her head. "That wouldn't be fair on

the other members," she said. "Nor our clients. No men on the premises, remember."

"I suppose," I said, chewing on my lip as an idea formed, "that he could stay at my house."

Max looked like he was about protest extremely forcefully, but before he could do so Mrs Finch spoke. "*That* is a very good idea."

I thought about it for a moment. It would be easy enough to keep Max away from Mama, and apart from Button there was no one else in the house. No one would be looking for the Duke of Roxton in the Stanhopes' townhouse. It was unthinkable.

"But the servants," Max said. "And your mother. What on earth will we tell them?"

"Don't worry about that," I said, hoping I sounded confident. "We'll go at once. Max, you'll have to slip round to the back door and anyone who sees you will only see a man coming to the servants' entrance. Could be any number of reasons for that. Leave the servants – and everything else – to me."

"Good." Mrs Finch was already moving papers on her desk. "And tomorrow we will reconvene here with the others to discuss our next steps."

With that we were dismissed, and we retraced our steps back outside, hailing another cab. We didn't talk at all on the journey. Max was drumming his fingers against his knee and I looked out of the window. The reasons that made my home the perfect hiding place were also the truths I had kept successfully hidden from all of society for almost two years, and Max was about to witness everything. The last of my secrets. He would be the only person to know them all. How had it come to this? My stomach churned uneasily, and I sent up a silent prayer that I was doing the right thing.

Not that there was much I could do about it now. We needed to keep Max safe and this was the best way to do it. When we drew up outside the house I paid the driver while Max slipped away round the back. Then I steeled myself, marching up to the front gate and letting myself inside.

When I appeared at the back door Max was already waiting there.

"Come in," I hissed.

He looked around the empty kitchen in confusion.

"I thought perhaps one of the servants would answer the door."

I dropped my hat on to the kitchen table, and pressed my fingers against the wood, staring down at them. "There are no servants," I said. "Well, none except Button, my mother's maid."

I dragged my eyes up to his, and the look of confusion on his face only deepened. "What do you mean?"

I sighed and went about filling the kettle with water and settling it on the stove – anything to keep my hands busy. "Nobody knows this," I said finally. "Nobody. Do you understand? Not Teresa, not the other Finches, not even my mother. Mrs Finch may have guessed most of it, but really it's only me. Just me."

The look of confusion had been replaced by one of alarm. "Izzy," he exclaimed, taking an involuntary step forward. "What is it? Are you in some sort of trouble?"

I laughed hollowly. "I suppose you could say that." I gestured to a seat at the table. "Sit."

He did as I asked, and I poured two cups of tea, finally sitting in the seat opposite him. I was cold, but the heat from the china cup that I cradled bit into my hands.

"My father died," I said. "A little over two years ago now. My brother Henry inherited everything, but Henry was only eight then and he has been away at school. My mother is … unwell and she keeps to her rooms."

Max nodded. I suppose that he knew all of this already. None of it was a secret.

I sat up straighter. "When Mama fell ill after Father died, I was the one to deal with the lawyers. That was when I learned that we had been left with very little." I pressed my lips together. *Very little* was an understatement. "My father made some poor financial decisions. He wasn't a business-minded person, you see, but he *was* a wonder with locks; he could pick any of them, it was a game to him, and he taught me everything he knew. What I hadn't realized was that he used that to generate an income, one that kept Henry in school and Mama and I clothed and fed, with a small number of servants in the house. When he died that income went away."

I lifted my eyes from the table to find Max listening, stone-faced.

I rubbed my forehead and pressed on. "Mama's

doctor has diagnosed a problem with her heart. He said that any sort of shock could be life-threatening. Henry is a sweet, carefree little boy who loves his school and has won many friends there. I needed to find a way to protect them both, to keep them safe and happy. To keep the parent I had left *alive*. At first I thought I could take over my father's work but I made a mistake. I introduced myself as his daughter and every door slammed shut in my face. No one wanted a woman to work for them. I sold pretty much everything in the house that wasn't nailed down. And then..." I trailed off.

"And then you met the Finches?" Max said gently.

I nodded. "They'd heard of my skill with locks. It was Sylla who recruited me. The money that I'm paid keeps everything running, and the lack of family and servants is actually an advantage in my line of work." I gave the ghost of a smile, but Max didn't return it. "I've been saving every penny I can. Through the Aviary and our clients I've found several excellent places to invest, and the money is growing. I hope that when Henry comes of age he won't find himself in such dire straits, and there will even be some left over for me to live independently. It's my ten-year plan." I couldn't keep the pride from my voice. Watching my small income grow, knowing that it was from my own hard work, was an unexpected source of pleasure.

Max's expression was still impassive. "Your mother is in the house but she doesn't know?"

I shook my head. "The rest of the house is a shell but her rooms are entirely as they were. Her maid Button is still with us and she takes care of Mama. Sometimes I think I should tell her, but she's so fragile ... I *can't* risk it; it's simply too much to gamble with. I can't lose her as well. Mama and Henry are the only family I have." I tried to keep my voice level, but it was becoming more difficult.

"But what if your mother changes her mind? What if her health improves and she wants to leave her rooms?"

As if I hadn't considered that, as if it wasn't a thought that kept me awake at night.

"I-I have to hope that doesn't happen before I can save enough to restore things to the way they were, or that if she decides to leave her rooms then it's because her health truly is better and she can handle a few unpleasant surprises." They were words I had said to myself over and over, but somehow they still lacked conviction. The truth was that I sometimes felt my life was a vaudeville act and I had no choice but to frantically keep all these separate plates spinning in the air and hope that nothing got broken.

"And your brother has no idea?" Max continued his curt interrogation.

"No. What could he do if he did? He's a child, and he would only feel guilty. I've kept him away so far with stories of Mama's illness. It won't work for ever, but he's rarely at home. For most of his holidays he prefers to go and stay with his friends in the country rather than be stuck in town, and I go and visit him whenever I can."

Max's fingers drummed against the table. "And Miss Wynter?"

I sighed. "She doesn't know. Teresa is my best friend and I love her like a sister. She'd be determined to help me – her family would get involved. At first, I didn't want to become a charity case, to risk upsetting my mother. Then I got the job at the Aviary, and I *couldn't* tell her. Our work *has* to remain secret. Besides, I'm perfectly capable of taking care of Mama and Henry on my own."

"And who," Max's voice was a low growl, "takes care of you?"

I felt the sudden hot sting of tears and blinked hard. It felt as if he had pressed on the tenderest part of a bruise. "I am also perfectly capable of taking care of myself," I said, though I was annoyed that the words wobbled a bit. I lifted my chin and looked him in the eye, daring him to pity me.

Except Max wasn't looking at me with pity. If anything, he looked furious.

"I know better than most how capable you are," he said finally. "But that is a heavy burden for anyone to carry, you shouldn't have to do so alone." While the words were kind his tone was stiff and formal.

I felt calmer now that the secret was out. "I'm not doing such a bad job."

If I thought this would lighten the look on Max's face then I was mistaken. He reached up to run a hand through his hair, and his fingers met the dark thatch of his wig. He snatched it from his head and threw it on the floor, eyeing it sourly, as if it had offended him.

"Why haven't you married?"

I froze. "Why haven't I married?" I repeated.

He seemed oblivious to my dangerous tone. "Yes," he said. "Why haven't you?"

"For one thing," I managed, my voice frosty, "I would never deceive a man about the circumstances he would be marrying into. I have nothing to bring to a marriage that would make me an acceptable candidate in the eyes of society—"

"Money isn't everything, even in a society marriage," Max interrupted. "You have so many ... I mean, there must be many... You are... I wouldn't..." He looked miserably embarrassed. Presumably he was realizing exactly how little I had to offer: no title, no fortune, no beauty. None of the things society valued.

"It's irrelevant anyway," I said firmly. "Once you've seen what I have of other peoples' marriages, it becomes clear that that particular institution should be a woman's *last* resort. I have no desire to live my life at the whim of a man. My own father was a good husband

and he and my mother loved each other. But he did a poor job managing his money, and kept his secrets, leaving his wife and children unprotected when he died. I don't want to be left feeling that vulnerable again. I'm much happier being responsible for myself."

This had the benefit of silencing Max completely. I could tell that I had shocked him, but I didn't care. I knew that what I said was true.

I rose to my feet, swirling away from him. "And now that you know all of my secrets, perhaps I should show you to your room."

CHAPTER TWENTY-SEVEN

That night I lay in bed replaying the conversation with Max in my head, trying and failing to fall asleep. When I finally did manage to stop thinking about it, it was only because I was reliving that moment in the train station over and over again instead: the touch of his breath against my cheek, the way his lips had skated over my neck, the press of his big, hard body against mine. It was not exactly restful.

When I eventually drifted off I was tormented by dreams of shadows and rubies, glinting dangerously in the dark, Mama's face crumpling in confusion as she looked around the empty ruins of our house, and then I was dancing, swirling around the wreckage in Max's arms, and he steadied me like he had at the Devonshire House ball. "Just breathe," he whispered, his mouth close enough to my ear, that I could feel the words against my skin.

I woke up hot and tangled in my bed sheets, and groaned as I remembered the first thing I had to do today: explain Max's presence to Button.

"What do you mean the Duke of Roxton is here?" she hissed when I cornered her in the kitchen, where she was preparing Mama's breakfast.

"It's only for a few days," I whispered urgently. "You mustn't tell a soul. He needed a ... refuge."

"A refuge?" Button's brows snapped together in suspicion. "The Duke of Roxton ... needs to stay here? Doesn't the man own a castle somewhere? Have you lost your senses, girl?" She narrowed her eyes at me. "If you're up to anything improper you'd better stop it at once, Isobel Stanhope. I won't have your mother upset."

"Of course we're not up to anything improper!" I snapped. "He's the *Duke of Roxton*! And I'm – well…"

"Mmmm, I suppose." Button looked me up and down, obviously finding me far from the sort of siren who would tempt a handsome duke into an indiscretion.

"I'm not sure what being a duke has to do with anything," Max's voice came from over my shoulder and I closed my eyes in mortification. "But I really am sorry to intrude on you in this ramshackle fashion. I can promise that Miss Stanhope's well-being is of great concern to me."

I swung round. He had that charming little half-smile on his lips, and I knew he was certain he would win Button round. Little did he know he'd met his match. I was almost looking forward to seeing Button tear him to pieces.

"Oh, Your Grace!"

Disbelief surged through me. Turning back to face Button, I saw the woman not only returning the duke's smile but absolutely beaming at him and dropping into a low curtsey.

"I hope my presence won't inconvenience you too much," Max continued.

"Not at all, Your Grace," Button murmured, her voice all breathy and not a bit how she usually sounded. "I'm only sorry circumstances prevent us from taking better care of you. I'm afraid the house is … in some disarray at present. Can I get you some breakfast? A cup of tea, perhaps?"

I huffed in astonishment. Button had *never* offered to make me a cup of tea, and did she just *bat her eyelashes*?

"That's kind, but I wouldn't like to put you out," Max said. "I can make the tea myself."

"Nonsense," Button gasped, clearly horrified by the very idea. "You sit down here, Your Grace, and let me get you settled."

"Actually," I said. "We have to go out. We have an appointment." Mrs Finch had sent a note early this morning and, as promised, the rest of the charm had been called in.

Button scowled, and her voice was needle-sharp once more when she turned to me. "You need to go and see your mother before you go out gallivanting again, young lady. She knows you're home and she's expecting you."

I stifled a sigh. "I'll be quick," I said to Max.

But he didn't seem too worried, and was already being fussed over by Button. I shook my head as I stomped up the stairs.

"Darling girl!" Mama exclaimed when she saw me, wrapping me in a tight hug. "How wonderful to have you home. Did you have a nice time? But of course you did, I know all about it thanks to those lovely newsy letters. So kind of you to send several every day – you know how much I love to hear about everything you're up to." She gestured to a stack of paper on her nightstand, which appeared to be covered in my handwriting.

"Oh," I said, wondering what Sylla had written. "Yes, the letters. I'm glad you enjoyed them."

"Well, of course I did!" Mama said. "And the Banajis sound utterly marvellous, especially Miss Banaji, so beautiful and generous and what a kind-hearted young woman, rescuing those kittens."

"Yes," I said suspiciously. "Sylla is all goodness."

"And after you fell head first into that pond in your own clumsy attempts!" Mama giggled. "Your letter made me laugh so much! I never knew you were such a vivid writer. The description of you as the sea monster, dripping in algae and the *smell*..."

"Yes, Mama," I cut her off, cursing Sylla. "It was very funny."

I chatted to Mama for another couple of minutes, during which time she regaled me with stories from "my" letters – most of which ended with Sylla rescuing me from my own stupidity.

"And I've had another letter from darling Henry," Mama said, pressing another sheet of paper into my hand.

"He needs to spend some time on his penmanship," I said, but I was already smiling, Henry's messy, exuberant scrawl was full of affection for us both.

...and please tell Izzy that I have been practising chess with Daniel and I am so much improved that next time we play I will be the one winning all our ha'penny wagers and

I won't cheat (even though I have learned
some sneaky tricks!) And Daniel's mother wrote
to him and told him to tell me to tell you that
Izzy is welcome to join us at their house
for the holidays which I do think would be
great fun because Daniel's family have simply
hundreds of dogs, and horses too, and their cook
makes a very good jam sponge and the only
thing that could make it better would be if
you were there, Mama, but I will write to you
every day...

"He sounds like he's happy," I smiled.

"Yes." Mama leaned back against the pillows with a
sigh. "It's such a relief to me that your father organized
everything with the school before he passed away – it's
going to be the making of Henry, I know it will."

"I'm sure you're right," I said and then turned the
subject to Mama's friends and all the town gossip,
which she was happy to share while I tried – yet again –
to stop thinking about the near-kiss that Max and I had
shared the day before.

"...and of course, poor Kitten Morland is quite under the weather," Mama sighed, the words bringing my attention sharply back to her.

"Oh, really?" I said, trying to sound only mildly interested.

"Yes, Andrea says she hasn't been receiving visitors for several days," Mama said.

"Did Andrea say what was wrong with her?" I asked.

"Some nervous complaint or other." Mama waved a hand. "Which of course I sympathize with, there's nothing worse." She leaned forward conspiratorially. "I did *wonder* if it might be because she was increasing. I mean, I thought the fact that he wanted an heir was one of the reasons Morland took such a young wife in the first place, but apparently not. Evidently he's quite upset over it all, calling in specialists and there's talk of a trip to a European spa. Such a doting husband, like he was with his first wife."

"Oh, yes, the first Lady Morland." I smoothed the bed covers with a casual hand. "She had an accident, didn't she?"

Mama sat back against her pillows. "Oh, Izzy,

it was awful. Eliza Morland – she was such a sweet thing, quiet and shy, and even before the accident – she fell down the stairs, you know – she hadn't been well. Bridget – Mrs Fargate, I mean – was quite close to her at one time and *she* said that towards the end Eliza was ever so skittish, nervous and jumping at shadows which is why she'd scaled down her social events and no one had seen her for weeks. There was even some talk that her accident hadn't been an accident, that she'd ... taken matters into her own hands..." Mama broke off here, a look of something like shame crossing her face and clearly feeling she'd taken the gossip too far.

I felt something twist deep in my gut, and struggled to keep my hands steady. "Suicide?" I murmured.

Mama waved a hand in front of her face, as if to bat the terrible word away. "No, no," she said quickly. "A nasty little rumour that was quickly squashed. I shouldn't even have mentioned it. Morland was devastated after the accident, very withdrawn and absolutely threw himself into his work."

"And yet, it was only a year after Eliza's death that he started courting Kitten," I said.

"Yes, well," Mama said with surprising cynicism. "He's a man of ambition, isn't he? He wants people to see him as a family man, wants to have children, perhaps. You can't fault him for remarrying, and from what I hear he's always seemed fond of his new wife, young as she is."

She must have seen the surprise on my face because she laughed and said, "Darling girl, you know not everyone is as lucky as I am – to marry for love alone. Your father and I..." Here she broke off, looking small and frail against the pillows and I took her hand, squeezing it gently.

"I do know that," I said. "You were lucky. Both of you."

Mama's voice was fervent, as she squeezed my hand back. "It will be the same for you one day, Izzy. I know it will."

I only smiled and turned the subject back to Henry and the care package we should send to him, something which Mama had a lot of – unfortunately expensive – opinions on.

Finally, I extracted myself and went to collect Max from Button's clutches.

When we reached the Aviary, Winnie and Sylla were both waiting in Mrs Finch's office. Maud hadn't yet arrived.

"Been out saving more helpless creatures, have you?" I asked Sylla.

"Only you lot, on a regular basis," Sylla said sweetly.

I stuck my tongue out at her, and she smirked.

"Mrs Finch showed us the brooch. A key." Winnie rocked back and forth on her heels excitedly. "What a fascinating turn of events. And the mechanism! Extraordinary."

"Indeed," Max said dryly. "If only we can work out what the bloody thing is for."

"Oh, don't you worry, Your Grace," Sylla purred. "We *always* get our man." She lit up when a puzzle got tricky like this. She loved the game, and now her eyes were bright with excitement.

The door slammed open then, and Maud whirled in like a tempest, red hair flying as she took Winnie's face between her hands and pressed a smacking kiss to her lips.

Sylla rolled her eyes. I glanced at Max who looked surprised for a moment, but otherwise gave no response.

"Maud!" Winnie exclaimed, flushing, though unable to hide her own delight.

"Hello, Your Grace!" Maud said cheerily, when her gaze fell on Max. "Still with us, then?"

"As long as Izzy'll keep me around," Max said lightly, smiling back at Maud. It was difficult to resist her when she was in this sort of mood. "And I'd rather you all called me Vane." *Vane. Not Max. Max was just for me, then.*

"*Vane*," Sylla said. "It suits you."

Max laughed. "It would be hard on any man's vanity to wear this monstrosity," he grumbled, tugging at his wig.

"What's got you flying high as a kite, anyway?" I asked Maud, tearing my gaze from Max.

"I finally got the bastard!" she crowed, flopping down into the seat behind Mrs Finch's desk and spinning it round. "I've got him like *that*." She slammed her fist into the palm of her hand.

"Tell us!" Winnie said, sitting up.

Mrs Finch came into the room, gesturing to Maud to get out of her seat.

"Well," said Maud, moving to stand in the centre of the room, obviously intending to relish her triumph. "I managed to sneak out of the servants' quarters. There's an alcove near Kitten's room and I hid there. It was gone two in the morning when I saw Morland's valet approach her room. I watched through the keyhole as he moved things around while she slept – rearranging her dressing table, that sort of thing. He poured some of her perfume away, hid one of her books under a cushion. After he'd done that, he left. But that's not all."

"What happened?" I asked. Maud had a real knack of telling a gripping yarn. Even Max looked hooked.

"I followed him all the way to the basement. Down there, he started hitting one of the pipes that obviously runs up to her room. The sound must echo right inside her bedroom door – but nowhere else in the house. It does sound horrible, sort of wailing and ghostly."

"And then?" Sylla asked.

"Well, then I confronted him," said Maud cheerfully.

"Of course you did," said Max.

"Thought I might as well. Told him I wouldn't tell anyone if he spilled. He's pretty dim, only following orders, he said. He's afraid of Morland, though, absolutely deathly afraid. Says it's more than his life's worth if anyone finds out. I'm not sure we'll get him to talk to anyone else."

We all turned to Sylla, who was looking thoughtful. "I wonder whether this is enough to take to Kitten Morland and tell her that she isn't losing her mind."

"I can show her how the sounds were made," said Maud. "Tell her I saw someone, even if I don't know who. But if she confronts Morland or doesn't believe me, then the gig is up. He'll have me out on my ear, or worse. We need her to stay quiet."

"We might need more, then, Maud. I don't know how much convincing she'll need. Does she trust her husband?" Sylla asked.

Maud tilted her head. "The servants all say she was fond of him once. Now ... I'm not so sure. She seems on edge around him. Frightened."

Everyone fell quiet. "I don't think this is the first time he's done this," I said.

"What do you mean?" Max asked sharply.

I told them what Mama had told me about Eliza

Morland. "Don't you think it sounds awfully familiar?"
I asked.

The grim silence that met these words said I wasn't
alone in thinking that Morland had used a similar
strategy with his first wife.

"I remember thinking something was wrong at the
time," Mrs Finch murmured almost to herself.

Max swore, his hands clenched into fists on top of
his knees.

"Sylla," Mrs Finch said. "Have you had any luck
looking into Kitten? Have you found anything useful?
Anything we can use to get her on our side?"

Sylla shook her head reluctantly. "Nothing we didn't
already know, though I do think there's more to her
than meets the eye. People talk about her as if she's ...
empty-headed but sweet, but I hear she had several offers
which she turned down before she accepted Morland.
It's not a love match so there was no reason for her to do
that unless she was making certain calculations about
Morland's political career."

"Do we know *why* Morland is going to all this
trouble to make Kitten think she's mad?" said

Winnie. "Is it really just to punish her? He must have a good reason to get rid of her – and I can't work out what."

"Vane suggested he may be trying to discredit her," Mrs Finch said. "Making sure no one would listen to anything she had to say. Perhaps she knows something she's not supposed to know."

Sylla glanced at Max. Their eyes met, then Sylla nodded slightly grudgingly, as if to say *perhaps you have got a brain after all*.

Maud shook her head. "Nice theory, but it's unlikely. Whatever Sylla reckons, Kitten is sweet but not exactly the sharpest. I can't see her having access to Morland's secrets. I mean, look at her diary ... the most boring, endless list of food and clothes and—"

"The diary!" I exclaimed, cutting Maud off as I leaped to my feet.

Five expectant faces looked up at me, and I struggled to catch up with my own thoughts, as though they were running fast down a hill. "Win." I turned to her. "Can you bring the notes you made from Kitten's diary?"

"They're right here on the desk," said Win,

producing a sheaf of paper. "Maud's right, though. Nothing interesting that I could see."

"But it's like you said, Maud. In the diary," I explained, "Kitten records everything she wears. *Including the brooch.*"

The air thickened.

"Remember what her maid said?" I went on. "Kitten hated that brooch, but Morland made her wear it to certain events. Which means…"

"We have to look for patterns," Max said, a slow smile spreading across his face. "Because Morland never does anything without a good reason."

"Win?" I turned to her, her brow already furrowed in concentration.

"Give me a pen and a piece of paper," she said. She began making a list.

The room was silent except for the heavy ticking of the clock on the mantelpiece, as we all sat and waited, until she pushed over a list. "Those are all the dates Kitten wore the brooch," Win explained.

We crowded around the list.

"There's no pattern that I can see," Win said. "Here

she wears it twice in a week – then there's a few weeks with nothing. I've cross-referenced it with the events, but there's no pattern there either. This time she wore it to a private dinner, but then here," she said, tapping the paper with her finger, "she wears it to a state function. A few times in a row she wears it at home, but then she also wears it to house parties."

"What about guests?" I said. "The people at the events where she wore it?"

Winnie's eyes lit up. "Now that will take some time," she said, with relish. I could almost see the gears turning in her head, and she caught her lip between her teeth as she worked on a new list, occasionally screwing up her eyes as if in deep concentration.

At last, she pushed across the amended list. As we pored over the paper I felt a thrill of excitement.

There it was. A pattern.

I looked at Max and I could tell that he had seen it too. There was a glimmer in his eyes that I was certain matched my own.

"Those three," I said, pointing at the sheet, and unthinkingly clutching at his sleeve with my other hand.

He nodded, and so did Sylla.

"Sir Alec Hudson, Sir William Pennington and Lord David Hartwell," Sylla read. "At least one of them is at every event where Kitten wore the brooch. Usually all three of them." She turned to Max. "What do you know about them?"

Max remained focused on the paper. "Three exceptionally ordinary men," he said. "They lead quiet lives, family men, no scandals attached. The only thing that might be relevant is that they're Morland's staunchest political supporters. They've helped him push through several bills ... some concerning the management of national security. They're powerful players, and they've certainly helped him climb the ladder over the last few years. He needs their support in his bid to become prime minister if he hopes to succeed."

"So why the brooch?" I murmured. "Perhaps they all have them? Some sort of club?"

"But why make his wife wear it?" Sylla said. "With Morland it's all about power. If you ask me he's a sadist."

I felt Max flinch beside me. I wasn't sure if he had

really come to terms with the fall of his idol yet.

"Lady Hartwell is an acquaintance," Mrs Finch said. "I could see if she could get her husband to talk to us."

I wondered if acquaintance meant client.

"Lord Hartwell has always seemed a decent sort to me. You think we could question him directly?" I said.

"I'm not sure it's a good idea." Sylla frowned. "What if the brooch *is* some sort of club insignia? You'd be revealing yourself to Morland. It sounds like they're in league with each other."

I thought about this. "I could meet with his wife, at least," I said. "That wouldn't cause any suspicion – and she may have information that could help."

"I'll go with you," Max said quickly. "You shouldn't go alone if it's dangerous."

"I think Lady Hartwell will recognize the Duke of Roxton."

"Not if I go in disguise," he said. "Not if she doesn't expect it. People see what they want to see."

"We can discuss it later," I said, and Max's chin lifted stubbornly.

"I'll write to her now," Mrs Finch said. "I can send

the reply on to your house when I get it."

"Fine," I agreed.

"Winnie," Sylla said as we rose to leave. "Will you show the duke your lab? I understand he was most interested the other day. Izzy, a quick word?"

The others left the room, even Mrs Finch going along to give Max a tour of the space, leaving Sylla and I alone in the office. She waited for the sound of their footsteps to recede.

"Well?" she said, her hands on her hips.

"Well, what?" I asked, confused.

"You and the Duke of Roxton, *Isobel*."

"What about me and the Duke of Roxton, *Sylla*?" I crossed my arms.

"What's going on between the two of you?"

My eyebrows shot up. "Nothing!" I spluttered.

"Then why does the man keep looking at you like you're the last cream puff in the bakery?" she snapped.

I felt myself blush down to my toes. "First of all," I said, "a cream puff? Thank you *very* much. Secondly, he doesn't look at me any special way."

Sylla scoffed. "It's so obvious. His eyes are all..." She

waved a hand at her face. "Sparkly."

"Sparkly?" I laughed. "The Duke of Roxton? I don't think so."

"And you're as bad." I could do less to deny that. After all, sometimes Max did make me feel sparkly.

"There's nothing going on between us," I said firmly. "His only interest is in clearing his name, and you can hardly blame him for that. It's exactly what you would want in the same situation."

"I am not so stupid as to get into this sort of situation in the first place," Sylla bit out. "You can deny it all you like, but I'm warning you … be careful. Don't let a handsome face cloud your judgment. We have work to do. This isn't a game. There are people depending on us."

"I know that," I protested, trying to hide how much it hurt that she thought I'd forget.

"We're all keeping important secrets here. Secrets that we risk by including him. Don't let yourself forget that once this is all over he'll go back to being the duke and you'll go back to being our wallflower," Sylla continued, and her words twisted like a knife. It wasn't anything I hadn't thought myself, but hearing someone else say it was somehow worse.

"I know that too," I snapped. "Now, if you've quite finished, I'll go and get on with it!"

I left the office in a swirl of skirts, ready to prise Max out of Winnie's lab and return home.

"*Cream puff*," I couldn't help muttering bitterly as we drove away.

"Sounds delicious," Max said hopefully, and then he looked confused as I laughed the rest of the way back.

CHAPTER TWENTY-EIGHT

I tried not to dwell on Sylla's comments that evening, but it was quite difficult given that I was locked away in a (practically) empty house with Max Vane.

We had been alone in the hut in Yorkshire, but this time felt different. For one thing it was a lot more comfortable here, and we had plenty to eat. I offered to cook something, but Max surprised me by making it clear that he was going to take charge of the kitchen.

"When did you learn to cook?" I asked, sitting at

the kitchen table and enjoying the sight of him whisking eggs by the stove. It was growing dark outside and I lit the candles, which seemed only to underscore the intimate atmosphere.

"It's just buttered eggs," he said. "I'm not sure it can really be called cooking."

"All right, where did you learn how to make buttered eggs, then?"

He smiled. "From Mrs Beeton's recipe book."

I laughed. "Mrs Beeton? I can't imagine you reading Mrs Beeton."

"Why not? I needed to learn to fend for myself so I went to the library."

"When have you ever had to cook for yourself?" I asked, trying to ignore the bizarre fact that I found the idea of Max consulting library books about cooking extremely attractive.

"I needed it when I was in France. In the countryside. Alone."

I raised my brows. "I take it that means you were working?"

"I may have been," was all the response I received.

"Fine, don't tell me. There's plenty I won't be telling you either."

"That I can well believe." He began melting butter in a basin over a pan of boiling water.

"How did you come to be working for Morland?" I asked curiously.

Max hesitated. "Morland recruited me," he said finally. He spoke with his back to me. "He knew my father, knew that I felt a sense of duty that extended beyond my own land and tenants." He darted a glance at me over his shoulder. "You'll think I was naive, I suppose, but I always thought it was a vocation. I'm aware my life is one of privilege, but I wanted to earn it, I wanted to … to *deserve* it somehow."

He tipped the eggs and the butter into a pan, swirled them around.

"I don't think that's naive," I said quietly.

He shrugged, his shoulders moving beneath the linen shirt he wore. I still couldn't see his face. "I was trained to suspect everyone. But it seems I have been too unquestioning when it comes to trusting my superiors. Morland always told me we were in the business of protecting people. Of keeping them safe. I believed him."

I winced. I couldn't imagine how betrayed I would feel if Mrs Finch behaved as Morland had – pinning her own crimes on me. She was one of the most important people in my life, and I trusted her completely. I had to; that was what our entire enterprise was built on. Losing that trust ... the thought of it had me pressing my fingers absently to my chest, as though to ease an ache there.

I fetched bread and a fat pat of butter from the pantry. I set the table, dug out a half-empty bottle of wine. Max piled the buttered eggs on to two plates. He placed one in front of me, the eggs were fluffy and golden, and smelled delicious.

"So, Kitten Morland," Max said, sitting across from me as I cut the bread. "Don't you think we should tell her the truth? It feels wrong to leave her in the dark any longer than we have to."

"I know," I said. "I think you're probably right, but it's difficult when we have to be so cautious about tipping our hand to Morland. He can't know anything about our involvement, or where the key is." I poured us both a glass of wine. "I wonder what she's really like ... as Sylla said, she could have married anyone with her money but she *chose* Morland. Perhaps that speaks to ambition. He *is* supposed to be the next prime minister, after all."

Max nodded, and placed the slice of bread he had buttered on my plate. I looked at it for a moment. Such a small thing, and yet it brought an unexpected lump to my throat.

I took a hasty sip of my drink. "Then, there's her diary," I continued. "It's mundane, but it's meticulous. She clearly has an eye for detail. And it was her maid Lorna who came to us." I chewed thoughtfully on my bread. (Was it possible that it tasted better because he had buttered it?) "That says something too. She inspires a lot of loyalty in Lorna. I think people underestimate her."

"I can't believe Morland would be so cruel," Max said heavily. "To play such tricks on his wife, a woman he's sworn to protect. It's so far from the person I thought I knew."

"Unfortunately, it's not the first time I've heard a story like hers." I looked into the depths of my wine glass. Sometimes I worried that those stories would crush the optimism out of me, given enough time, but then I reminded myself that we were doing something to try and make things right, that we were fighting.

"It's fortunate for women like Kitten Morland that the Finches exist," Max said with his half-smile. "Fortunate for me too."

That's true," I said, cheering up. "You wouldn't have lasted five minutes without me."

"I like to think I'd have lasted more than five minutes," Max protested, but I shook my head, spearing the last mouthful of eggs with my fork and popping it in my mouth.

"I had to save you twice, and the second time you were bleeding in my lap."

"I only got stabbed in the first place because I was helping you!"

I did feel guilty for a moment, but I saw the light of humour in his eyes. "You weren't helping me, you were interfering. Wading in to a well-honed plan. I had everything perfectly under control."

Max poured us some more wine. "D'you mean when

you were hanging off the side of a building, dressed as a boy, surrounded by thugs who wanted to kill you? It was all perfectly under control then?"

"Yes," I grinned. "I'd have worked something out. I always do."

He laughed then, really laughed. That lovely, giddy laugh that had smacked me in the heart a year and a half ago. And this time I could laugh with him. To sit in the kitchen with him, the candles flickering around us, as we laughed together – it was heaven. I knew if Sylla could see me now she'd despair. The thought was enough to cut my own laughter short.

"Will you..." I hesitated, afraid to voice the question, but knowing that it had to be asked, that I needed to know. "Will you keep our secret? My secrets?" The words came out in a rush.

Max looked startled.

"I know you're a stickler for the rules," I said awkwardly. "But we can only do our work at the Aviary because no one knows about us. And for me, it's not only my life at stake, you see, it's my family I'm risking..." I trailed off, toying with my glass.

"Izzy," Max said gently and I lifted my eyes to meet his. "Your secrets are safe with me. All of them. I give you my word. Whatever happens, no one will know about you or the Finches because of me."

His gaze was utterly unwavering, and I knew that he meant it, that I could trust him. I think I had known it for a while. It felt like a burden lifted from my shoulders, an actual physical lightening, to share everything with someone I trusted. I wondered for a moment if I would simply lift off my chair and float away. It was then that I realized I had somehow let Max Vane into every single part of my life, all the pieces that I kept so separate: my home, the Aviary, my society life, my friendship with Teresa … he was the only person who had seen it all, the only one who knew the whole truth.

"Tell me about *your* family," I said, changing the subject.

Max leaned back in his seat. "My father died when I was quite young. I was still at school when I became the duke, with all the responsibilities that come with it. My mother lives in our house in the country and I see her as often as I can. We're close, but she doesn't know about my work. So I know all about keeping secrets from the people you care about. I know..." He hesitated here for a second. "I know how lonely that can be."

I felt a tightening in my chest at his words. Perhaps we had more in common than I thought. "And you have a sister?" I asked, though I already knew the answer.

His eyes lit up. "Felicity. She's sixteen, not out yet. God help us all when she is, she'll run rings around society. She's got a real talent for getting in trouble. Mostly because she's a hundred times more intelligent than other people, and she's not afraid to tell them so."

"I like her already," I said.

"She'd love you," Max said with a certainty that had joy uncurling in my chest. "She'd be absolutely beside herself if she saw Miss Phillips's lab."

"Winnie is proud of it." I took a sip of my drink. "I'm glad Mrs Finch found her, or her gifts would be wasted. She's brilliant, you know."

"The same could be said of you." Max rubbed a hand along his jaw. "Your gifts could have gone to waste too."

"Yes," I said. "It's funny to think that if my life

hadn't gone so horribly wrong I'd probably have been married off to some dreary man, and I'd have never found all the things I was good at, the work that I love." I glanced at him. "You see? Things worked out in the end."

Max raised his eyebrows. "Are you trying to make an optimist of me?"

"I wouldn't change a thing about you," I said lightly.

Just like that the atmosphere shifted. Our eyes caught and I was tangled in his gaze for a moment. My mouth was dry, and my stomach felt like I was falling from a great height at great speed. He swallowed, and I looked at the movement of his throat. Why had I never realized what a nice throat he had before? People really didn't talk enough about what a nice throat he had.

I reached out for my wine glass, but my hand was shaking and I didn't want him to see so I curled it into a fist and put it back in my lap.

When I looked up, Max still had his eyes on me, and for a moment I thought I saw what Sylla had been talking about. For a moment there was heat there that trembled through me like a touch.

Max's gaze dropped to my lips, then back to my eyes. He placed his glass down with a deliberate gesture, and opened his mouth, as though to say something.

And then I almost leaped out of my seat as someone began banging on the front door.

Max had already risen from his own chair. "Stay here," I said.

He looked like he was about to disagree, but then he nodded reluctantly. I made my way quickly upstairs and through the hallway, trying to brace myself for whatever I was about to find.

By the time I reached the door I could hear someone shouting. "Let me in! I need to speak to Miss Stanhope *immediately*!"

I pulled the door open and exclaimed, *"Teresa?"*

My friend stood on the doorstep, her fist still raised, her mouth open. She looked at me in astonishment. "Izzy!" she exclaimed. "You're here! Why are *you* answering the door? Where have you been?"

"Yes, I'm here!" I said, ignoring her other questions. "And you'd better keep it down or you'll upset Mama."

Teresa's eyes darted up to the top of the house then,

and she looked guilty. "I didn't think. But I've been so worried..." Her eyes snapped on to me with suspicion. "Do you want to tell me what's going on?"

"There's nothing going on," I said, as easily as I could. "Except that you're here in the middle of the night practically knocking my door down."

"Oh no, you don't." Teresa actually wagged her finger at me. "Don't go acting like *I'm* the unreasonable one. I'm calling in on my way back from the Penningtons' reception, which *you* were supposed to attend."

I stifled a groan. How could I have forgotten?

"I haven't seen or heard from you since you disappeared halfway through the Devonshire House ball," my friend continued in a whispered hiss. "A ball which was *burgled* by *criminals*, by the way. Then I hear that you've been whisked away by Sylla Banaji, of all people, and *then* you didn't come for tea with Nick and my grandmother yesterday. I thought you were *dead*!"

"Ah," I said helplessly. "Yes, I can see how you might have been worried. I hope Nick wasn't too offended..."

"My idiot of a cousin is not the issue here, Isobel!"

Teresa crossed her arms over her chest. "Well, aren't you going to invite me in? I've sent Great-Aunt Louisa home."

I started. "Teresa, it's getting awfully late. I'll come and see you tomorrow and explain everything then, and—"

"Izzy." Teresa cut me off coolly. "How long have we been best friends?"

"Eighteen years," I said.

"So don't you think I know when you're hiding something from me? Something is up, I know it. I won't be put off any longer. I want an explanation right now."

I hesitated. My friend's face was pinched with worry, her eyes enormous.

"Iz?" she whispered.

"Oh god, fine," I snapped gracelessly, my whole body jangling with nerves. "You can come in but, Teresa, not *one word* until I say, all right? I really don't want to disturb Mama. It's important."

Teresa nodded, and I opened the door more fully to let her in. I guided her back towards the kitchen and I heard her gasp as we passed the empty rooms, shrouded in shadows. That was nothing however to the sound she made when we entered the kitchen, and she found the Duke of Roxton anxiously pacing the room in his shirtsleeves.

"Izzy!" she squeaked. "Can I talk yet?"

Max's eyes met mine, full of confusion and I shrugged hopelessly at him.

"Yes, Teresa, you can."

But Teresa only looked at Max, and then at the kitchen table – which I'll admit with the candles and the wine and the two empty plates did look quite intimate – and then back at Max again. She blinked several times.

"Teresa, are you having a stroke?" I asked. "You've never gone this long without talking."

She let out a great whoosh of air and spun round to face me. "Don't you dare make jokes at a time like this, Isobel Stanhope. You have got *the Duke of Roxton* hidden in your kitchen."

"Good evening, Miss Wynter," Max said politely, as if the situation was completely normal, and I struggled to hold back a laugh.

"Don't you Miss Wynter me!" She strode forward,

pressing her finger into his solid chest, and glowering up at him. "What do you think you're doing, trying to seduce my best friend? I'll have my cousin call you out for this! No, forget that, I think I'll kill you myself with my bare hands."

"Teresa!" I exclaimed, horrified. "He's not trying to seduce me!"

"I think I know what someone trying to seduce someone looks like!" Teresa snapped, her glare still on Max. To make matters worse, he burst out laughing.

"For goodness' sake," I sighed, pulling her towards the table. "Please, sit down and I'll explain everything."

"I think perhaps I should go upstairs," Max said, and Teresa who had been about to sit in the chair shot to her feet.

"*Upstairs?!*" She strode towards him, alight with the fire of an avenging angel. "You ... you scoundrel! I really am about to kill you. Izzy, we'll finally be able to bury a body in the garden."

Max let out another surprised splutter of laughter. "Go!" I hissed at him, and he had the good sense to disappear.

"You," I said firmly to Teresa. "Sit down."

She fell into a chair with a huff. "Fine, but I insist you tell me what is going on at once."

"That's what I'm *trying* to do."

Teresa gave a harrumphing noise that made her sound exactly like her grandmother.

I began at the beginning – not with Max, but with Father's death. I told her about the money, about Mama's heart and Henry's school, about selling the furniture, about letting the servants go, about the lies and lies and lies I had to tell to keep everyone safe. I told her about the Finches and being recruited by Sylla. I told her about the sort of cases we worked on, and that the one I was currently working on had something to do with Max, that he was being forced to hide out here. By the time I'd finished the story, Teresa was practically sitting on my lap, both arms wrapped around me.

"I can't believe you didn't tell me, Iz," she murmured. "All this time you've been living like this. Taking care of everyone without any help, anyone to talk to."

"I knew you'd want to help," I said apologetically. "And I couldn't let you. I-I didn't want you to look at me any differently. I didn't want things to change."

"Of course I want to help!" Teresa exclaimed. "But I wouldn't have pushed you into anything you didn't want. I would have supported you with your plans, you must know that?"

"I love you, Teresa, but you know that's not true." When she opened her mouth to protest I pushed on. "I mean, before I joined the Aviary and had a plan, you would have involved your family, I know you would. I couldn't do that. I couldn't risk Mama finding out."

Teresa sighed. "I would have done what I could to protect you. I'm not going to apologize for that, Izzy. You never even gave me the chance to try and understand."

My heart clenched at the hurt in her face. "You're right," I said. "I'm so sorry."

We hugged for a long time, and when we pulled back, both of our faces were wet with tears.

I gave a watery chuckle. "I'm so glad you know the truth now," I said. "It's been horrible keeping it from you."

"And the Duke of Roxton is involved somehow?"

Teresa frowned.

I nodded. "But I can't tell you everything about that or what he does. Not yet. It's dangerous, and Max being here has to remain a secret."

"Oh, I see," said Teresa, a sly look in her eye. "He's Max now, is he?"

My eyes slid away from her and I toyed with the butter knife. "It's part of our cover story."

"Oh, yes, the cover story where you had to pretend to be *married* and travelled across the country together." Teresa was gleeful and I was glad that I had held back the part about sharing a bed in the abandoned shepherd's hut because I was sure she would spontaneously combust. "That explains the way he looked at you when you walked in the room," Teresa mused.

I looked up sharply then. "Not you as well!" I exclaimed. "You're as bad as Sylla. She said he was all sparkly."

"That's it exactly!" Teresa agreed. "His eyes were all soft and shiny like glittering emeralds." She sighed dreamily.

I snorted. "You're determined to turn everything into a romance novel. Speaking of which, it's a good job you didn't meet Oliver Lockhart, or James St Clair would be forgotten."

"Impossible!" Teresa grinned, her own eyes shining. "I'm absolutely, totally, completely lost over him. Besides, it's too late. James St Clair as good as proposed tonight."

"What?" I exclaimed. Fear spiked in my veins. I still wasn't sure how James St Clair fitted into Morland's schemes. How much did he know? Could we trust him? And now he was about to be engaged to my best friend. Teresa's heart had been thrown into the mix, and it seemed the stakes in this game were constantly getting higher and higher.

My friend batted her lashes innocently. "I'm not sure there's much to say except that we're hopelessly in love and that we both admitted it tonight, and he's going to call on Father. He's wonderful, Iz. Funny and kind and handsome and he makes me feel ... oh, so safe, and so exhilarated all at the same time."

"That's wonderful," I said hollowly. "Listen,

Teresa – there's something else you have to know. This organization Max works for – who are after him – well, James works for them too. I don't think he's involved, but—"

Teresa snapped her fingers.

"I understand what he meant now! Of course he couldn't tell me the details," Teresa said. "But James told me he did some work for the government – that's why he was away for so long in France." She thought for a moment. "In fact, James seemed worried about Roxton, said something about a terrible mistake, but ... then he kissed me and so I was a bit distracted." Teresa blushed. "So they're both spies together?"

I nodded. "Yes," I said. "Only, Teresa, you *can't* tell James you saw Max. Do you understand?"

Teresa's eyes widened. "Izzy, you can trust James. He'd never hurt Roxton. The two of them are like brothers."

"I'm sure you're right," I said. "But it's too serious. We can't risk it. I'm asking you to keep my secrets. Every single one of them."

She nodded thoughtfully. "Very well." The spark reignited in her eyes. "But only if you tell me *everything* that happened in Yorkshire. I can tell when you're keeping something back from me."

I tried to make my laughter sound carefree. "Fine." I poured out the remnants of the wine. "Prepare to be scandalized."

CHAPTER TWENTY-NINE

By the time Teresa left (reluctantly, and only after I had described what Max looked like in a wet shirt several times), it was late and I assumed Max had long since gone to bed. I did the same, lying awake for a long time, turning over the feelings that flooded through me at the thought of him.

When had things changed, when had infatuation tipped over into liking and then something more? I thought back to Teresa's words about James, how he made her feel safe and exhilarated at the same time, and knew she could be describing my own feelings. This had the potential for catastrophe. I had told Max all of my secrets ... *all* of them. For a moment I had felt that I didn't have to do everything on my own, like I had someone who could help carry the burden. It was almost dizzying to think of the relief that would be, but it was a temporary illusion. Sylla was right – I couldn't let myself be distracted from the job I had to do. When all this was over, we had to go back to being the Duke of Roxton and Isobel Stanhope the wallflower. That thought was disturbingly crushing.

All in all it was a restless night and I slept later than I usually would. I washed and dressed, then made my way towards Mama's room; I had been neglecting her lately. As I approached the room I heard Mama laughing and I paused. My mother had a wonderful laugh, bright and musical. It was almost as nice as...

Then I heard it. Max's laugh. Max was laughing *with* my mother. I burst into the room.

Mama looked up from her seat by the fire where she sat, wrapped in a pretty silk gown, a lace cap arranged over her head, her face still lit with laughter. Max saw me and rose.

"Mama," I said, hurrying to her side. "Are you well?" I shot Max a look that I hoped said, *what are you doing here?*

Mama looked back at me in surprise. "Of course I'm well, Izzy, stop fussing!" She turned to Max. "You must forgive my daughter, Your Grace. Isobel is a worrier."

"I-I..." I trailed off, hopelessly confused. I turned, bewildered, to Max.

He took my fingers in his own, squeezing them reassuringly for half a second before stepping away.

"Good morning, Miss Stanhope," Max said evenly, as though nothing peculiar was going on at all. "I told your mother that I've called to take you for a drive. She heard me talking to her maid in the corridor and invited me in to meet her." He turned his smile on Mama, who dimpled. "And very pleasant it has been too."

Button! I was going to murder her. I glimpsed her in Mama's dressing room, putting her gowns away, a smug look on her face. I was almost certain she'd arranged this on purpose, luring Max up here on some pretence, thinking it would be a treat for Mama to have such a handsome visitor. Seeing Mama's face, so bright and happy, I had to admit that part might have been true, but *still*.

Then the rest of it sunk in. *Called to take me for a drive.* That was why Mama had agreed to see him, and why she was grinning at me like the Duke of Roxton was a unicorn who'd wandered in off the street. She thought the man was showing an interest in me.

"Did we arrange a drive?" I said, striving for indifference as I took a seat across from my mother. "I'm afraid I forgot."

Max looked at me impassively. Mama frowned. "Isobel, I don't know what's come over you. She must be shy," she said conspiratorially to Max.

"Oh, Miss Stanhope is one of the most interesting young women of my acquaintance," Max said, and Mama beamed at him with approval. "In fact," he said, his eyes meeting mine, "I wouldn't change a thing about her."

My mouth fell open. I was trying to remain professional, to remember our jobs, our roles. How was a young woman supposed to steel herself against comments like that?

"You and Izzy met at the Perrys' ball, did you? She never mentioned it to *me*." My mother darted a reproving glance at me.

"I'm not sure I created the best first impression." Max came to stand beside me, his hand resting lightly on the top of the chair I was sitting in. He didn't touch me, but somehow it was as if I could feel the heat radiating from him. "I find such occasions overwhelming at times," he continued. "And it can make me appear a little forbidding. My sister berates me about it constantly."

I was surprised by the admission; I remembered how kind and helpful he'd been at the Devonshire House ball, how he'd seemed to understand exactly what I needed when I was overwhelmed by the crowd.

"That wasn't my first impression of you," I blurted out, without thinking, and then I coloured as both Max and Mama looked at me in surprise. "I mean," I faltered, "I'd seen you before."

"Across a crowded ballroom," Mama sighed.

Max was still looking at me. "Or somewhere else?"

he suggested.

"I saw you at the Scott-Holland ball," I said. I couldn't seem to help myself; it felt almost as though he was pulling the words out of me through some sort of hypnosis. Perhaps this was why he was an effective spy, I thought wildly – because he was gifted in the art of mesmerism. Or perhaps it was because, inexplicably, I wanted to share this memory with him. "I'd gone out for some fresh air. I saw you – you were trying to get a dog to cross the stream. You fell in the mud. And then ... you laughed."

The words hung in the air between us.

"Oh dear, how unfortunate," Mama said, clearly confused.

"I thought I heard someone," he murmured. "I had needed a rest from the crowds too. So that was your first impression of me?"

"The one I remember, yes," I said, and it felt like all of my words sounded wrong, as if it was obvious that they were drowning in all the longing and the infatuation of the last eighteen months, as if I might as well tattoo my true feelings across my forehead. I absolutely had to stop this, had to stop lowering my guard around him, had to stop *feeling* all these things. It was going to make it so much worse when he disappeared.

I cleared my throat, feeling colour burning in my cheeks. When I shifted in my seat, the back of Max's hand brushed the nape of my neck and I shivered. I was a mess, I was falling apart, hot and cold and unable to think clearly, and *my mother was there*, and she was grinning. This was a nightmare. How had I ended up here? I leaped up from the chair.

"Well, Your Grace," I said. "Shall we go for this drive?"

Max said an unhurried goodbye to my mother, and I felt that great overwhelming, extremely unwelcome rush of tenderness towards him again as he made her laugh and complimented her and listened to a long, convoluted story about the Marchioness of Hurst and her first husband, chuckling when Mama reached the end.

Finally, I managed to drag the two of them apart, trying to ignore the look of radiant joy and excitement Mama sent me before I quit the room.

We walked in silence down the corridor and then, as

soon as we were out of earshot, I turned towards him, fighting the impulse to shake him by the lapels. "What were you thinking?" I hissed.

"I know." Max held up his hands in surrender. "I'm sorry, but Button said it would make her happy, and, honestly, it was happening before I even knew I'd agreed to anything. One second I was minding my own business and the next I was being introduced to her."

I sighed, because that sounded like Button, all right. "But now she'll think that you're – that we're—"

Max looked bemused. "What?"

"Calling on me, taking me out for a drive," I choked out. He waited. He was going to make me say the words. "She'll think you're courting me." I swallowed thickly.

"Oh, is that all?" Max exhaled. "You made it sound like something awful."

"That *is* awful!" I exclaimed.

"Oh." Max frowned, and I wanted to howl in frustration. Of course he didn't realize how bad it was, how when things went back to normal, and he disappeared, my mother would be horribly disappointed. He probably just thought anyone would be pleased to be driven around by the Duke of Roxton.

Then another thought occurred to me, one so terrible that I gripped his arm. "She'll tell *everyone*," I gasped. "She'll be beside herself, having a duke come to call and showing an interest in me. I'll bet you anything she's in there right now writing letters to every person she's ever met describing everything about you down to the colour of your waistcoat."

Max looked down at his borrowed clothing in alarm. "But this is a dreadful waistcoat," he murmured. "Do you think she really noticed it? I wanted to make a good first impression. My valet's going to flay me alive."

"Max!" I snapped. "We have bigger problems than your tailoring! Don't you understand? *Everyone will know where you are*."

The words sunk in and his eyes widened.

"I'll have to intercept the post for a couple of days. God, Sylla's going to *love* this," I muttered.

Max grimaced. He was definitely afraid of Sylla; normally that would make me laugh, but right now I had too many problems to think about.

"So I take it your talk with Miss Wynter went well

last night?" Max asked, his hands clasped behind his back as we walked side by side back down the stairs. "Given that I have not yet been murdered and buried in the back garden."

Something loosened in my chest. At least one good thing had happened – Teresa knew the truth. I had my best friend, and she wasn't going anywhere. Whatever happened next, I wasn't as alone as I had been. "Yes," I said with a smile. "I told her everything, and I feel so much better."

"I thought it was nice," he said. "How she defended you. Even if it was against me, which was extremely unnecessary."

"I think she's serious about Mr St Clair," I said. I glanced at Max. "What sort of man is he?"

"The very best," Max said unhesitatingly. "You have no need to worry about your friend on that score, and for what it's worth I know James is sincere in his feelings for her. I've never seen him like this before."

"I don't know that I've seen Teresa like this before either," I said, recalling the softness in her gaze as she spoke about him. "But do you think he is in this scheme with Morland?"

Max sighed. "I've been thinking and thinking and – no, I don't. I think he's been duped, the same as me. I'd like to believe that, whatever else, James is on my side … he's been my best friend since we were children. I only wish I could talk to him, but I know how persuasive Morland can be, and there's so much at stake…" He trailed off miserably.

When we reached the front door it was to find a note on the mat on Aviary stationery. I scanned the message from Mrs Finch.

"Lady Hartwell will be happy to receive me," I said to Max.

"To receive *us*," he replied.

"Max," I sighed. "You can't seriously expect to waltz into Lady Hartwell's sitting room. Her husband is probably an accomplice of the man who is trying to have you arrested and tried for treason."

Max scowled. "If you go, I go."

"I don't need a chaperone."

"I'm not trying to be your chaperone!" Max exclaimed. He pushed a hand through his hair. "Izzy, can't you understand how useless I feel? All this time I thought I was doing some good in the world, it turns out I've been working for a villain! I want to help. I need to be doing something, I can't go home, I can't go out, I'm hiding here. I need answers. This is my life we're talking about."

I chewed on my lower lip. "Fine," I said reluctantly. "We'll go together, but you'll have to go in disguise."

"Whatever you want," Max agreed.

"How on earth will we explain why you're there?" I thought for a moment, then felt a smile play across my mouth as an idea formed.

"What is it?" Max asked. "Why are you looking at me like that?"

CHAPTER THIRTY

"You'll have to excuse my Aunt Geraldine," I said to Lady Laetitia Hartwell, as she received us in her elegant sitting room. "She insisted on chaperoning, but she's something of an invalid, and deaf as a post so you needn't mind her."

Lady Hartwell only nodded and smiled politely at my "aunt". In truth Max made rather a formidable-looking old woman.

Sylla and Winnie had arrived on my doorstep in record time. Sylla brandishing a voluminous gown that had once belonged to a statuesque opera singer, and Winnie with wigs, cosmetics, and a box full of other curiosities.

"You'd better walk with a stick," Sylla had said. "That way you can stoop and you won't look quite so tall. You really are irritatingly enormous for a fugitive we're trying to hide."

"Shouldn't have eaten all my vegetables," Max mumbled around the cotton pads Winnie had had him stuff in his cheeks to alter the shape of his face. "My nanny did warn me."

Winnie giggled, and Max winked at her. Sylla had clicked her tongue and stuck another wart to Max's chin.

Sitting beside me on the sofa now, Max was absolutely unrecognizable. His hair was hidden by a lady's wig of grey curls. His body had been padded, generously rounded and swathed in the dark gown. He was muffled in scarves and a huge shawl with an Indian design that Sylla had lent him. On his nose a pair of thick spectacles were perched to hide his eyes. As Sylla had pointed out, even if anyone suspected something amiss, no one in their right mind would expect the Duke of Roxton to be hiding underneath such a disguise. It was utterly, fantastically absurd.

"So," Lady Hartwell said crisply, after the servants had brought in tea and a selection of perfect little cakes (Max eyed these mournfully, his disguise preventing him from being able to chew them, and I decided I would slip one into my reticule for him to have later). "I understand that you are a ... colleague of Mrs Finch. What is it precisely that you have come here to ask me about?" She was poised and calm, her movements graceful, her gown expensive but understated.

"I'm here to discuss Lord Morland," I replied tranquilly. Mrs Finch seemed to think that honesty would be the best strategy here; I was still unsure.

The poise disappeared. Lady Hartwell's face blanched and her teacup shook in its saucer. It had obviously been the last thing she expected me to say. "Lord Morland? W-what do you want to know about him?"

"Please don't worry," I said gently. "This conversation is between you and I, Lord Hartwell will never know. I know that he and Lord Morland are friends."

"That man is no friend to my husband," Lady Hartwell spat. The fear in her face had turned to rage.

I sat back in shock, unsure what to say next. There was a brief but heavy silence.

"I was under the impression that Lord Morland and your husband were political allies," I said. "That you spent a lot of time in the company of he and his wife."

"Politics often has little to do with friendship," Lady Hartwell said, pressing her lips together. "I will say this to you, Miss Stanhope, as a friend of Mrs Finch – stay away from Samuel Morland. Stay as far away from him as possible."

The grip on her teacup was so tight that her knuckles were white.

I decided to tell her at least some of the truth. "What if I told you that my interest was in striking against Lord Morland?"

She blinked. "*Against* Morland," she murmured, placing the cup and saucer on the table in front of her with a clatter.

Another thick silence fell. I noticed that Max was careful not to move a muscle beside me. For such an extraordinary-looking character, Aunt Geraldine was doing an amazing job of blending into the background.

"I think," I said, my words breaking the quiet, "that you know something of the work we do at the Aviary?"

Lady Hartwell gave a tense nod.

"Our initial interest in this case was the treatment of Lord Morland's wife," I continued. "She was in some distress, caused, we believe, by her husband. But our investigation has led us in a different direction. To a piece of jewellery."

Lady Hartwell's hand leaped to her throat, and she let out a choked sound. "That damned brooch!"

I felt Max tense beside me.

"What do you know about the brooch?" I asked.

"What do *you* know about the brooch?" Lady Hartwell countered.

Again, I hesitated. This wasn't something I could get wrong. Too much was at stake. But my instincts were screaming, and I decided it was time to listen. Mrs Finch had sent the brooch over with Sylla and Win, telling me to use it should I need to.

I reached into my pocket and took out the ruby, placing it on the table beside Lady Hartwell's teacup.

She eyed the piece of jewellery as if I had set a poisonous snake down in front of her. Her mouth moved several times as though she was trying to speak but nothing came out. Then she started to laugh. It was not a pleasant laugh – it was harsh, gasping, edged with hysteria.

"You have the brooch!" she managed finally. "Morland doesn't have it. He must be going wild. *He doesn't have it!*" These last words were almost yelled in triumph. She stood and tugged on the bell that called the servants.

I scooped up the brooch and stood, ready to run or to fight, if necessary. Max did not move. His eyes behind the spectacles were hard to read, but I could tell he was watching Lady Hartwell closely.

When a maid appeared at the door, Lady Hartwell simply instructed her to, "Fetch Lord Hartwell. *At once!*"

We waited in agitated silence for only a minute or so before Lady Hartwell's husband came into the room.

David Hartwell was roughly the same age as his wife, fair and good-looking with an air of gentle solicitude. He had always struck me as kind. On entering the room his eyes flew anxiously to his wife, before moving over Max and settling on me.

"David." Lady Hartwell sank back into the chair. "This is Miss Stanhope." She recalled Max and added, "And her aunt. Miss Stanhope works with Mrs Finch. They've come about Morland. Show him." She turned to me, her voice imploring. "Show him what you have."

Reluctantly I held out my hand, uncurling my fingers from around the brooch. When he saw what I had in my grasp, Lord Hartwell seemed almost to sway on his feet, and when he looked at me I saw raw fear in his eyes.

"Perhaps we should all sit down," I said calmly. There were so many emotions flying thick and fast around the room, and I didn't understand them. What did seem clear, however, was that the Hartwells were no friends of Lord Morland – and that opened up all sorts of interesting possibilities.

"How do you come to possess Lord Morland's brooch?" David Hartwell asked, dropping into a chair.

"We ... acquired the brooch following the Devonshire House ball," I said.

Hartwell flinched. "The Devonshire House ball? So it was part of the collection of jewellery that was stolen?" He frowned. "But what on earth was it doing at Devonshire House?"

"It seems that Lady Morland gifted the brooch to the Duke of Devonshire," I said, and Lord and Lady Hartwell exchanged a look of surprise. "So you didn't notice it there on the night of the ball?"

Hartwell shook his head. "We never visited the retiring room. Most people would have gone to admire the jewels later on in the evening. I had no idea that the brooch was out of Morland's possession." His face grew grim. "He made sure that I didn't know."

"And he wanted it back urgently before you could find out," I mused aloud. "Which is why he arranged to have it stolen in such a risky way."

"You mean to tell me *Morland* was behind the robbery?" Hartwell looked stunned.

His wife however gave a short, humourless laugh. "Can you really be surprised by anything that viper would do?"

Hartwell turned back to me. "How is it that you came to be involved?"

"Our organization was originally retained to protect Lady Morland from her husband's cruelty," I said. "During our investigation, we discovered Morland's scheme to steal the brooch and intercepted it. We want to find out its importance – and help Kitten Morland before it's too late."

"That poor, sweet girl." Hartwell shook his head. "I knew she'd end up on the wrong side of Morland eventually. I don't imagine he took her gifting the brooch in good humour."

"It would seem he did not," I said.

Lady Hartwell's eyes closed briefly. "He's doing it again, isn't he? What he did to Eliza? As soon as I heard the rumours, I knew. That poor child."

"You believe Morland was responsible for the death of his first wife?" I tried to keep my tone neutral.

"I know he was." Lady Hartwell's fingers twisted in her skirts. "I knew Eliza from the day she was born – the man bullied her out of her wits. He did his best to cut her off from her friends, never left a mark on her physically, as far as I could tell, but the games he played with her mind... I think it was when he realized she couldn't give him an heir, when he realized she wasn't useful to him any more..."

She trailed off here, and I felt bile rise in my throat. Stories of Morland's viciousness shouldn't surprise me any more but I couldn't contain the shudder that passed through me.

"In the course of our investigation," I said, forcing my mind to return to the matter at hand, "we came to realize that Kitten Morland was forced to wear the brooch on many occasions. We found a pattern – she only wore it when at least one of three men were in attendance. I think you must know, Lord Hartwell, that one of those men is you."

"Oh, I know it well enough," Hartwell said hotly. "The man's a sadist, having his wife parade it about in front of me. Watching me squirm." Lady Hartwell took his hand in her own, squeezing gently.

I shifted in my seat. "So the brooch isn't just a key. It's a message," I said slowly. "One that you understand?"

He shifted in his seat. "Yes, I suppose it's a message.

It's Morland's way of reminding me that he has me under his thumb."

"Blackmail," I said, the pieces finally sliding into place. "He flaunts the brooch to remind you to stay in line. And the key is to wherever he's holding the material he uses to blackmail you?"

Hartwell's jaw clenched and his eyes moved to his wife.

"I believe we can confide in them, David," she said. "They work with Mrs Finch, and you know she's a trusted friend. They're trying to bring down Morland. Perhaps they can help us."

"We can," I said with certainty. "If you'll let us, we can put a stop to all of this."

"Very well," Hartwell said heavily. "If you think it is the right thing, Letty..."

"I do," his wife said.

He squared his shoulders. "Then, yes, Lord Morland is blackmailing me. He has certain ... photographs, and letters in his possession which could see me in prison, and humiliate my wife." He paused and looked at me with pain in his eyes. "I hope I'm right to put my trust in you. The truth is that my wife is my best friend, one of the most extraordinary people I know, and my closest confidante for over thirty years." His hand was still in Lady Hartwell's and I saw her squeeze his fingers again. "However my feelings towards her – towards *any* woman – are not of a *romantic* nature. I have another relationship for that, one which must remain secret. Do you understand?"

His voice was strained, and I nodded. The current law made romantic relationships between men illegal, even in private, and Oscar Wilde had only recently been released from a two-year prison sentence for gross indecency. It was a cruel, brutal piece of legislation. I understood what David Hartwell was trying to tell me, and precisely what he stood to lose by doing so.

"And Lord Morland is using this material to secure your political support?"

"Yes," Hartwell said. "I believe he targeted me from the start because I have the connections to help him climb the political ladder. Only a few years ago he was relatively unknown. Now, he's on his way to becoming the leader of this country, God help us all. He wants my support passing a key piece of legislation."

"And this legislation is about the country's defence system?" I asked, remembering what Max and Mrs Finch had said.

Hartwell nodded. "Morland believes our country to be under threat, that war is on the horizon. He's not necessarily wrong about that, but the particular legislation he has drawn up concerns me because it's so heavy-handed and extreme. It would give the prime minister a great deal of autonomy. That prime minister might well be Morland himself. Knowing what I do about him – how he craves power – I wouldn't put anything past him. The size of the armada he wants to build, it's a dangerous amount of power for one person to wield. It's possible that Morland wouldn't wait for war, that he may provoke it himself if he saw an opportunity in it. But the man is virtually unstoppable. He buys off any opponents – or buys favours and votes. Those he can't buy off – like me – he pressures in different ways."

I felt my blood run cold.

"How is he paying for all of this?" I asked.

"No one knows where Morland's money comes from exactly." Hartwell's frown deepened. "His wife, of course, brought a great deal to the marriage, but making a ministerial bid is costly. I have no proof of impropriety but I know he has been working alongside some unsavoury characters. I only have one name that I heard by chance ... Andrew Sharpe."

Everything stood still for a moment as the name rang through the air. Sharpe. The villain we had been undermining for months at the Aviary, the one whose letter to Wyncham had provided the final nail in his coffin. The last name I had expected to hear spoken in this room.

"You're certain of that name?" I asked.

"Yes, though I have no idea who he is."

How on earth did Andrew Sharpe fit into this? I thought back to my conversation with Joe. He'd said that Sharpe was part of something bigger, that someone was creating ripples in the criminal world. I cleared my throat, trying to focus on getting all the information I needed. "Tell me about the key."

"There's only so much I've been able to discover.

Morland has a special safe in his home," Hartwell said. "I don't know where exactly but I do know that it's top of the line, a customized, fireproof Diebold – impossible to crack."

I drummed my fingers against the table. "And the brooch holds the key?" If we possessed the key to this unbreakable safe, then perhaps things were looking up.

Hartwell shook his head wearily. "The brooch holds *one* key. The other is hidden in a tiepin that Morland always wears. Both keys must be used simultaneously or else it won't open – Morland took great pleasure in explaining that it had been tested by the greatest safe breakers in the world."

I thought for a moment. "Without this brooch, then, Morland can't open it either," I pointed out. "He's a victim of his own hubris. Morland cannot open the safe to access the blackmail materials himself. Not without destroying the safe and potentially whatever is inside along with it. Which explains why he was so keen to recover the brooch before any of his victims realized..."

Hartwell's eyes lit up. "Yes," he said softly. "We may

all become a lot less amenable to his plans."

We had that on our side, at least – what we didn't have was time. Morland was close on our tail. "Lord Hartwell, Lady Hartwell," I said. "Thank you for your time."

"But what do you intend to do?" Lord Hartwell leaped from his seat. He looked panicked and careworn and I found myself thinking about Morland's victims: the Hartwells, Eliza, Kitten, the girls Sharpe had used, and Max, whose life was in danger every moment he evaded the trap Morland had set for him. And those were only the ones we knew about.

"What do I intend?" I smiled dangerously. My eye met Max's, under his heavy wig. "I intend to bring Lord Morland to his knees. You can count on the Aviary for that. Your secrets will be your own again. I promise you both."

"Thank you," Lady Hartwell murmured.

I nodded at them and then swept from the room, followed by my "aunt".

I felt like I did when I first put on my Medusa costume: powerful and wild and sure. It was time to put an end to Morland's schemes.

There was much to be done.

That evening, the candles burned low in Mrs Finch's office as we discussed our strategy. From down below the sound of merriment spilled out of the salon. The distant plinking of the piano and the hum of chatter usually made me feel warm and comfortable, but tonight I was still reeling from all we had discovered about Morland. The truth was even worse than we had imagined.

"Tell me more about this Sharpe character," Max said. He was sitting beside me on the sofa, having shed his Aunt Geraldine disguise. His face was taut, his jaw set. There was no longer any chance of denying Morland's villainy, and the truth had settled around him like armour. He was ready for battle, but he still didn't truly understand the stakes – he didn't know what the name Andrew Sharpe meant.

"Sharpe came to our attention about eight months ago," I said. "My friend Joe told me several girls had disappeared, the kind of girls the law doesn't worry about too much, but Joe was worried and asked us to investigate. It turned out that they were being kidnapped and sold. The man behind it was Sharpe – a thoroughly nasty character. We set about dismantling his business. As well as the kidnapping he had some other interests – money laundering, possibly counterfeiting and opium too. He was well connected and we thought he might be working for someone else."

"And we were right, of course," Sylla said grimly. "We compiled a dossier for the police, one that they couldn't deny, and we sent copies to the papers too. It's precisely the sort of sensational story they love."

"Including a letter to a Mr Wyncham with some extremely damning evidence." I smiled at Max. "One that was liberated from him and copied during a recent performance of *Manon Lescaut*."

Understanding dawned in Max's eyes. "Sharpe is our link to Morland. Find Sharpe and we can follow this trail all the way to the top, and—"

"He's dead," Sylla said flatly.

"He's *what*?!" I exclaimed. "Sharpe is dead?"

"It happened while you were in Yorkshire," Winnie

said. "With everything that's been going on we must have forgotten to tell you. We thought his case was over ... we didn't know it was connected to any of this."

"How did he die?" I asked, trying to gather myself.

Sylla shrugged. "It was a bar-room brawl. I thought it well-timed, suspiciously so – after all, we knew he had friends in high places who wouldn't want him to talk. But we had no idea *how* high this little conspiracy went. The police, of course, have no interest in the case now that his operation has been shut down. Nor do the press."

"You think Morland had him killed?" Max asked, his voice low.

I shivered, and he shifted his posture, moving a fraction closer to me. I wished that I could curl up against him, but I settled for the soft brush of his jacket against my arm, the reassuring warmth that seemed to emanate from his large body.

"Of course Morland had him killed," Sylla snapped. I sensed something under her usual impatience – fear. This case seemed to be made of so many layers, peel one away and there was something else waiting beneath: clues hiding clues, villains hiding more villains. "He must have known that Sharpe was finished. Morland almost certainly has sources inside the police. He was scared that Sharpe would blab and so he shut him up for good."

Max nodded grimly. "Tying up loose ends. It's something Morland always drilled into us."

"What about Wyncham?" I asked, already knowing the answer.

"Gone," Sylla said.

"We thought he'd done a runner," Maud put in. "But I suppose he's dead too."

"So what are we going to do?" Winnie asked. She stood in the window, her arms wrapped around her middle.

"If we destroy the brooch then Morland's blackmail is over," Max said. "The safe is inaccessible without it. He would lose all the support he needs to win the election and pass this legislation."

"But without the brooch we won't be able to prove your innocence," I said sharply. "And who's to say this is the only scheme Morland has up his sleeve? The man seems to have snaked his way into every corner of this corrupt system. He could still win the election, with or without his victims. He could still find a way to blackmail those men. No – we need him gone. We have to recover the blackmail documents and destroy them. Then we need to tie Morland to Sharpe's crimes and hold him accountable. We need to root out his influence and destroy him once and for all."

There was silence. Max was looking at me as if I were wearing Sylla's Valkyrie costume and the warmth in his gaze made something flutter in my chest.

"If the safe is in Morland's house then I have a few ideas about where it could be hidden," Maud said thoughtfully. "I can draw up plans, with Winnie's help."

"We'll need both keys for the safe. Someone will need to steal Morland's precious tiepin," Sylla mused, her eyes on me. "Perhaps the lightest-fingered pickpocket in the city?"

"Kes," I nodded.

"No, not this time." Sylla tapped her chin thoughtfully. "I believe this is a job for Miss Isobel Stanhope, the plain little wallflower he'd never suspect."

Max looked puzzled. "Izzy's not plain."

All eyes turned to him. Sylla's eyebrows were raised. Then she turned back to me. "I told you this was going to be a problem," she said.

Maud choked on a laugh.

Max continued to look bemused while I longed to sink into the ground. This chivalrous nature of his kept putting me in embarrassing situations, giving people very wrong ideas about us.

"Morland will be on alert with everything that's going on," I said, continuing with burning cheeks. "We'll need a decoy pin, something I can replace it with." I turned to Max. "Do you know the tiepin that Hartwell was talking about?"

Max nodded. "He wears it all the time. I can draw a pretty good version of it."

"I can make a copy," Winnie said.

"Then all Izzy has to do is swap the two," Sylla finished.

"But how?" I frowned. "We won't have much time. We'll need to find and break in to the safe straight after the swap, before Morland notices the real pin is missing."

We fell into a taut silence.

"It seems to me," Mrs Finch said, speaking for the first time. "That we need to return to where this whole thing began." A smile lit her face, one that did not bode well for her enemies. "I think it's time that we spoke to Kitten Morland."

CHAPTER THIRTY-ONE

"Are you sure that I should be here for this?" I asked Mrs Finch the next day. I was waiting in her office for the arrival of Kitten Morland. "Kitten will recognize Isobel Stanhope."

"She's not going to see you," Mrs Finch replied, opening the door to her office and gesturing for me to follow. She led me to the storage cupboard next door – it was a small space, lined with shelves and filled with odds and ends that didn't fit anywhere else – a few old

432

crates, some of Win's old equipment, stacks of spare linen, that sort of thing.

Mrs Finch moved over to the wall that was shared with her office and climbed up on to the bottom shelf, which was empty, then she shoved a box aside on a higher shelf. There, in the wall behind it, was a small metal grate, and when she slid it to one side it created a spy hole through which you could see and hear what was happening in the room next door.

"How did I not know that existed?" I asked.

Mrs Finch smiled. "Because you didn't need to know. Until now. I think you should hear everything Kitten says first-hand."

"Shouldn't it be Sylla doing this?" I asked.

"It was Sylla's suggestion that you do it," was all Mrs Finch replied. "They'll be here any moment." She brushed down her skirts. "Make sure you stay quiet – you can hear us but that means we can hear you too."

With that she was gone, shutting me inside the cupboard – the only light was that spilling through from the grate. I climbed on to the bottom shelf and positioned myself so that I could see through – the grate was somewhere in the wall above Mrs Finch's desk, and it offered a perfect view of the whole room.

I was just in time, because the door opened and Mrs Finch led in three women: Maud, Lorna and Kitten.

"Lady Morland, Miss Smith," Mrs Finch said. "Please, take a seat."

I looked closely at Kitten. Maud had planned to show her the trick with the pipes before they came – to offer some proof of all we had to tell her, and to explain Lorna's visit to the Aviary. In the end we had decided that the best thing we could do was lay the whole story bare and hope Kitten could be trusted to play out the game with us, and keep Morland in the dark. My instincts said it was the right move, but we were about to find out. Kitten's face was pale and pinched, her hazel eyes wide.

Still, she watched Mrs Finch carefully, and when she sat it was with perfect poise. She was dressed simply but neatly, her blonde curls artfully arranged. Lorna sat in the seat beside her, her inclusion vital in convincing Kitten that we were telling the truth, and Maud stood at the back of the room, making herself as unobtrusive as possible.

"I think, by now, you have some idea of why we asked you here," Mrs Finch said gently.

"It has been a strange morning," Kitten replied, her voice sweet and musical. I had been expecting her to be nervous, flustered, but instead she seemed oddly calm.

Mrs Finch sat in the chair behind her desk so that her back was to me, but I heard the sympathy in her voice when she said, "I know the revelations about your husband's behaviour must have come as a shock…"

"Let us call a spade a spade, Mrs Finch," Kitten said composedly. "My husband has been trying to convince me – and everyone else – that I have lost my wits."

Lorna, who had been silent until now, shifted in her seat, as if she wanted to comfort her mistress, but didn't want to overstep.

It was as if the whole room held its breath. This was not the Kitten Morland any of us had been expecting.

At last, Mrs Finch nodded. "Very well, Lady Morland – we shall call a spade a spade. It would seem that your husband has become involved in some unsavoury activities and it is possible that you witnessed something you shouldn't have. He is determined to undermine you – by convincing you, and the world, that you are not a credible witness."

Kitten frowned. "Morland conducts a great deal of business at the house." She spoke slowly. "But if I know something, then I don't know what it is, I'm afraid." She sighed. "I thought all of this had something to do with that horrible, ugly brooch."

"It seems that the brooch is also a key to a special safe – one that contains blackmail material. Lord Morland had you wear it in front of his victims to remind them of the power he holds, to keep them in line." Mrs Finch spoke plainly, and the truth was brutal.

For the first time, Kitten's face showed some emotion – her mouth opened, and her face paled further, her eyes filled with tears. "How cruel," she managed. "You mean all this time I was causing people pain – just by walking around, wearing that terrible thing?"

"You didn't know, my lady," Lorna broke in here, her tone fierce. Kitten gave a watery smile and took Lorna's hand, squeezing it briefly.

"I still wouldn't, if it hadn't been for you, Lorna."

The maid's face flushed.

"Does the name Andrew Sharpe mean anything to you?" Mrs Finch asked.

Kitten frowned again. "Sharpe? No, I don't think so."

"Or has your husband welcomed any unusual visitors recently?"

Kitten thought about it for a moment and then nodded. "A few weeks ago there was something strange. It was just after I gave the brooch away to the Duke of Devonshire. I had thought Morland would be so pleased because the duke was absolutely beside himself at the gift but, well, we all know how that worked out. He lost his temper, like I'd never seen before. Then he seemed to calm down … almost to be sorry about it. I had hoped the matter was forgiven.

"Then one morning I was going out shopping, only I forgot my reticule and had to come back. I had last had it in the library that morning, but Morland was in there with the door ajar. He was talking to a man who looked like a rough sort. He looked up and saw me, and seemed furious when he realized I'd seen them talking, though I was only there for a moment and I didn't hear anything of significance." She gave a small shrug. "But that man wasn't called Sharpe."

"Do you remember what he was called?"

Kitten's brow wrinkled. "He had a funny name. I heard Morland say it. It was the name of a bird ... Magpie or..."

"Rook," I whispered, at the same time as Kitten said the word. *That's* what Kitten had seen: a meeting between Morland, future prime minister, and the man who was to break in and steal from the Duke of Devonshire.

"Do you know the whereabouts of Morland's safe?" Mrs Finch asked.

Kitten shook her head. "No, I had no idea about these secret keys or the safe, or any of it. I suppose it's in his study, but Morland's so careful, it could be anywhere in the house." She gave a wry smile. "It seems my husband is rather good at keeping secrets."

"So you know nothing of the blackmail material?" Mrs Finch asked, and there was a thread of steel in her words.

"Absolutely not." Kitten's words were emphatic.

"I didn't know about any of this. You may think me a fool, but until the last few weeks Morland has been an absolute model husband – kind, attentive, indulgent even. I was busy congratulating myself on my own good taste, I assure you."

"And of course he was in the running to be prime minister," said Mrs Finch, almost idly. "Quite the prize."

Kitten lifted her chin. "I would have thought, Mrs Finch, that you're not someone who would be shocked by a woman with ambition."

"I'm not," Mrs Finch said coolly. "Only by how far some will go to achieve that ambition."

Lorna made a sound of protest, but Kitten sat forward in her seat. "You're asking, I think, if now that I know my husband for the monster he is, I'll throw my lot in with him anyway?"

"Women don't always have a choice in the matter," Mrs Finch said.

Something leaped in Kitten Morland's eyes. "That is true, but let me be clear," her voice had risen, stronger and more certain, "I'm here today because I will do whatever it takes to bring my husband to justice and to tear off the smiling mask he wears, revealing the villain underneath. I'm here because he stole something from me – I have spent weeks living in a state of fear I can hardly begin to describe. I thought... I thought..." She broke off here, swallowing hard, before composing herself. "I want him to pay for what he did to me, and for what he has done to others. From what Maud tells me, this is the right place for that. I'm offering you my help, Mrs Finch. Whatever you need."

There was a moment of silence, and Mrs Finch leaned back in her seat. I could hear the smile in her voice when she replied, "In that case, Lady Morland, welcome to the Aviary."

The rest of the plans were made fairly quickly. When Mrs Finch explained that we needed access to both Morland and the safe in their house, Kitten had thrown herself into the scheme. It turned out she was much tougher than she looked. A kitten with claws, in fact.

It had been her suggestion that she throw the sort of party Morland couldn't refuse – one full of guests with influence. It would be Kitten's way of apologizing for her erratic behaviour, of showing her desire to be useful to him. The guest of honour – thanks to Mrs Finch's little black book and a result of her calling in several favours – would be Bertie, the future King of England. Morland would surely jump at the chance.

Mrs Finch had suggested the ball be a masquerade. After the disastrous Devonshire House ball, people would be longing to get dressed up and engage in some debauchery. It had all been arranged with relative ease. We weren't going to break in to Morland's house at all; we were going to be invited through the front door.

By the time Kitten and Lorna left, my body was aching from being cramped into the uncomfortable position in the cupboard.

"Well?" Mrs Finch asked when she opened the door with a flourish.

"It sounds like the perfect plan," I said, rubbing my neck. "Making it a masquerade was clever – I can't see Max agreeing to sit this one out, and at least this way he'll be able to sneak in without having to resort to the Aunt Geraldine costume again."

"My thoughts exactly." Mrs Finch smiled, but then

all humour left her face. "Did you believe her?" she asked. "You trust that Kitten Morland is on our side?"

"Absolutely," I said without hesitation. I had seen it written all over her face. She was furious with Morland. "She wants him to pay – and not just for what he did to her. I don't blame her at all."

"No, neither do I," Mrs Finch sighed.

"We do see some terrible things," I said quietly. "All these awful marriages."

Something flickered in Mrs Finch's eyes. "It's difficult not to let this work harden you."

I nodded, and there was a moment of quiet between us.

"I should get home," I said. "Max will be climbing the walls. Either that or he'll be wooing my mother again."

Mrs Finch smiled, and the dark mood lifted.

Fortunately, when I arrived home Max had kept his promise and remained below stairs, though I did find him pacing the kitchen like a caged animal.

"Finally!" he exclaimed when he saw me. "How was it? Did she believe you? Will she help? Did you make a plan?"

"We did," I said, unpinning my hat and flopping into a chair, while Max busied himself pouring me a cup of tea and fixing it just as I liked. I told him everything Kitten had said.

"At last," he exhaled. "We're nearing the end now, aren't we? We're going to get the bastard."

"We are," I said, my own voice hard as I looked at him over the top of my teacup.

We were interrupted then by a tentative knock at the back door. I set the cup down, as Max turned quickly in the direction of the noise.

"Who can that be?" I murmured, moving forward.

"Maybe you should ignore it," Max cautioned. I edged closer and rested my ear against the door.

"Izzy?" a voice came on the other side. "Are you there?"

"It's Teresa," I said, and Max's shoulders relaxed as I unlocked the door, pulling it open.

Only it wasn't just Teresa. Standing there, behind her, was James St Clair.

I pushed the door closed fast, but James wedged his foot inside, preventing me from shutting it. Max leaped forward, pulling me behind him as the door swung open and the two men stood frozen, staring at each other.

"Teresa!" I managed.

"I didn't tell him, Iz, I promise!" My best friend gave James a shove, pushing him through the door and closing it behind her. "He worked it out himself, I don't know how. He told me he was coming and I had no time to warn you. But he's on your side. Aren't you, James?" She nudged him in the ribs. "Tell them."

"How did you know I was here?" Max growled.

"You think I don't know my best friend when I see him? Even if he's wearing a dirty old wig?" James scoffed. "I saw you two together at the train station, of course. Once I knew Miss Stanhope was involved it was easy to work out you were here. And Teresa has a terrible poker face."

"Or maybe that's what I want you to think," Teresa grumbled.

"You saw me at the train station," I repeated blankly.

A grin spread over James's face. "Yes," he said. "I saw you, even with this great lummox wrapped all around you."

"Wrapped all around her!" Teresa squawked, looking delighted. "You didn't tell me that part."

Max was eyeing James in silence, one arm still extended in front of my body though I don't think he was even aware of it.

"Come on, Rox," James said softly. "Time for me to help *you* out of a scrape for once."

There was another fraught moment, and then Max laughed and the two men were hugging and thumping each other loudly and manfully on the back.

"Oh, thank goodness," Teresa exhaled slumping against the wall. "It would have been awkward if the Duke of Roxton had killed my future husband in my best friend's kitchen."

James extracted himself from Max's arms, and pulled Teresa tight against him. "Excuse me?" he murmured. "I'll have you know that I could take Rox in a fight any day of the week. Ask him who won last time?"

"We were eleven," Max said. "I hadn't had my growth spurt yet."

"Always was a sore loser." James rolled his eyes at me.

Teresa swatted him on the arm. "You needn't have worried, because I'd have avenged your death anyway."

"Thank you, my love." James kissed the tip of her nose. "That is most reassuring."

"I'm sorry," I said, finally catching up with the conversation. "Teresa, did you say *future husband*?"

"Oh, yes." Teresa turned a fetching shade of pink. "James spoke to my father this morning. It's all arranged."

I felt a brief pang of something, something dark and complicated like fear and envy and loss all swirled up together, but I pushed it firmly aside. Then it was my turn to throw myself into my best friend's arms, and we were diverted for several tearful, joyful minutes, until James said, "I don't mean to bring the mood down, but I do think we need to have a conversation about Morland."

All traces of happiness left Max's face, and I felt my own smile drop.

"You'd better have a seat," I said. "There's a lot we need to discuss."

PART FIVE

Morland House, London
July 1897

Chapter Thirty-Two

Lord and Lady Morland
Invite you to a masquerade
At Morland House
July 10th, 1897
9 p.m.
Grand unmasking at Midnight
Carriages at Dawn

"Are you sure about this?" I asked, adjusting the silver-edged lace of the mask around my eyes. "What if someone recognizes Max?"

The carriage wobbled along the cobbled street. The smoke haze of the city was heavy tonight, and the world outside the window was shrouded in thick silver cobwebs of mist, though it was still warm with the lingering heat of the day.

"Stop fussing," Teresa tutted across from me. "This is his job, isn't it? Secrets and disguises and thrilling adventures?" She sighed dreamily. "Do you think I'd make a good spy?"

"No, I think you'd be terrible. Probably fall in love with a foreign agent."

Teresa dimpled. "That's what James said too. Then he said there'd be a duel for my hand, and I think I'd almost like that, only the thought of anything happening to him is too terrible."

"It must be love if you'd turn down a duel over your hand," I teased.

"Must be," Teresa agreed and we both laughed.

"Don't worry," she said, after a moment. "Everything

will be all right. After all, I'm on the team this time. What could go wrong?"

Actually, there was quite a lot that could go wrong, but Teresa's words still gave me a lift. Morland may be a formidable opponent, but tonight he faced us all, together, and I knew what we were capable of.

Teresa and I were in her family's carriage, headed to the masquerade while a masked coachman guided the horses with a light hand. We had fudged the facts a little, meaning that Great-Aunt Louisa had the night off from chaperoning, as Teresa's newly minted fiancé was going to be there, making sure we were well protected. The fact that he was going to be joining us in ransacking our host's house had not come up.

The carriage drew up to the Morlands' residence, and I smoothed the skirts of my new dress. It was one of Iris Grey's creations, and it had arrived that morning like a gift from fate. I had asked her to help bring me out of half-mourning and what she had made was perfect. The gown I wore tonight was ice-blue silk, simply cut, utterly plain without a ruffle or a bow or a trim in sight. It was cut wide across my shoulders, fitted perfectly over a loosely laced corset, and then fell into a pool of liquid silk, spilling down to the ground. The sleeves were short and flat – defying the convention for voluminous puffs – and the long silver gloves I wore matched the silver mask on my face.

"Here we go, then," I said.

"Is it always this exciting?" Teresa squeaked.

The door to the carriage opened, and the coachman stood there, tall and broad, clad in a midnight-black suit. The black silk mask that covered the top half of his face gave him the air of a menacing stranger, but the green eyes that looked back at me were familiar. I put my fingers into his outstretched hand, his black glove wrapping around my silver one.

"Oh, yes," I said, in answer to Teresa's question. "Yes, it is."

The night air was thick and sultry, heat still seeming to emanate from the paved roads. Teresa and I made our way inside. There was a giddy atmosphere in there, a feeling of anticipation. After the drama of the Devonshire House ball, it seemed as though society had been waiting feverishly for some sort of release, and an impromptu masquerade was just what the doctor ordered.

Not that there was anything impromptu about the set-up. Kitten Morland was an accomplished hostess, and creating a party fit for royalty on only several days' notice seemed not to have tried her one bit. The house was lit only by candlelight: candles hanging from chandeliers, candles lining the staircase in glass jars, candles skewered in enormous baroque silver candelabras, there were candles everywhere, and the flames flickered, sending shadows trembling across the walls. There was deep green foliage wrapped around banisters and mantelpieces, twined with heavily perfumed roses the colour of plum jam – so dark a purple they were almost black.

The guests moved around, sly grins underneath their masks, greedy eyes taking it all in as an orchestra played. We followed the sound, and made our way through to a ballroom, the walls clad in ornate gold-framed mirrors that reflected back a kaleidoscope of images of masked dancers whirling in brightly coloured gowns. The orchestra was hidden, the music of the waltz seeming to drift from nowhere, sultry and compelling, the candlelight danced here too, refracted as a thousand glittering stars around us.

"Goodness," Teresa murmured. "This is decadent."

Decadent was the word, I thought, as I accepted a saucer of champagne from a man in black livery, his waistcoat the same purple as the rose petals that floated in the top of my drink, turning the champagne the palest lilac. I took a sip, the bubbles mixing with the perfume of the rose, sweet and heady.

As I glanced about I kept my eyes peeled for the others. Sylla was there in the corner, talking to a gentleman and looking bored. Maud, I knew, was working somewhere in the background in her capacity as the Morlands' maid, and Winnie had seconds ago walked through the door, graceful in a spring-green gown, her blue eyes wide behind the gold mask she wore as she took in the scene in the ballroom.

"Dance with me." The words came from behind me, and I found myself being spun against a wall of muscle, pulled into the arms of a man in a black mask. I heard Teresa's laugh as she plucked the champagne from my hand and then I was twirling away from her, guided by the warm hand on my back.

"You managed to sneak in, then," I said.

"Maud was waiting for me, as arranged," he said. His dark suit was immaculate. "Teresa's idea of coming as your driver was a good one."

"Your eyes are too green," I sighed. "It's not good for your disguise, everyone will recognize you."

"Now isn't the time to lose your optimism, Izzy," Max murmured, those green eyes crinkling softly.

That warm, sunshine feeling unfurled in my chest then, and I allowed myself to lean into Max's arms, a tiny, snatched moment of bliss, imagining what it would be like if he were really mine, if we were really together. If he wasn't the untouchable, impeccable duke and I a girl on the edge of society with too many secrets. We danced in silence for several minutes, and I knew I should have been looking out for Morland, for threats to our mission, that I should have been thinking about the job I had to do, getting the key, finding the safe, but instead all I could see was the girl in the pale blue dress, held tight in the arms of the dark, handsome stranger, reflected back at me a hundred times, as they danced through the stars.

"Don't you wish you could write poetry at times like this?" Max said.

A surprised laugh escaped me. "Where did that question come from?"

Max shrugged, and I felt the movement underneath my hand. "Something about this room, I suppose."

"How do you know I *don't* write poetry?" I asked.

A smile twisted the corner of his mouth. "Do you?"

I sighed, but couldn't keep the grin off my face. "No, I tried once but it was a disaster. Absolutely terrible. I think I should leave the poetry to Teresa. I'm a very prosaic person."

The music stopped, and Max held me for another second. He looked down at me, and smiled. "Isobel Stanhope," he said softly. "I don't know where you've come by this idea of yourself. You're a sonnet."

I stood, staring at him for a moment as my brain struggled to understand the words that had come out of his mouth.

"I – you – that—" I stammered, which was extremely

unfair given his eloquence, but Max was ignoring me now. He stilled, and his eyes slid away from the doorway that he was facing, he stood closer, his mouth pressed softly to my ear as he murmured three little words, just for me.

"Morland is here."

CHAPTER THIRTY-THREE

I spun around to face the entrance to the ballroom, and there he was: Lord Samuel Morland.

Of course I had seen him before, though we had never been introduced, but he had become something from a fairy tale in my mind – a villain cloaked in shadows, evil dripping from his fingertips, head thrown back in a cackle of brutish glee, and so it was something of a shock to see the man in the doorway.

He was in his early fifties, middling height, with sandy hair starting to grey at the temples and a boyish smile. He wore a pale blue mask, but I could see his eyes, which were a deep navy, full of warmth and he was talking to one of the guests, throwing his head back in good-natured laughter. His clothes were clearly expensive, and tailored to fit him perfectly, but they weren't showy. He was neither fat nor thin, tall nor short. He was, in fact, completely and utterly ordinary.

At his side, Kitten Morland was all fragile elegance – on the surface, at least. Glossy blonde ringlets were piled on her head. A heavily embroidered gold mask framed wide hazel eyes and her mouth was a pink rosebud. There was nothing subtle about her gown, which was made of heavy gold brocade, with enormous, wide skirts and a jewelled bodice. She stood poised, at ease, with all eyes on her. Morland looked down at her, nothing but doting affection in his eyes.

I shivered.

"It's time," Max whispered, and I nodded. The butterflies in my stomach took flight, and my heart began to beat faster, loud and insistent. That familiar excitement took hold of me, and as Max briefly brushed his hand against mine before disappearing into the crowd, I saw a mirror of my own feelings in his eyes. The fear, yes, but also the thrill of it all, there was nothing like it.

"Are we really doing this?" Teresa asked, appearing at my side.

"We really are."

"Are you sure about him, Iz?" She wrinkled her nose in Morland's direction. "He doesn't look like a master of the criminal underworld."

"I know who he is," I said in a low voice. "Where's Mr St Clair?"

"Here I am." James arrived, slipping his arm around Teresa's waist, and leaning in to plant a kiss on her cheek. My best friend made the same face she used to make when presented with all her Christmas gifts wrapped in shiny bows. "You look beautiful," he murmured, and Teresa flushed with pleasure, clashing quite badly with her vibrant orange dress. ("I'm sure it was more of a pale apricot in the dressmakers, Iz.")

"Miss Stanhope." James gave me a small bow. "You're also looking lovely this evening." His face tensed as he cast a glance at Morland. "Let's go," he said now, pulling Teresa's hand through his arm. "I want to get this part over with as soon as possible."

The three of us headed straight for Morland who was still busy greeting the crowds.

"Morland!" James exclaimed, and the man himself turned.

"St Clair!" Morland reached out, clasping James's hand. A delighted smile spread across his face as he took in Teresa. "And this charming lady must be Miss Wynter, who I've heard so much about. I understand congratulations are in order."

Morland twinkled down at Teresa in an avuncular fashion that set my teeth on edge. Perhaps my friend would make a better spy than I gave her credit for because she managed the perfect blend of shy happiness at being introduced to her future husband's mentor.

"It's a pleasure to meet you, Lord Morland." Teresa gazed up at him. "It's the greatest honour, and privilege, to meet the man who James has spoken of so warmly, as a hero to him really, so thrilling, so..." She was getting carried away now, her eyes filling with the tears that I knew she could summon whenever she wanted to get her own way, and I stepped hard on her toe. She cleared her throat. "So nice," she murmured.

"The pleasure is all mine," Morland said, bowing over Teresa's hand. "I'm extremely happy for you both. This young man is one of the best and brightest there is." He clapped James on the shoulder and James beamed back at him.

"This is my friend, Miss Isobel Stanhope," Teresa said, and I felt Morland's compelling gaze move to me.

"Miss Stanhope," he murmured taking my hand gently in his. "I knew your father, of course, I was so sorry to hear of your loss. He was a wonderful man."

His voice was sincere, the full weight of his attention strangely thrilling. I felt a fleeting sense of doubt. *Could this man – warm, urbane, sympathetic – be capable of such terrible things?* "And this is my wife, Lady Morland." He pulled Kitten to stand beside him, and though she smiled brightly and said all the right things, I saw his fingers grip her arm a touch too hard. My eyes met hers and behind the façade of gracious hostess was something taut and afraid.

That moment of doubt vanished, and as Teresa

moved towards Kitten, knocking her shoulder into mine, it was the easiest thing in the world to let myself stumble into Morland's chest. His caught me before I could fall.

"Forgive me!" I stammered, straightening up, and palming the pin in my hand off to James, who stood behind me. I glanced at Morland's tie where the false pin Winnie had made gleamed innocently. It was a perfect lift, one Kes could be proud of.

"That was my fault," Teresa giggled. "I'm afraid I always turn into a clumsy fool just when I'm trying to be impressive!" She pouted and we all laughed.

"Well, sir," James said with another smile for Morland. "We should stop monopolizing our hosts and let you greet your other guests."

"Join me for a cigar later," Morland said, shaking his hand again.

"You may count on it," James replied.

The three of us made our way towards the entrance hall and the winding staircase, stopping on our way to pick up drinks and say hello to one or two people. When I glanced at Morland he wasn't looking at us, but you couldn't be too careful. We continued our leisurely stroll up the stairs, as I stopped to point out the beautiful flowers winding up the banister, to bury my nose in one of the dark blooms, keeping an eye out for anyone observing us, but I could see no one. And really, why would there be? The only people Morland would be looking for were Max and Kes, and he had no reason at all to suspect either of them would be here tonight.

Upon reaching the landing we followed James when he opened one of the doors and ducked inside. I was the last over the threshold and I closed the door behind me. When I turned, it was to find that we were in the library, a big, beautiful room filled with floor-to-ceiling bookcases, and we weren't alone. Sylla, Max, Maud and Winnie were waiting for us.

"Right," Sylla said without preamble. "Now we're all here, Izzy, do you have the key?"

I looked to James and he pulled it from his pocket. The tiepin was gold and shaped like a sword. The pommel of the sword contained a small emerald, and the hilt was engraved in a design like a chain. We had to work fast; Morland wouldn't be fooled by Winnie's copy for long; we were banking on him not noticing the exchange at all until we could swap the pins back.

I took the pin from James, looking at it closely. I pulled gently at the top and when that didn't do anything I tried twisting the pommel on the sword. With a click the pin opened up to reveal a narrow, fine-toothed key. The work was so fine, so precise, that I began to understand why it would be impossible to pick such a lock.

"Yes," I said triumphantly. "I have the key."

"Then we stick to the plan." Sylla was brisk. "Maud has shared all the possible locations for the safe. Morland's study seems most likely, but as Kitten told us, her husband is careful. The safe could be anywhere. We will work our way systematically up the house. Teresa and James will return to the ballroom and keep an eye on Morland. If he looks like he's on the move then do your best to detain him but *don't* draw suspicion. Winnie and Maud will search the east side of this floor together, and I will take the west. Izzy and Vane, you have this room."

We all nodded. This had been agreed upon in

advance, and tension rippled through the air as we prepared to put our plan into motion.

"We meet back here in forty minutes," Sylla said, and then without another word the group disbanded.

Max and I were now alone in the library. It was the biggest room and the most likely place for the safe to be on this floor of the house. We knew – after all – that it was in this room that Morland had met with Rook. Maud hadn't seen any sign of it in here but we couldn't discount the idea of a hidden door like the one in Oliver Lockhart's library. There was a lot of ground to cover.

"You start that side." I pointed to my right. "And I'll start over here."

We worked our way methodically around the bookcases, tapping on joints, pulling out books, feeling the surrounds, but there was nothing. The work was painfully slow, and each shelf had to be checked. By the time Max and I met in the middle, most of our time had passed.

"Where else is there to look?" I asked, frustration growling through my voice.

We both cast our eyes around the room. "The fireplace?" Max said.

"The desk?" I added.

Max went over to the fireplace while I made a start on the desk. It was clearly not Morland's work desk – that must be up in his study – but a more ornamental affair. The drawers were filled with headed notepaper scented with lilac, and pale pink wafers. It must have been the desk where Kitten wrote her correspondence, and it was too delicate a piece of furniture to conceal a serious safe, but I still searched it carefully to be sure.

"Anything?" I asked Max.

He rose on his heels and shook his head. "Nothing." He stood and made his way over, standing beside me and looking down at the open desk drawer which contained little more than a few open bottles of ink in different colours.

I sighed, pushing the drawer shut as Max leaned back against the desk, his eyes half-closed. "We knew it was unlikely that we would find it straight away," I said, trying to sound cheerful. "Perhaps the others have had better luck—"

I broke off as the sound of voices approaching the door reached my ears – and then the handle turned. I had only a moment to take in the widening of Max's startled eyes before I hurled myself into his arms and tugged his head down, crushing his lips to mine.

CHAPTER THIRTY-FOUR

For a second Max was still, then his arms came around me, pulling me into the cage of his body with a ferocity that drew a gasp from my mouth. His lips softened beneath mine at the sound, and he made his own murmur of appreciation before I found myself being thoroughly, enthusiastically kissed back. His big hands lifted so that they cradled my face, the tips of his fingers curling into my hair as he drew my mouth more tightly to his own.

My hands wound round the back of his neck, and

I pressed closer to him, standing between his legs. I wanted to melt into him, wanted to leap out of my body and sink into his skin. The kiss was so many things: tender and hungry, soft and lazy, sharpening into something giddy and desperate. I ran my fingers across his broad shoulders, and it wasn't just the feel of him that overwhelmed me – I could taste him, sugar and peppermint, and the clean, sharp, fresh-air smell of him enveloped me. My senses were alight, full of this man, the man I had wanted for so long, and yet I was hardly aware of the door opening.

"Get out," Max growled, his mouth leaving mine. "Can't you see we're busy?"

There was a chuckle, a strangled apology and the door closed again. I stood panting, listening to the ribald comments drifting away from the door that indicated our surprise visitors were truly leaving.

I took a step back, clinging desperately to the side of the desk. It was the only thing holding me up, my knees trembling madly. I lifted a hand to my lips. They felt swollen. *More*, my body sang. *More*.

I forced myself to look at Max, and he was still,

staring at me with wild eyes gleaming behind the dark silk of his mask. I felt my body swaying towards him, and I saw his throat move.

"I'm sorry," I blurted out.

"What are you sorry for?" he asked, his voice rough.

"You shouldn't kiss a person without asking first." My eyes dropped to his mouth and then away, I focused on my own hand, my fingers still clutching the edge of the desk. "It was ungallant of me."

There was a moment of silence, and then I forced my eyes to meet his, and saw laughter dancing there.

"Izzy." He said my name softly, like it was precious. "Let me be very clear: you may kiss me any time you like."

"W-what?"

He nodded. "Yes, whenever the whim takes you. In a library, at a party, in the morning, on a Tuesday afternoon. I'm absolutely amenable to being kissed by you at any opportunity."

"I-I." The stammering and gawping seemed to be sticking, oh, good. "*What?*" I managed again.

Max laughed, and he raised a hand as if to run it

through his hair, only to remember the mask there before lowering it again. "I see I've been doing a terrible job here, but I thought it was so obvious. I mean, even James took one look at me and knew what was going on, and I love the man like a brother but he's not usually the most sensitive soul – apart from when it comes to your friend, of course – but still, he said—"

"Max," I cut into this rambling monologue, finding some sort of poise now that he was the one who sounded nervous. "What are you talking about?"

"About loving you," Max replied. "I mean, about being in love with you. That I love you."

"You—" I broke off.

"Love you," Max nodded ruefully. "Yes, I think that has been established. I'm sorry I'm not being more eloquent. I've never professed my feelings before; it's actually a lot more difficult than I thought. Perhaps I should start again?"

I stared at him, completely stunned. It was as if the words were coming from far away, as if they were taking their time, travelling towards me, and I was trying to make sense of them. He loved me? How could he love me? And what did that *mean*? Emotions rose up in me in a furious storm – a piercing golden happiness, mixed with something close to panic.

"I—" I began again, but then Sylla swept into the room.

I sprang away from Max, my nerves jangled completely. Sylla paused on the threshold.

She sighed. "Your hair appears to be coming down from its pins, Isobel."

I lifted a hand, feeling the loose coils of hair falling around my face. "Oh, yes," I said brightly. "I never manage to pin it up properly." I bent down to pick up the scattered hairpins, sticking them back into my hair almost at random. I could feel the hot flush of mortification on my face.

Not that Max seemed embarrassed or worried. No, he seemed positively *cheerful*, beaming in a way that was actually quite unnerving from a man who usually looked so serious, and was currently involved in a fight for his freedom and possibly his life.

"I take it you didn't find the safe," Sylla sniffed. "Or were you too busy to look?"

"Of course we looked," I said indignantly.

"It's not in here." Max pulled away from the desk. "We checked everywhere."

"We didn't find it either," Maud said, entering the room with Winnie.

"Nor me," Sylla replied.

Silence fell.

"Right," Sylla said in a rallying tone. "We all knew that this was going to be a possibility. We need to search Morland's rooms on the next floor. Maud, you said that the rooms are locked?"

"That's right." Maud nodded. "I've never been up there. Only his valet goes in there and never alone."

"So we need someone who can pick a lock." Sylla's eyes slid to me and I lifted my chin. "Which means Izzy has to go. I'll go with her. I'll stand the best chance of explaining our way out of this if we're caught."

Max didn't look happy about it, but he nodded. "We'll all keep lookout," he said, and the others murmured in agreement.

I followed in her wake as she swept through the door and we began climbing further up the staircase.

A velvet rope had been pulled across to stop guests from going any higher up into the house, but Sylla and I slipped around it. We didn't speak as we crept silently up the stairs, listening for any sound that might indicate someone else was up here.

We reached the landing and paused.

"Maud said it was the third door on the right," Sylla whispered.

I nodded, but we didn't need the instruction – it was clear enough which door was the right one and there was a serious-looking lock gleaming on the frame. I crouched down in front of it, pulling the long hairpins from my head. Sylla stood beside me, poker straight with energy quivering through her, like she was a live wire set to shock anyone who came near her.

Unsurprisingly, Morland took his locks a lot more seriously than the Duke of Devonshire had, and this one was putting up a fight. I felt my hands grow clammy as I manipulated the brass cylinder pins, waiting for that telltale click. Tense seconds slipped by and I forced myself to breathe deeply, to steady my fingers as I tried again. This time I felt the pins slip into place, felt the give as the lock sprung open under my hands.

I reached out and turned the handle, and Sylla and I streamed through the door, silent as ghosts. I pulled it closed behind me with a soft click. Everything was still and quiet, except the clock on the mantelpiece, which ticked heavily. The room was shrouded in a gloomy darkness, and Sylla hurried to turn a lamp on, leaving it burning low enough that it cast only the faintest ghoulish illumination over everything.

"Quick, efficient, undetectable," Sylla murmured.

We began our search of the room. It was actually three rooms linked together – the breakfast room, which we were standing in, was a sort of gentleman's sitting room with a small dining table, a sofa and a comfortable armchair, a bookcase and a coffee table covered in periodicals. I leafed through them, noticing that Morland seemed to subscribe to every newspaper available, even the scandal sheets. Sylla's words rang in my head as I made sure everything was replaced exactly as I had found it – not a sheet of paper an inch out of place. Morland struck me as the sort of man who would notice a detail like that.

The first room searched, we moved on to Morland's bedroom and dressing room. Here, the furniture was old-fashioned. An enormous four-poster bed dominated the room, and the dressing room was lined with immaculately pressed and well-ordered suits in sober shades of blue, black, grey and brown. Morland's valet was clearly of a meticulous nature; everything was organized by season and colour, and even his shoes were lined up and labelled for different occasions. There was less to look through here and we moved with relative speed through to the final room: Morland's study.

As soon as we walked in I felt anticipation cresting like a wave through my body. The safe was in here, I knew it was, and inside it were the secrets we had been looking for all along. I began sifting through Morland's desk. Several of the drawers were locked and I picked these as speedily as possible, finding papers inside that related to his work in the government. Some of it was classified, but there was nothing particularly startling, and I knew that I wasn't going to find what we were looking for here.

I moved to join Sylla in knocking on the walls. In the

alcove that sat behind Morland's desk we finally heard it: a hollow sound that indicated something was hidden there. I tapped up and down, but whatever it was, was concealed beneath the ornately patterned wallpaper – a design of scrolling gold on midnight blue.

"There must be a lever," I hissed, pushing desperately on the skirting board.

Sylla was by my side, and she reached out to a brass wall sconce in the shape of a flaming torch. It gave easily in her hand, and the hidden panel swung open revealing an enormous iron safe, sitting in a receded space.

I ran my fingers over the safe door. The unflinching iron was chill beneath my hand. It was a serious piece of equipment, with two different-sized keyholes. I had never seen anything like it before, and I was relieved that we had both the keys – this whole thing was clearly custom-made, and I was unsurprised by Morland's claims that it had been tested against the best lock picks in the world.

Sylla pulled the brooch from her pocket, twisting it to reveal the key, and sliding it into the larger of the locks. She turned it sharply to the right, and I heard the tumblers falling into place as the first lock opened.

"Now the tiepin," Sylla murmured.

I removed the pin, twisting the emerald at the top to reveal the key, and pushed it into the second lock. It was something like threading a needle.

"Ready?" I asked Sylla.

She nodded tensely.

I turned the key, waiting for the feeling of the lock releasing.

But nothing happened.

CHAPTER THIRTY-FIVE

"What's going on?" hissed Sylla. "Open the bloody safe!"

"I'm trying." I flinched, pushing on the key until it felt like it might snap. "It's not working."

"What do you mean it's not working?" Sylla asked and I felt my stomach drop, as if I was standing on the edge of a great ravine, looking down, down, down at how far I could fall.

I pulled the key gently from the lock and looked at it. "It's not the right key," I said.

Sylla's face was a mask of confusion. "How can it be the wrong key?" she demanded. "It's the tiepin, it has a hidden key – one that fits this stupid, tiny lock."

"I don't know, I don't know," I murmured, my mind racing like mad, trying to work out what on earth was going on. "It must be a decoy pin – a fake. Morland is being extra cautious because he knows Max has the brooch."

I sat back on my heels, fear and disappointment weighing on my bones. We had failed. We had been given an opportunity to end Morland's devious plans and we had failed. Everything that we had worked towards ended here, and with it any hope for Morland's victims. What would become of his wife? Of Max? Of the countless others caught up in his schemes. For that matter, what would become of a country led by such a cruel and dangerous man?

I felt a familiar tightness in my chest, felt panic rolling in like thunder clouds, dimming the light in my eyes. My hands were prickling, my breathing was too fast, and I could hear it, too loud in this quiet room. Tears welled in my eyes.

"Stop right now," Sylla said, and she crouched down to look at me. Her eyes were burning, twin amber flames. "I can see what you're thinking," she continued. "But we're not done yet. Just breathe, Izzy. Concentrate, breathe in, and breathe out. You're not alone, I'm here with you."

Her voice had dropped low and soothing, and her hand was rubbing surprisingly gentle circles on my back. I closed my eyes and concentrated on pulling air into my lungs. I felt the tightness ease a fraction, and I focused on that feeling, counting in my mind as I drew the air in and out.

"What else can we do?" I asked finally, when my breathing had settled, when I knew I had cost us several precious minutes that we couldn't afford to lose. "Without the key we can't open the safe. If we can't get into the safe we can't retrieve the blackmail material and whatever else is in there. We can't connect Morland to his crimes."

"So we break into the safe," Sylla said, shrugging her shoulders like the answer was obvious.

"It's an *unbreakable* safe," I hissed, more tears of

anger and disappointment clouding my eyes. I swiped at them with the back of my hand. "No one can pick it."

Sylla took my chin in her hand, turning it so that I was looking straight at her. "You can."

"I can't!"

"An unbreakable safe is only one that hasn't been broken *yet*," Sylla insisted, letting go of my face. "You are the best lock pick in this country. You have beaten unbeatable odds again and again. Despite being a gently bred, sheltered young woman you have become one of the most dangerous, capable, brilliant agents that the Aviary has ever known. Together we have saved lives. We are not about to be defeated by a tiny little man like Morland. You can do this. I know that you can."

Sylla had never spoken to me like this. Never. The words wove around me like a magic spell, I could feel my spine straightening, feel the power of Sylla's certainty. I felt myself beginning to believe her. She was right, Sylla was always right, I could do this. I had to.

"Did you just call me brilliant?" I asked, my voice unsteady.

Sylla rolled her eyes. "I can't remember," she said. "Now get to work."

I crouched down and placed my picks in the lock. I could only use the finest parts at the end, and the space was so small, it was almost impossible to even get a feeling for the tumblers inside. I pressed my ear to the safe door, remembering what my father had taught me: that breaking a lock wasn't only about touch, that there was a music to it as well, if you only knew how to listen – a sweetness to the pins as they were manipulated into place.

I don't know how long it took. I got close several times only to have it slip out of my grip. If it wasn't thwarting me at every turn I would have been able to appreciate the beauty of the safe. It really was a work of art – a devious, infuriating work of art.

My tongue was between my teeth and beads of sweat rose on my brow. The world narrowed down to this spot, a pinprick of light, the slightest of movements, a gentle coaxing. Finally, finally, I heard it, the sound of the lock clicking into place. I leaned back, my eyes wide, and Sylla looked at me expectantly.

"Well?" she asked.

I reached up, turning the large wheel on the front of the safe door, and then giving it a tug. The door opened, uncomplainingly, on silent hinges, swinging open to reveal a fat folder full of documents, a box of photographic plates, and an envelope of developed images. All of these were sitting on stacks of bank notes and two rows of gold bars. A fortune.

"I did it," I murmured in a daze.

"So it would appear, Miss Stanhope," a voice came from behind us, and Sylla and I swung around, confronted by the sight of Morland pushing Max into the room ahead of him. In Morland's hand a gleaming silver service revolver was pressed tightly to Max's temple.

"Get away from the safe." Morland's voice was almost conversational.

I stood slowly, my eyes glued to Morland's gun. Then I looked at Max. His mask had been removed, a trickle of blood ran down from his hairline. His mouth was grim, but his eyes were all for me. Sylla and I moved to the side, putting distance between us and the open safe door.

"You really are a most impressive young woman, Miss Stanhope," Morland said, his voice a rich baritone, and I noticed that he had removed his mask as well. "I must thank you for the return of my brooch. I have been quite concerned about its disappearance, but it seems you've been keeping it safe all along. First you steal my brooch from Rook, then you lift my tiepin without me feeling a thing, and now you break my unbreakable safe. Your father would be proud."

My spine stiffened and Max made a warning sound in his throat, but Morland only smiled, pressed the gun a little harder. The sight of his finger hovering on the trigger, the barrel unflinching against Max's skin was something out of a nightmare.

"Oh, yes," he said, drawing my attention back to him. "Didn't you realize? Your father modified that safe for me himself. Told me even he couldn't crack it without both keys; that no one could. It seems he had underestimated your own skills."

"It would seem so," I said, finding my voice. I was surprised by how calm I sounded.

Morland's smile widened in response. "But I think

perhaps you're used to being underestimated, aren't you, Miss Stanhope?" His blue eyes crawled over my face. "It's no wonder my young protégé here is so taken with you. Foolish enough to follow you into this wild scheme, to allow himself to be identified by one of my men."

Max winced at that. "Let them go," he said, his voice hard and flat. "It's me you wanted; they have nothing to do with this."

As I was currently standing over the man's open safe, I thought Max's chivalry was misplaced, but I almost smiled that he hadn't been able to help himself.

Morland clearly had the same thought because he let out a bark of laughter. "Noble to the bitter end, Roxton," he said, and then he raised his hand, bringing the gun down on the side of Max's head with a sickening crack. Max's legs crumpled beneath him as he fell to the floor.

"Max!" I shrieked, throwing myself at him, regardless of the gun, which was now trained on me. "Max, Max," I whispered, cradling his head in my lap, my hand on his cheek. Max's eyelids fluttered, and I let out a gasp of relief. He was alive. But he wouldn't be for long, not if I didn't intervene. This time I was not Kes, crouched over him with a knife. This time I was only Isobel Stanhope.

My eyes darted round to Sylla, who was watching Morland with a calculating expression. Morland's attention was all for me, and if I could keep it that way then perhaps Sylla could get the gun off him. I brushed Max's hair back from his face, laying his head gently on the carpet as I got unsteadily to my feet.

"You shouldn't have done that," I said, danger crawling through my voice. "You've taken enough from him."

Morland's eyes flickered to Max's prone form. "A shame," he said with what sounded like genuine regret. "He was a good soldier. Given time, I think he could have been extremely useful. Of course he has far too finely tuned a moral compass. Sees things only in black and white." He looked at me intently. "But you and I, Miss Stanhope, we know that the world is made up of shades of grey."

"I am *nothing* like you," I spat, taking another

488

step away from Max, and Morland's gun followed me, unwavering. Sylla made an almost imperceptible movement towards him.

"Oh, really?" Morland cocked an eyebrow. "Because it looks to me like you operate fairly widely outside the law yourself."

"We do what we need to do to protect people," I replied. "You do whatever you like for your own gain. Regardless of who it hurts."

"That is a narrow-minded view," Morland sighed. "What I do, I do for the good of the country. If a few weak people, some of the rabble, are lost in the pursuit of those ideals then so be it."

"Ideals?" I scoffed. "Since when are kidnapping, blackmail and murder lofty ideals to be protected? Or are you referring to the opium smuggling and counterfeiting?"

Morland smiled then, like a benevolent uncle. "I'm even more impressed. What a thorough little investigation you've been running. However you shouldn't be so short-sighted. Power must be taken by force, Miss Stanhope. Protecting a country – no – an *empire* like ours is not a small undertaking. One needs ... resources."

"You're mad." I shook my head, taking another step away from Sylla, who I was dimly aware was edging round outside of Morland's sight line.

"Mad?" Morland frowned. "Not at all. The world stage is growing unstable. It's in the best interest of the country for us to be appropriately armed, for our war chests to be full, for us to be ready to strike first even ... should the need arise. Why limit ourselves to holding on to what we already have when there is so much left to gain? There is more than one country that would benefit from our civilizing influence."

"*Civilizing?*" Nausea swept over me at the use of that nasty little word, the one that covered so many sins, but Morland nodded.

"We are leaders of an empire on which the sun never sets. I mean to keep us that way."

"Through crime?" I said.

"It was such a simple idea," he said, sounding pleased. "London has a vast and profitable underworld. The criminal class are precisely that: they commit crime because it is in their nature to do so. There is nothing you or I can do about it. We have only to make the best of the situation, why not capitalize on it?"

"You were working with Andrew Sharpe. He was kidnapping young women off the street, selling them. That's the sort of business you want to *capitalize* on?"

His eyes narrowed. "Sharpe was a fool. I'll admit that some of his activities were distasteful, but what happens in the slums is hardly a priority for any good leader."

Sylla was edging ever closer.

"And blackmailing people for their support? Bribing and cheating your way into power? Are those the qualities of a leader?" I asked.

"People cannot always be relied upon to choose the leader that they need." Morland shrugged, a light in his eyes. "And whatever you might think, they do need me. *You* need me. Her Majesty's health is failing. Her son is a profligate fool, a wastrel concerned only with his own selfish appetites. We are about to enter a storm and this country needs a firm hand guiding the ship. Everything I do is for the greater good."

Sylla was almost beside him now. She may not have had to fight on the streets like I had, but Mrs Finch made sure we could all defend ourselves. Morland wouldn't expect it, I knew she could disarm him, and I would be ready...

As if reading my mind, Morland's other hand reached behind him and with one smooth movement he pulled a second gun from his waistband and pointed it straight at Sylla.

"Ah, ah, ah, Miss Banaji," he chided, the barrel disturbingly close to her forehead. His hands were perfectly steady. "Let's not do anything rash now, shall we? Back over there, next to your friend, please."

"You can't possibly hope to get away with this," Sylla said tightly, as she moved back to stand beside me.

"Of course I'm going to get away with it," Morland said, as though explaining something to a small child. "In fact, I'm going to be a hero, catching the treasonous villain, the Duke of Roxton, who I found trying to break in to my safe. He also kidnapped and murdered two of my guests – innocent young women. They'd hang him for sure." His eyes narrowed. "On second thoughts,

492

that may be too messy. I will simply have no choice but to shoot him, defending myself. A traitor to the Crown, brought to justice. The Duke of Devonshire's jewels will be found in his home. They'll throw me a parade; it will all but ensure the election. Think what a time the scandal sheets will have with the story."

My blood ran cold at the casual ruthlessness of Morland's plan. "If you kill us then the women we work with will come for you," I said, but my voice shook.

"*Women?*" Morland laughed. "You think a group of women will bring me down? Who will believe them? You really know nothing about how this world works, do you, Miss Stanhope? Don't worry, Miss Banaji, you'll be following straight after your friend here. I'm sorry to do this to you both, but – ah, well, – sacrifices must be made."

With those words he cocked the gun and I knew I was about to die. My eyes closed, just as the sound of the gun firing ricocheted around the room.

"Izzy!" I heard Max roar, and then there was pain, and I fell to the floor as the world turned to darkness.

CHAPTER THIRTY-SIX

"Izzy! Izzy!" I was dimly aware of Max's voice, of the feeling of his hand against my cheek.

"Did I die?" I croaked, because honestly, if there was a heaven, then I thought lying in Max's arms was a fairly likely place to end up.

My eyelids fluttered open, and there he was, his face pressed almost against mine as he made a sound that was somewhere between a laugh and a sob.

"Of course you didn't die." Sylla's scowling face

appeared over Max's shoulder. Perhaps this wasn't heaven after all. "You were barely grazed by a bullet and then you collapsed in an unnecessarily dramatic fashion while Romeo here flung himself at your body and started weeping."

"I wasn't *weeping*," Max protested, though his eyes definitely gleamed with unshed tears.

"Pfffft." Sylla made a sound of derision, and Max took my elbow, gently helping me to sit upright.

"I'm really not dead," I said in wonder. "But then..." I swung to look at Morland, a sharp stab of pain in my side protesting the movement.

Morland's body was on the floor, a pool of blood seeping from beneath him, leaving little question as to the state of his health. Standing behind him in the doorway, a neat revolver with a mother-of-pearl handle still smoking in her hand, was a woman in a scarlet ball gown and a matching mask.

Mrs Finch.

In a fluid motion she blew on the end of the gun and then dropped it into her red silk reticule.

"Quite the party," she said.

"I'm glad you could join us." I winced, as another spike of pain shot through me.

"Where is she?" I heard a voice cry from behind Mrs Finch and then Teresa ran into the room, skating past Morland's body as if she barely registered it, flinging herself down on to the floor, wrapping her arms around me. "Oh my god, Izzy! We lost track of Morland and I heard a gun going off! I thought you'd *died*! Again! But you're all right?" she demanded.

"I'll be better if you stop squeezing me," I managed.

"She's injured," Max said sharply. "Be careful."

"I am being careful, I think I know how to take care of my *best friend*." Teresa scowled at him.

"Teresa!" James sped into the room then, and he certainly *did* do a double-take when he saw Morland on the floor. He yanked his coat from his body, throwing it down to cover as much of Morland as possible, before Teresa cast herself into his arms and burst into noisy tears.

"Now, now," James whispered soothingly. "Don't look at him. There's nothing to be frightened of now."

"I'm not frightened." Teresa raised a tear-stained

face to him. "I'm furious. He hurt Izzy and I wish I'd killed him myself."

James smiled down at her. "Don't worry, my love, perhaps you'll still have the opportunity to bury him in the garden." And on that romantic note he caught Teresa's mouth with his.

"Well, I'm glad that the corpse in the room is doing little to dampen your romantic spirit," Sylla said sourly. "But perhaps we should come up with a plan?"

"Sylla's right," I said, clinging to Max's arm as he helped me to my feet, holding me as if I were a precious glass figurine. "We got the safe open, so I'd imagine there's plenty of evidence in there to connect Morland to his crimes."

"Izzy cracked the uncrackable safe," Sylla said, and I thought I heard a note of pride in her voice.

"Of course she did," Max said, looking down at me so fiercely that I wondered why he wasn't kissing me already.

"Max," I said, but my voice sounded as if it were coming from down a long tunnel. The world began to wobble around me, and I saw Max's hand come away from my side, covered in blood.

"Izzy!" His mouth moved but the sound didn't seem to come out at the same time.

"I think it might have been more than a graze after all," I slurred. "I'm sorry, Sylla, but I'm going to be dramatic again."

I was caught up against Max's chest. *What a way to go*, I thought, and then everything receded into darkness once more.

This time when I came around I found myself at the Aviary. I was tucked into Maud's bed, and I was dimly aware that two people were there with me, sitting on either side of the mattress. As I continued to fall back into my body, awareness tingling in my limbs, I realized that they were each holding my hands.

I fought to open my eyes, and I found Mrs Finch leaning over me. "You're awake," she smiled.

I licked my lips, my mouth dry. "What happened?" I croaked.

"The bullet hit you in the side. It didn't do too much damage, but we didn't realize how much blood you were losing. I stitched you up and you'll be right as rain in no time. Though I'd recommend avoiding any gun-wielding madmen for a while."

"Noted." I blinked, the events of the evening becoming clearer in my mind. "You killed him," I said.

A shadow passed over her face, but her voice was calm, as she replied, "I did."

We were quiet for a moment, letting the words settle over us, then I turned my head. The person holding tightly on to my other hand was slumped over the bed, asleep. "Sylla?" I whispered.

"She's been here all night." A smile played around Mrs Finch's mouth. "Telling us all very loudly how little she cares about you."

"She helped me break into that safe," I said. "She told me she believed in me. Do you think she's quite well?"

Mrs Finch chuckled. "Izzy, why do you think Sylla suggested you listen in on my conversation with Kitten? *She* recruited you. Of course she believes in you. She thinks you should be running your own charm, she's been giving you space to prove it, and I'm inclined to agree with her."

I started in surprise, wincing as I felt the tug of the stitches in my side. The movement woke Sylla who sat up, snatching her hand from mine.

"You're finally awake, then?" she said.

"Yes, thank you for sitting with me."

Sylla shrugged, already getting to her feet. "Just wanted to make sure you weren't going to start spilling blood everywhere again. You made a mess of my gown, you know."

"I'm sorry," I said meekly.

"Well, if you think you're quite finished with all the theatrics then I'll go home?" She swept towards the door but turned to raise an imperious brow at me.

"I'm finished," I said. "No more theatrics from me, I promise."

"Good." Sylla brushed down her bloodstained skirts and wrinkled her nose. "I'll see you tomorrow so that we can get back to work. Morland's demise will create a lot of fallout for the Aviary to deal with." And with that she was gone.

I slumped back into my pillow, and let out a sigh. "You'd think getting shot would mean I get a day off."

"That's not how the Aviary works," Mrs Finch said. "Now, shall I tell that young man of yours that he can come in and see you? He's probably worn a hole in the floorboards, pacing up and down out in the hallway."

"Max is here?" I asked, dazed. "I thought he'd have other things to see to."

"I get the impression that you're the most important thing for him, Izzy."

I didn't say anything then, only stared down at my lap.

"Is there something wrong with that?" Mrs Finch asked. I lifted my eyes to hers, and I saw her face full of quiet understanding.

"I-I don't know," I confessed, pushing unruly strands of hair back from my face. "He said … he said that he loves me." The words came out in a rush. "But I don't know what that means. He's so honourable, he must mean – he must want to *marry* me? *Me?* It would be a huge scandal. He's the most eligible bachelor in the country and I'm a wallfl—"

"If you call yourself a wallflower one more time, I'll be rather disappointed," Mrs Finch said sternly. "And you know why. That's not the reason you're hesitating."

"You're right," I said. "It's everything else. It's this job. I love it. I love my work. You mentioned me leading my own charm, and I want that. I believe in what we do, I think there are women who need us. But how could I do this job if I was married? Especially if I was married to the Duke of Roxton?" I traced the pattern on the bed sheets with my fingertips. "And then ... there's the whole idea of being married at all. If I was Max's wife, I'd be like his property, I'd be at his mercy. Look at all the marriages we see – the imbalance in power, the pain that can be caused, even by *good* men." I thought again about my own father, about the position my mother had been left in.

Mrs Finch took my hand in hers. "If you don't want to get married then don't," she said calmly. "Marriage is not the answer for every woman, and it is absolutely not your only recourse. The choice is and always should be entirely yours, Izzy. But not all marriages are bad. Some marriages are true partnerships, unions between people who love and respect one another, who want to lift each other up, rather than curtail each other's freedom."

"Is your marriage like that?" I ventured.

For a moment I thought she wouldn't answer, but then something in her face softened.

"It is," she said steadily. "It really is. Although, it hasn't always been easy, and we've had to overcome our own obstacles. But don't forget: in this line of work you will always see more of the bad than the good, you'll always see people at their lowest, at their most vulnerable, most hurt – it's the nature of the work we do and it's *why* we're so important. But there is still good out there, plenty of it. Now." She got to her feet. "I've said my part, and you are the only one who can make this decision, but I expect you'd like to speak to him now? He'll be relieved to know you're awake."

"Yes," I said, my head still spinning. "I want to see him."

I did; that was the trouble. I *always* wanted to see Max. I was wild about him, the big, beautiful, kind, funny idiot, but it didn't change any of the anxieties that gnawed at me. What would I have to give up for him?

But Mrs Finch had already let him in and he was moving towards me, worry carved into his face that eased only when he saw me sitting up.

"You're really awake!" he exclaimed. "How do you feel?"

"Sore," I said. "Not sure I'd be up to running around London, chased by flying bullets. I have a whole new respect for you."

A smile pulled at his mouth as he dropped into the seat beside me. Mrs Finch left the room, closing the door behind her.

"I was only stabbed," he pointed out. "You were shot."

"True," I agreed. "What's a little light stabbing between friends?"

"That's what I always say," Max agreed and he took my hand in his own, lifting it to his lips. "Thank god you're all right. I don't think I've ever been so scared in my life."

"It will take more than Samuel Morland to get rid of me," I said, and I removed my hand from his, repositioning myself against the pillow. "I'm surprised to see you here. I thought there'd be a lot for you to sort out at Morland's house."

"I've never seen a more efficient conclusion to a

case." His eyes scrutinized my face even as he spoke lightly. "Mrs Finch and Sylla wrapped it all up in a bow for the investigators. James and I were barely needed at all, although we did have the authority to bring in further help from the agency. The stack of evidence you found left no one in any doubt whatsoever about Morland's dealings. The powers that be have decided it's better covered up, so the official story is that Morland had a heart attack during the party, leaving Kitten a very merry widow."

"What about you?" I asked anxiously.

"Completely cleared," he said. "Thanks to you. They've even offered me Morland's job in the service."

"Will you take it?"

He nodded. "I think so. Everything is different for me now. I see a lot of things more clearly. Perhaps it's a helpful perspective for a leader to have. Maybe things can begin to change. Perhaps *I* can change things … from the inside."

I felt warmth gathering in my chest.

"Izzy." He paused. "There's something I need to say…"

"Do you think it could wait?" I murmured, closing my eyes. "I'm sorry, but I think I need to sleep."

"Of course," Max said at once. "You should rest. You've been through a lot. We have all the time in the world."

And with that he stood quietly and left the room, while I lay in bed, cursing my own cowardly ways.

CHAPTER THIRTY-SEVEN

Almost two weeks later I was standing in the beautiful ballroom at Earl Wynter's London home, and I was still the greatest coward alive. Two weeks of avoiding Max and blaming my recovery while he sent me notes and flowers were going to come to an end tonight, and I was jittery with nerves. I still had no idea what to say to him.

"Doesn't everything look beautiful?" Teresa was rapturous. "It was so kind of Nick to let us hold our engagement party here. Most unlike him, actually."

"I'm sure your grandmother had quite a lot to do

with it," I said. But Teresa was right, the ballroom did look beautiful – full of romantic sweeps of pale pink silk and frothy arrangements of flowers tumbling from various Grecian-style urns.

"How rude of you to impede my honour," a voice drawled over my shoulder, and I turned to find Nicholas Wynter himself sauntering towards us. "It barely needed any psychological manipulation for our grandmother to con me into throwing this party for my favourite cousin." Nick pressed a kiss to Teresa's cheek and sighed. "What an interesting choice of gown, Teresa. What do you call that colour? Puce?" A delicate shudder passed over him. Nick, as usual was dressed in the height of elegance, his startling good looks thrown into sharp relief by the simplicity of his tailoring.

"It's called pink, you ass," Teresa said, unfazed.

Nick did not dignify this with a response but turned his gaze on me, taking in my sage-green dress, the airy overlay of gold tulle. "At least you look well, Iz, finally a ball gown that doesn't look like a greengrocer's sack."

"Ever the charmer, Nick," I sighed. "Shouldn't you be getting things ready for your guests? I thought I saw the dowager countess looking for you a minute ago."

"Where?" Nick's head swung round. "Do you know, I think I've remembered something I needed to do … in my study." On that note, he hurried off like a hunted man.

"Is your grandmother still trying to marry him off to the nearest eligible female?" I asked.

"He *is* the earl now." Teresa shrugged. "But I'm much more interested in talking about *my* wedding."

"Of course!" I exclaimed. "It's going to be the wedding of the season, I promise."

"The wedding of the year," Teresa said sternly. "We already discussed this."

"The wedding of the decade, I won't settle for anything less," James St Clair's voice interrupted us as he appeared, slipping an arm around Teresa's waist. "I'm sorry to disturb you two, but your grandmother says we need to get ready to begin greeting the guests, and she is not a woman I want to argue with."

"Yes, go, go!" I exclaimed, shooing them away. "Everyone will want to see the two of you looking disgustingly happy."

"Don't hide away in a corner all night, Iz," Teresa

called over her shoulder as James led her away. "I'll be sending my spies after you."

"Less of the spy talk, please, darling," I heard James murmur.

Ignoring Teresa's instructions I went and found myself a nice little corner where I could watch the guests arriving, could see the ballroom filling up around me – a swirling mass of light and colour, the hum of excited chatter, the gentle swell of string music. At the top of the stairs James and Teresa welcomed their guests, and I didn't think I'd ever seen my friend look so happy, so radiant.

I, on the other hand, felt rather flat. It was depressingly easy to fall back into the role of watchful wallflower, sitting here in the shadows while things unfolded in front of me. There was still no sign of Max, and that was probably a good thing. If I saw him then I was going to have to explain how I felt, and I barely knew how to explain it to myself.

Someone came and sat beside me. "So here you are," Sylla said. "Feeling sorry for yourself."

"I'm just doing my job," I said, unable to hold back from sighing. "Blending in to the scenery. Watching the world go by."

"Waiting for Prince Charming to turn up, more like." Sylla angled her head. "Where is Vane this evening?"

"I don't know," I said. "He hasn't arrived yet."

"Trouble in paradise?"

I frowned. Sylla was the last person I would usually turn to for advice about feelings. I could already imagine the scowl, the dismissive mutterings, but she was here, she was asking, and maybe, just maybe, she cared about me more than I realized – hadn't she shown me as much recently? "I don't know how to choose," I said. "Max or the Aviary."

There was a brief silence as Sylla considered my words, and then she shook her head. "Who's asking you to choose?" she said. "Has he? Have we? Why not have both? Izzy, if you're lucky enough to be able to choose it, why not have it *all*?"

I looked blankly at her. "How can I?"

"Well, it would be up to you two to work out the logistics, I can't do everything for you, but I can think of several advantages to having one of our agents married to the head of the government's secret service." A feline smile spread across her face. "In fact, there are one or two particular files I wouldn't mind getting my hands on."

"I'm not going to marry someone just so that you can get into his files..." I laughed. "That came out wrong."

"Well, no," Sylla said sensibly. "You should probably marry him because you love him. The files would simply be a nice bonus." With that she got to her feet. "Anyway, it seems like a conversation that the two of you should have. Once you're done, come and find me. We have work to do."

With her usual impeccable timing, Sylla glided away, just as Max appeared, right there at the top of the stairs. My breath caught in my throat. His hair shone gold in the soft light, his dark suit clung to his broad shoulders. Why did he have to be *so* beautiful? It was extremely unfair.

His eyes scanned the room, and even here, in the gloomiest corner, half-hidden behind a pillar, they came to rest on me almost at once. A smile illuminated his face, and I saw the people around him trying to work out who he was looking at. The Duke of Roxton wasn't known for smiling, they didn't usually get to see him like this – all lit up and glittering. That was for me.

I got to my feet and gestured towards the French doors, which led out on to the terrace. He nodded in silent agreement and began making his way through the crowd, stopping occasionally to politely return a greeting.

I slipped out of the doors to wait for him. The night was warm, the air filled with the smell of summer – cut grass and jasmine, soft and dreamy. I heard the door open, and felt Max come to stand behind me.

"Here you are," he said, and I turned round to face him, holding back from simply throwing myself into his arms. I had missed him so much, and it was such a strange feeling; after all, I had been on my own for so long.

"Max, I—" I began, but he held up a hand and cut me off.

"Izzy, would you mind if I go first? I have some things I need to say. It's important." He looked serious, and my heart dropped. I'd been worrying for nothing. What an idiot! Of *course*, now that the case was over, everything was going back to the way it was, and Max was only going to apologize for what he had said in the heat of the moment, and try to save me some embarrassment.

"Certainly," I murmured, willing the ground to

swallow me up.

"I've been thinking a lot the last couple of weeks," Max said earnestly. "About what happened between us, and what a difficult situation I put you in."

"It was nothing," I managed, trying to cut him short, but he was not to be deterred.

"It wasn't nothing." His voice was firm and it did strange things to my knees. "These last few weeks, you've challenged me, opened my eyes to so many things, but I still went blundering in with my feelings without talking to you about it, without imagining how it would be for you. When you started avoiding me I thought at first that you didn't feel the same way I do, but now I've had time to reflect, I think … I *hope* that's not true."

"What are you talking about?" I asked, confused.

He smiled ruefully. "You see, I'm making a mess of it again. That's why I wrote it all down." He reached into his pocket and pulled out a sheet of paper. "I know you once told me that marriage should be a woman's last resort, and I understand now why you said that, I really do. So I made a list of things that *shouldn't* need to be said, but that I have to make plain. So…" His eyes went to the piece of paper, and he cleared his throat, sounding nervous. "First: I would never ask you to give up your work. What you do is important and honourable, and it allows you to use your not inconsiderable gifts. I will never interfere with that. Second: what's yours is yours. Your money, your possessions, *you* will never belong to anyone else, especially not me, and I will have paperwork drawn up to make that legally clear. If you ever wanted to leave I would not cage you – you are, and will always be, utterly, wildly free. Third: I love you. I should probably have said that first but I'm saying it now. I'm in love with you. I have been for a while. I love your spirit, your intelligence, your kindness, I love *all* of you. I want you as my equal, my friend, my partner. I want to help carry your burdens, and I want you to help carry mine. I can't even begin to describe what I feel for you, I love you so much, Izzy, I…"

"Stop talking," I said and, pushing the sheet of paper aside, I launched myself into his arms, and he held me, my feet not even touching the floor as we kissed each other like the world would end if we stopped. One of his arms was locked around my waist, pinning me to his chest, his other hand cradled my face, warm and gentle but sending desire shivering across my skin. I lost all sense of time and space, and there was only this: his mouth against mine, the feeling of him, all of him, wrapped around me.

When we finally broke apart he relaxed his grip, slowly, slowly, so that my feet found the floor.

"Marry me," I said, and I was rewarded with the sort of smile that could light up an entire room.

"That was supposed to be my line," Max smiled, leaning down towards me. "You didn't let me get to the end of my list."

And then he was laughing against my mouth and we were kissing again, and I wondered if it might be possible to simply explode with joy.

Several minutes later, I pulled away, flushed and dizzy. "You know we have to keep this to ourselves tonight?" I said, jabbing ineffectually at my hair with the pins that had come loose. "It's Teresa's big night, and all the focus should be on her. You and I are going to cause quite the scandal."

"I think it may be too late for that," Max said,

looking over my shoulder.

I swung round and there, standing in the doorway, were Teresa and James, and crowding behind them were plenty of their guests, gleefully taking in the scene.

I looked at my best friend, who was grinning like a maniac.

"Oh dear," I said.

"Well, if we're going to be a scandal anyway..." Max murmured against my ear.

"We might as well really give them something to talk about?" I finished his thought on a laugh, turning and pulling his face down to mine once more. The kiss he gave me then made me feel like a living, breathing flame.

Dimly, over the outraged gasps, I heard my best friend's voice, bright and carrying.

"I *knew* he was trying to seduce her, James! Didn't I say so? I told you I'd make a wonderful spy. Don't you think a double wedding will be lovely? The wedding of the century."

ACKNOWLEDGEMENTS

First of all, I have to thank Louise Lamont, Gen Herr and Sophie Cashell who have been my pals and collaborators on so many books now. Thank you for making writing (a notoriously lonely pursuit) feel like a team sport, without the matching T-shirts. (BUT SHOULD WE HAVE MATCHING T-SHIRTS NEXT TIME??) Working with you is so much fun, and I think this is our best (and most fun) work yet.

Thank you to the whole team at Scholastic who have championed me for EIGHT years now! I can't believe all the things we have done together. Special thanks to Lauren Fortune, who has always made me feel so supported and who has the handsomest cats in the business. Thanks to Harriet Dunlea and Hannah Griffiths, who have literally taken this book around the country and pressed it into people's hands. I appreciate your creativity and the work you do. Thank you to Sarah Dutton, Susila Baybars and Jenny Glencross for polishing everything up until it shone. Thanks to Jamie as always for a stunning cover, and to Mercedes for reaching into my mind and bringing Izzy perfectly to life. Thank you to the whole team at Bounce, who make me feel giddy with appreciation whenever I have a new book that I am nervous about.

Thank you, thank you, thank you to the bloggers, BookTokers, and Bookstagrammers who make such beautiful content and share my books with their audiences. I probably don't need to tell you how much your passion and creativity make a difference, but they do, and I'm so grateful to you. Thanks to all the readers who have been so kind and vocal about my books from the start – you are the reason I am able to keep doing this.

In particular, I'd like to thank Jo Clarke, Liam James, Sifa and Beth of #UKYASpotlight, Rachel Goodson-Hill, Beth (@Booksnest), Lauren (@fictiontea), and Kate Poels. Thank you to all the writers I admire, who have also supported me so much, especially Sarra Manning, Louise O'Neill, Katherine Webber, Cat Doyle, Amy McCaw and Maria Kuzniar.

Thanks to my friends and family who are the reason I have this job that I love and manage to hold on to my sanity at the same time. Special thanks to my husband, Paul. We sat at a restaurant in Cornwall and spent the whole fancy meal plotting out this elaborate mystery, and it's one of my favourite memories. I love you and I like you.

Laura Wood is an academic and writer. She loves Georgette Heyer novels, Fred Astaire films, travelling to far flung places, recipe books, Jilly Cooper, poetry, new stationery, sensation fiction, salted caramel and Rufus Sewell's cheekbones.

Other achingly romantic stories from Laura Wood:

Want to read more about Iris and Nick?
A Single Thread of Moonlight is available now.

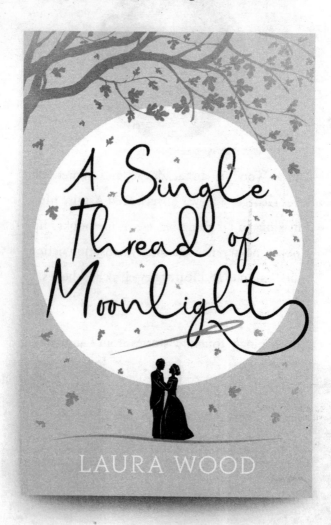